ISBN: 978-0692451113

Blue Columbine

Printed in the United States of America
First Printing, 2015

Cover Design by Roseanna White Designs,
www.RoseannaWhiteDesigns.com
Cover photos from www.Shutterstock.com and www.Lightstock.com

Edited by Sally Bradley and Janet Kerr
Author Photo by Larisa O'Brien Photography
Published by Rooted Publishing
McCook, NE 69001

Scriptures taken from the Holy Bible, New International Version®, NIV®. Copyright © 1973, 1978, 1984, 2011 by Biblica, Inc.™ Used by permission of Zondervan. All rights reserved worldwide. www.zondervan.com The "NIV" and "New International Version" are trademarks registered in the United States Patent and Trademark Office by Biblica, Inc.™

All other Scripture quotations taken from the New American Standard Bible®, Copyright © 1960, 1962, 1963, 1968, 1971, 1972, 1973, 1975, 1977, 1995 by The Lockman Foundation Used by permission.

Contents

For those who wander.
The Father is waiting. Come home.

Jennifer Rodewald

"...the younger son gathered everything together and went on a journey into a distant country..." Luke 15:13

Prologue

"Wait up!" Eight-year-old Jamie Carson scrambled out of the aspens, calling to the boys as they charged ahead without her. Figures. They didn't want her at their fort—why had she hoped they'd wait? She was, after all, the cootie-filled, freckle-faced girl of the bunch. If it wasn't for Andy, she'd never get to do anything fun.

She jumped from the lowest branch, landing against a board left on the ground. A burning sting jammed through her foot, and she ripped the air with a high-pitched scream.

All four boys came running.

"Jamie," her older brother, Cole, scolded. "You promised not to scream!"

Tears streamed down her face. "My foot…"

Four pairs of eyes dropped to her blue tennis shoe.

"The nails!" Andy pushed the other boys out of the way. "She landed on a nail."

Jamie sucked in a whimper as Andy dropped to the ground beside her and tugged her foot free.

The other boys snickered and he scowled. They spun away, snickering as they ran down the trail.

"It's okay, James." Andy stood and squeezed her elbow. "I'll help you. It'll be okay."

He walked by her side while she hobbled back to her house. Of all the rotten luck—Cole had said no girls allowed, poking a stick in her face as if she were some kind of threat to the forest.

"Don't worry, James," Andy said. "It'll quit hurting soon. We can play stick people or something until then."

Don't worry? Yeah, right. It wasn't fair—her brothers would never let her go to the fort again. They'd only put up with her because Andy had argued her case.

Andy and Jamie reached the house just as the older boys burst from the front door.

"Let's go, sissy-boy." Devon slugged Andy's shoulder. "Mom says we have to come home for supper."

Andy pushed his bother away. "In a minute."

"It's okay." Jamie moved away. "I'm fine, Andy. You can go."

He frowned, so she forced a smile. "I'll see you later."

Andy hesitated before he nodded, then the Harris boys left for their own home down the dirt road.

Jamie took herself inside and found her mom waiting with a bowl of warm water. "A nail, huh?"

"Two." Jamie dropped into the chair Mom had pulled out. "Now I'm stuck here."

"It's not the end of the world." Mom chuckled, patting her head. "Good thing you've had your shots."

That was the only good thing. And it could be the end of her world. What was she supposed to do all summer while the boys ran off to play at the fort? She sank into gloom as she soaked her foot. Why did she have to be the only girl? *Life stinks.*

Forty minutes and a couple of Tylenol later, she was in her bedroom, lying on her back staring at the ceiling. Andy appeared through the doorway, blue columbines flopping over his fist.

"I'm sorry you got hurt, James." He pushed the flowers toward her.

She sat up, careful not to jostle her throbbing foot, and reached for his gift. "Thanks, Andy." She sighed, attempting a smile.

His shoulders dropped. "Does it hurt real bad?"

"No, not really." She flopped against her pillow.

"What's wrong, then?"

Jamie studied the textured pattern that circled the light fixture, biting her bottom lip. She blinked back her tears, looking back at him. "I'll never get to go again, will I?"

His eyes grew thoughtful, as if he was arranging an argument in his head, and then he shrugged. "I don't see why not. It was our fault anyway. We shouldn't have left the board like that."

Never failed. No wonder he was her best friend. "Thanks, Andy." She sat up and grinned. "You're the best."

He mirrored her smile, showing a flash of braces, and messed with her hair as if she were a puppy. "Just don't forget it."

Chapter One

You are more than this.

Andrew Harris glared at his smartphone while his mother's text burned into his mind. How many times had he stared at those five digital words? They came at him like a dull knife thrust between his ribs. And yet he kept opening it. It'd been months since she'd sent that text.

Just trash the thing and be done with it. His index finger hovered over the delete icon... and then slid to close his texting app instead. Apparently he enjoyed torture.

"Ladies and gentlemen, we have arrived at Denver International Airport."

The voice beckoned Andrew from his self-inflicted misery. His mother dealt out enough disappointment for both of them. He didn't need to swim in it. Shifting against the dense padding of his first-class seat, he pressed his leather loafers to the floor and cracked the knuckles in his right hand.

"...a comfortable eighty-two degrees. Please wait until the seatbelt sign has been..."

The captain's mellow voice set anticipation buzzing in his head, and Andrew discarded the jab of guilt. He reached to the floor for his carry-on, ready to be on his feet. Ready for the fresh start he'd paved for himself. This time failure wouldn't trip him up. Not here.

He ducked his head through the shoulder strap of his messenger bag while enabling his cell to receive calls. Leaning forward, he caught a glimpse of the view outside the small oval window. Beyond the tarmac and past the wide plain saturated with city life, the Rockies ascended to the sky with royal dignity.

Colorado. It'd been a long time. Somewhere tucked securely in the folds of those majestic peaks, life had made sense.

Rising from his seat, he shifted his attention to the attractive woman across the aisle—the one he'd caught eyeing him before they landed. She stood, adjusted her tight-fitting blouse, and acknowledged him with a flirtatious look.

He cleared his throat. An attractive woman—an attractive, interested woman—made for the start of a good weekend. What better way to kick off his redirected future?

You're a better man than this.

Ugh. That voice. Again. Forever intruding upon his life. What more did Mother want from him? He'd graduated from Stanford Law. He was a successful lawyer. Why couldn't she just be proud of him, rather than digging up his personal flaws and flinging pointy shards of metal at them? His chest seemed to cave, and a sharp ache pressed against his stomach. Great. Even halfway across the country and without actually saying a word, Mother's disappointment could needle his gut.

Not today. Do-overs weren't like the sunrise—they didn't happen every day. The space he'd gained from his family would allow him to breathe, to be whoever he wanted. No pressure, explanations, or apologies required.

Glancing back to the woman, Andrew set his focus on the anesthetizing pleasure of physical attraction. "After you." He swept a hand across the small space.

Her dark, perfectly plucked eyebrows rose. "A gentleman?"

He winked. "Maybe."

With a sultry grin, she let her eyes roam over much more than his face. The tip of her tongue grazed subtly along her bleach-white teeth.

He swallowed a self-satisfied chuckle, certain how this little interlude would end. "Are you home or here on business?"

She smirked, as if she might hold out on him. "Who's asking?"

This game he knew. Well. Touching the small of her back, he nudged her through the exit. "Andrew Harris."

"Business." She flipped her dark hair over her shoulder as they passed through the Jetway. "You?"

"Relocating."

"So you're new to town?"

A nod would suffice. She didn't need to know his life story.

"That's too bad." Her bottom lip poked out in a flirty pout. "Now you can't show me around."

Smooth laughter rumbled through his chest. "You might be surprised." He winked again, and then his cell went off. Checking the ID, Andrew smothered a groan. Anthony Locke wasn't to be ignored. Not when the powerful attorney was now his overseeing senior partner.

"I'm sorry." He tipped the phone toward her as if she'd have a clue who the man was. "I have to take this."

The willowy brunette put a hand on his bicep and slipped him a business card. "Call me," she mouthed, pointing to the cell number. Her dark curls slid off her shoulder as she tipped her chin in a way that exposed her neck, and Andrew waved as she stepped away.

**

Andrew woke up alone. He'd called Diana from flight 1287, and they'd gone out for drinks. But Cheryl had called somewhere around eleven, and that had put an end to the night.

Stupid conscience.

Running a hand over his stubbled chin, he shuffled into the kitchen. His loft was mostly bare, but a coffee maker sat on the counter with a bold blend at the ready. He growled at the empty room, willing the ache in his head to subside.

After a half hour and two strong cups, Andrew decided the day should begin. Huh. What to do? Rinsing his mug, he took inventory of his loft. He ought to go shopping for furniture. Couldn't sit on boxes forever.

His phone chirped from somewhere near his bed, and he rummaged through the pile of dress clothes lying crumpled on the floor. Where was that thing? Wait. His jeans. He'd changed before he'd gone to the bar last night. Locating it before the call went to voice mail, he checked the number and groaned.

"Hello, Mother."

"Hi, Andy. How are you this morning?"

"Mother…" Clearing his throat, he tried to conjure up something that would pass as a respectful tone. "Why are you calling me so early?"

"It's not that early. Did you forget to reset your watch?"

He shut his eyes and held his head. Late nights didn't escort pleasant morning phone calls. "I slept in today."

"Of course. Listen, I know the timing is fishy, but Yvette Bright is sick—it doesn't look good. She's at Saint Joe's there in Denver, and I'm coming to see her."

"Who's Yvette Bright?"

"Oh, Andy, surely you remember."

Uh, clearly not. "No, Mother. I don't."

Her voice cracked. "Pastor Bright's wife?"

The silence gave him time to think. Good thing, because if it involved a pastor he'd have to go way back. All the way to— "Oh, from the mountains, right?"

"Right." She sighed. Disappointed or relieved? "Anyway, I'll be there Monday night."

"Mother, I'm not ready for company." He raised a fist to his forehead, bumping it as though he could smash the fiery headache. Did she have to call when he was hungover?

"Don't worry." Her voice turned sharp. "I'm not staying with you. I've booked a room downtown. I won't be in your way."

His hand fell to his side, and he blew out a puff of air. "When does your flight get in?"

"Not until eight."

9

Grinding his teeth, he searched a cabinet for the bottle he'd opened the night before. Right where he left it—thank God—and enough to make do. Rum went with coffee, right? "I'll pick you up by the baggage claim. Call me when you land."

"All right." She took a breath, and the pause made him edgy. "I miss you, Andy."

Great. Manipulation first thing in the morning. He tipped the bottle again, splashing more liquor into his mug. "Mother, it's Andrew, and I just moved."

"I know, but I feel like you're walking out of our lives."

As if she'd let that happen this side of her fabled rapture. He brought his rum and coffee, minus the coffee, to his lips. Good ole Morgan burned down his throat. "That's not what's going on."

She sighed, firing those arrows of disappointment as only she could. "Fine, Son. I'll talk to you later."

Click. Done. A jolt sizzled in his head, and his skull felt like it was going to crack. Andrew walked over to his unmade bed and dropped onto the mattress. He stared at the ceiling, wishing the day was done. He needed a distraction.

Turning his neck, he caught sight of the tourist pamphlets scattered across the floor.

Explore the Rocky Mountains.

A trip home would be just the thing.

***

Jamie Carson parked in her usual spot as the sun crept over the hills. Watching the light seep through the peaks, she breathed in the new day. Camping in her meadow connected her to the past—reminded her of the things she'd cherished. It was the perfect way to begin her summer break.

After a twenty-minute hike on a path she'd known well, she reached her campsite. Barely visible through the trees, the old house stood as a familiar stranger. Stopping to adjust her backpack, she gazed at her childhood home. Memories played out before her—playing hide-and-seek, chasing butterflies, and waging snowball wars—beautiful, haunting shadows from a time long gone. She lifted her camera, and her hands trembled.

Why did she cling to those days?

She turned to the trees across the meadow. Faint scars, brown in the white aspen bark, bore testimony to the fort they'd built so many years ago.

"Jamie," Andy's adolescent voice cracked, "promise me..."

Forcing the air from her lungs, she turned away, cutting the memory short. How stupid to hang on to something that had happened so long ago. They'd been kids. Too innocent to make meaningful promises. Too young to feel so much.

She pushed against the twinge of regret. It shouldn't be there. Lifting her camera, she snapped a picture of the tiny mountain house. One more to add to the hundreds she'd collected. After forcing her shoulders straight, she swallowed. Forward on in life. God had never left her. Not once.

Chapter Two

Black Hawk wasn't the ghost town Andrew remembered. Monstrous buildings clung to the blasted mountain walls, their neon lights proclaiming great wealth. Loose slots. Easy money.

Yeah, right. Alluring facades to tax the poor.

He recognized very little, as though this hadn't been his childhood home. The old buildings and houses along Main Street had been replaced by flashy hotel casinos and massive parking lots. His quiet hometown had morphed into a painted giant, once again luring droves of gold diggers into the historic mining town.

A little red-brick church sat among the glitz, dwarfed by the steel and glass. Andrew wasn't sure why the visual awkwardness of the building bothered him. He'd long since escaped the entanglements of religion. But this had been home for almost sixteen years, and that small church... well, perhaps some things were still sacred.

His head began to pound again. He wasn't sure what he'd been looking for, but a tourist trap wasn't it. Andrew turned around in the nearest parking lot and headed back toward Highway 119. On a whim, he turned left instead of right. Dory Lakes waited twenty miles farther up the mountain.

Instead of an isolated little patch of houses, the old neighborhood had transformed into one of those trendy, expensive, showy-destination-home kind of places. He felt like an intruder as he cruised the winding road. Massive log homes mocked the modest seventies-style structures, and his old house had become the eyesore of the block.

Why had he tortured himself? Disgusted, he floored the gas. Less than a mile down the road, however, he jerked to a stop. Their path was still there. He pulled into the ditch and killed the engine. As he climbed out of the Mustang, the magic of his childhood beckoned him into the trees.

The trail snaked past two houses and into the forest. Emerging from an aspen grove, the foot path led him to an open expanse of grass and wildflowers. The meadow. It hadn't changed. No bulldozer, developer, or weekend resident had destroyed it.

He and Jamie had played here once upon an enchanted time. He could picture her clearly, an adorable girl with strawberry-blonde hair and a melodic laugh.

Suddenly it was worth the drive. Andrew felt like Andy, the carefree kid he'd been so long ago. Sheltered by the fortress of the woods, life had been good.

As if pulled by an unseen force, his attention shifted to the grove of aspen where their fort had been. To the sight of his favorite childhood memory. The bittersweet moment replayed. Her hand in his. His thumb brushing at her tears. And the last thing he whispered before he kissed her.

"Denver's not that far, Jamie."

He hadn't seen her since.

So many years had passed, and life didn't look anything like he'd planned. Like delicate stemware carelessly dropped against a wood floor, the forest's spell shattered. The hypnotic power of this place— of their past—wasn't reality. Beauty was deceptive. The world was rushed and uncaring. People were selfish. Hope was an invention of the imagination.

Andrew turned away from the scarred aspens, intending to go back down the trail. A twig snapped behind him, halting his steps, and he turned to see a woman step into the clearing.

"I thought I heard someone." Her voice was calm, but her eyes held caution.

Flashing a smile, Andrew took her in from head to toe. Her light-brown ponytail held a hint of red and poked out from a blue ball cap. Lightweight pants draped an athletic build, and a green cotton tee shirt highlighted her emerald eyes. An expensive camera dangled from a strap around her neck.

Hello, Jungle Jane. He took another visual tour.

She drew back, and her eyes narrowed. "Are you lost?"

His ego ruptured. "No, I'm sorry." Andrew glanced away, shoving his hands in his pockets. It'd been a long time since he'd met a woman who didn't welcome his notice. "I grew up here. I just came to see it again."

Her jaw dropped. "You grew up here?" She tilted her head suspiciously. "Where?"

When he pointed northwest, she laughed. "Andy?"

His study turned curious, and this time she didn't react with offense. A slow smile returned as the girl from his memory slid into the woman standing before him. "Jamie Carson. You have to be Jamie."

Her giggle sounded girlish, familiar—like when she'd stolen his baseball cap and flung it into the trees. Laughter tickled in his chest.

"Of all the people to run into, I find one of my favorites." Delight painted her face. All hesitation vanished as she moved to hug him.

The embrace was innocent, her joy sincere. It touched the deep reaches of his heart, a tender place he'd abandoned when life had turned ugly. "I was reliving some of the days when we were kids." He glanced to the stage of his memories. "I wish some things had never changed."

Her attention also drifted to their hideout. He studied her at his side, wondering which scene she saw in those trees. Questions lurked in her eyes, and the last words he'd said to her drifted through his mind. An implied promise... one he hadn't kept. Breathing suddenly became difficult.

Why?

Don't ask, Jamie. I guarantee you don't want to know.

She blinked, as if she'd heard his silent plea, and a tiny smile tilted her mouth. "Are you up for a cup of coffee?"

His chest relaxed. "Yeah, that'd be nice."

Following her around the tree line, he discovered a small dome tent sheltered in the evergreens. After settling her blackened coffeepot in the white-hot ashes of her fire pit, she joined him on a log.

For the first time in his adult life, Andrew sat with a desirable woman without a game plan, without an ulterior motive. He felt a genuineness that had long since become foreign. "Do you often camp in your own backyard?"

Jamie snickered. "It's not my backyard anymore. We moved a couple of years after you did. And yes, I often camp here."

"Your parents don't live here anymore?"

"No." Her posture wilted. "My father lives in Iowa. He remarried eight years ago, and his wife's family farms there."

"I'm sorry." The words tripped off his tongue. Remarried? The Carsons had been such a solid family. "I didn't know they'd separated."

Jamie tilted her head, her eyes sadly curious.

What had he missed?

"They didn't." She looked at the ground. "My mom died."

Air rushed from his lungs. "I'm so sorry, Jamie." Resting an arm on his knee, Andrew rummaged his brain for answers. "What happened?"

"Cancer." She cleared her throat. "She got sick not long after you left. We moved to Denver, too, to be closer to Saint Joe's, but she just couldn't beat it."

Andrew scanned their childhood playground as a heavy silence pressed against him. Why hadn't he known? Their families had been close—very close. His gaze found her again. Raw emotion etched her profile as her jaw clenched. Something sharp split his gut. All their growing up, he and Jamie had been inseparable. He *should* have been there for her.

"How old were you?"

"She died two weeks before I turned eighteen." She bit her lip and looked at the ground.

On instinct, and with a familiarity time had not diminished, he settled a long arm around her shoulders.

She rested her head against him. "I haven't talked about my mom in a long time." After drawing a long breath, she moved for the steaming kettle and poured the coffee. A peaceful smile graced her face as she returned.

His calloused heart softened a little. "I wish I'd known…"

She picked at the bark on the log, and a long stillness hung in the air. Peeking up, her eyes locked on him, and an unvoiced question penetrated the silence. *Where were you?*

His jaw clamped hard. *Please don't ask.* He could little remember that particular year, much less explain it.

Jamie shifted and stared into the aspen grove, absently sipping her coffee. After clearing her throat, she leaned away. "It was a long time ago."

She wasn't going to ask. Andrew barely squelched a sigh of relief, though he lamented her retreat.

"My mom was amazing." Jamie squared her shoulders and turned her eyes to his. "I don't remember a single day that she didn't find something to thank God for."

It wasn't trite. Should have been, but it wasn't. Her passion took him captive. And pushed him away. He tried to ignore the growing chasm between them. There wasn't a good reason to feel inadequate. It was perfectly logical to reject fairy tales.

Why, then, did he suddenly feel like a traitor?

He swirled the coffee in his cup, fighting against the self-reproach that still lurked in his conscience. The suffocating silence needed to end.

"So what do you do now, James?" A safe subject, maybe. Unless she was a missionary. Or a pastor's wife.

She studied him, and he quivered at the feeling that she saw into the deep and ugly places he'd accumulated over the years.

"I'm a teacher." Her penetrating scrutiny relaxed, relieving his fear of exposure.

"A teacher?" That didn't seem right. "I can't imagine you trapped in a classroom all day. I would have guessed a forest ranger, or a botanist, or something."

Her laughter rippled with the leaves of the quaking aspen. "Well, I teach earth science, and I get the kids out into God's creation as much as I can."

There was that God thing again.

"And when I'm not taking more classes or going to conferences, I spend my summers hiking and camping." She sipped her coffee, inspecting him again. "What do you do?"

"I'm a defense attorney."

He felt trapped in her gaze. She was measuring. He was bound to fall short.

"I could see that." Her approval surprised him. "You were always good at standing up for others—making sure justice was properly distributed."

Andrew cringed. That was hardly the kind of law he'd been practicing. He looked for angles and loopholes, and questionable characters paid him a pretty penny to do it well. That wasn't exactly distributing justice. But he'd come to Colorado for a fresh start. That must count for something.

Jamie waited, looking bewildered. "Do you like it?"

Andrew shrugged. "I started at a new firm this week, so I guess that remains to be seen."

"What'd you do before?"

"I joined a practice in California right out of law school. I was there for three years."

"But now you're here." A question hung in her statement.

Andrew picked up an evergreen twig and snapped it. The less said, the less to explain—or defend. He glanced away, not willing to meet her eyes. "It was time for a change."

Her unwavering stare convinced him she could read the things he kept hidden. He couldn't take any more of her silent probing. It stirred up things he'd worked hard to sweep into a dark corner.

"It's getting late." He pushed himself off the log and gulped down the remainder of his coffee.

She stood, uncertainty and a trace of disappointment settling in her posture as she turned toward the trail. "I hope you find what you're looking for."

Nodding, Andrew shoved his hands in his pockets. "It was good to see you, James."

She lifted her eyes to his, and they softened. "I've often wondered about you." Her hand touched his elbow. "I'm glad to have run into you again."

His stomach twisted, and his lungs felt too small. She was still Jamie—sweet and forgiving and full of life. His James. He was not her Andy, though. Best to walk away now. He began to turn for departure, then paused. "Can I call you sometime?"

Oh no. Did he really ask that? They had nothing in common anymore. And being near her made him feel… deficient.

She shrugged. "Sure."

Not the gushing response he usually received. Andrew hardly knew what to do with the anomaly as he punched her number into his smartphone.

"Maybe we could go hiking or something?" That would be safe. Not a date. Not even a drink. Did she drink? Whatever. Just a walk.

Jamie grinned. "You'll have to break in those boots first," she sassed. "You'll be hurting something awful otherwise."

He looked down at his fresh-off-the-shelf footwear and back at her, sheepish under her grin. "Okay, so it's been a while. You could pick something easy, right?"

She laughed as they moved around the trees and into the bigger clearing. "I'll be back in town in time to go to church tomorrow." Her tone turned tentative. "You could go with me, if you wanted."

He stopped at the edge of the meadow. *No.* That would have been his immediate response. But he didn't say it.

The scent of pine swirled on a breeze, and across the meadow—tucked against a boulder—blue columbine bobbed unpretentiously against the gray granite. Andrew took in the scene of his childhood, and life refocused. Made sense. Going to church with Jamie Carson was the most natural thing in the world.

"All right, Jamie."

Her smile bloomed full, and his heart did a strange hiccup. She gave him directions, and he set out for home.

But the illusion faded as he stepped onto the road. What had he just done? Church? No way. He'd stand her up, because he wasn't going there. Not in this lifetime.

He stopped short of climbing into his car and turned back. Jamie had vanished, but he could make out the gabled end of her old house. Something powerful gripped his insides. Defiance drained away, and his shoulders slumped.

Maybe for Jamie.

***

Rain splattered against the dome of Jamie's tent. She snuggled deeper into her mummy sleeping bag, wishing there was a way to right her world again. Images from their childhood had pushed into her sleep, specifically a bouquet of blue columbine and a sweet boy's smile.

"Thanks, Andy. You're the best."

He mirrored her smile, showing a flash of braces. "Just don't forget it."

She hadn't forgotten—a friend like that didn't vanish from memory. She still had those flowers, in fact, perfectly preserved, just like that moment from so long ago. Before he vanished from her life completely.

Andy, Lord? After all this time he shows up now?

He'd promised to stay in touch after he moved, and her young heart had innocently believed him. When the months went by without a word, she had retreated into loneliness. The solitude intensified the following year as she watched her mother painfully transform under the cruel decree of cancer.

Through it all, she'd wished for his shoulder to cry on, for his wit and for his protection. But she'd never heard from him. Something burned in her chest. He'd been her best friend. Forever. Why hadn't he been there? He hadn't even bothered to come to the funeral— though his parents sat right next to her the day she buried her mother. Jamie had asked about him, and she couldn't shake the way Kathy Harris's voice had dropped to a sad whisper.

"He's not who you remember," she'd said.

No, indeed, he was not.

Chapter Three

Andrew sat in his Mustang and stared at the sprawling church. Why had he agreed to this? Why was he following through with it? Sundays were sleep-in, lazy, kick-around-in-sweats days. Not get up at eight, dress-up-and-get-going days. Religion was such a noose.

He heard her footsteps before he saw her. Within seconds, Jamie's lovely face dropped by his open window, and Andrew pulled in a breath. Still the cutest girl he'd ever seen. How had she managed that?

"Hey." She smiled pleasantly. Not flirty. Not conceited. Just kind. So not normal. "You found it."

"I did." He should tell her this wasn't for him, but that innocent charm of hers paralyzed his tongue. Jamie stepped back, and he climbed out of the driver's seat.

His attention wandered to the church, its tall steeple piercing the deep blue sky. The white cross at the top mocked him. *Poser.* He tried to ignore the icon and that annoying little voice.

Jamie waited at his side. Andrew forged a smile. Her hair was darker than he'd remembered—closer to brown than blonde—but strawberry highlights still gleamed in the sunshine. Clothed in a red v-neck dress, she looked more like an accomplished woman than a rambunctious girl who loved a good sword fight.

"No Wild Jane today?" He debated which version he found more endearing.

Jamie rolled her eyes. "I did take a shower, thank you."

He grunted a laugh, and they moved toward the front of the building.

"Melissa." Jamie addressed a dark-haired woman as they neared the door. "This is the friend I was telling you about."

The woman smiled and held out her hand. "Hi."

"Melissa, was it?"

She nodded. "That's right."

"Andrew Harris."

Jamie touched the other woman's shoulder. "Melissa is my housemate."

"I see." Andrew shoved his hands into his pockets. "Are you a teacher as well?"

"No, I'm a nurse." Petite in build, she looked like the run-a-marathon, outdoorsy type. "I work in surgery at Lutheran Medical Center."

Andrew nodded.

"Jamie tells me you grew up in the mountains together."

"We did, for the most part. My family moved away when I was almost sixteen."

"It's beautiful up there." Melissa smiled. "You two were lucky kids."

Paradise lost. How lucky was that? Andrew searched for a response, but music beckoned from inside. Jamie and Melissa took to the steps, and Andrew found himself walking into a large sanctuary before he could think of a good excuse to leave.

Church hadn't changed much. The music was different—he didn't know any of the upbeat choruses. He tried to picture the drum set in the small, red-brick mountain church and smothered a laugh. The rest, however, wasn't new or impressive. Friendly people pretending to have it together. Bibles available under the chairs for any poor sap who needed to numb the emptiness of life with mythical promises. Pastor Whoever's voice droning on about some passage that surely would change a life—or something.

Whatever.

How had Jamie bewitched him into coming?

Relief spiraled through him when the final benediction was pronounced. Jamie laid a hand on his elbow, leading him out of the sanctuary. She cheerily introduced him to several people as they went, and he tried to ignore the itch to run.

"We missed you this morning, Jamie," an older gentleman spoke as they neared the exit. "Were you camping?"

"Yeah. It rained a little last night, so everything took more time. Was it a good class?"

"It was." The man nodded and looked at Andrew.

"Pastor Bartley, this is my childhood friend, Andy." Stepping to the side, Jamie introduced him. "Andy, this is one of our pastors, James Bartley."

"It's nice to meet you, Andy."

Andrew. He swallowed the urge to correct the man. "It's nice to meet you as well."

"Are you new to the area?"

"Sort of. I grew up next door to Jamie, but I've lived in California since college. I just moved back."

"I see. I hope we'll be seeing more of you."

"Thank you." *Not a chance.*

Jamie finally led the way out the door, and Andrew smothered a sigh of relief when they made it to her car.

"I'm glad you could make it." She unlocked the door.

He nodded, and then his brain went haywire. "How about lunch?"

What was he thinking?

Quiet moments skipped by while Jamie examined him. She was going to reject him. Probably for the best. Yet he couldn't let it go.

"You're suspicious of me." He crossed his arms.

Caution filled her green eyes. "You've changed."

You haven't. He shrugged. "It's been thirteen years. Who hasn't changed?"

She tucked her lips between her teeth.

Who was he kidding? He couldn't fit into her world any more than she could his. Then again, his world needed some tweaking. She could be just the thing.

"You're right, James. I'm not the same, but all of my favorite memories have Jamie Carson in them."

Her eyes softened, and a gentle grin lifted her mouth. "There's a Mexican place a mile down the road." She reached for the door handle. "I'll meet you there."

Tension rolled from his shoulders as he breathed a silent sigh. It'd been a long time since he'd had an honest friend.

***

Jamie pulled out of the church lot, her mind racing. All of those childhood memories slammed against the reality of who Andy had become.

She'd felt his discomfort all morning, even before he'd stepped out of his Mustang. His eyes darted around as if he were afraid somebody would point him out as a fraud, and she didn't miss his white-knuckled grip on the steering wheel. Clearly they had moved in opposite directions. What was she to make of that?

What was he after with her? His initial survey of her face and form had offended her—she knew the type. But all her memories with him were precious. And evidently he felt the same. She couldn't write him off.

What was she getting herself into?

Lunch. She was just having lunch with an old friend. Not that big of a deal.

Andy waited near the front door, and by the time she left her car, the waves in her stomach had calmed. Hanging out with him wasn't going to tilt her world.

"So, are you settled?" Jamie leaned against the table, fiddling with the straw in her drink.

"No, not really." Andy took a slow swig of tea. "Actually, I was hoping you could do me a favor."

"What's that?"

He crossed his arms and leaned back. "I had to shop for furniture yesterday, but they can't deliver until tomorrow—they said two. I have to work until six."

She caught on before he was done. "Andy, I'm not sure I'm the right person for—"

"Please, James? I need someone to accept it. They'll set the furniture up however you tell them."

Red flares exploded in her mind. *Caution: quicksand ahead.* "I'm not an interior designer. To be honest, my stuff comes from thrift stores and garage sales. I wouldn't know where to put anything."

Fixing puppy-dog eyes and poking out his bottom lip, Andy folded his hands in dramatic plea. "Look, I'm literally begging you. Please?"

His face looked so comical, Jamie couldn't help laughing. *Warning. Warning. Warning.* She pulled in a long breath, ignoring the buzzer in her head. "Do you have Internet?"

He snapped his fingers. "Lightning fast."

Jamie grinned, consenting against her better judgment. "There'd better be chocolate waiting for me."

Charm oozed from his eyes as he gave her a cockeyed 'I win' smile.

Oh, brother. What have I done?

"On second thought…" She tipped her head and held his gaze. "I think you'll owe me more than chocolate."

He sat straighter. "Really?" His eyebrows twitched with an ornery challenge. "What's that?"

"Come with me tonight."

Interest warmed his gaze, and his voice dropped. "Where are we going?"

Yeah, right buddy. Do you think I can't see through you? Jamie swallowed back a sudden wave of nausea. "ABF." Did she just squeak?

"ABF?"

"Adult Bible Fellowship."

Frost eclipsed the heat in his eyes. Andy dropped back in his chair.

"Jamie…" He drew a long breath. "Church really isn't my thing. It's all good that you're still into it, but I got out a long time ago."

Jamie examined the man, a stranger with familiar eyes. "I'm not sure church is really anyone's 'thing.' It's not about doing stuff, or being in a building. It's about me and God. You and God. Anything less would be bondage."

Andy said nothing.

***

Monday afternoon found Jamie in Andy's loft in a revitalized LoDo district. One of those trendy, overpriced areas that attracted the young and unattached. It suited Andy.

She took a tour around his living space. Boxes were stacked neatly against exposed brick. Large windows lined the entire outward wall, and sunlight gleamed off the dark wood floors. It was all clean, modern, and expensive.

A jolt of inadequacy rippled through her gut as she slid into a bar stool opposite the kitchen. Andy had done well for himself. His mom had said he'd gone to law school—Stanford—but Jamie hadn't imagined what success would look like on him. How it would have changed him.

Her phone jingled from her purse, and she shelved her tumbling thoughts.

"What are you doing?" Andy's voice had already become familiar, making her smile. Maybe he wasn't so different.

She put him on speaker as she opened her MacBook. "I'm getting ready to upload some pictures."

"Did my stuff come yet?"

"What stuff?"

"Hilarious."

She thought she could actually hear his eyes rolling, which bubbled laughter in her throat.

"Did it?" he persisted.

"No, but it's only two-fifteen. Deliveries are always late. Thanks for the cheesecake."

"Of course." His voice smiled. "That coffee on the counter is for you too. Take the bag after you brew yourself some."

Jamie slid off the stool and rounded the counter to the sink where Andy kept his coffee maker. She picked up the bag of gourmet brew and inhaled. Ah… The strong scent of coffee held undertones of a nutty smoothness. How did he know? She grinned as her eyes traveled over his kitchen. A lone glass rested in the sink. Otherwise, the area was pristine.

Curiosity had her picking up the used glass. A tiny ring of amber liquid rested in the bottom. Apple juice? Andy hated apples—he'd always been an orange guy. She held the glass up to her nose and sniffed. *Whew!* The pungent odor of alcohol stung her sinuses, making her eyes water. Definitely *not* apple juice. Did he drink that this morning?

Andy interrupted her alarm. "Do you want to go to the airport with me tonight? I'm sure Mother would be excited to see you again."

Clearly he didn't realize that Kathy had maintained contact with her over the years. She set the glass back in the sink and swallowed. "You should meet your mom on your own, Andy. I still have laundry that smells like campfire."

Silence. She wondered if he was thinking up an argument. Hoped he wasn't. Her stare focused on that empty glass, and apprehension clawed in her chest. She seemed uncommonly powerless under Andy's persuasion—certainly a vice that could get her into trouble.

***

"I ran into Jamie Carson." Andrew settled into his new club chair across from his mother. He grinned as he scanned the room. Jamie had done a good job.

"You did?" Mother looked pleased. "How is she?"

"Doing well, as far as I can tell. She's a teacher out near Golden." She smiled. "It must have been fun to see her again."

"It was. I went up to the old house—she happened to be there." She laughed but didn't comment.

After a space of quiet, Andrew continued. "Why didn't we know about Mrs. Carson?"

"We did." Her eyes moved to the floor.

"I didn't."

Sighing, his mother stood. Without a word, she made her way to the kitchen and refilled her glass from the tap.

Andrew scowled. "Why didn't you tell me?"

She took a sip, settling a steady look on him. "I did."

Rarely did she become somber with him anymore, and he understood what she was not saying. Heat crept up his neck, but it annoyed him that she made him feel guilty.

"You did *not* tell me." His lawyer's voice took over. "I would have remembered something like that. I felt like an idiot when Jamie told me."

Mother kept a cool gaze. "How well do you remember your brother's wedding?"

Not very. Andrew swallowed as anger simmered in his gut.

"That's what I thought. He was married the same year Stacy Carson died. I doubt you remember much of anything your freshman year of college, and I'm not going to shoulder that for you. Your father and I both told you about Stacy. And we flew back for her funeral."

Without him? They came, they were with Jamie, and he wasn't? No wonder she kept him at a safe distance.

Chapter Four

Andrew groaned as he unlaced his hiking boots. Why hadn't he listened to Jamie? Three miles into their hike, and his ankles were starting to swell.

"Sore?" Jamie unsnapped the buckle at her waist and eased out of her pack.

He laughed, pulling off his socks so he could dunk his feet into the mountain stream. "Yeah, I didn't wear these at all before today."

She sent him a sympathetic pout. "We can have lunch here and turn back."

Andrew wanted to argue. The falls were just another two miles up. Except two miles ascending a mountain past timberline would take at least an hour, not to mention the return trip.

"It's not as if we can't do more another day." She settled against a tree a few feet away. "Besides, I can snap some decent shots right here, so you'd actually be doing me a favor."

Like that was the truth. Andrew's foot twisted in a cramp. He couldn't take a couple more hours. Dipping half a nod, he conceded before he reclined against an aspen.

Jamie smiled as she fidgeted with her camera.

He watched her switch out a lens. "That's an expensive-looking piece of equipment."

Her grin peeked from under the bill of her hat, though her focus remained on her work. "It was."

"Hobby?"

She shrugged. "More or less. I took a few classes in college."

"Do you do portraits?"

"No, just nature. I don't have an eye for arranging people and props. I capture what God has already put together."

Andrew sat up, leaning toward her. "It's digital, right?"

She nodded.

"Can I see?"

Jamie slid the strap over her head and passed the camera to him. He browsed through her snapshots, recognizing some of their childhood haunts. Impressive. Very impressive.

"Have you ever tried to sell any?"

"I have." She smiled her shy, self-conscious smile.

It tugged on his heart, awaking the old desire to see her happy. "Well?"

"I've sold a few—enough to pay for that." Her head indicated the camera he still held.

"Do you have a gallery or something?"

"Just online. It's mostly a hobby, though. Not something I could make a living doing."

"These are very good, James." His eyes held hers while he handed her camera back.

Her skin turned pink as a look of humble appreciation crossed her pretty face. Andrew waited, sensing she wanted to say more. Hoping she would.

"My mom was into photography." She sounded timid. "Do you remember?"

Andrew thought back. He remembered Mrs. Carson often had a camera, but he hadn't make the connection before. He nodded anyway.

"When gambling was approved in Black Hawk, things began to change. It made my mom sad. She said it was criminal that people would never be able to see the raw beauty of the area."

"So that's what you capture—the raw beauty of Colorado?"

"Yeah." Her eyes misted. "I guess I want to put together a book someday. For my mom—for her memory. I don't know that it will ever happen, but it's a dream in my heart."

It would happen. Andrew was certain of it. His gaze locked on her, and something in the moment felt intense.

Jamie grew still. Her eyes widened, and the pink on her cheeks blazed. She blinked and then snatched her camera from his hands, darting away as though she were in danger.

"So…" Andrew swallowed back whatever had just sizzled between them. "Teaching, hiking, and photography. Is there anything else you do?"

Jamie flipped the camera strap over her head. "I do love a good ride."

"Ride?"

"Mountain biking. Nothing extreme or technical, but off the pavement and in the hills."

"Sounds fun." He grinned, his heart rate coming back down to normal. "I haven't been on a bike that goes anywhere since we were kids."

"I don't know why you would ride any other kind."

"I'm sold. Now I've gotta get one." He poked her with a stick. "You know that means you'll have to go shopping with me, right?"

She rolled her eyes. "Are you always this helpless?"

"Helpless?" He sat forward and made a face. "Helpless? May I remind you, my dear friend, how many times I went to bat for you?"

Jamie laughed. "You're pathetic."

He hiked an eyebrow, then chuckled. "Seriously, though. Will you help me find something decent? I don't know anything beyond a Huffy."

She shrugged. "I'm not an expert, but I'll take you to the shop that tunes mine. It'll have to wait, though. I've got the next three weeks pretty well booked."

He nodded, squinting curiously. She was setting a boundary, keeping some sort of distance. Which would be better for her.

Something unsettling sparked, and a flashback played unbidden.

You're capable of so much more. He couldn't shut his mother's voice out. *I've known you to be a young man of outstanding character. Why have you become less?*

The memory twisted his gut. That day should have been an apex in his life. He'd graduated from Stanford Law. Didn't that demand some sort of accolade? The sting pierced deep, but he attributed the ache to anger. He was almost able to ignore the fact that Mother had been the one to pick him up from county jail. Almost. Minor detail. At any rate, it'd been his graduation. He'd been entitled to a certain amount of celebratory liberties.

Mother didn't understand. He didn't have a reason to be who he'd once been; the effort was taxing and the payoff had been less than acceptable. People didn't care about character. The bottom line was the only thing that mattered. How he got there was irrelevant.

Oh, but then there was Jamie. Consistent, honest, and upright. And she did care about the journey. Andrew felt a stab of guilt with her subtle sense of caution, as if his life had been wasteful.

Wasteful? Relative concept. He shrugged away the old wound. He was successful. The rest didn't matter.

"My mother was glad to hear I'd bumped into you." He leaned back against the tree again.

Jamie's eyebrows darted upward.

"She was always quite found of you—of all of you."

"Your mom is a darling." Affection softened her voice. "Her fondness has always been returned."

A darling? Ha. Andrew studied his toes while Jamie went back to her camera. She lay back, pointing her lens through the aspens, clicking away as the leaves danced above.

Such a little puzzle. Adorable, though. Surely there was a man in her life. "Are you seeing anyone?"

Her attention snapped back. She looked sideways at him, her eyes wide. Why did he hope she'd say no? Clearly they'd never work. She was too pristine and he was… Never mind. He maintained a casual expression, and after a breath that she seemed to have held, she began to relax.

"No." She shrugged. "Are you?"

Yikes. Should have seen that coming. How much to tell? "Sort of."

"What does that mean? How do you 'sort of' date someone?"

So she was still black and white.

Who cared? Didn't really matter what she thought. "I've been with a woman, Cheryl, for about a year. It's not serious, though. More of an open relationship."

Jamie sat up, and her brows went higher.

"You disapprove?" Why was he baiting her? Her approval was irrelevant, right?

She shrugged. "It's your life—and hers, I guess. I'm not sure why either of you would want to waste your time if you knew it wasn't going anywhere, though."

How completely archaic. The logic hardly bore argument, though. Unable to conjure up anything clever, he sighed as he tipped his head toward the sky. "It's nice to have someone to claim, I guess."

Wait for it… Surely he had a sermon on Christian ethics heading his way.

But Jamie held a steady gaze and then went back to her viewfinder.

Her silence left him perplexed.

***

Jamie stumbled as she rushed out of the university lecture room. A hundred pairs of eyes zeroed in on her as her phone jingled. She should've turned the thing off and stayed for the rest of class, but Andy's name flashed on the screen. Pushing *accept*, she slipped out, hoping the lecturer wouldn't recognize her later.

"Hello?" Her whisper echoed in the vaulted hallway.

"Hey, James. It's Andrew."

"Hi." She smiled, despite her embarrassment. "What's going on?"

"Nothing, I was just finishing up for the day and wondered what you were up to."

"I'm in Greeley."

"Greeley? What are you doing there?"

"I've been up here all week. Continuing Ed. Listen, I really need these hours, so can I call you back a little later?"

Digital air hung undisturbed. Jamie felt a warning in the silence.

"Sure." He cleared his throat. "I'll talk to you later."

She caught his disappointment. What was she supposed to do? It didn't matter. Andy hung up, leaving her with dead air.

The hike flashed through her memory as she stood in the empty hall, their conversation jumbling up her emotions.

Are you seeing anyone?

So. Maybe she was naïve, but she could only think of one reason a man would ask such a question. Apparently she and Andy didn't share the same mental model. Good thing, too, because he was a flat-out no. He wouldn't have been—her old Andy had been special. But Andrew Harris, all grown up? Total disaster.

He was putting her to some sort of test, asking such things and announcing that he was in an "open" relationship. What did that mean anyway? Open to what? Mistrust? Abuse? Heartache? No thank you.

Where had that old Andy gone? Why'd he have to grow up and become… whatever he was now? And why'd he have to dance back into her life, swirling disappointment in her heart?

Jamie jammed her phone into her back pocket and sighed. Trouble. That's what Andrew Harris was. How much was this going to hurt?

***

I just need a fresh start.

Andrew had given his boss that explanation three months before. Though successful in court, a series of legal issues had put him on professional probation.

"Clean up so you can do your job." That had been his ultimatum.

He did for a while, but it just didn't stick. Within the year he landed himself in a bar fight, earning another professional censure. He resigned. He'd be happier somewhere else. A new job, a fresh start, a new life.

Cheryl wasn't thrilled. "Open" summed up their relationship perfectly, but it had nothing to do with honesty. *Quid pro quo* was more accurate. And he couldn't live up to his end of the bargain halfway across the country. She was quick and consistent to point that out.

Just break it off.

He couldn't. For all his bravado, he just couldn't. What he'd told Jamie was the raw truth. It was better to have someone to claim than to be completely alone.

A new life.

Hard to accomplish when one was still entangled in the old one. Cheryl had called earlier in the day. With all the authority her position as assistant DA afforded, she demanded he hop the next plane west. She had an engagement and needed a date.

Not an option.

She had a few choice words to burn into his ears before she'd hung up. His mood took a downward turn, and a familiar thirst began to build.

He snapped his laptop shut and gathered his things. By the time Jamie called him back, he was settled next to a twenty-something blonde. With green eyes. They'd moved well past the entry-level beers. Knocking back something more potent, the warm, numbing relief traveled through his limbs.

Jamie asked about his earlier call. He dismissed it. She said they would talk tomorrow, and that was the end of that. Ignoring the annoying prick in his anemic conscience, he lost the rest of his troubles in the anesthetizing effect of drink and the pleasures of a pretty and willing woman.

Apparently old habits carried into fresh starts.

***

"I called you Saturday morning." Jamie leaned her elbows against the table. The diner was packed, thanks to the after-church crowd.

"I know." Andy popped another fry into his mouth. "I slept in and then had some work to do. That's why I called today."

Elusive. And not convincing. "Anything going on?"

He shrugged, wiping his mouth with his napkin. "Cheryl called, and I was annoyed. I'm sorry I bothered you."

"No bother." She raised an eyebrow. "Are you two okay?"

"I haven't heard from her since Friday, but I'm not really worried."

Jamie straightened her shoulders, pushing her back against the padded rest behind her. This man was not boyfriend material. Why did he bother?

Skip it. He lived by his own set of rules. Moving on.

Except she couldn't. Scanning his face while making a conscious effort not to stare, Jamie took inventory. Bloodshot eyes? Check. Jittery? Check. Aspirin with his Coke? Check. Definitely a hangover.

Maybe it was time to nudge him out of her world. Her lungs seemed to shrink, and her chest burned.

Andy caught her looking and froze. He could read her mind—she felt sure of it. Something in his gaze begged her not to turn away.

He shifted, looking down to his drink and stirring the ice with his straw. "Do you know what you'll call your book?"

Why did he do that? Just when she was sure that he was nothing like the boy she remembered, he reached out and poured sunshine onto the fledgling hope that he was. He wanted her to believe he was still that kid. Andy had always been the one to believe in her. He'd cheered her on in every sword fight, every bike race. Deep down, he must want her to cling to those memories, to see him with that backdrop.

She couldn't help but comply. "Not really. I don't have the language skills you have, and I don't know that it'll ever happen, anyway."

Warmth filled his eyes. "It'll happen."

There he was, the hero-boy from her childhood—buried, maybe chained—but not gone. How could she reject him?

Chapter Five

"You've got your front wheel on backwards."

Andrew's shoulders dropped, and Jamie laughed. She'd had her bicycle put together and ready to ride for several minutes, and he was still fumbling with the chain and cog set, feeling like an idiot.

"I could help you, if you'd quit being stubborn. Waterton is waiting."

He raised an eyebrow. "I'll do it, little Miss Hurry-Up."

"Just sayin'. I'd like to be back before it gets dark."

"It just barely got light." He glanced at the pale eastern sky to confirm the early hour. "When did you get so ornery?"

Smirking, Jamie sat back on her saddle. "We could've been a mile down the road if you hadn't insisted on the Mustang."

Spunk, huh? He liked that. "Your car's not much bigger than mine."

"It'll take a bike rack."

Andrew rolled his eyes. "Done. Are you ready yet?"

"Just a sec, let me check my hair."

Her cheeky grin made him chuckle. He playfully popped her on the helmet, which was already fastened in place.

Within seconds, they were pedaling down a dirt road.

The summer had flown, and it was August already. Realizing out of the blue that Jamie would be back in school soon, he'd called the day before, set on a mission to get a bike. She'd met him at her favorite shop, and after a couple hours' worth of test rides, he'd left with a mid-level mountain bike.

Jamie had said Waterton Canyon was an easy ride—six miles on a Jeep trail to a dam. A good place to get started. After the first two miles, his muscles took to the rhythm of pedaling. He settled in the saddle, enjoying the granite walls, scattered scrub vegetation, and the rush of the river as it tumbled over boulders, carving a timeless path.

After four miles, Jamie slowed the pace. They rounded a corner where the South Platte took a drastic turn, and she eased to a stop near a green meadow shadowed by a sheer cliff. Twelve bighorn sheep perked to attention.

The animals examined them and Andrew and Jamie kept still. After a brief interlude, the sheep bounded across the narrow river before making an amazing ascent up the steep granite.

Andrew watched as white puffs of wool bounced from rock to rock. "How'd you know they were here?"

"They often are. I look for them every time I go this way."

She turned with a grin, and he mirrored her expression. With the ease of a long stride, she dismounted, walking her bike off the path. Andrew followed, and they stretched out in a patch of sunshine.

They sat in easy silence, still eyeing the impossible trail the sheep had effortlessly climbed. Warm August air was tempered by the cool, north-facing cliff. Across the thin, sweeping grass the river rushed and swirled—nature's music. Movement was everywhere, but peace undergirded it all. Jamie tipped her head back as if she were soaking in delight.

This was the girl who had captured his young heart. Her countenance beckoned to him. *Come, know this peace.* The whisper settled deep, and a cold fist gripped his heart. He struggled against it, not wanting to acknowledge that voice.

The silence became too much. "Will you miss your freedom when school starts?"

She stretched her arms up, then fell back on her elbows. "I always miss the summer, but I like teaching."

"You teach science, right?" He scowled, still not free from the chill of that hand.

Nodding, she sat forward. "What was that look for?"

He shook his head. Jamie leaned against her knees, obviously expecting an answer.

"I was just wondering how that works." He rubbed his chin, wishing he'd kept his mouth shut.

Jamie's forehead wrinkled. "You don't think I'm a good teacher?"

"No, that's not it." He tugged at the grass and then stared at the Platte. "It's the science part that has me. How can you teach it and still cling to the Bible? They don't agree—so do you just ignore that?"

Jamie squinted, and a frown scrolled her mouth.

What was he doing? She could believe what she wanted. Shouldn't matter to him.

Come...

Except her life jabbed him in a place he couldn't define.

"Don't be mad, James." He shrugged. He needed to let it go and get back to the fun. "It's just that they can't both be true. It seems hypocritical."

That was letting it go?

Jamie pierced him with a long look. Was there accusation in her eyes? *Traitor. You took the easy out when life got hard.*

Stop with the voice, already.

Her silence left room for introspection. He hated introspection. "That's all you're gonna do?"

What the heck? Words just kept coming out of his mouth. Baiting her? To what end? Either she'd continue drawing that stupid voice in his head, or he'd have her lose her faith. Which would be terrible. Jamie wasn't Jamie without her beliefs. They defined her, propelled her life, and made her the person he... adored?

Her eyes narrowed, and her jaw set hard. "Evolution is a theory, Andy. Not a fact. It doesn't have conclusive observations, and it can't be reproduced in the lab."

Whoa now, Crusader. Let's get our information straight. "What are you talking about? Every respectable institution of higher education has embraced evolution. Because it's a fact. The fossil record confirms it, and we're able to change things like crops using the premise of evolution." He picked up a rock and tossed it toward the river. "I think you're out of your league."

She glared at him and then shut her eyes—like she was reaching for composure. "I think there's a lot of information you don't have. We do see genetic variations, and we can use those to improve some things, such as corn production. However, it's a matter of selecting the best genetic characteristics that are already written in the code. That's the point; it's already there."

"I don't buy it." He shook his head and leaned an arm against his knee. "How about all of the fossils that confirm the process of evolution? Just go to a museum."

"Go to a *museum*?" Anger sizzled in her voice. "That's called artwork, Andy. Not science. We don't have real proof that animals mutate into another kind of animal. It's not in the fossil record. No fossils show an animal in transition. If evolution were true, we'd see that all the time."

Andrew kept still. What had he gotten himself into?

"You have to dig deeper. Did you know that there are over one hundred different renderings of Lucy? Based on the same bones, every one of them shows a different face—a different creature. You can't form your conclusions based on artwork." Jamie caught his eyes and held them. "There's tremendous detail and complexity in life. I've studied that detail, and I don't see random chaos. I see the handiwork of God."

He couldn't turn away. The connection beckoned. ***Come back and know…***

Know what? Resentment surged hot. He jerked his gaze away, silencing the call. "Whatever, Jamie."

She didn't move. Andrew fought against the urge to glance her way, but he couldn't resist. She sat with her shoulders hunched over, her eyes sad. She looked crushed, like when her brothers would call her "sissy-girl" and tell her to go away. It was the very expression that had him championing her ever since she was five.

His heart deflated.

She stared at her hands and forced a timid voice. "Have you ever heard of irreducible complexities?"

We're continuing this? "Irreducible what?"

"Complexities. Mouse-trap systems that require everything to work together, or they don't work at all. Like that scar on your chin."

Andy fingered the narrow line in his skin. It was hardly noticeable, but he remembered the day they'd raced their dirt bikes down the long hill. He'd hit a partially buried rock and lost control, splitting his chin against his handlebars.

Jamie took his silence as an invitation. "You have a scar instead of a coffin because your blood clotted—a complicated process that wouldn't function without all of the pieces in—"

"Enough." He sliced the air with his hand. "I don't really care."

Tension settled in the canyon. The magic of the day vanished.

Jamie climbed to her feet. Trembling. Watching her walk away, Andrew's throat closed over.

She replaced her helmet and straddled her bike, staring down the dirt road while she waited. Andrew eased to his feet and followed, his stomach rolling. He snapped his helmet in place. She still wouldn't look at him.

"Jamie..." He touched her arm and felt her shaking body sag. "I'm sure you're a great teacher."

She swallowed, turning tormented eyes on his, then nodded. Without a word, she pushed forward and pedaled down the road. Andrew hurried to follow.

Silence ruled their ride back to the parking lot. He'd ruined the morning. Maybe the day or—for Jamie—the whole weekend.

That was unacceptable.

They made it back to his car, and he loaded their bikes. He filled the awkward air with chatter about the upcoming Broncos' season as he cruised C-470. He asked when she would have to report back to the classroom and what the week of preparation was like before the students came. He even pulled into the Jamba Juice near Denver West and wouldn't hear of Jamie paying for her peach-raspberry smoothie.

She managed a tiny smile. Forgiveness. They'd be okay.

***

The day simply moved on. Andy had shifted back to Mr. Nice Guy and let the rest go. It should have been comforting, but Jamie wrestled with anxiety. She told Melissa about their argument as the sun hid behind the western peaks.

"It seems that it's done." Melissa swirled her spoon in a bowl of fudge mint ice cream. "Why is it bothering you?"

"I still see my old friend in him." Jamie leaned against the table. "I miss him. What if he hadn't kicked God out of his life?" She stared at her bowl of melting ice cream. "Plus, I didn't handle it well."

"Sounds to me like you handled it fine." Melissa's eyebrows drew downward. "You don't need to feel guilty about defending your faith. Especially when he provoked you."

Jamie slouched against her chair, her eyes stinging. "I just don't want to push him away from God."

"People choose what they want to believe." Melissa chewed on her lip and drew a long breath. "Jamie, don't take this like I'm coming down on you, but this guy has you pretty tied up. You've been… preoccupied all summer, ever since you ran into him. Are you sure he's good for you?"

Jamie's tongue felt thick, and her stomach ached. Was he good for her? No, not really. He made her feel all knotted inside.

But maybe she was good for him.

Chapter Six

Andrew raked the room with his gaze, ignoring the irritating squeal of the steel guitar saturating the bar. Better than the silence in his loft, though. Too much room to think—to hear Jamie's voice echoing in his head.

What the heck were irreducible complexities?

She wasn't dumb—and he hadn't really studied anything she'd been talking about. Made him feel dumb. She couldn't be right, though. Plenty of really smart people said she was dead wrong. Evolution had been proven, which meant God wasn't real. Or if he was, he wasn't much to worship. Which was why he didn't care either way.

"You gonna just stand there, handsome?"

His attention slid over to the blonde behind the bar counter. Star. That was her name, right? Pretty sure. She was a flirt, but it never went anywhere with her. "Nope. Not if you're pouring."

"Whatcha want?"

He focused his gaze on her face, then let it slowly travel over her shape. "Whatever you've got."

One corner of her mouth tipped up, and she patted the top of the counter. Star played the game well, which was probably why Manny kept her around.

He dropped onto the stool in front of her and laid an arm across the bar. "As long as it's strong, I don't care."

She flipped a tumbler onto the space in front of him."One of those nights, eh?"

Every night was one of those nights. He closed his fingers around the glass and barely let her finish pouring before he tipped it back. Hot. Pungent. Not enough. He slapped the glass down and nodded toward it.

She tipped her bottle again, but didn't pour. "Alone tonight?"

No, he wasn't. Between the reel of Jamie's lecture and that crazy voice that wouldn't shut up, he hadn't been alone all evening. Was he losing it? With two fingers under the bottle in her hand, he sloshed another shot into his glass. "Just keep it coming."

***

Jamie's phone jarred her awake. Through the blur of sleep, she glanced at the clock. Two a.m. Who would call her at two a.m.? Ringing demanded her attention again, and she checked the ID.

Andy.

Awesome. Suddenly she was wide awake.

She answered. "Andy?"

"No, Miss, I'm sorry. Listen, this is Manny, down at the Bull Pen. Your boy Andrew is here, and I need someone to come get him. I called the usual guy, but he's not answering, and I'm closing up. He said 'call Jamie.' Anyway, can you come get him?"

She tossed her covers off and set her feet on the floor. "Where are you?"

"The Bull Pen. Two blocks from Coors Field. Could you come?"

Jamie rubbed her eyes, trying to digest the information. The Bull Pen? A bar. Had to be.

"Uh, yeah." She was going to drag Andy out of a bar. At two a.m. Pretty sure her daddy wouldn't approve. "It'll take me about twenty minutes. What street are you on?"

Manny gave her the address, and Jamie threw on some clothes. Nearly half an hour later, she was walking into a place she never would have entered voluntarily—especially at that hour.

"Hey." The man behind the bar smacked the form slumped over the counter. "Your ride is here."

The form moved, and Andy's face emerged from his folded arms.

"James…" He gave her an idiotic grin and stumbled toward her. His arm dropped over her shoulders, and she glared at him.

She turned to the bartender. "You don't happen to know where his car is, do you?"

"Doubt he brought it." The man shrugged into his coat. "He's smart enough to leave it home when he intends to get smashed."

It really wasn't shocking, but the information knotted Jamie's stomach. "This is a habit?"

Manny snorted a small laugh. "Something like that." He walked them out the door, helping her steer Andy to the sidewalk. "Will you be okay?"

Stupid question. They'd have to be. Clearly Manny wasn't going to get Andy home. She walked toward her car, Andy staggering beside her, and opened the passenger door. "We'll be fine." Jamie pushed Andy into the seat. Manny stepped away as she slammed the door shut, and she walked around the car and slid behind the wheel. *God, please let us be fine.*

She'd barely driven a block when Andy flipped the knob on her radio. "Why don't you listen to real music?"

She smacked his hand, then hit the power button.

"That's right." He rolled his head to look at her, speaking in his most disdainful voice. "Miss Priss does not lower herself to such drivel." His hand hung in the air, and he laughed.

Blinking, Jamie refused to cry. It was juvenile to get all weepy because he was a mean drunk. He was too gone to know the difference, and he didn't mean it. She bit her lip. Tears were only for really bad moments.

Andy continued his sharp monologue, critiquing her "squeaky-clean life," her "unrealistic church world," and anything else he felt was utterly ridiculous.

Jamie remained silent.

The minutes were few to his loft, but it felt like forever before she was asking for his keys. Once inside, she shoved him into his leather club chair. Andy stared at her through glassy eyes while she moved to the sink to fill a glass with water.

"You're really hot."

Jamie met his eyes and held them. There was only one thing to say to the vacant, wasted man. "Goodnight." She dropped his keys onto the granite counter and took quick steps out the door and down the five flights of stairs.

Her vision was blurry the entire drive home.

***

Jamie peeked through the window beside her front door. Yep. Andy. She jerked on the knob, and sunlight spilled onto her floor. Glaring at the man slouching on her porch, she folded her arms across her chest.

He looked at her and then at his feet. "Hey, James."

She stepped back and leaned against the wall next to the door. "Hi?"

After stepping inside, Andy pushed a paper coffee cup into the space between them. "Thanks for coming for me."

Her stomach knotted as she continued to stare at him. The reality of what he'd become—of the downward spiral of his life—made her nauseated. And she really wasn't ready to see him again.

Silence drew a long divide between them before he nudged her hand with the cup. "A truce? Please?"

Coffee? That was his version of "I'm sorry, it won't happen again"?

Would it happen again?

"Look, I went out because Cheryl and I..." He rubbed the back of his neck, then set the coffee on her scuffed-up coffee table. "I was mad, and I got a little carried away. Okay?"

Sure. No problem. Everyone drinks themselves stupid when they have a fight—totally normal. She watched him as he dropped into her overstuffed chair like he belonged in her home. What did he and Cheryl fight about all the time, anyway?

"Does Cheryl know you hang out with me so much?"

One eyebrow cocked upward. "Why are you worried about Cheryl?"

She swallowed, staying her nerve. "Maybe that's why she's so hard on you. Maybe it bothers her."

"I wouldn't worry about it."

Scowling, she took a step closer. "You wouldn't worry about something bothering your girlfriend?"

"Jamie, quit." He stood, hands perched on his waist. "Cheryl isn't anything like you, and you have nothing to do with the things that come up. And to tell the truth, if it came down to a choice, it'd be an easy decision."

Was that supposed to be a compliment? She blinked. "Why are you with someone you could so easily toss aside?"

"Just, really, don't worry about it." His sharp tone ended the conversation.

Jamie dropped onto her couch in silence as questions tumbled around in her head. How could he be such a great guy and then turn into such a jerk?

***

Andrew wiped the water from his face as steam floated around him. After a five-mile run, he'd been sure a hot shower would melt away the rest of his tension. His leg muscles felt better, but his head continued to pound.

Why did Jamie bring up Cheryl today? Clean out of the Colorado blue sky, she had to rip that one out and ruin a day that had already started badly. Couldn't she just accept his apology and move on?

Never mind that she was right.

He cleared the mirror and stared at his murky reflection. Clean shaven, the scar on his chin caught his eye. He fingered it as Jamie's voice echoed in his memory.

Instead of a scar, you'd have a coffin.

Nice. The day went from bad to worse. That conversation continued to jolt him more than he cared to admit. It just wouldn't die. Instead, Jamie's words mingled with older ones—not from her—making him miserable.

"It's wrong, Andy." Mother, though in tears, had been emphatic. *"What you're doing is wrong, plain and simple."*

"Who says?"

Her shoulders dropped. *"You're seventeen. It's illegal. And more importantly, God says to keep away from drunkenness."*

"The law is only to keep the deadbeats off the street." He shook his head and rolled his eyes. *"And I've already told you, I don't believe the Bible. It's irrelevant and juvenile, and I'm not going to be bound by it."*

He hated that he could hear his contemptible voice as clear as if it'd just happened, and even more, that his mother's heartbroken expression etched in his mind like one of Jamie's perfectly framed photographs.

Die. Just die, stupid memories.

He glared at the image in the mirror and turned away before the horrible, empty nothingness consumed him. Wrapped in a towel, he stomped to the kitchen and searched the cabinet beside his refrigerator. Waiting like a faithful friend, a bottle of amber liquid promised reprieve.

"It's wrong, Andy."

He didn't care. About any of it. He just didn't care.

Chapter Seven

"Hey, Teach, whatcha doing?"

Jamie pulled in a sharp breath as she tossed her bag into her car. He hadn't called since his pathetic apology Monday night. Silent the whole week. She thought she'd wanted the distance, but it had been agonizing. "I'm going home. What are you doing?"

"I'm at work." He sounded completely normal, as if nothing had happened. "So listen, there's a deal on the slopes, and I think we should go."

"Skiing?"

How could he switch gears like this? Conflict rotted inside her — she had replayed their arguments over and over until she'd almost been convinced that *she* needed to apologize. He seemed to shed all of it like water off a rain slicker. So not fair.

"Right. Tomorrow. Are you up for it?"

Was she ready to see him again? No, that wasn't the real question. What she should be asking was could she stand up to him in person? He'd crossed a line and taken advantage of the fact that she hated conflict. "Andy, I haven't been on skis since high school. I'll look like an idiot."

His laughter tickled a smile from her mouth. She was such a rag doll.

"An athletic girl like you?" He snorted. "Not at all. You're going—I've finally found something you're not going to smoke me on the first time out, so it's a done deal."

She remembered sliding down snow-packed trails. It'd been a blast. She bit her bottom lip. Maybe they could talk—iron out this whole problem and be okay. "You're on. What time?"

"I'll come by your place about seven-thirty."

That gave her the whole evening to map out her speech. One where she drew a line, confronted his behavior, and redefined their relationship.

Jamie was ready to go when his blue Mustang pulled up in front of her house Saturday morning. Andy strode up her front walk, sporting a new, gray ski coat and carrying two cups of steaming coffee. She mentally calculated his expensive new attire. Money ran through that man like water down a drain.

"Ready?" He held the door open, tipping his head to his car.

She took in his blood-shot eyes. Hungover again? This was a bad idea. *Say something.* "Sure, but I'm not riding up to the Eisenhower tunnel in that rear-wheel drive. I think we should take my car."

Yeah, that totally addressed the real issue.

He eyed her. "Chicken."

She shrugged and moved the opposite direction. Maybe in the car she could bring up this drinking habit of his. "Besides, my car will carry skis. Let's go before you have an ego fit."

Andrew laughed. With a click of a button, he locked the Mustang, following her to the garage.

Steven Curtis Chapman's greatest hits played softly from the rear speakers as Jamie's Honda took the curves on I-70 West. She tapped her fingertips on the steering wheel, wondering how to begin her outlined talk. *A*—she wasn't at his beck and call. *B*—he owed her a real apology—like the words, accompanied with humility. And *C*—he drank a lot. Too much.

Got it. Ready, go...

"Is this guy still popular?" Andy dipped his head toward her stereo.

"Chapman?" He recognized the voice? Huh. When was the last time he'd heard the man sing?

Wait. That wasn't what they were going to talk about. It'd be rude not to answer, though. "Think so. I still like him."

Andy nodded, but he seemed annoyed. Not a good time to bring up last weekend.

"I was going to call you last night to see if you were up for pizza." He turned down the volume. "Some other things came up, though."

Okay. "Not a big deal. I got my laundry done and some tests graded." And prepared a speech…. Yes, that.

Andy stared through his window, raking his fingers through his hair. Jamie felt his tension, and worry turned in her stomach. Maybe this wasn't a good idea. Any of it.

"You'll make some lucky man a fine wife, James."

Whoa, wife? Her eyebrows pulled together. "Doing laundry is what qualifies a 'fine wife?'"

He chuckled. "No—although I'm sure it couldn't hurt. I just meant that you're a good person."

Where was this coming from?

Conversation paused for nearly two miles before Andy filled the silence. "Were you ever close?"

"Close?"

"To marriage. Were you ever with a guy you thought you'd marry?"

Jamie laughed quietly. What on earth was going through the man's mind? Was it even possible that he and Cheryl were discussing marriage? *That* would be a disaster.

"Not really. The guy I dated my freshman year in college—we talked about it some."

Even from his profile, she could see Andy's brows go up. "What happened?"

She kept her focus on the road, not sure how to explain.

Andy's head jerked forward, and his spine went ramrod straight. "Did he break your heart?" Ferocity edged his voice.

Jamie snorted. "You're awfully worried about it."

He rubbed his jaw and shrugged. "You're my friend."

Huh. His overprotective reaction was sweet, in a weird, long overdue sort-of way. If only he'd been around ten years ago...

"Well, I wasn't really heartbroken. I was—" She licked her lips, fumbling for words. "I just needed to get some things straight in my head, and in my heart. He wasn't ready for the burdens I came with, and I wasn't in any position to be unloading those on anyone but Christ."

Andy clenched his fist. "What does that mean?"

"It hadn't even been a year since my mom died, and my family was scattered. I was terribly lonely. He was a good guy. A lesser man would have taken advantage of my vulnerability, but he made it clear that he couldn't walk with me through the things I needed to deal with."

"He couldn't go with you through grief? *That* sounds like a 'lesser man.'"

Jamie shifted her attention to his face for the tiniest breath. If only he could understand.

"Andy, at the time it hurt, but what happened was honestly for the best—for both him and me. He couldn't be the net underneath me. I needed to be okay without him. There are places in the heart that man cannot touch, and this guy had enough discernment to know that. At the time, I guess I didn't. When we broke up, I had to start pouring my pain out to God. I had to come to Him for the love I was aching for."

Andy stared out the windshield, and out of the corner of her eye, she could see his expression harden. She held her breath, expecting an argument.

"So what happened?"

Worse than an argument. He'd brushed her off.

He turned his attention to her. "Do you know where he is now?"

"I do." She forced a smile, ignoring the sting of Andy's indifference. "He's in Texas working for a cartography company. He's married, and as of last Christmas they had two little boys."

Awkwardness took over and the conversation died. She'd been sincere—she was happy for the couple, even if she was slightly jealous. Not because she'd loved the guy, but because she hadn't planned on entering her thirties as a part of the singles crowd. But that was a different conversation—and not one she wanted to have with Andy. Besides, the day was too beautiful to waste on disappointment.

Chapman's voice filled the silence. Andy seemed to ripple with aggravation. Something was poking him inside. Maybe beneath all his bluster, he was lonely.

Of course he was. Why else would he fill his life with the superficial? He had to be lonely. Afraid. And lost.

Her heart ached, and the last vestiges of anger about the weekend before vanished. He needed her to be his friend—to show him the way back to who he'd been.

Andy smacked the power button on her radio as if it were a mosquito needling his skin.

Could he read her thoughts?

***

Andrew battled irritation as they neared the Eisenhower Tunnel. Mother loved that song. He hated it.

Actually, he'd been annoyed before he'd dragged his hungover body out of bed that morning. Cheryl had called the night before. She seemed to hate him.

Why would he stay with her?

Because he couldn't bring himself to end it.

How did Jamie live the way she did? Clean. Safe. Dare he say, boring? But she seemed happy. Didn't need the comfort of someone to claim. It was puzzling, and yet envy seemed to rot inside his gut.

The drive up hadn't helped. Why couldn't she just put on some punk music and let loose? She was little Miss Mary Poppins; always perfect. Even in how she handled heartbreak. Who lived like that?

Jamie Carson, that's who. She was such an anomaly. Such a strange, cute, perplexing, addictive woman.

And maybe she was his ticket out of trouble. Her lifestyle was the perfect avenue for self-reform.

Jamie exited off I-70 just below the tunnel. Time to shift gears. He didn't need to waste a Saturday on psyche garbage.

Plows had worked to clear the parking area, creating a brownish ring of gravel-packed snow, but the powder on the slopes sparkled clean and brilliant in the morning sun. Colorado blue skies contrasted against pure white ski runs, inspiring a rise of anticipation.

Andrew looked at Jamie.

She smiled.

So addictive. Rolling the tension from his shoulders, he took in the cold air, as refreshing as Jamie's calm presence.

Let it go. It was just a song.

"Are you ready for this?" He knew full well she was.

"Sure." She grinned as she pulled her stocking cap over her ears. "No laughing at me, though."

He chuckled, provoking a look of warning. In little time they had their boots snapped and were clomping over white powder, a pair of skis balanced over each of their shoulders.

They managed to clear the first challenge—safely mounting the chairlift—without looking like rookies. Andrew was relieved for Jamie's sake. She'd looked like a timid rabbit as they'd approached the block. An instinct to protect brought his hand to her elbow, and the moment passed without incident.

Or not.

Jamie wasn't frail. She took on life—and the people in it—with boldness. With him, however, she seemed… exposed. Raw in a way that kept him spellbound.

Had she been that way with Mr. Texas? Had he seen her courage melt, leaving an uncertain girl in the shadows?

Probably not. No man alive could resist that kind of paradox.

So what had he been like? What had *she* been like? Whatever did she mean—he couldn't be the net beneath her? The tension in his shoulders returned as he replayed Jamie's explanation.

Just say he wasn't the one, James. Don't excuse his unworthiness. Anger wasn't foreign to Andrew, but this fierceness felt deeper. Justified. His thoughts had threatened to pour out of his mouth in the car, but by some unusual feat of self-control, Andrew kept them unspoken. He listened to her prattle on about the other man's life while the embers of offense smoldered in his chest.

I'll bet she went to the wedding, smiled all the way through it, and wished them great happiness.

Why should the thought make him angry?

"Are you okay?" Jamie's intrusion brought him back to the slopes.

"Fine." He forced a smile. "Just going over a case in my head." Sort of.

"Is it a tough one?"

Andrew's eyes rested on her. He couldn't see her face beneath the winter gear and tinted goggles, but he could imagine her genuine expression.

"Baffling."

"Will you win?"

Will I win? I can't begin to understand. What will I win, if I do? "I don't know."

Thankfully, Jamie let it rest. His mind returned to the drive up, and suddenly the music haunted him. The lyrics to "His Eyes" pressed against his conscience, and the stirring in his gut felt like indigestion. Against his will, more words began to echo from the past.

Where can I go from your Spirit... if I plunge into the depths, you are there.

Andrew groaned, lamenting the AWANA program he'd attended as a kid and the verses forevermore tattooed on his brain. Why was he bent on torture? Today was supposed to be fun. Glancing at Jamie, who sat perfectly content, he pulled out his smartphone and snapped a shot of them together.

"Those are always silly." She leaned into his shoulder to peek at the screen. "Nobody takes good pictures with their arm stretched out as far as it can go. Did you see if you cut our faces in half?"

Tugging on his gloves, Andrew rolled his eyes, relieved to be back in the present. "Be nice, or I'll take you on a black."

***

Jamie's memory had been correct—skiing was a blast.

By lunch her legs were well on their way to Jell-O, feeling like they had after she'd run the Bolder Boulder. They dropped their trays of grossly overpriced food at a table near a huge window, and she reached to undo the boot straps.

"Sore?" Andy's movements mimicked hers.

"Getting there."

"Me too," he confessed. "The first time out is always brutal."

Jamie smiled as she stretched her stocking feet, reaching for her hot cocoa. "It sure is beautiful, though. Thank you for the invitation."

Andy grinned.

She held his eyes; they seemed clear again. His moods ebbed and flowed. If only she could understand the tides. *Save him, Jesus. He's drowning.*

They ate in easy silence, both captivated by the scene beyond the lodge. Hills rose up in every direction, some gradually, some severe. Evergreen trees contrasted against the snow-covered ground, making the paths easy to see. Skiers slid down without any predictability. Some were graceful, their edges dancing in harmony with the powder. Others were choppy, kicking up snow haphazardly and often landing on their backsides.

Her mind wandered, replaying their conversation in the car. *What* had he been thinking? If he were seriously contemplating marriage, she'd need to force an intervention.

"So, what was going on in your head earlier today?"

"Earlier?"

"The marriage stuff." She paused, and Andy shifted in his chair. "Were you ever engaged?"

He laughed. "Um, no."

She waited, expecting something more.

Andy set his coffee down and leaned both arms against the table. "I don't think I'm the marrying kind."

"Mmm." Jamie chuckled, though not because it was funny. Sadly true, actually. "Then what brought it up?"

He shrugged and leaned back. "Because you are, I guess. I'm surprised that you're not. It seemed a bit of a mystery to me."

Dropping her stare, she felt her face warm. "I'll take that as a compliment, I guess."

"It is."

She nodded, too aware of his unhindered admiration. What exactly did he feel for her? Sometimes she saw the reflection of her childhood tomboy self in his gaze and felt safe. Other moments, however, like this one, she was sure he saw her as a woman — an attractive, interesting woman. That felt... delicious. And dangerous.

He leaned on the table again. "Are you going to Iowa next week?"

"No." She looked at him, and the safe friend stared back. The ball in her stomach softened. "Thanksgiving break isn't long enough to make the twelve-hour drive worth it."

Andy nodded. "My parents are flying in. Do you want to join us?"

"I usually go to church. We play games and eat junk all day." She paused, studying his expression. The pull of his silent persuasion tugged her to indecision. It'd be like having family again. "I'd love to see your folks again, though. It's been a long time."

He crossed his arms with a shrug. "They'll be here all weekend. What if you came over on Friday? That way you could do both."

Trepidation spiraled deep in her stomach as she agreed. Such a pushover. She knew Andy pretty well. She also knew Rick and Kathy enough to know there was bound to be conflict. Somehow she'd landed herself somewhere in the middle of it.

Chapter Eight

Clinking stemware and soft music overtook the clamoring noise of the 16th Street Mall. Andrew opened the door to the restaurant, and Jamie passed through. They barely made it to the table he'd reserved before his parents swept upon her.

"Jamie!" His mother was all joy as she gathered Jamie into her arms.

Andrew stayed back. Jamie fell into his mother's embrace as if they were related. Hadn't she said that it'd been a long time since she'd seen them? That would make them near-strangers. This was crazy.

As soon as his mom released her, Dad pulled Jamie to his side.

Andrew began to feel like an intruder.

His father smiled tenderly. "It's been way too long."

Jamie nodded and laughed as enthusiasm animated her eyes.

Andrew drew upon his courtroom manner, assuming a neutral expression. This was over the top. She was acting as though his mother was her long-lost best friend. Which was, in fact, his title—and he hadn't received this kind of greeting upon their reunion.

He wasn't given much time to ponder Jamie's connection with his parents. Their waitress arrived with menus, and the hungry quartet plunged in.

His father settled a napkin over his lap. "How are your Dad and Karen?"

Andrew's head snapped up from the menu. How did his father know about Karen?

"They're both well." Jamie fingered the fork in front of her. "Karen will retire from the college this year, and Dad is planning to hang up his badge in five years."

"Does he miss the mountains?" Dad asked.

"Not as much as I thought he would. He comes back once a year or so, though, and we find some rocky slope to climb."

"I don't remember your dad climbing," Andrew said, still feeling like an outsider.

"He didn't, not when we were little." Jamie's green eyes fell on him as she sipped her water. "He started when I was in college. I think he saw it as something we could share."

How could he stay mad when she turned those emeralds on him? Plus, Andrew caught an underlying tone, one he was sure she didn't intend. He recalled her comment about being lonely after her mother's death, and something sharp jabbed his heart. Mentally, he filed it, wondering if he'd have a chance to ask her about it on his own.

Dinner moved on, but Andrew couldn't relax. The invitation he'd extended to Jamie was just as much selfish as it was benevolent. And his aim had been dead on; she did make things easier. Except he hadn't banked on this sort of reunion.

They'd clearly kept in touch, and Jamie knew more than she let on. All of it? God help him.

She still treated him like her best friend, though. That deserved some latitude. Plus, he was using her as a shield from his parents. His throat constricted. What if she knew that too?

They stayed at the restaurant for more than two hours before they caravanned back to Andrew's loft. He turned on the Xbox, and the night slipped by as they took turns playing Wipe Out. Jamie yelled and laughed like she had when they were kids, and his parents joined her antics. It had been years since time with his family had felt so easy—fun.

It was late, even for a Friday night, when his parents donned their coats to head back to the hotel. Jamie mirrored them, slipping her arms into her own ski coat, but she stilled when Andrew put a silent hand to her elbow.

They bid his parents goodnight, and he closed the door. Jamie stood nearby, pulling on her gloves.

"What's up?"

"I'll walk you down."

"I could have gone down with your folks."

He squeezed her shoulder. "I have a favor to ask."

She nodded and waited for him to retrieve his coat.

Andrew held the door for her and followed her to the elevator. "What time does church start?"

She examined him, her lips pressed together in a frown. The elevator chimed, and they both stepped on.

"What's that look for?" He knew perfectly well, but he didn't think she'd actually voice what was in her eyes.

"I'm not lying for you, Andy."

She sounded calm but resolute, and Andrew weighed his arguments. If he were charming, she might shrug off her irritation, but lying to Jamie didn't seem like a solid long-term tactic. A direct approach would probably spark an argument, but at least it would be honest.

"I'm not asking you to lie. It's just that they'll want to go, and it will save me from a guilt-riddled afternoon if we just do it. So, please, tell me what time it starts."

"Deceiving your parents is the same thing as lying."

He cocked an eyebrow. "You deceived me."

Her mouth fell open. "What?"

"You never told me you kept up with my parents."

"You never asked. Your mom writes to me a few times a year, and I write back. I can't tell you how much that helped—especially after Dad remarried."

Her glare bore into him, though he was sure she didn't mean to flare his guilt.

"You could have mentioned it."

She shrugged. "I didn't know it mattered. I wasn't trying to deceive you."

Typically innocent. Andrew crossed his arms. "Whatever. Just help me out here."

"Why?"

Her disappointment could have crushed his resolve, but he stubbornly blocked it out. "Because you're my friend, and you want what's best for me."

"What's best for you?" She tilted her head like she was scolding a child. "Lying is never what's best for you. You could be honest. Better yet, you could be the man they raised you to be."

"Enough, Jamie." He sliced the air between them, hating that she flinched. "That's not your business. I'm not asking *you* to lie. I'm just asking for a time."

He hadn't meant to use that condescending tone. But it came so readily. Was it that unreasonable to ask her to help him with this?

The doors slid open, and they walked down the deserted hall and out the door to the parking garage. Andrew pushed a hand through his hair. Swallowing his ire, he switched to charm.

"Please, James?"

Jamie unlocked her vehicle before she made eye contact. She stared at him as though she could see through his façade, but her face softened.

He couldn't squelch the grin that was sure to clinch his cause.

She sighed and her shoulders dropped. "I go to the eleven o'clock service."

He opened her door, his boyish smile in place. "Thanks, James. I'll see you Sunday."

Her mouth set with disappointment as she reached to shut the door herself.

Andrew worked to keep guilt at arm's length.

***

Sunday morning Jamie found Andy still intent on his cover. Somehow he managed to time his appearance with hers, and she walked into the church alongside the Harris crew. To say that Kathy looked pleased would have been an understatement, and anger burned in Jamie's stomach.

The four of them sat together, and after the service Pastor Bartley recognized Andy, which played neatly into his charade. Jamie sent him a glare when she was sure she had his attention alone. He didn't smile, but his eyes were pleading. She looked away, her shoulders sagging.

Rick and Kathy asked her to join them for lunch. Jamie pulled at the belt of her wool coat while she debated. She couldn't stand watching Andy deceive his parents. She didn't know when she would see them again, though, and having Kathy love on her touched a spot in her heart that still ached for her own mom.

She agreed, and the afternoon was mostly enjoyable. She couldn't swallow her indignation with Andy, though. She didn't even feel guilty giving him a mild taste of the cold shoulder.

He ignored it.

***

"I know you were upset with Andy yesterday." Kathy leaned toward Jamie, her voice soft. She had called the evening before and asked Jamie to an early breakfast before school.

Jamie froze with her fork loaded and halfway to her mouth.

"And I know why." The older woman finished her thought. "He's not fooling us, Jamie. I'm sorry he put you in an awkward position, but we know the truth."

Jamie set her fork down, the bite of food still waiting.

"You've probably figured out that Andrew has been floundering," Kathy continued. "He has been for quite some time. I just wanted you to know that while we're very pleased that you and Andy have reconnected, you need to be on the cautious side."

Kathy fiddled with her napkin, folding it neatly, and then crumpling it in her hands. "That sounds a little cruel coming from his mother, and to be honest I would love to see you be the reason he comes back to us. But we don't expect you to save him."

Jamie's lips pressed together as her head bowed. "What happened?"

Kathy sighed. "He spiraled. I don't know how else to say it, and I'm not clear why. He was so angry when we moved to Denver. Angry with me, mostly. He didn't understand, and, truthfully, he still doesn't know the full picture. After that, it seemed there was one small step after another, and then one day he was just gone."

Kathy paused, sniffing as her eyes welled up."My Andy became Andrew. Had it only been the name, who cares, you know? But he became pompous and rebellious. His freshman year in college he spent more time drunk than sober. He nearly lost his scholarship. He had a full academic scholarship, and he very nearly threw it away. It was as if he didn't care. His father finally made it clear that we were *not* paying his way if he lost it—we couldn't afford to even if he was a model student. He managed to beg his way back through his college advisor, but oh, was he ever mad at us."

Kathy inhaled, slumping against the back of the booth. "He absolutely hated it when we moved out to the coast, sure that we were stalking him. It never occurred to him that his father's career was still a little important. Teaching at USC was a dream job for Rick.

"Anyway, Andy's not quite as cold anymore. There were a few things that happened in California that chipped off his arrogance. I don't know the whole story—some trouble at work, I think. He decided that his life needed a new direction, and now he's here."

Jamie digested the story. She could fill in some of the blanks— namely drinking. A lot. The 'spiral' still didn't make a whole lot of sense, though. Unless 'ungoding' his universe put him in a tailspin.

"Why did you move from the mountains?"

Kathy drew a long breath, and Jamie felt bad for pushing. "I'm sorry, Kathy. That's not any of my business, and I certainly didn't mean to imply that it's—"

"I know." Kathy stopped Jamie with a hand on hers. "Life is messy sometimes. That's why we moved. Rick and I were in way over our heads, financially. We were in a mess, and everything was horrible. The boys and I rarely saw Rick, and our marriage was pretty rocky. We couldn't afford to live up there in the first place, and commuting was brutal. In the end we had to leave. Our house went into foreclosure, and we didn't have a choice."

"I'm so sorry." Jamie reached for Kathy's shoulder. "Oh, Kathy, please forgive me for prying."

"It's all right." Kathy leaned toward her. "In many ways, our story is a miracle. Rick and I were just about done. I didn't think we were going to make it. When we moved to Denver, we got an apartment together, but I thought Rick would stay there and I'd find something else. God intervened. We found a church and a counselor, and we began to rebuild our life together. Unfortunately, Andrew was lost in the storm."

"What happened to Devon?"

"He was eighteen when the whole situation boiled over. He went to college and started his own life. He followed in his father's footsteps, and now he's in the math department at Baylor."

"Andy never talks about him," Jamie said. "Did they have a falling out?"

Kathy gave a sad little laugh. "Many."

Jamie didn't have the heart to ask why. "Andy smiles the same when his guard is down." She squeezed Kathy's hand. "I can see in him the kid that always stuck up for me."

Kathy's mouth tipped with a small smile. "You always brought out the best in him."

Chapter Nine

With the holiday over, life became hectic. Finals were less than four weeks away, and school demanded more of Jamie. When Andy called on Friday, however, she made time to talk. They hadn't spoken since Sunday. It was time to call a truce.

"Hey, Andy. How was your week?"

"Long." He paused.

Oh, *that* tone. She'd come to know it all too well. Why in the world did he stay with a woman who grated on him?

Andy sighed. "Do you want to go somewhere tonight?" She could picture him jamming a hand through his hair. He always did when he was frustrated.

"I really can't, Andy." She hated to turn him down, but she did have a life beyond him. Thankfully. "I'm babysitting for a couple from church tonight."

Silence fluttered between them.

"All right." He sighed. "I'll catch you later."

"Andy?" She caught him before he killed the call. "What's up?"

"Nothing." Another pause, then another sigh. "I talked to Cheryl. I just needed to go clear my head. Don't worry about it, though."

Jamie hesitated. How far should she push? "Why do you do this? Why are you hanging on to something that makes you crazy?"

"Not helpful, James."

She groaned. It was always the same. If he'd just had a fight with Cheryl, she probably should leave it alone. Drawing a breath, she changed the subject. "Did your folks get home safe?"

Andy growled. "Why are you so taken with them?"

"What?" Bad shift. Apparently everything was off limits tonight.

"You're continually pointing out that they're good people," he barked, "that I'm lucky to have them, how much you admire them. What's the deal?"

She wasn't continually praising his parents. They hardly ever came up in conversation. Her body stiffened as her voice turned hot, matching his. "I don't know what you mean."

"Come on, Jamie. You do it to reform me. Like you think I'll change if you keep reminding me that I have good roots."

Her mouth fell open. What on earth?

Andy didn't let up. "I don't know why you admire them so much. They're not as flawless as you seem to think. In fact, they almost disowned me."

Enough. She wasn't stupid, and she knew the real story. "Telling you that they're not going to pay for your college education isn't anywhere near the same as disowning you, Andy. I'm not so innocent that I can't read between the lines. Even if it wasn't a financial issue, they were well within reason, and you and I both know it."

Silence. Had he hung up on her? With this kind of mood, he would. Why did she put up with him? Maybe it was about time he knew what she really thought. "What happened to you, Andy? Your parents love you. What was so tragic in your life that you think you have the right to be so mean?"

Andy snorted. "Listen to you. Did you minor in psyche? Look, I know in your perfect little world there's a cause and effect for everything. That way you can fix what you don't like. But I'm fine, there's nothing wrong with me. I don't need some tragic sob story about my mother dying or my parents rejecting me or anything else. If you want to figure me out, it's really quite simple. My parents drive me nuts, I don't believe in God, and I will live however I see fit. These are the facts, and you're not going to change them."

She sat stunned, her head pounding. His rant felt like an arrow through her soul. Silence rang painfully in her ears. Pulling the phone away from her head, she found her hands shook. Her thumb slid over the screen, and she tapped *end.*

Tossing her cell to the couch, she glared at it as if she could see him sitting there. *End.* She needed out. Being Andy's friend could only lead to heartache.

***

Andrew jammed his hand into his hair. What had he just spewed out of his mouth? This entire week had been a disaster. From the moment his parents had landed, he'd been tied up in knots. Mother disapproved of everything. His car—"Isn't it a bit pricey for a new job?" His loft—"Must cost a fortune to live downtown." And of course she had to open *that* cabinet. She'd said nothing, but he'd heard everything. *You're headed for trouble. Again.*

What did she know? Mother couldn't understand the pressures he worked under. Criminal law was a tough field. Everyone he knew took the edge off. Somehow.

None of that was Jamie's fault. He swore under his breath as hot guilt throbbed through his veins. She hadn't deserved it. Jamie was the sweetest, most sincere person he knew. Manipulation wasn't in her playbook. What was wrong with him?

He reached for the phone he'd chucked across the room onto the club chair. His call went to voicemail twice before she finally answered.

"Jamie," he whispered.

Nothing.

Andrew wasn't sure what was worse, imagining the anger in her green eyes or hearing it loud and clear in her silence.

"Jamie." His voice wavered. "That was really horrible. Please…"

Still dead air. Was she there?

"Please, James?"

She sniffed. "I'll talk to you later."

"Wait. Please, let me buy you lunch tomorrow or something." Andrew clutched the cell in his hand. "Don't run away from me."

"Don't run away?" Her voice bit hard, stinging deep. "Sound advice coming from a man who refuses to deal with anything in his own life."

"James…"

"Don't." Not a trace of tears laced her angry voice. "Don't play me like that. Just give me some space. You're a lot to deal with. Sometimes I think I really don't know you at all."

The death silence returned. A hard lump in his throat made it hard to swallow.

"Maybe I'm just hanging on to a memory." Her voice cracked just a bit at the end.

Nausea swirled in his stomach as the call dropped. She *was* hanging on to a memory—but he wanted it to be true. Once upon a time, it had been true.

Surely he could still be that person.

***

Saturday morning. The sun had come out, just like little orphan Annie would sing, but her heart didn't feel the warmth. Showered and clean from her morning ride, Jamie still felt cold and muddy on the inside. Maybe a change in scenery…

Snow covered the meadow as she crossed to her campsite, but she settled on the log as though she intended to stay awhile. Usually she lost herself here. She could shed her cares and frustrations, the feelings of loneliness and the questions about God's plan for her life. They would all roll away, like Pilgrim's burden at the cross. But not today.

Turbulent thoughts remained her companions. She'd prayed as she drove the rolling road through Golden Gate Canyon, prayed as she walked the faded foot path to the meadow, and prayed as she sat in nature's silence, waiting for peace to wash over her. The stubborn ache continued to throb in her soul.

Distant memories flooded back. Most of them were happy. Andy had defended her. Andy made sure she was included. He smiled, he laughed, he was fun.

One particular memory stood out from the others. It had been a rare day, one during which Andy hadn't smiled at her in the halls of their secondary school. He didn't save her a seat on the bus, nor did he wait to walk her home. She knew him well enough to know he wasn't angry with her, but he needed to talk.

She'd found him exactly where she supposed he would be; in the very spot she sat as the memory played out.

"Hey," she spoke to him before he looked up.

His baseball cap came off, and he threw her a quick glance. "Hey."

She sat next to him, wondering why he was so down, but she didn't press.

"We're moving to Denver." He tossed his hat across the field.

Jamie's shoulders sagged, and her breath came out in a rush. Not knowing what to do, she nudged his shoulder, and he leaned on her.

"Why?" She wanted to cry.

"My mom," he spat. "She doesn't like it here. She says we never see Dad, that commuting is too much."

Jamie folded her arms, not knowing what to say. They sat together in wordless ache.

"Hey, Jamie?" Andy's adolescent voice cracked.

She looked at him and waited.

"Promise me we'll always be friends."

She swallowed hard, pushing away the anxious feeling that everything was about to change. "I promise."

She'd meant it.

That moment seemed to mark the end of her childhood. Life had never been the same. Andy would never be the same. Why did she keep holding on?

***

Andrew's head pounded as he poured his morning coffee. And not from a hangover, for once, but from lack of sleep. Anxiety had tortured him, and in an attempt to be the man Jamie thought he should be, he used every shred of self-discipline he could summon to avoid the cabinet next to his fridge.

Probably wasn't worth the effort. At least he would have slept...

After dropping onto one of his kitchen bar stools, he rubbed against the pain throbbing in his temples. Losing Jamie couldn't be an option. Somehow he'd give her a real apology, make things right.

Close to an hour later Melissa answered when he knocked on their door, looking surprised to see him.

"Is Jamie home?" He tried not to look anxious.

"No, she went hiking." Melissa opened the door wider so Andrew could step inside. He didn't. "I thought you were with her. She said something about heading up to the old house."

"Is she camping?"

"I doubt it. It's still pretty cold up there."

Andrew nodded. Slowly he turned and stepped down the steps of their front porch. "If she gets back before this afternoon, will you have her call me?"

Melissa nodded, looking concerned. Andrew didn't stay long enough to entertain questions, though. He fished in his puffer vest pocket and removed his keys, waving mildly as he went.

Their meadow—sacred ground for both of them. The perfect spot to regain their friendship. If he'd believed in God, he might actually thank Him.

She was exactly where he'd guessed she would be. And oddly, she didn't seem that surprised when he stepped into the clearing. She simply sat, watching his progress across the patches of snow until he lowered himself beside her on the log.

Stillness extended between them. The forest to the left and right, the hills that rose up in every direction—even the sun seemed to pause.

Jamie stared into the trees. "I was just remembering."

He stretched out his legs and leaned back on his hands, hating the tension between them.

"It seems so strange—those days feel like a lifetime ago, and yet they're so vivid in my mind. Sometimes I really believe I'm still that kid and that nothing has changed."

"What were you thinking about?"

"The day you told me you were moving."

He remembered. How appropriate.

"Jamie, last year, when I ran into you—" He shifted to face her. "It was the best thing that's happened to me in a long time."

She looked into his eyes, and he could feel the comforting shadows of their childhood in her soft expression.

Promise me we'll always be friends.

"I know I've changed." He covered her hand and held it. "Not really for the better. I can be a huge jerk—I could think of another word, but I doubt you'd appreciate it." His breath released in a ragged sigh. "The fact is, James, our friendship is the best thing going for me right now."

She nudged his shoulder with her own, and he leaned on her for a moment.

I promise.

Her head rested against his arm, and the last traces of strain evaporated. "We're still friends."

Chapter Ten

Sometimes heartache is a scheduled affair.

May sixteenth came on a Wednesday. The day was hardly noteworthy for anyone else, but for Jamie it was always something.

Eleven years.

Her mother had endured so much pain, and she bore a heartache few could truly understand. She faced death knowing that she would never hold her first grandchild, due in three months. She wouldn't see her middle child graduate from college and continue on to medical school. And she would never watch her daughter walk down an aisle, dressed in white—all things a mother ought to see, joys that were crowning moments in motherhood.

Stacy Carson never complained, though. She whispered words of love and encouragement to her children and her husband. Even with her last breaths, she praised God for the opportunity to love them. The woman had hardly been recognizable to her teenage daughter, and part of Jamie had been relieved to let her go. But oh, how she missed her.

Jamie left school as soon as possible. Her home was quiet, and she pulled out the worn notebook she kept in her dresser. Inside were wildflowers she and her mother had pressed over two decades before, a note her mom had sent in her lunch box her first day of junior high, and the letter that her father had given her a week after the funeral—one her mother had written only a month before.

She lovingly touched each treasure. Precious memories of an amazing woman. *Thank you, Father, for such a mother.*

After finding a pen, Jamie stopped in front of an old frame on her wall—the only decoration that hadn't come from her camera. She fingered the papery blue flowers behind glass. Mom had helped her preserve them. A memento of two of the most important people in her young life. In many ways, they were both gone.

Blinking, she took her journal to the deck out back. She soaked in the warm afternoon sunshine and the slight hint of lilacs as she let her heart speak to God.

You tuck me safely beneath Your wings.
If on my own I grow in You,
I'll rest in Your good plan.
If on my own You'll sing to me, I'm content to hold Your hand.

Jamie let her pen rest and closed her eyes. Cradled in the arms of her Father, she dozed in the comfort of His love.

"Jamie?"

Her eyes fluttered open and she blinked.

Andy stepped to the top of the stairs. "Are you okay?"

"I'm fine." She smiled as Andy moved to the chair next to hers.

"I was thinking about you today." Kindness warmed his amber eyes as he handed her a pot. In it, a tuft of clover-shaped leaves was topped with purple-blue flowers. "I thought it might be a hard day."

"Blue columbine." Her eyes went from the plant to the man. *Not gone.* "How did you know it was today?"

"I asked my mom." He paused, then covered her shoulder with his hand. "I wish I'd been there for you."

He hadn't been, though. Because he'd been too drunk to hear, or care. *I needed you.* Jamie swallowed, managing a small smile. He was here now. He'd thought of her and acted on it. That was something.

"Thank you, Andy."

Andy locked her gaze, and the tenderness in his expression caught her breath. He was her Andy. The boy who'd picked her favorite flowers when she'd been hurt. The young man who'd walked her home from the bus stop nearly every day for a decade. The only man to have offered her anything to ease the pain of losing her mother.

Her heart hiccupped and her limbs felt warm. Sitting up and moving from his touch, she dropped her eyes to the flowers, trying to understand what had just happened.

Andy nudged her arm. "I think you need to get moving."

"Moving?" Jamie reeled, still trying to sort through her tangled emotions. "Where?"

"Let's go for a ride."

She considered a moment. It was an emotional day. That was explanation enough. And Andy was right; doing something always lifted her spirits.

Two hours later, sweat trickled down the sides of her cheeks, and her entire body felt soaked. She dropped to the ground, gulping lukewarm water from her bottle, still panting between swallows.

That hill. Wow…not for the novice rider. What was he thinking? "When did you decide to go technical?"

Andy grinned under his helmet. He was also drenched, but looked pleased with himself.

"You can't be better than me at everything." He removed his headgear and plopped down beside her. "I've been going to the clinic the Cyclery has on Thursdays. The guy there thought this would be a good ride for me to try some of the techniques they've been teaching."

"You're gonna kill me," Jamie lamented, half-serious.

"Nope, we're going to keep coming until you can ride that hill."

Jamie was not enthusiastic. Not that she didn't enjoy a challenge, but the steep, shale slope they'd just attempted seemed impossible. She didn't have enough air in her lungs to argue, though. Lying back in the dirt, her heart pounded in her ears as she slung an arm over her head.

Squinting against the bright sun, she changed subjects. "Can I ask you something and have you promise you won't make fun of me?"

Andy looked down, examining her. Vulnerability spiraled through her chest.

"Sure. I promise."

She sat up, feeling stupid. What was she doing? Why would she talk to Andy about this? Melissa would be the better choice. Her roommate was stable, logical. But Andy… well, actually he knew her better. Better than anyone, really. He saw the good, the bad, and the ugly—the latter two mostly because he provoked her like no one else. He was always honest with her, though. That was something of a rarity.

Drawing a deep breath, she plunged in. "Well, when I went to pick up my bike last week, I kinda met somebody. Sort of. I don't really know him, but we were both waiting in the service department and started talking. He'd just moved here from Ohio and was asking about some trails. Anyway, long story short, when I was leaving, he gave me his card and said if I was ever interested in riding with him to call." She finished lamely, holding the business card she had pulled out of her pocket. *Ryan Anderson, CPA.*

Andy's left eyebrow raised.

Jamie's neck warmed. "Was he hitting on me?"

Andy laughed.

Perhaps she'd overestimated his reliability.

"Oh, James." He reached to give her shoulder a shake. "I don't know how you've managed to stay so innocent. Yes, he was hitting on you."

"You said you wouldn't make fun."

"I'm not." Sincerity washed over his expression. "I hope you never change. I mean it."

Jamie stared at her shoes, certain her cheeks were about the color of an apple.

Andy gave her that teddy-bear kind of squeeze. "So did you call him?"

"No." She plucked a blade of grass.

"But you liked him?"

"Yes." She shrugged. "Well, I guess. I mean, it was all of a ten-minute conversation."

"Why didn't you call him?"

"I don't know. It just seemed awkward. I feel so stupid." She glanced at his face. If anyone could explain men, maybe it'd be another man. "Anyway, why didn't he call me?"

"Um, did he have your number?"

"Oh." Yeah, that. Jamie felt her face go yet another shade of red. "No."

Andy chuckled again. "How long ago was this?"

So, so dumb. What on earth was she thinking? "Monday night."

"Call him, Jamie." Andy shook his head and gave her a soft push. "Poor guy probably thinks you just wrote him off."

"What if he's a freak?" Jamie jerked her head up. "I don't usually go out with a man I don't really know first—or at least someone a friend knows. What if he's crazy or weird—or worse?"

Andy sat for a moment, staring at her. She knew she looked younger than she was anyway, but at the moment she felt more little girl than woman. Surely, though, even Andy would have to admit that her concerns weren't paranoid. His profession allowed him to see more than enough "freaks" to know that a woman needed to be cautious.

"Tell you what." Andy dropped his hand from her shoulder and leaned against the ground behind her. "You call him and then let me know where you're going. Cheryl flies in tomorrow. She and I can just 'happen' to bump into you."

Well, that was nice—but presumptuous.

"He asked to go riding."

Andy gave her a confident smirk. "He'll ask you to dinner."

"How do you know?"

"I'm a guy, and I've seen your pretty face. Trust me."

Jamie eyed him, flattered, but not convinced.

"Let me see that." He reached for the card she was fumbling with, plucking it from her fingers. He pulled out his phone and began punching numbers.

"Wait!" Jamie reacted with a high pitched squeal. "What are you doing?"

"He's waited all week." Andy continued dialing. "You're torturing him."

Jamie snagged his phone, clearing the number. "I'll call him."

Andy sat back and cocked his head, a look of expectation crossing his face.

"What? Now?"

He shook his head. "You're just being mean."

"I am not."

"*Call* him."

"Fine." Jamie punched in the number on her own cell. A man's voice picked up on the second ring and she nearly choked.

"Um, hi. Is this Ryan?" She dropped her head, trying to hide her face, but she didn't miss the grin spreading across Andy's lips.

"Yeah, that's me," the man on the phone answered.

She couldn't remember the last time she'd felt like such an idiot. "This is Jamie Carson. I met you at the Cyclery on—"

Ryan's chuckle tickled her ear. "I remember, Jamie. I'd about given up on you."

She tried to tuck her smile between her teeth. "Yeah, I'm sorry about that. So were you interested in riding?"

"Sure, sometime." He cleared his throat. "Actually, I was wondering if you were busy Friday night?"

"Friday? As in the day after tomorrow?" Jamie tucked her chin into her shoulder. "No, I don't really have plans."

Andy actually laughed out loud. Jamie eyed him, biting her lip.

"Good." Ryan sounded relieved. "How about dinner?"

She quit trying to hide her smile. "Sure."

"What are you up for?"

"Just casual. I'm not really a fancy person."

Ryan suggested a local restaurant near her home—which happened to be one of her favorites—and Jamie agreed to meet him. She flipped her phone shut and sighed.

"He asked you to dinner."

Jamie nodded.

Andy's brows went up again. "Say it."

She laughed. "Okay, you were right."

Andy shoved her arm. "So, Cheryl and I will meander in around eight. If it is bad from the beginning, just text me a SOS, and I'll get there sooner."

Chapter Eleven

Ridiculous.

Jamie sat in the restaurant's parking lot, five minutes early, contemplating whether or not she'd stay.

It was ridiculous that a grown woman was so unsure when a man noticed her, ridiculous that she should be so nervous about going out with him, and ridiculous that she'd had to ask another man's advice about the whole thing.

What was wrong with her, anyway? It wasn't as if she'd never been on a date before. Although, she had to admit, it'd been a while. Even before she'd run into Andy, dating had been lower on her priorities. The whole scene had long since proven to be a lesson in disappointment. After she and Andy reunited, well, he'd kept her busy. That had suited her fine. She no longer dealt with disappointing encounters with eligible men, nor did she have to battle loneliness nearly as often.

Why Ryan Anderson caught her attention and unnerved her was mystifying. Good looking, intelligent, and athletic were among his assets, but he wasn't the first man she'd run into with that resume. Andy filled the list just as well, and he didn't make her stomach flutter in a sickish, excited sort of way.

She was being ridiculous.

A black Jeep pulled in next to her Honda. A man she vaguely recognized climbed out the driver's side and sent a small wave through her passenger window. He made it to her side as she was stepping out, and he held her door until she stood clear.

"Hi, Jamie." He smiled, and her stomach began to calm. His brown eyes were soft, radiating a gentle confidence, and his stance embodied peace. "Sorry to keep you waiting."

He was nice. Now she remembered. That's what snagged her attention in the first place. Not just nice looking, although that was definitely true, but his smile was kind.

She grinned, glancing to the ground. "You didn't. I was early. I really hate being late."

He closed her car door and gave a small laugh. "I feel like I should introduce myself again."

Jamie echoed his chuckle. "Right. Jamie Carson." She held a hand out, and he accepted the gesture.

"Ryan Anderson. I'm glad you came." He motioned toward the restaurant. "Shall we?"

They waited in the foyer while a table was readied, filling the time with small talk. Jamie discovered the basics—Ryan was an accountant and had just joined a group at the Denver West complex. They were seated in short order, and as they settled in, Jamie began to relax.

"What brought you from Ohio?" she asked.

His dark eyes looked self-conscious as he grinned down to his hands. "My brother is up at CSU. When he transferred last year, I helped him move, and that was it. I hadn't been west before, and I didn't know what I was missing. So I started looking for a job, and now here I am."

"Fort Collins? Why didn't you end up closer to him?"

Ryan laughed again. "We're close, Nate and I, but I'm seven years older. When I started talking about moving this way, he made it clear that he didn't want his big brother checking over his shoulder."

Jamie nodded. "How long have you been here?"

Their waitress showed up right after Jamie found out he'd been around town for six weeks. They ordered their meals, and a small lull settled at the table.

Ryan crossed his arms and leaned on both elbows. His face seemed to naturally relax into a pleasant smile. "Did you grow up here?"

"I did." She settled back into her chair. "Up in the hills, mostly, but we moved down my senior year in high school."

"Is your family still around here?"

"No." Trepidation coiled in her stomach. She hated talking about her mom. People had a hard time seeing past pity, and she wanted so much more than charity. "I have two brothers. John is the oldest, and he's a pilot; he's stationed in Charleston. Cole is a doctor. He married a girl from Washington State, and they live there with their two kids."

Their food arrived and Jamie turned the conversation back to Ryan. He was the oldest of three. His sister, Katie, was three years younger. She was married and living in Indiana with her husband and two-year-old son. And then there was Nate, whom Jamie had already heard about.

"My mom was a little crushed when I decided to move." He finished his story. "Not one of her children stuck around. She and Dad are good travelers, though, and good sports for that matter. They'll be around."

Jamie sipped on her Coke, unable to think of anything else to say.

"Are your parents still around here?"

She hadn't avoided it after all.

"Jamie!"

She nearly choked on her soda. Evidently Andy had a flare for drama. Turning, she fell speechless at the sight of the woman standing under his arm. She'd assumed Cheryl was pretty, but the perfect size two, raven-haired model was far beyond pretty.

"Hey, Andy." Jamie swallowed a lump of inadequacy.

Ryan's eyes moved from her face to the other man's with nothing but friendliness.

Jamie swallowed again, recovering from her whiplash. "Ryan, this is a friend of mine."

Andy held out his hand before Jamie could finish. "Andrew Harris."

Ryan gripped his hand, and Andy introduced his date. "So, James, this is Cheryl. She just flew in this afternoon, and we thought we'd get a bite."

"Why don't you join us?" Ryan gestured to the table. "Our food just arrived, and we've hardly touched it."

The invitation was sweet and selfless—and maybe a little bizarre. Jealousy sparked as she looked at the beauty Andy had introduced. When she looked back to Ryan, though, his eyes moved from Andy's face to her own, completely bypassing the other woman.

Andy touched Jamie's shoulder, concern on his face. "Do you mind, James?

"Of course not."

It was done. He pulled out a chair for Cheryl, forgetting that he didn't introduce Jamie to her, and settled himself in between the two women.

"Jamie, was it?" Cheryl's voice was cultured, if not a bit edgy.

"Yes." Jamie felt her face grow hot. This was not what she'd expected.

Ryan waved their waitress over to inform her of the seating change and then plunged into a conversation. He was completely pleasant as he asked both Andy and Cheryl about themselves, and eventually Jamie relaxed enough to participate in the conversation. Somewhere in the mix, more food was ordered and delivered, and the topic turned to how Andy and Jamie knew each other.

"We grew up together." Andy grinned at Jamie. "We were neighbors in the mountains."

"I thought you were from Denver." Cheryl's piercing blue eyes flashed.

Jamie nearly flinched.

"I graduated from a Denver high school." Andy dropped his hand to the back of Jamie's chair. "My family moved down my sophomore year."

Cheryl stabbed him with a look. Andy met her gaze without moving. The chill that passed between them set goose bumps on Jamie's arm.

"Jamie was just telling me that she grew up in the mountains." Ryan rescued them all from awkwardness. "I have to admit, I'm a little jealous. What a playground you two must have had."

"It was pretty great." Andy appeared unscathed. "I hated it when we moved."

Jamie couldn't speak, even if she could have thought of something to say. She peeked at the woman across from her. Absolutely beautiful. But her voice had been stone cold, and her narrow eyes were like daggers. Was Andy really that shallow? Certainly he couldn't be that desperate.

This was all wrong. Why had she allowed Andy to intervene?

Because she was a chicken, that's why. She shouldn't have told him. Now she was caught in some kind of cold war between Andy and Miss Universe. And her first decent date in forever was sitting on ice.

"Why did your family move, Jamie?" Ryan turned his attention back to her.

They were back to that topic? She drew a long breath, her misery stacking up by the moment. "My mom got sick. She was being treated here in town, and we moved to be closer to the hospital."

The table went still, and Jamie could feel both men's eyes on her.

Cheryl's brows went up. "Did she get well?" That voice was still sharp, still cold.

"She died," Jamie answered softly. Her eyes settled on Ryan's, gauging his reaction. She saw the expected sympathy, but there was also a light that made her relax.

"I'm sorry," he offered.

At that moment, she knew why she'd been attracted to him. Somehow, with two words, Ryan was able to communicate the hope, the peace, of a fellow believer, and he gave the slightest nod as if to confirm.

"Thank you." Jamie felt a fresh boldness. "God is good, though, and my life has been blessed."

Andy and Cheryl both balked at the claim, but Ryan's calm smile remained in place, and once again his head bobbed ever so slightly.

Andy changed the subject. "So, Ryan, do you mountain bike?"

Jamie eyed the man. He was going to make her spinelessness obvious if he kept talking.

"Definitely." Ryan sat back and grinned. "Ohio had some pretty decent trails, and I've been on part of the Appalachian Trail, but I haven't pedaled in the Rockies yet."

The air seemed to relax and move on.

"You should take him to Waterton, James."

She smiled, pushing away the strain of the previous moments. "Sure, but it sounds like it would be a kindergarten level to him. I've heard about the Appalachian Trail. How much have you done?"

"Not anything crazy." He shrugged. "What's Waterton?"

"It's just a Jeep trail through a canyon. Easy, but really pretty."

"Sounds great. What if we all went tomorrow?"

Jamie could hardly believe he'd be so easy going.

Andy didn't think twice. "Sure, that'd be fun. Cheryl spins, and she's not seen much beyond downtown. What do you think, James? Would Melissa lend her bike?"

Jamie studied Ryan. He wasn't driven by competitiveness; she couldn't detect any angles, any underhanded agendas. He was just nice. An all-out grin spread across her lips. "I'll ask her."

And the plan was set.

Andy and Cheryl finished their meal and set off. Ryan and Jamie followed not long after. They sauntered to her car, and she thanked him for the evening. His reply was immediate, but then he stood, silently examining her. "I get the feeling I've just been scouted." Kindness never left his eyes.

Jamie couldn't stop the blush, or a small laugh, as she dropped her head forward. "I'm sorry. I don't usually go out with someone I know nothing about."

He grinned wider. "It's understandable, so don't apologize." Another pause extended and his voice dropped. "I hope I passed."

***

Jamie pushed her foot into her sock as her phone rang the next morning.

"Hey, we're not going to make it," Andy's gravelly voice whispered. "Is that going to be okay?"

"Yeah." She pulled on her other sock. "What's going on?" Uh, did she want to know?

He laughed, but not happily. "Cheryl spins in a gym. She has an aversion to dirt, and mornings."

Jamie had the impression he was in trouble.

"Hey, James?"

"Yeah?"

"He's a nice guy."

She sank back against her pillow and sighed. "Yeah, he is."

"Have fun, okay?"

"Thanks." She couldn't help her smile, even if it was the silly girl sort. Good thing she was alone in her room. "Have fun with Cheryl."

"Right." He didn't sound cheerful. Definitely in trouble.

Jamie couldn't help but feel bad for him. The phone call ended, though, and there was nothing she could do anyway. Ryan's Jeep pulled up ten minutes later, and they were off to spend the day under the Colorado sun.

Their morning ride turned into lunch and then an afternoon at the batting cages—something Jamie hadn't done since she was fourteen. Ryan was a relaxed, fun person, and he confirmed what Jamie had suspected.

"I grew up in church," he said while they walked to Dairy Queen. "My parents are both Christians, and I gave my life to Jesus when I was seven."

Jamie smiled and shared her own similar story.

"It must have been tough, losing your mom so young." Ryan slid into an outdoor picnic table, his dipped cone half gone. "Did you ever doubt God's love?"

Jamie sighed, stirring her soft-serve vanilla. "I don't know that I doubted so much as I couldn't feel it." She set her dish on the table. "That doesn't make sense, does it?"

His eyes, warm and serious, held hers. He slid his hand to hers, and she wove her fingers with his.

"It makes sense." He squeezed. "We all long to feel the love we know is there. But knowing it's there will get us through the dark times."

Jamie's heart sighed. If only Andy could understand too.

***

Andrew took the long way home from the corner coffee shop. The walk should have taken about four minutes, but he reached his building in a smidge under twenty. The weekend had been unbelievably long. The only good part had been meeting Jamie and Ryan Friday night. He'd guessed Cheryl wouldn't be thrilled with it, but he was willing to risk her wrath for Jamie. Anyway, given a few drinks, her sharp personality would wear off, and he'd enjoy the only good part of their relationship.

He hadn't banked, though, on how angry she really was. She didn't say a word during the drive back to his loft Friday night. When he'd mixed her a margarita, she'd leveled him a look of disdain before dropping his stemware on the wood-planked floor. She'd walked away, leaving a frigid wake.

"Did you really fly halfway across the country to deliver the silent treatment?"

Sapphire eyes turned into spears. "I certainly didn't come to witness whatever weird relationship you have going with that woman."

"My relationship with Jamie isn't weird."

"Right." Cheryl didn't raise her voice, but her sneer shouted her anger. "I know you, Andrew Harris."

"You don't know me at all."

Her eyebrows shot up. "I know you better than she does."

Steam crept up his neck. "Look, I was doing her a favor, that's all. She was nervous about meeting a man she didn't know and—"

"Since when do you do favors that don't turn to your benefit?"

He felt his ears set aflame. "Fine, Cheryl. Think what you want." He spun on his heel and marched to the door.

"Don't call me for a ride." She crossed her arms. "I'm not going to endure the humiliation of your drunken stupidity. Again."

He let the door slam without a backward glance.

Andrew woke up on his couch Saturday morning. With his head throbbing, he'd called Jamie and then decided an apology to Cheryl might salvage what remained of the weekend. Coffee was always a good start, so he headed out to track down the fancy kind Cheryl liked.

Now at his door with her skinny soy latte, Andrew pulled in a long breath. Was this really worth it? Why did he stay with someone who made him crazy? Who brought out the very worst in him?

It's nice to have someone to claim, I guess.

Deep emptiness swallowed every kind of logic and sound reasoning. Turning his key, Andrew smothered the penetrating abyss.

She sat primly on the arm of his leather sectional, her small suitcase at her feet. He shut the door without a word, turning to face the ice beauty.

"I'm leaving."

He stepped toward the kitchen. "I thought your flight wasn't until tomorrow."

"I've made other arrangements." Those blue eyes didn't flinch.

What could he say? *Good. Why? Don't come back…*

"Andrew, I don't know what you thought this thing between us was, but it's not what I thought." He nodded and she continued as though she were simply stating the facts in an arraignment. "You were right, I don't know you. I never knew you lived in the mountains. I had no idea you spent your spare time as an outdoorsy boy scout. And since when does anyone call you *Andy*?"

"She's been a good friend since we were kids. That's who she knows me as and—"

Cheryl held up a single hand. "You never even mentioned her." She held his eyes, daring him to defend himself.

He did nothing.

"I've tried, Andrew. I've been out here three times. You haven't been on a plane since you moved. I call you. You never call me."

Did her voice just waver?

She drew her shoulders straighter. "We're done."

Andrew dropped his eyes. He should feel relieved.

She stood, tugging on her wheeled luggage. "I'll get myself to the airport."

"I can take you."

For the tiniest moment, a flash of hurt sparked in her eyes. It was brief, however, and the all-too familiar coldness returned. "Don't bother."

Angry heels pounded across his wooden floor, then the door opened and shut with a thud.

Andrew sighed, waiting for relief. Now he was alone. Really alone.

Dumping the coffee, he searched for something that would dull his unending misery.

***

By the time Jamie was dressed for the morning service, she wished she'd invited Ryan to church. She'd thought to, but held back. How headlong did she dare fall? She shrugged at her reflection in the mirror. Maybe next week.

She sat in her usual spot in the third row next to Melissa. All morning her mind had bounced back to Ryan. By the time class was done, Jamie had gained nothing from it.

Jeff and Mandie Kendricks, a young couple and friends to both Melissa and Jamie, approached the two women. Mandie was sharing a funny story involving a worm and their two-year-old when Jamie caught sight of Ryan across the room. He smiled, and heat crept over her cheeks as he made his way to her. He seemed comfortable as he stepped beside her, and Jamie introduced him. Their conversation was short as the second worship service was about to begin, and in only a few minutes the group scattered.

"I thought about asking you to come here today." She glanced at her Bible. "I didn't know if you'd found a church yet."

Ryan laughed. "I've visited a couple of places, and Applewood Bible was next on my list." He gave her a warm smile, which she returned.

"Have you gone to service yet?"

"I did, actually." He sounded regretful. "Had I known you'd be here I'd have waited."

A tingle of pleasure ran down her spine. Still, she couldn't think what to do next.

Ryan touched her arm. "Is it too much in one weekend to ask you to lunch?"

She smiled as the warmth of his touch traveled down to her fingertips. "I'd love it."

Chapter Twelve

Go to sleep, you feather head.

The clock read a quarter after midnight, but Jamie giggled to herself. It'd been such a long time since she'd felt… giddy. She smiled for about the millionth time, but when she took another peek at her clock, she rolled her happy eyes. She planned to drive to southern Colorado to explore the Great Sand Dunes for the week, and she wanted to get an early start. It didn't seem likely as the minutes ticked closer to one. Somehow, though, she didn't mind.

She wasn't any closer to slumber when her phone buzzed on the bedside table. Looking at the ID, her heart sank. "Hello?"

"Hello, miss. It's Manny at the Bull Pen."

Jamie groaned.

"I'm sorry. He's bad tonight. I tried Shawn three times, but he's not answering. We're not closing, but he's been here since early afternoon. I'm not interested in sending him to the ER."

Jamie rubbed her head, agreeing with a sigh.

She drove through the streets of Denver, anger building with every mile. Why did he do this? And why was she called on to rescue him?

Manny hadn't been exaggerating. Andy could hardly stand, and when he did, his stomach emptied at her feet. With the bartender's help, she managed to get him in her car, but she had no idea how she'd get him up to his loft.

Once again he slurred out insults and demeaned Jamie's life, although he qualified his critique when Cheryl suddenly made her way into his intoxicated mind. If Jamie thought he was mean to her, she was straight-up mortified at his rage toward his girlfriend.

By prayer alone she managed to get him into his home, but she was afraid to leave him. He vomited again as they passed through the door, then passed out on the couch. What did alcohol poisoning look like? Should she call Melissa? She sorted through the options while she cleaned up the putrid mess. It'd be best to call the ER.

The nurse sounded as though she'd been through this phone call a few times. Questions came rapid-fire. How long had he been drinking? Manny said he'd come in early afternoon—but she had no idea if he'd had anything before. Had he eaten anything? Not a clue. Age, weight? Thirty, maybe one-eighty? Does he drink often? More than he should.

"You seem sketchy on your answers, ma'am."

"I'm honestly not sure. He's a friend. The guy at the bar called me to come get him, and I really don't know the rest. I just need to know what to do."

"It would be best to bring him in."

"He's out. I can't move him by myself."

The woman sighed. "Look, professionally speaking, I have to say that getting him here would be your best option. But, to be honest, more often than not, they sleep it off. Make sure he's breathing, and if he vomits blood, call an ambulance. Otherwise, you'd be fine watching him there. But that's off the record."

"Thanks." Not so helpful. Calling an ambulance seemed over the top. Staying with him seemed... indecent.

What do I do?

She checked Andy. He was still out, but breathing steadily. Heavy-hearted, she crumpled into the club chair and closed her eyes.

Please guard me, Father. I can't just leave him here. I don't know if that's wrong—if that gives the appearance of evil, but I don't know what to do.

Resigned, Jamie called Melissa. She explained the situation and paused before she added that she was staying with Andy.

"Are you sure?" Melissa sounded concerned, but not shocked.

No, she wasn't sure. "I don't know what else to do."

"You know what? We haven't had a chick-flick night in forever. I'll just grab some of our faves and be there in a bit."

"Melissa, you have to work in the morning. Really, I'm okay."

"It won't be the first time I've pulled an all-nighter. I'll be there soon."

Melissa ended the call before Jamie could argue. Relief washed over her. Maybe nobody would ever know, and her intentions were only concern for a friend. But if anyone ever stumbled on the fact that she'd stayed at Andy's that night, Melissa would be her voucher. What other choice did she have?

***

A woman slept on the opposite side of the sectional when Andrew attempted to focus his eyes. Her hair was dark, similar to Cheryl's, but much shorter. Had she cut it? Was Cheryl still here? Andrew pulled in a deep breath and tried to think. It couldn't be her. Cheryl had left, and he'd gone out alone.

He blinked, his eyes on fire, as he tried to recall who the woman was and why she was on his couch. How had he gotten home? As he pulled himself up, a low groan rumbled through his throat, and his head pounded furiously. He hunted half-blindly for the remote, desperate to turn the television off.

Shifting gingerly, he spotted another woman balled up and wrapped in a blanket on his club chair. Her face was hidden, but he knew her hair and form. Andrew closed his eyes, swallowing the bad taste of puke and guilt.

He moved slowly—because everything hurt—but the urge to vomit swelled in his gut.

"James." He lowered himself on the arm of the chair, forcing back the bile.

She woke with a start, jerking upright. Her stare was wild before she regained her bearings. "What time is it?"

He shook his head, then held it as if it were going to fall off.

She scrambled out of the blanket and checked her phone. "Five-thirty." With a sigh, she pushed her fingers through her hair. Her eyes scanned the room, and she looked relieved to see the other woman sleeping.

Andrew followed her gaze. Melissa. The other woman had to be Melissa. He closed his eyes again. "What are you doing here?"

"You drank too much," she snapped. Then her face crumbled.

She was going to cry, and it was his fault.

"It was either stay with you or take you to the hospital. I thought you would prefer this."

"I'd have been okay," he argued quietly, hating the moment. Hating himself.

"I didn't know that." She glared, her eyes hot with anger. "You puked twice in ten minutes, and the guy down at the bar said you were worse than usual. I couldn't just leave you. People die from alcohol poisoning, you know."

Andrew gulped. Anyone else would have left him. He would have deserved it. His shoulders sagged, but the apology in his head didn't find his voice.

Jamie got up and folded the blanket she'd used before she moved toward Melissa.

"Thank you, James."

She turned to face him, coldness passing over her expression. "Is this who you really are?"

Andrew remained silent. Yes, but not really. It was just a bad day. Maybe a bad decade.

Jamie pressed her lips together, her expression revealing the tearing of her heart.

"What is wrong with you, Andy?" She stepped closer, her voice harsh. "It's like you want to be miserable. Maybe that way you think you have the right to be mad at God. But it's your doing, Andy. It's all you."

Shaking, she returned to Melissa, waking her up. Together they made a quiet exit.

Alone in his loft, Andrew cursed the burning pain in his skull and attempted to diminish the anxiety in his heart. But her words cut deep. Perhaps a visit to church would renew her confidence in him. It would be worth the hour and a half of his time.

***

Melissa followed Jamie into their home. She hadn't said anything on the drive over, but as soon as the door shut, she spoke. "Are you okay, Jamie?"

Jamie slid onto a dining chair, dropping her keys on the table. She couldn't meet Melissa's eyes. "No."

"I thought not." Melissa's arms wrapped around her shoulders, and Jamie leaned into them. "I know it's been a long night, so if this isn't the time to talk about it, just say so. But I'm worried about you. I don't think this is a good friendship for you."

"I know." Jamie pulled in a long breath. She'd thought that very thing as she sat listening to Andy's breath come and go. Prayed about it while her tears rolled one on top of the other. She was desperate for direction. "He's not always that way, Melissa."

Melissa moved to a chair opposite, sitting forward, ready to listen.

"My old friend is still in him, locked away." Jamie leaned in, pouring herself out. "Did I tell you he brought me flowers on my mom's anniversary? He encouraged me to call Ryan when I didn't have the confidence to. And he came for me, even though it was totally stupid for me to be so worried. Melissa, he's still there, and I feel like he needs me."

Melissa nodded, considering slowly. "Have you prayed over this?"

"I have." Jamie squared her posture. "I know Andy's difficult, but I still feel like this is where God wants me. Perhaps He can use me to call Andy back."

Again her roommate nodded. "Just be careful, Jamie." Melissa sighed as a frown pulled on her mouth. "I've worked long enough in a hospital to see some really horrible stuff. Drunk people can do incredibly stupid things—things they would never dream of doing sober."

Jamie gulped. So far Andy had only ever been verbally mean. But what if… No. Not Andy. He would never forgive himself if he hurt her. He simply couldn't.

**

Andrew got a call from Ryan while Jamie was out of town. Something sank inside him. Maybe Jamie had told him.

The fear was short lived. Ryan had asked Jamie for his number and wondered if Andrew played racquetball. They met at the gym on Thursday, and Ryan schooled him in two sets. Later, he invited Andrew to go mountain biking a week from Saturday. It was an event with his church group—Jamie's church group. Surprised by the offer, Andrew agreed, hoping it would please her.

That Saturday morning was spent in a couple of low-gear climbs and some challenging switchbacks. The ride was fun until the guys topped it off with a late breakfast and group devotion. Andrew tried to hide his discomfort.

Both men showed up on Jamie's back deck shortly before noon. Jamie and Melissa both sat with mud-laden legs stretched out in late summer sunshine. Dressed in cycling gear and the tell-tale streak of mud up their backs, Andrew assumed they'd just returned from their own ride.

"Where'd you go?" Ryan plopped down on a deck chair.

"Mt. Falcon, over in Morrison." Jamie's eyes collided with Andrew's.

The last time he'd seen her she'd been hopping mad, but today she smiled. Intentionally? A knot unraveled in his gut. He couldn't believe how relieved he felt that she'd let it go. Relieved that instead of rebuked, he was silently invited to fit in, to belong.

"Have you been there yet?" Her attention had gone back to Ryan.

"Nope." Ryan laughed. "Looks like your trail was messier than ours."

Jamie and Melissa exchanged a grin. "Just a few slick spots, but they sure left a mess."

"How many went with the guys?" Melissa asked.

Ryan turned to Andrew. "What were there, eight of us?"

Andrew nodded numbly. He didn't fit with this crowd. They talked easily, shared readily, and were completely transparent. Jamie wanted him to belong, but this world was too clean for him.

No, that wasn't it. He was too tarnished for it.

Except that maybe it was what he needed. To keep him on track. To balance out the part of his life he kept from Jamie. Mostly.

"Jamie got some pretty great shots of the castle." Melissa broke into his thoughts. "The sun hit it perfectly this morning."

"Shots?" Ryan leaned forward. "Like pictures?"

Jamie nodded, and Andrew piped in. "You haven't seen Jamie's photography?"

See, he could fit in.

Ryan looked at him and then back to Jamie. "No, I didn't even know to ask."

"James, you've got to show him." Andrew turned his attention back to Ryan. "Seriously, she's really good."

Jamie sat mute during the exchange. What was she thinking? Had she forgiven him yet?

"Can I see?" Ryan's warm gaze settled on Jamie.

Andrew's gut clenched, and he looked away.

"Sure." Jamie stood and walked sock-footed across the wood planks and into the house. She retrieved her laptop, which was in the dining room, while the conversation on the deck continued.

Lost in some weird introspection, Andrew lost track of it all.

Their friendships were peaceful—sincere and alluring. Nothing like the relationships in his other life. He could lay it down—the darkness of late nights, the instability, the roller coaster of knowing the people he was with would disappear without notice. Perhaps there was something to a predictable life. They weren't boring. They were settled.

Maybe just what he needed.

Chapter Thirteen

Jamie sighed, fingering the silver pendant lying against her neck as she leaned back in the bistro chair. They'd been together for four months, and Ryan had surprised her with jewelry. A sweet gesture—although Jamie wasn't much for bling—and a gift that should have made her heart puddle.

It didn't. After opening the small, velvet box, her emotions traveled from relief—*it's not a ring*—to unsettling doubt

This means less to me than it should.

She couldn't see a clear future with Ryan. She liked him, liked hanging out with him. But... well, just but. Maybe they needed to give it time.

Ryan returned to their table with steaming hot mugs of cocoa. They'd spent the evening wandering through a community garden when Ryan had presented his gift in the moonlit gazebo. Jamie had laughed, hoping it sounded like unexpected delight rather than a nervous giggle. Afterward he'd guided her back to his car. A small, no-name coffee shop was their next stop, and while Ryan got their drinks, she'd worked to set her mind straight.

He was a great guy, and they were a good match. Never argued, liked almost all the same things... about the closest to the perfect couple anyone could hope for. If only...

Her phone vibrated against the table as Ryan slid into his chair.

"Who's that?" His grin wasn't the annoyed kind.

Jamie glanced at the screen, and her heart rate picked up. "Andy." She didn't look at Ryan as she focused on settling her rolling stomach. It was only ten o'clock. No real reason to panic. Drunk calls should be a good two or three hours away.

"Hey, Andy." She forced a calm tone as she finally found Ryan's eyes.

He smiled across the table as he sat back.

"Jamesss," Andy slurred, "I need a beaufuller ride..."

Oh no. "Where are you?"

"I dunno." He shouted a laugh, and then started to sing. "Can't get her out of my mind..."

Jamie huffed and caught Ryan's darkening look. There went his perfectly planned, romantic evening. She shifted so she could look out the window. "Give the phone to someone I can understand."

The air clattered in her ear and then several seconds of rustling passed before another man started talking. She got a location while Ryan sat forward. Jamie swallowed, meeting his eyes again. His expression hardened, igniting a burn in her chest.

She punched the end button and shifted to get up.

Ryan covered her hand, still planted in his chair.

She pulled away from his hold. "Andy needs a ride."

"Why?" His voice was not the least bit curious.

Certainly Ryan could guess. Jamie's irritation escalated. "Because he's intoxicated, and apparently the boys he went out with left him alone."

"He can walk."

"He's three miles from his loft, at least." Jamie glared across the table and then stood. She was going, whether he came or not.

Ryan didn't move.

"Fine." She shoved a hand, palm up, between them. "Give me the keys. You stay, I'll go."

"You're not serious."

"I'm completely serious." She frowned and snagged the keys from the table.

"I'm pretty sure that's called stealing. And I'm really sure you don't need to run off rescuing some guy who should have enough sense to take care of himself."

"I'm not going to bed knowing Andy's wandering LoDo drunk. So you can either take me home so I can get my car, give me the keys to yours, or come with me."

Ryan's expression grew colder, but he conceded—begrudgingly. It took an hour to pick Andy up and get him to his loft. During that time, Ryan and Jamie didn't speak.

Andy was safely deposited in his home with the door closed before Ryan readdressed the issue. "Does this happen often?"

Jamie sighed. Who was she really mad at? Andy. Why did he keep calling her like this? Her posture crumpled. "A few times."

Ryan settled a stiff gaze on her. "Jamie, you're a beautiful woman, and you have no business wandering the streets of Denver in the middle of the night, going into a bar alone, and dragging your drunk friend to his home by yourself. What are you thinking?"

"What else am I supposed to do?"

"He can find someone else."

"Ryan, he doesn't have anyone else."

He looked back at the door, glaring as if he could see the other man through the steel. What was she supposed to do?

They didn't settle the matter in the hall, or on the way back to Jamie's. In fact, it wasn't until he walked her to her door that he said anything further at all.

"Don't go alone." He was still very much upset, but his eyes were pleading. "If he calls you again, don't go by yourself. Call me."

***

Andrew forced himself forward toward Jamie's doorstep the next morning, a latte, his typical peace offering, in hand. "Thanks for picking me up."

Jamie frowned. "Thank Ryan."

"Were you out last night?"

"Yes."

Andrew dipped his head. This was definitely not good. "I'll stop over at his place."

A look of disappointment crossed her face—the same one he remembered from that morning at his loft. It pierced the part of him that could still feel. Of all the really stupid things to do… Why did he keep dragging her into his messes?

"What were you doing?" Jamie's disappointment stabbed into his guilt.

"I don't know." His voice caught in his throat.

"Does Cheryl know—"

"Cheryl and I are done." One disaster out of his life. Sort of. He felt empty when he was with her. Why had he expected the vacant spot to close when she left?

Jamie's eyebrows dropped. "When?"

She was hurt that he hadn't told her. Was it wrong that her reaction actually made him feel a little better? "The last time she was here."

"That was awhile ago. You didn't say anything."

Andrew looked away. "Yeah. Things change, James." He brought his face back to hers. "I'll see you later."

Leaving without another glance, he considered whether he would actually go talk to Ryan. Under normal circumstances, he would blow it off.

But Jamie wasn't normal.

That meant he was going.

Ryan answered his knock with a jerk on the door. Andrew stepped back, surprised. Ryan's lips formed a line and his eyes narrowed, but he said nothing. The door opened enough for Andrew to pass through, and suddenly he felt like he was heading into an interrogation.

"How often does Jamie have to drag you out of a bar?"

He didn't know. Not for sure. Maybe a half-dozen times? Andrew looked at the floor, his shrug more guilt than an answer. "I'm not sure."

"Do you think that's a good idea?"

Andrew's stomach churned. He hadn't really considered it.

"Look at me and tell me it's a good plan to have Jamie come downtown for you when you're *drunk*, in the middle of the night."

Andrew gulped. Nothing had ever happened. Jamie was fine. He made her cry, sometimes, but… The lump resurfaced, larger and more stubborn. He swallowed it back again. Ryan was standing up for Jamie—something Andrew usually did. Something he should do.

"It's not." Andrew drew in a long breath, then squared his shoulders. "It's not a good idea at all. I just didn't think about it like that."

Ryan's mouth opened as though he had more to shovel out but then snapped shut. He seemed to weigh his speech. "Look, you and Jamie are good friends. I can deal with that. But the fact is you look out for you, and she looks out for you. So who's going to look out for her?"

That wasn't true. Andrew had spent half his life looking out for her. Wait, that was another life, mostly. A life Ryan hadn't seen, didn't know.

He couldn't formulate an intelligent reply.

"I consider you a friend, Andrew." Ryan pushed a frustrated breath out. "But I'm not going to let this go. You can't do it again."

Pride wanted to argue. Normally it would. Andrew didn't take mouth from most. But there wasn't a good argument. He'd put Jamie in a bad spot. If he were Ryan, there'd be more fists than words in this conversation.

His head bobbed. "It won't happen again."

The tense muscles in Ryan's arms relaxed, but he continued studying Andrew. "Can I help you with this?"

Andrew's posture jolted straight. "With what?" he snapped.

Ryan cleared his throat. "You drink a lot. It worries Jamie. It worries me. I'll help, however I can, if you'll let me."

"You can help me?" Andrew scoffed. "There's nothing to help. I gave you latitude when it concerned Jamie, but your interference will stop there. I don't need help—yours or anyone else's. Period."

Ryan looked more sad than offended.

Andrew's jaw tightened and his fists balled, but he managed enough self-control to leave without throwing one of them.

Maybe he didn't want to belong with them after all.

Chapter Fourteen

April, thank goodness. Winter was finally uncurling its grip in Colorado. Jamie ached for the warm days of summer. Or maybe it was that she longed for the fun days of last summer. When life wasn't as complicated, or confusing. Almost eight months dating an amazing Christian man. She shouldn't feel this way.

But summer was coming, right? Besides, maybe her gloom had more to do with Andy than Ryan. That had to be it.

She glanced at Ryan from her passenger seat in his Jeep as he pulled up to the curb in front of her home.

He met her eyes, but didn't smile. "Are you up for a walk?"

Ryan had barely spoken all morning. His invitation should have brought relief, but his hesitant tone set off a warning. Jamie eyed the sidewalk just outside her front door. Early spring snow lined either side of the cement, but the sun was bright.

"Sure. Can I change first?" Jamie tried to sound cheerful despite the knot tying itself around her middle.

Ryan nodded and they went into the house still swathed in tense silence. They'd been to the Kendricks' for lunch after church, but even that hadn't brought Ryan out of the funk he'd been in all morning. He was upset. Not angry, but definitely upset.

Jamie pushed against the ball in her stomach. "I'll be out in a minute."

It took very little time to change, but she sat on her bed for several minutes, replaying their blowout the week before. The whole reason for her gloom, and most likely for his withdrawal.

They'd gone to the IMAX. The showing was late, and it had been a last minute decision, but Jamie loved the documentary on Everest. She'd seen it before; it'd been made several years before, but the climber in her never got enough of it. And it was fun to share with Ryan.

Right up until Andy called. It'd been a couple of months since the last call, and Jamie had begun to think that maybe that part of their friendship was done.

It wasn't. He was wasted.

Ryan was not the least bit gracious. They left before the film was over and he was angry. Silent, but angry.

Jamie was too. But she wasn't sure which man she was more frustrated with. She understood Ryan's point of view, but why couldn't he see hers? Did he honestly expect her to simply leave Andy to fend for himself? What if something really terrible happened? What if Andy got hurt, or he hurt someone else? How was she supposed to live with that?

Ryan helped her, though he was not kind to Andy. Jamie wasn't sure why that made her more upset, but it did. She vented her anger by raking through Andy's kitchen cabinets. He'd stashed something in every single one, and in the big cabinet beside the fridge he had a whole liquor store. She hadn't consumed half that amount of alcohol in her entire life. How much did the man drink?

He was done for the night. She'd see to it for sure. By the time she was finished opening and dumping, he didn't own a drop of alcohol.

"So that'll fix it, will it?" Ryan jabbed the garage button as the elevator door closed.

Jamie kept her cold gaze forward.

Ryan didn't let up. "There's a bar two blocks from here, and a liquor store at the end of the street."

"What am I supposed to do?" Jamie's voice rose angrily.

"*Stop!*" Ryan matched her exasperation, taking her by both shoulders. "Stop rescuing him, Jamie! You're not helping."

Hot tears spilled over by the time they reached the garage. Ryan was right. But she couldn't stop. Oh, she was in such a pickle.

His anger mellowed before they reached the car. Rather than opening her door as he always did, Ryan tugged on her elbow and wrapped her in his arms. Jamie cried in the silence, and their fight ended there. But the week following had been strained, and Ryan had been nothing like his usual self since she'd met him at church that morning.

Jamie found Ryan in her overstuffed chair, slumped over in a posture of prayer. He straightened when she finally made it back to the front room, making an attempt to smile. She stooped to snag her running shoes before she settled on the couch across from him.

He sat quietly, but Jamie knew thoughts were tormenting him. She wanted to break the silence—to have something to say that would beckon a real smile.

Ryan stood and moved to her adjacent dining table.

She swallowed, praying they wouldn't fight again.

"Jamie, where do you see us going?" He didn't turn to face her until the question was out.

She glanced up from tying her laces, but only for a second. Dread, bigger than the fear of a fight, shot through her veins. *Please don't do this.* "To Clear Creek, as soon as I get these shoes on."

Deflection. Maybe he wouldn't pursue this course if she could give him a reason to hang on.

Ryan's gaze remained on her, begging for an honest answer. She didn't want to do this. She wasn't sure he did either. Her attention went back to her shoes, but she could feel the warmth of his body as he came near.

Please, please don't do this.

"Jamie." He couldn't disguise the emotion as he softly called her name.

Jamie's hands stopped, and her eyes closed.

With a gentle hand, Ryan raised her chin and waited until her eyes met his.

Without a doubt, she knew where this was going, and her heart cried. She waited in aching silence, watching Ryan search for the right words. Watching him resolve.

"Is this about Andy?" Maybe they could just talk through it. Maybe he could give her more time.

"I'd rather this be about you and me." He shook his head, rubbing the back of his neck. "But maybe that's not possible."

Jamie's gaze dropped to her hands. Silence stretched uncomfortably.

"I'm not going to fight him for you." Ryan squatted in front of her. "Not because I don't think you're worth it—I know you are—but because I'm pretty sure I won't win."

"I don't want you to fight with Andy. Ryan, that was the point. I need your help—"

Ryan stopped her tumbling words with a long, heartbreaking look. Jamie's core trembled while he worked his lips between his teeth.

"Do you love me?"

Did she love him? She was not prepared for that question. She wished desperately she could say yes. She should love him—he was about the best man she'd ever met. There was not a single reason not to love him.

But she didn't.

The awful, silent moment was acutely revealing.

Jamie's breath drew in sharply. "Ryan, I—"

He grasped her hand in both of his, stopping her protest. "Jamie, I'm not fishing. But I need to be honest with you. And I need you to be honest with me, even if it hurts."

She flinched, and he squeezed the hand he still held captive. "You're an amazing woman, and I care very much for you. But I don't think you can give me your heart."

Her face crumbled and he faltered. He paused, maybe waiting for her to argue. But silence proved to be a confirmation. He was right, and they both knew it.

"I don't want to continue on this path only to end up in love by myself."

She could beg him not to do this, to give her more time. Surely she would fall in love with him. But they'd been dating long enough to know that although she admired and cared for him, she was not in love.

Ryan waited as the tears rolled down her cheeks. It was several moments before she realized his dripped from his chin. He sniffed and wiped them away, the action crushing Jamie's heart.

"I'm sorry, Ryan." Jamie choked on the words.

He stood, pulling her up with him and into his arms. She hugged him back fiercely until he pressed a kiss to her forehead and pulled away.

"Goodbye, Jamie."

***

"Jamie!"

Jamie jumped, spinning away from the door she'd just come through to face Melissa. She breathed relief and jerked her earbuds out. "You startled me."

Usually they would have laughed, but neither broke a smile. Melissa eyed her curiously. Jamie removed her shoes and set them by the patio door, keeping her eyes averted.

"We missed you in ABF." Melissa moved to the refrigerator. She grabbed two water bottles and returned to the table where Jamie had dropped, still panting.

Jamie wiped her face with the sleeve of her sweatshirt, keeping her focus on the sliding glass door. "I just needed to go for a run."

Melissa eased into a chair, watching with concern. "How far did you go?"

"To the brewery."

"Coors?"

Jamie nodded.

"Seven miles... that's a ways." Melissa paused and swallowed. "The Bolder Boulder isn't for a while yet. Are you training early?"

Jamie tried to smile. It didn't work.

Melissa sighed as she bit her bottom lip. "Ryan said you weren't feeling the best. Are you okay?"

Jamie finally brought her gaze from the door. So Melissa knew. That made it official.

"Is he okay?"

Melissa's expression sank. "He seemed upset. What happened?"

Jamie shook her head.

"Did you have a fight?"

Again, Jamie shook her head, but it was several seconds before she found her voice. "We broke up."

Melissa's eyes rounded. "What? What happened?"

Jamie focused on the deck beyond the window.

Melissa rose to get the tissue box. After setting it on the table, she pulled the nearest chair close. "Jamie?"

"We didn't fight. He asked me if I loved him, and I couldn't answer." Her throat tightened painfully, but she wouldn't give in to more tears. "He told me he didn't want to end up in love alone, and so now he and I are—we're done."

Melissa examined her. "Do you love him?"

Jamie looked away. "No."

"Are you sure? He's such a good man."

Good? No, Ryan was next door to perfect. What else was she looking for?

For some stupid reason Andy's face flashed through her mind. Probably because he was the only thing she and Ryan ever really fought over. Guess that wasn't an issue anymore.

"No, I don't love him."

Something must be seriously wrong with her.

***

Jamie's stomach growled, but she continued working. The desks, the halls, even the office were all empty—school had been over for more than three hours—but she couldn't stand to be at home. Her mind was best occupied so she wouldn't have to think about Ryan or Andy. Or how disappointing life had suddenly become.

Her phone chimed from her purse, forcing her to stop working on the labs she was grading. She fished through her bag to retrieve her cell and was both relieved and disappointed to see Andy's name on the ID.

"Hi, James."

She sighed. "Hey, Andy."

"Wow, don't sound so glad to talk to me, I might get the wrong impression."

"Sorry." Jamie straightened her shoulders, hoping the new position would carry through in her voice. "What's happening?"

"Nothing, I was just finishing up here. Word has it that the trails are fairly dry. I was hoping you'd be game for a ride."

Jamie thought for a moment. She was a little achy from her long run the night before, but the distraction might be good.

"Sure," she finally answered. "What were you thinking?"

"Maybe out at Dakota Ridge?"

"Okay, I'll meet you there." She pulled her phone away to end the call.

"James?" Andy's voice caught her short.

"Yeah?"

"Are you okay? You sound upset."

She swallowed hard. She'd cried enough for one week. After clearing her throat, she drew a cleansing breath. "I'm okay. Thanks, though."

"Are you sure?"

"Yeah, I'll see you in a while." She ended the call, not giving him a chance to push further.

Chapter Fifteen

The giant hill waited. As she pulled into the trailhead parking lot, Jamie shifted her mind, resolving to take it on, to beat it.

Andy was tightening down the quick-release on his front wheel when she pulled next to his Mustang. He flashed a grin and a small wave, and Jamie felt confident that the nice version of the man had shown up today.

The thought wasn't new, but for the first time Jamie really pondered it. Andy could be the best—the best listener, the best encourager, the best friend. He could be the kid who played her hero in all of her favorite childhood memories.

But he could be a real jerk too. Sarcastic, insulting, and downright mean at times. Those times didn't dominate him, and usually they involved alcohol. Still, they were disturbing.

She'd seen a change in him since they'd reunited, though. Subtle, but there. Maybe Andy was softening. The thought lifted her heart.

A knock on her window jerked her back to reality. Andy stooped to peer through the glass as she cracked the window. "Are we riding today or what?"

A small smile crept across her lips, the first one in twenty-four hours. "Sure, sorry. I got lost in thought."

The corners of his brown eyes crinkled as he smiled. "Pop your trunk and I'll get your bike."

The Colorado evening did not disappoint. Snow still lay in patches along the trail, but the mud was negligible. It was good to get out and breathe deep.

They'd ridden a few miles when they reached the dreaded hill. Still not a strong technical rider, Jamie fell behind, but she attacked the incline with a fresh determination and met Andy at the top. They both dismounted, dropping their bikes off the path and panting for breath.

"Whew!" Andrew snapped the buckle under his chin loose. "That hill just doesn't get easier." He grinned at Jamie, sweat dripping from his nose and chin.

She nodded and removed her own helmet. "At least you've figured out how to keep your weight in the back while you climb. I can't seem to get it. I kept spinning out every three strokes."

Andy dropped onto a large chunk of granite. Jamie dug through her saddlebag for her trail mix and joined him. They munched in comfortable silence while they regained a normal heart rate.

Jamie had just packed a handful of food into her mouth when Andy suddenly searched her face. "So what's going on, James?"

"Huh?" she mumbled around a mouthful of nuts and raisins.

"You sounded upset earlier, you were 'lost in thought' in the car, and we just rode the fastest and hardest ever. What's up?"

Jamie examined her hands before wiping the salt off. She couldn't meet his eyes and only managed a shrug.

"Right. You haven't changed since we were kids. I always know when there's something wrong. Did you and Ryan have a fight or something?"

She sighed heavily, locking her arms around her knees. "Not a fight. We broke up, though."

Pushing up off his elbow, Andrew turned to face her. "Whoa," he said softly. "I did not see that coming." He examined her while she worked to remain stoic. "Do you want to talk about it?"

Jamie looked away, feeling hollow. "No."

The back side of the Hog Back blocked the city view, but the traffic from C-470 moaned through the pines. She needed to get away. Away from people and noise and life. Just for a while.

The man next to her stirred, and her mind took a left turn. Suddenly she stepped back in time, and she and Ryan were at the IMAX. Would she have done anything differently if she'd known getting Andy would end their relationship? Her mind stopped on that to ponder it honestly. No. No, she wouldn't. And that really wasn't what ended it.

Andy was undeniably her best friend. He could be difficult and frustrating, and his drinking habit was a growing concern, but he was and always had been her best friend. How was another man supposed to accept that?

Maybe Ryan could have—if she loved him. But she didn't, and her loyalties proved it.

"Are you okay, James?" Andy's voice snapped her back to reality.

She hoped desperately that he could not read her thoughts. She drew a deep breath and let it out slowly. "I'll be fine."

Reaching across the stone, he squeezed her foot, and Jamie finally looked him in the eye. He slid over and dropped a long arm around her shoulders. The gesture was more big brother than anything, but Jamie couldn't help but think, *This is the reason,* even as she leaned into him.

"How about I treat you to dinner? There's gotta be a Fazoli's nearby somewhere. You can eat all the bread sticks you want. I won't tell a soul."

She managed a laugh as she gave him a slight elbow. "I'll take it. Thanks."

***

Andrew couldn't sleep. At all. Jamie wouldn't leave his head. She stayed, sweet and lovely, capturing his desire.

Tormenting him.

Up on the hill, when she'd said she and Ryan were done, something sparked. Something he'd only been slightly aware of before, like the rebirth of a hope he hadn't fully realized existed.

He wanted her. And she was available.

But not for him. If a man like Ryan Anderson—everything a Christian woman like Jamie would want—if he couldn't win her heart, then Andrew Harris didn't stand a chance.

But he loved her. He was absolutely certain of it. He could change for her, if that's what it would take. Already, he'd been making a serious effort. A few drinks here and there—a quick stop at the bar after work. Nothing crazy or stupid. His drinking was under control. If she'd only seen how hard he was trying, how well he'd been doing.

He could take care of her; fill that spot deep in her heart that wallowed in loneliness, the spot she kept carefully tucked away. He could make her happy. Couldn't he?

Is this who you really are?

She'd despised him that night.

You're a lot to deal with.

She'd hung up on him in disgust that day.

Who was he, really?

Not anyone she belonged with.

The riotous thoughts raged into the night. Frustration gnawed at him, giving rise to the demands of addiction. Andrew tossed aside his sheets, marching out of bed to search his cabinets. When the large one beside the fridge failed to produce what he needed, anger boiled over. Doors slammed loudly, accompanied by growling curses, as every shelf turned up dry.

Vague images flittered across his memory.

Andrew's eyes blazed from the sink to the leather club chair and back again. Not long ago Jamie had brought him home sloshed. He'd slumped in that chair, not really conscious, and she had every last bottle of alcohol he owned lined up on the counter.

You need to stop this, Andrew. Her voice had not been kind, but it sounded more hurt than angry. *It will rob you of everything. Everything!*

And then it all went down the sink. Every. Last. Drop.

The piecemeal memory made him livid and then ashamed. His pulse thundered, his ears roared. Need surged. Demanded. *Now!*

A quick glance at the microwave clock read three a.m. The bars would be closed. He sent a glass sailing across the room; it shattered against the brick wall. A second followed. Still no satisfaction. Andrew roared ravenously. The monster unleashed.

Storming into the bathroom, the vanity mirror shattered as he ripped the cabinet open. Sleeping pills slid down his throat. One, two… how many could he handle? Anything he put down. He clawed at an unopened bottle of Nyquil and a half-used bottle of Listerine. A heinous cocktail.

Angry with himself, angry with Jamie and her unattainable perfection, and angry that life was not what it should be, he slammed down both bottles.

Black relief finally overcame unrest.

***

"Hello?" Jamie spoke into her Bluetooth as her car sped past the Nebraska state line.

"Hey, James." Andy's voice wasn't a surprise. "What are you doing?"

"I'm driving."

"Where?"

"The interstate."

"Oh yeah?" He sounded mildly surprised. "Which direction?"

"East."

"East?" His voice rose. "Why are you going east?"

"I'm going to see my dad for the rest of the week."

"Jamie." His tone was a soft rebuke. "Why did you tell me last night that you were all right when you weren't?"

"I was. Am." She paused, then sighed. "I have a few days off for Easter, so I thought I'd go for a visit."

That was a cop-out, but it was all she had. She still ached over Ryan, and she didn't want to have to see him on Sunday—Easter Sunday at that. Plus, Andy confused her. She needed an escape for a while.

"You should have called me," Andy said. "I could've taken a day off and driven out with you."

Jamie was glad he couldn't see her face, or he would have known how odd she thought that offer was. "Thanks, Andy. I'm really fine, though. I've driven this road many times."

Andy didn't answer, and she could picture him rubbing his upper lip while his mind concocted some fail-safe rebuttal.

Not today, Andy. Not on this.

"All right, James. Drive safe."

Relief. Jamie pushed *end* and turned the radio back up in time to hear "Unredeemed" by Selah. She hoped very much that the words they were singing would prove true—that all of the broken things in her life would not go unredeemed.

***

Andrew slid his phone across his desk, his mind still on Jamie.

She wasn't okay. Neither was he.

He'd woken up that morning with his face smashed against the cold subway tile in his bathroom. Covered in green puke. So strung out that he couldn't focus his eyes. And late for work.

What if she were around when the monster in him cut loose? She'd rescued him more times than he could remember, but thus far he hadn't been that bad.

Last night? He'd been out of control. Blind rage had seized him.

Downing sleeping pills like they were candy? Drinking cold medicine and Listerine? Who does that?

Alcoholics.

Na-uh. That was *not* him.

He pictured the mess that awaited him at home, the whole night playing over again. The whole, ugly scene.

And then he mentally put Jamie in the middle of it.

Andrew raked his hand through his hair, willing the images to stop. He had to make all of it stop.

Even as the thoughts formed, his legs propelled him to the small refrigerator he kept in his office. He banged against the false panel below and pulled out a half-empty bottle of bourbon.

Just one drink.

Jamie would never settle for such a spineless man. She shouldn't, not when she deserved so much better.

Chapter Sixteen

Dad's home hadn't helped much, especially since she'd only been able to stay for a couple of days. The long drive home led to a long week at school, followed by a long and lonely weekend. Which wasn't getting any better. Church suddenly felt uncomfortable. Jamie's stomach hurt, and she set her feet toward the exit.

Everyone knew them as "Ryan and Jamie." When they were invited anywhere, they were invited together. Several women had even hinted at wedding plans. Now she was just Jamie and he was just Ryan, and she had no idea how to face that reality in this context.

She'd considered changing churches, even going so far as to look up statements of faith and service times, but the thought made her heart ache. She loved the body she was a part of.

You'll just have to brave up and get through it.

She compromised on her courage by going to first service. Now it was time to go. She'd be braver next week and return to ABF.

It had seemed like a good plan. Until it was sabotaged by a woman with a knack for interference.

Mrs. Batey caught her before she hit the exit doors. "Jamie, dear, we've been missing you in class."

Jamie wanted to pretend she hadn't heard, but the woman had her by the elbow. There was no way to ignore her politely.

"Will you be joining us today?"

"Uh…" She scanned her brain for a quick excuse. Nothing. "Yes, I'll be up as soon as I refill my coffee."

She made a move toward the coffee bar, but the older woman stopped her again. "Listen, sweetie. Are you coming this afternoon?"

"Um…"

The woman didn't give her a chance to fabricate an excuse. "Now, you don't want to miss our picnic."

Jamie's eyebrows dropped. What was she talking about?

Mrs. Batey rolled her eyes and shook her head. "How typical of a man. Ryan didn't tell you, did he?"

She went still, chewing her bottom lip. Words wouldn't form in her head, and even if they did, she was certain she couldn't get them past her dry mouth.

"I'm sorry, Mrs. Batey." Ryan rescued her from behind. "Jamie and I haven't had much of a chance to talk this week."

The woman raised an eyebrow and gave Ryan a scolding look. "You can't just expect a girl to be ready for anything at any moment, young man."

She released Jamie's arm with a pat, and left her awkwardly alone with Ryan. Running suddenly seemed like a good option.

"Can we talk?" He put a hand on her shoulder.

Why had she come this morning?

You're a big girl, now act like it.

She nodded.

Ryan led the way out the side door, taking her around to the back of the building. Jamie's mind flitted to her childhood, and the moment felt something like when her father had taken her out to impose some discipline on her backside.

"I haven't seen you in a while." His statement sounded more like a question.

She breathed in deep, swallowed, and took another breath. Still, she couldn't meet his eyes. "I went to my dad's for a few days."

He nodded as his hands went into his pockets.

Her lungs seemed to collapse. How long did he want to drag this out? What did he want, anyway?

"Jamie, are you okay?"

Wait. She had broken his heart, and he was asking if *she* was okay? How could she not love this man? Biting her lip, she nodded.

He rejected it with a slight shake of his head.

"Nobody knows," she whispered.

"No." Ryan's shoulders sagged. "I didn't know how to tell anyone, and you were gone. I didn't know what to do."

"Ryan, I'm not sure I can face this." She hugged her Bible. "I think I should find another church."

"Please don't do that." His hand warmed her shoulder again. "Listen, it didn't end ugly. It just didn't work out like either of us hoped. That's all anyone needs to know. It's going to be awkward for a while, but then it'll be okay."

"But what do I say when the other women ask what happened? That I have a foolish heart? That I don't know a good man when I meet him?"

Ryan's features fell. "Don't say that. I meant what I said that day—you're one of the best people I know. I think it would be awful if we couldn't get through this and still be friends."

A measure of optimism lifted her spirit.

He wrapped one arm around her shoulders and squeezed. "Don't worry, I'll tell Mrs. Batey, and the deed will be done. Everyone will know by noon and will be over it by dinner."

Jamie forced a smile and Ryan squeezed her again.

"Ready?" He nodded to the church.

She stared at the building. No. Still not that brave. "I think I'm just going to go home." She was such a coward.

Ryan looked at her for a few breaths, then let his arm drop from her shoulders. "It'll get better."

She hoped so, but for the moment, she felt like a fool.

***

Andrew shoved the file he'd been staring at to the side of his desk. It didn't matter how long he looked at the affidavit. He couldn't concentrate.

Jamie needed a distraction.

He thought long and hard over that. Not the distraction—that would be easy. Anything outdoors would do. He thought over her melancholy—her heartbreak—and his sudden hope. The one he knew logically he shouldn't have.

He'd called her twice while she was in Iowa, just to make sure she was okay. He didn't even use a pretense to disguise his concern. He didn't have to. He loved that about her.

He thought over that. Maybe that was enough. If she could love him, maybe he could be the man she wanted—needed. She'd be the reason he would finally overcome the demons that still clawed at his life.

Jamie needed a distraction. He needed her. The time was opportune.

He glanced at the clock before he dialed. Three-thirty. What time did school get out? He should wait to call her when he knew for sure she'd be done. But he couldn't retrain his mind on his work. He had to talk to her.

"Hello?"

Success. Andrew grinned. "Hey, James, how are you today?"

"Okay. The kids are always hard to bring back after a long break, but we made it through. How are you?"

Vague. Andrew concentrated on her voice. Did it still sound hollow?

"Andy? Are you there?"

"Yeah, sorry. I was working on something."

"Oh." She paused. "Well, if you need to go, I've got some stuff to catch up on, so we could talk later."

This was not going in the right direction at all.

"No." He answered a little too fast. Good idea, freak her out by being weird. He cleared his throat. "I mean, yeah, I've got to get back to work, but I was thinking about you. Someone around here was talking about Homestead Meadows. Have you ever hiked there?"

"Up by Lyons?"

No idea. But it had perked her interest, so that was a good start. "I think so."

"No, I haven't. I thought it was too close to Estes. What have you heard about it?"

She sounded like Jamie. Fun, enthusiastic, and easy to be with. Andrew smiled. "That it's a great hike—really pretty, not heavily traveled, and lots of history." That's what the online reviews had said. Leaning back into his leather chair, he let himself relax for the first time all day. He had her. "Do you want to go?"

"I have conferences coming up next week, Andy. I'm not sure I can spare the time."

So not Jamie. What just happened? Andrew's mind raced as he sat forward again. "Not even a Sunday hike?" He was grasping. He never did that. But he needed to see her. "I could meet you right after church."

She hesitated, leaving him room to wonder how transparent he actually was.

"I guess I could just go to first service."

Andrew considered carefully. Very carefully. Nothing had changed between him and religion. But...

"I could go with you, James." His voice dropped softly. It was the first truly selfless act he'd offered. Well, sort of. "If it would make it easier for you, I'll go."

Silence.

He'd shocked her speechless.

***

This was a bad plan.

Jamie scolded herself in the mirror. She should have known it straight off, but Andy's offer was both the distraction and excuse she'd needed. Now she had a legitimate reason not to go to ABF. And it seemed like having Andy with her would be an overall win. No one would approach her about her split with Ryan while Andy was beside her.

The reasoning seemed sound until she told Melissa her plans. Her roommate had frowned, and Jamie mentally stepped back. "Do you think it will upset Ryan?"

Melissa gave her a long, strange look. "I doubt it'll make him smile."

Jamie searched her brain for an explanation, an out, anything to make this uncomfortable conversation turn."Ryan usually goes to second service." Dumb. But it was the best she could do.

"People talk, Jamie, even in church. Especially in church."

"But they've seen Andy before." Jamie laid out her defense—mostly for her own benefit. "They know we've been friends forever."

"He came with you twice and met maybe three people. Most people who know him do so from riding and associate him with Ryan, not you. All they're going to know is that you broke up with Ryan three weeks ago and are now showing up with his buddy."

"He broke up with me."

Melissa's shoulders dropped, and she looked stuck. Suddenly Jamie knew her friend was aware of more than she let on. Melissa knew exactly why Ryan had broken it off.

"I don't mean to make this more difficult, Melissa," Jamie sighed, looking at her feet. "And I never intended to hurt Ryan."

Melissa's voice fell compassionately. "I know." She moved to hug Jamie, and Jamie slouched in her arms with relief. "Sometimes things just don't work out."

Jamie had slept fitfully after that talk. She couldn't back out with Andy, and truthfully, she didn't want to. He was her shield, as he had always been, and he was going to church, which by itself was a good thing. Life would just have to move on. Even through her bad plans.

***

"Self-reform doesn't work!"

Andrew shook his head, trying to dispel the pastor's voice. It didn't work.

"Christ himself is telling us here that even if we manage to clean up our mess, we come out worse than before. Look at Matthew 12:45, and take a close inspection near the end. Jesus says 'the final condition of that person is worse than the first.' Paraphrase: self-reform doesn't work."

Andrew shoved away irritation. He could change, he could free himself. He didn't believe the Bible, so it shouldn't matter what some delusional preacher-man said about it, anyway. It didn't matter.

If he could just shut off the voice in his head…

Jamie's voice cut out the preacher's. "Do you know how far back the homesteads are?"

Ah…relief. Andrew stopped behind her and pulled out the trail map he'd downloaded. She sipped on her CamelBak while he unfolded the page against an aspen.

"We just passed the switchbacks." His finger traced the trail, and Jamie's eyes followed. "So this should level out and dump into the meadows. Not too much farther."

Jamie nodded with a grin before her eyes caught something above them. "Hang on."

Her camera came up, and Andrew followed the direction of her lens. A perfectly formed spider's web glistened with dew in the filtered light.

Her grin returned as she showed Andy the screen.

"Nice." He squeezed her shoulder.

She recapped her lens, and they continued upward for another forty-five minutes.

Outside and doing what she loved, she seemed normal; she seemed okay. Not so much at church, though, which made him sad for her. Church was her home base, it didn't seem right that it would become uncomfortable.

He hadn't seen Ryan. Certainly a relief to Jamie, but he was a little curious. How had the other man handled the breakup? He assumed she'd ended it. He simply couldn't imagine that Ryan had. Not with the way he'd intervened for her, doted on her, obviously loved her.

Andy trailed Jamie as he recalled the times he'd spent hanging out with her, Ryan, and Melissa. She'd been happy with Ryan. Suddenly it didn't make sense. She'd been happy, and now she was really bummed. Why had she done it?

A clearing opened as the trail leveled out. Off the path and down a slight hill, a rough cabin stood lonely and abandoned. Jamie diverted wordlessly, and Andrew followed, still pondering.

They didn't fight. Jamie had said they just broke up. He'd never seen them fight. In fact, he hadn't seen much passion out of them either way. They were the type of couple that kept only their friendship on the surface.

But Jamie had been happy. What had changed her mind?

Andrew followed her into the tiny building, ducking to enter the less-than-six-foot door frame. He scouted the room. Twelve by twelve, at best. Hardly a home by modern standards.

Jamie laughed. "You wouldn't fit in this house." Her camera came up and she snapped a photo of him dwarfing the interior. "Isn't it amazing how living standards have changed?"

Andrew grinned—because she'd smiled. He sat down on the ledge of a square cut-out where a small window would have been and held a hand out. "Let me see."

Jamie ducked out of the camera strap and passed it to him. She didn't stand around, however. Her curiosity took her outside the house and had her peeking around every corner of the homestead.

Andrew stayed put while she wandered, looking not only at the snapshot she'd just taken, but through the entire memory card. Three hundred and forty-two frames. "Hey, why do you have so many pictures on this thing?"

Jamie poked her head through the window next to him and he tilted her camera so she could see the count.

She shrugged. "I haven't uploaded any of them."

Weird. Very weird. "Why not?"

Her green eyes met his. "I just haven't."

Something was off. "How long has it been since you've updated your gallery?"

"August." Her attention left the screen and she wandered off.

Andrew stood from his perch and ducked out the door, following her to the remains of an oxcart. She leaned against the wheel iron, which was sunk fast into the dirt, and he studied her with concern."Why so long?"

Again, a shrug. "It's not real life, Andy."

He felt like an invisible hand had just smacked the wind out of him. "What do you mean?"

Jamie's gaze darted to him, then dropped back to her shoes. Her shoulders moved, which was supposed to suffice as an answer.

Suddenly he was angry. "Did Ryan tell you that?"

"No." Her eyes flew back up. "He didn't say that."

He'd offended her. Or hit a nerve. "What did he say?"

She slouched back against the iron again. "Nothing."

"He didn't say anything about your photography?"

Jamie shook her head.

"He never asked to see your work?"

"Not since that day on my deck." She drew herself straight. "Look, it doesn't really matter. It's just not reality, and it's okay."

Well, he wasn't okay with it; it did matter. Jamie's dreams mattered. A lot. And they should have mattered to Ryan. "Did you tell him about your book?"

She laughed a little. Not a happy giggle, but a sound almost of mockery. "I don't have a book, Andy. It was just a silly dream. It's not real life."

The boiling heat in his gut simmered.

Jamie pulled herself away, slowly moving back to the cabin. Andrew's eyes dropped to her camera, still in his hands. He filed through the frames, taking in Jamie's point of view. Loving her point of view.

Finding what he'd been looking for, he scanned the homestead and sought her out again. She'd stopped at the threshold and leaned against it.

He didn't speak until he passed her camera back. "I'd have walked right by that." He nodded to the picture he'd brought up on her camera. "I never would have known it was there."

Her attention dropped, studying the perfectly formed web.

"You see the world differently, James. You see the beauty most of us miss." He paused, soaking in the warmth from her eyes. He couldn't resist contact, and his hand curved over her cheek, warm in the glow of the sun. "Don't give up."

She stayed for a moment, still and lovely as her eyes closed.

His Jamie.

But it was only a moment. In the next she moved away, and Andrew resented the fleeting panic that passed over her expression.

Chapter Seventeen

Jamie slid into the booth next to Dale Carter. Ugh. Four other teachers, and she landed next to *that* guy. How had he wormed his way into the group in the first place? He was everyone's least favorite colleague, not that he'd notice.

The man was as arrogant as they came—apparently an expert in all matters pertaining to anything and everything. He was sure that anyone and everyone should be impressed by the fact that he was a high-ranking member of the Colorado Bicycle Club and had run in three marathons. He loved to drop that bit of personal information at every opportunity, which is to say, whenever anyone was having a conversation about bicycling, running, walking, exercising of any sort, being tired, being worn out, being busy, or any other nearly or not so nearly related topics.

The man drove Jamie nuts.

He didn't belong with the group gathered for dinner that Friday night. His first year teaching had been a disaster, followed by a second, greater disaster that was still playing out as they began the meal. The only reason he'd landed the coveted position in the social studies department was because of his grandfather, which also proved to be the only reason he managed to retain the same job after a complete first-year failure.

Those who can't, teach.

He was the reason that phrase still lived. That offended Jamie the most.

It would have been nice to sit next to Jack, the ancient teacher who'd been instructing students in arithmetic since Pythagoras perfected his theorem. He was funny and non-threatening. Or Mary, known to their students as a no-nonsense teacher but was actually quite witty when fifteen-year-olds weren't looking. Or Ellen, the younger woman across from Jamie, whose talkative energy matched her fun, boing-ing hair which stuck out in all directions. People she enjoyed, people with whom she could relax.

Which was the point of this outing. The week of parent-teacher conferences was exhausting. The end of it always made Jamie feel like *she'd* run a marathon. It was time to hang out, to be Jamie instead of Ms. Carson.

The five of them had piled into a large round booth, and Jamie swallowed her distaste for Mr. Carter while the others began exchanging animated stories of their meetings. A shadow cast over the table, and a familiar masculine scent filled the space.

Andy.

Jamie looked up, her eyes wide. She hadn't mentioned her plans to him, and he was a good distance from his home turf. An uneasy quiver moved in her stomach, the same sensation she'd had when he'd cradled her face on Sunday afternoon.

"Hello." He looked at her warmly, then encompassed the rest of the group with his gaze.

"Hey." Jamie gave him a half-smile. He'd been so sweet, so attentive over the past few weeks. But his stares were becoming too intense, and she was getting too attached. "What are you doing all the way out here?"

"I had a meeting with a client. I've been here since three."

Not stalking her. What a dumb worry, anyway. She relaxed. "Oh, how'd it go?"

Andy shrugged with his hands in his pockets. "The usual. He's a new client, so it took a while. How did conferences go?"

"I think we're all glad to be done." Jamie's summation was confirmed by nods all around.

"I'm sorry," Dale Carter spoke after a moments' lull. "I could be the only one, but I don't think we've met."

"Oh." Jamie looked from the man sitting to the one standing. Did she have to introduce him to Dale? "I'm sorry. I thought you'd all met my friend Andy before."

With a professional mask Jamie knew wasn't genuine, Andy extended his hand to the man next to her. "Andrew Harris."

"Dale Carter."

Andy retracted his hand and scanned the other faces. "I think I've met everyone else at one point or another."

Dale motioned to the full booth, his tone dismissing Andy. "I wish we could offer you a seat, but we're pretty packed in as it is."

Jamie attempted to cover her scowl. Her heart rate notched up as Andy's eyes darkened. Not good.

Across the table, Jack raised an eyebrow at Dale and patted the table. "You could just pull a chair over. There's plenty of room."

Andy eyed Carter, then snagged a chair from a neighboring table.

Their waitress appeared as he folded his legs under the table. "Will you be staying, Mr. Harris?" she asked.

"Just for a bit."

"Lemonade?"

"No, I'll just have some water, thanks."

The young woman smiled and left.

"She was sure here lickety-split." Dale grinned as if he were making a joke. "You must tip well."

Andy cleared his throat.

Please be civil tonight.

Andy civil while in a bad mood? Not likely.

"Well." His eyes leveled the man across the table. The lawyer hath arrived. "When you occupy a space for four hours, it's only right to weigh your tip. I'm sure you would do the same."

Dale nodded, but didn't seem abashed in the least. "What exactly do you do, Andy?"

"Andrew." His gaze was cold.

"I thought Jamie called you Andy."

With a raised eyebrow, Andy wordlessly made his position clear. "I'm a lawyer."

Jamie inwardly groaned, knowing the condescending tone well. She crossed her legs, purposely kicking him as she moved. *Please don't embarrass me.*

He looked at her innocently—a bad sign.

"Really?" Dale answered in a made-up cheery tone. "The actual law kind or the divorce-court kind?"

Oh my goodness, he didn't just say that. Jamie's head snapped up, and she glared at Dale.

Hers wasn't the only disapproving look at the table. Dale apparently felt the heat and tried to recover. "I'm sorry." He laughed as if he'd actually been funny. "That was a bad joke. Really, Andrew, I was kidding."

Accepting the apology with a slight nod, Andy moved his attention to Jack, whom he'd met while helping Jamie with a new shelf the year before. The conversation began to relax again, but it didn't last.

The evening turned out to be one long, miserable sparring match between Dale and Andy. Dale managed to squeeze in by name every race he'd ever run since high school—like anyone actually cared—dropping in his times for each race for good measure. And, hey, by the way, had Andrew ever heard of the Continental Divide Trail? Well, guess what? He'd ridden *all* of the Colorado section.

Jamie's head throbbed. The man was such an idiot. Couldn't he see that everyone was bored?

Andy remained unimpressed. He didn't dip in the appropriate *oh*s and *ah*s, nor did he invite further information. Clearly put off, Dale moved on to professional accolades, adding in more jabs at the legal profession as he made up his own stellar resume.

Andy had enough. "So, you should be training for the Olympics soon, right? I'll look for you on the medal stand—which event do you think will capture the most attention?" One eyebrow hiked up, and he stared at him with dry sarcasm. "I think talking. You excel at that."

The air hung heavy and deathly still. Jamie's blood turned hot. Mad as she was at Dale, whom she couldn't stand in the first place, she was livid with Andy, because... well because she just was. He was embarrassing her, making it worse. Couldn't he just indulge the fool?

The check finally came. Jamie set down three tens, not bothering with change. She managed a civil farewell to the group and speared Andy with a glare before she left.

She'd been home for less than ten minutes when Andy knocked on her front door. She stared at him while she blocked the entrance, and he matched her defiant look.

"What are you doing here?"

"What do you mean, what am I doing here?"

She hated that lawyer voice. "This is my home, and we're done for the night."

"Oh no we're not." He spoke with authority. As if she owed him something.

A jogger passed by on her front walk, and the car next door pulled in, all of which Jamie became keenly aware of.

Andy followed her gaze, then pinned her with a cold look. "Do you want to do this out here in front of all of your neighbors, or are you going to let me in?"

She could slam the door in his face, but it would only delay the inevitable. She had some things to say about the evening, anyway. She stepped aside, still fuming.

"Is Melissa home?"

"No, she's at her parents' for the weekend."

"Good." He turned to face her with his hands on his hips. "What the heck happened back there, Jamie? And why do you think you get to be mad at me?"

"What? Are you crazy? You humiliate me, and then you can't think why I would be upset?"

"I humiliated you? You've got to be kidding. Were you even at the same table? That man you were with began insulting me before he even knew my name, and you did absolutely nothing. What kind of friend does that?"

"Right, and you were so much the better man that you just let it roll right off your back." Jamie's livid voice dripped with sarcasm. "Come on, Andy, you can give as good as you get, and you more than proved that tonight. Why did you have to spar with Dale Carter anyway?"

"Why? What's so special about Dale Carter?" He waited for an answer, but she gave none. His eyebrows rose in disapproval. "So that's how it is. You did better with Ryan, James. In fact, I'm not sure how you could stoop so far as to move from him to a guy like that."

Jamie added shock to anger. "There is nothing between Dale Carter and me. He's a jerk, but he's also my boss's grandson, and as you may have figured out, he doesn't know when to shut his mouth. So, thank you for the pleasant conversation tonight. I look forward to hearing about it later."

Crossing his arms, Andy rocked back on his heels. "You're more worried about how some guy at work is going to talk about you than you are about a friend? Nice, Jamie. I didn't think it was in you to go that low."

She shook her head and folded her arms. Stepping forward, she barely thought about the words rolling off her tongue. "Low? Oh no, Andy. You've got that one all to yourself. How many times have I had to endure your insulting behavior? How many times have I come to get you when you couldn't even stand upright? Do you know how awful you are when you're in a bad mood—and how much worse you are as a drunk? Don't you dare begin to tell me I've been a bad friend."

With blazing eyes, Andy held her glare in silence. Something changed in his expression, almost painfully, before he marched across her living room and let himself out.

Jamie stood glued to the floor.

Andy slammed the door and gunned his Mustang before she really heard the words she'd just spat out. She'd been cruel, and completely out of line. Andy was right. His anger was justified this time.

Her stomach turned, and her eyes burned. She needed to call him. Needed to apologize.

First thing in the morning.

***

Andrew sped down Colfax without regard for law or safety.

So maybe it was true. He'd been pretty awful to her in the past. But he'd never stand to let someone else treat her badly. He wouldn't sit mutely and let some stranger badmouth her like she had tonight. How could she think that was okay? And how dare she be angry at him over it all?

He could have held his tongue.

You were so much the better man that you just let it roll right off your back.

Her sarcasm pierced. Why does she have to be so perfect? Like anyone could ever attain to her lofty heights.

Andrew turned at a neon sign somewhere between Jamie's house and his downtown loft, his wheels squealing against the asphalt. It wasn't a familiar neighborhood, and he knew better than to park his car at a bar from which he fully intended to leave hammered. But he was angry, and consequently thirsty, and reason and logic had no pull for the moment.

Music blared, and smoke screened the cheap night scene, but Andrew was only seeing red. He saddled a stool nearest the bartender and wasted little time with his order. The fiery shots couldn't come quick enough as he attempted to drown out her spiteful words. To numb the inescapable knowledge of his complete insufficiency.

***

Jamie jolted upright in her bed. Her clock read just after one, but she was sure she'd heard something crash out front. With a racing heart, she grabbed her phone from the night stand and threw on a sweatshirt, wishing that Melissa was home.

The doorbell rang and she jumped. Someone pounded on her front door, and she shivered as she squeezed her fists tight. She wasn't sure what to do, but if someone had had a car accident, she didn't want to ignore them.

The banging sounded again, shaking the front window as Jamie cautiously stepped toward the door. She scanned through her favorite contacts in her phone and tapped Ryan's name, hoping he would answer.

"Jaaaimmmeee! Come open the door!"

Closing her eyes, Jamie groaned. "Andy, what are you doing?" she whispered.

"Hello?" Ryan's gravelly voice came through after the fifth ring.

"Ryan." Her voice shook. "I'm sorry, but I need your help. Andy's at my door. He's drunk, and Melissa is gone."

"I'll be there in a minute."

"Jaaimmmmeee Carrrsonn, wake up!"

The door rattled again. Jamie stood in indecision. Ryan only lived two miles away. It wouldn't take him long to get there, but she couldn't have Andy shouting on her front step.

She unlocked the door and opened it, gasping when she saw blood dripping from Andy's forehead.

"Andy! What happened?"

"I think I ran into your car," he slurred as he stumbled into her home. "You shouldn't park on the street like that."

Jamie peered through the doorway. Sure enough, Andy's Mustang was buried in her Accord.

She stared at him, dumbfounded. He rocked back and forth like an incoherent child. "What are you doing here?"

His eyebrows rose, and he stumbled back toward the door. "You don't want me here?" He swiped at the gash with the back of his hand, leaving a smear of blood from the middle of his face to his hairline. "Fine. I'll leave."

"Not with a car, you're not." She stepped in front of him and closed the door. The vehicle probably wouldn't even work, but she wasn't going to play the odds. "Give me your keys."

He stopped, and a slow leer crept across his face. He patted his pants pocket. "Why don't you come get them?"

Nausea twisted in her stomach, and her heart seemed to tear in half. But she couldn't let him see it. "Fine. Go get yourself killed." She stepped around him and headed for the kitchen as bile burned in her throat. She willed the horrible sensation back, praying Ryan would get there soon.

"Where are you going, James?"

"To get you some water."

"You're not going to get my keys?"

He was ruining everything. He would expect her to forget—because he wouldn't remember. But this was more than just a stupid insult she could discard. He was picking at emotions she'd not realized were there. "Knock it off, Andy."

He followed her, swaying until he reached the counter, which he used to steady his world. Jamie tried to ignore the fact that he'd stopped too close, but when his fingers drifted down the side of her neck, she broke into a cold sweat.

"Come on, James." His voice dropped to an intimate whisper. Leaning toward her, he left no room for separation. "We've been dancing around this forever. It's always been you and me."

Pulling away from his touch, Jamie fought against panic. Another time, another place, and from a different version of the same man, the words would have melted her. Now they sounded vulgar and threatening. She slammed the glass she'd filled on the counter, making a move for the other room. He blocked her passage.

"Andy, please don't." She couldn't hide the quiver in her voice. Her heart pounded against her ribs and her limbs began to tremble.

Andy either didn't notice or didn't care. His long fingers wrapped around her wrist. When she backed away, he followed, his grip tightening. Suddenly she was wedged between him and the counter.

"You're scaring me," she whimpered.

He traced her jaw. "Don't be afraid."

She moved away from his touch, but he pulled her back by her chin. She could smell the awful stench of fermented barley and burning liquor on his breath, and when his lips pushed against her mouth, she cried out.

His kiss was demanding, and his hands took possession of her body. She hadn't realized how large his frame was—how he towered over her, overpowered her—until she felt the full force of his body pressed against hers. If he was determined to have her, he would.

He wasn't her hero anymore. She felt something inside rip apart and die. It was by far the worst thing she'd ever known. Worse than her mother dying, worse than being alone.

A surge of anger empowered her with fresh strength. She grabbed a handful of flesh on his chest and squeezed. He jerked away, and her hand flew. The hard smack of her hand against his face burned her palm.

"Geeze, James," he yelled as his hand rubbed his jaw. "Why'd you do that?"

She could hardly breathe, let alone speak. Andrew didn't move toward her again, but she retreated anyway.

"You didn't mind the last time I kissed you."

"The last time?" It took a moment for her to catch her breath, but when she did, she stood straight and let anger take over. "The last time? I was fifteen! And here's a newsflash for you, Andrew Harris. You were a much better person back then."

She darted to the other side of the room, grabbing her purse from the far end of the counter. She'd laughed when her father gave her a can of pepper spray.

It wasn't funny now.

"You and your high-minded principles." He didn't follow her but yelled from his spot by the sink. "Nobody could live up to your impossible standards."

A knock sounded from the front door, and Andy frowned, his livid eyes piercing hers.

"Jamie?" Ryan called. "Andrew?"

Andy shook his head. "What'd you do, call in the Cavalry?"

"You need to leave," she seethed. She put away her self-defense and set her shoulders straight.

Ryan rounded the corner in his sweats and put a hand on Andy's shoulder.

Andy glared before he turned to Ryan. "I guess you get to babysit." Staggering out of the kitchen, he stopped at the table to deposit his car keys. "I believe you asked for these."

Jamie turned away. Ryan stood at her side for several seconds before he pulled her against him. She stiffened, pushing him away.

"Jamie, are you okay?"

"I'm fine," she answered woodenly.

Ryan studied her, and she felt her heart crumbling. No, she wasn't okay. Her best friend—her childhood hero. The man she'd defended, depended on, and confided in had just betrayed her. Crushed her. Terrified her.

She was anything but fine, but she couldn't possibly tell Ryan. "Jamie..."

She shook her head, fighting to keep the trembling unseen.

"Just get him out of my house," she begged. "Please, Ryan, just get him out."

Deep lines carved into his forehead. But after a moment he nodded. A knock at the door snapped their attention, which was followed by Andy's slurred curse.

"Couldn't leave it at just your boy-wonder?" Andy's growl chilled her spine.

Jamie stepped from the kitchen and around the front room to answer the door. Cherry lights flashed in the night's black depth. Awesome. If the neighbors weren't awake yet, they were zombies.

Who had called the police? Ryan? For some unexplainable reason, resentment kicked in her chest. Dumb—she shouldn't be angry about that. Andy deserved to go to jail for a night. At least.

A uniformed man stood on the other side of the door. "Ma'am. I'm Officer Johnson. We had a call about a crash...I can see the damage out front. Is anyone hurt?"

Depended on what he meant by hurt. "No."

"Is the driver here?" he asked.

Ryan came from behind her. "Yes."

That burning punch hit her stomach again.

The officer's eyebrows tipped. "You?"

"No." Ryan gripped the door and swung it wider.

Jamie turned and found Andy shooting an icy stare into Ryan's back. "Way to keep it on the down low, sellout."

Oh no. Andy was in so much trouble.

Officer Johnson stepped over the threshold. "That your mustang?"

Andy shrugged, swaying again. "That your squad car?"

"Okay, buddy, let's wander outside." Johnson clapped his hand over Andy's shoulder and started for the door.

"Don't wanna."

Jamie's gut cinched down harder.

Johnson looked at her, his stare an odd mixture of stern compassion. "Does this man live here?"

Her lips quivered. "No."

"Do you want him to stay?"

She hugged her burning stomach, desperately wanting this whole night to end. Ryan rubbed her shoulder. How did she end up here? The man she *should* have loved standing behind her, and the one that tempted her heart was shredding her world. This wasn't how this story was supposed to go.

The hand on her arm squeezed gently. "Jamie?"

"No." She sniffed and forced herself to look at Andy. "He needs to leave. Now."

The dark scowl Andy zeroed on her said it all. Their friendship had shattered.

Chapter Eighteen

Every muscle screamed. What had he done? Felt like he'd sent himself through an automated car wash a few times. Without his car.

Where was his car? Skip that. Where was he?

Smelled like metal, wool blankets, urine, and drunks. Jail. He was in jail, stuck on the wrong side of the bars.

What the heck happened last night?

For the moment, irrelevant. He'd get out, and then sort through whatever mess he'd tangled himself in.

Pushing up slowly, because if he moved too fast his brain might fall out of his skull, Andrew shuffled to the bars. "Hey."

Nothing.

He put a little more force in his voice. "Hey!"

A uniformed man meandered around the corner. "Morning sunshine. Enjoy your stay?"

Andrew scowled, which also hurt. "What are you holding me for?"

The man checked a file on his mobile device. "Drunk driving? Nice. Topped off with a wreck." He looked up again. "That'd be an aggravated DUI, sunshine."

A felony. So not good. Andrew rubbed at his temples. "How long are you going to keep me here?"

"Well, I guess since you managed *not* to injure anyone while driving illegally, you can go. For now."

Officer Sarcastic unlocked the door and led the way to the front. He read off a list of Andrew's personal belongings, returning them one by one, and then folded his arms over his chest. "That does it for today. Probably want to push to get that hearing scheduled. The sooner the better."

Yeah, thanks. Went to law school. Andrew shoved his keys into his pocket and jabbed the home button on his phone. He'd have to look over the charges to know what he was dealing with, but there was no way he wasn't going to fight an aggravated DUI. His career couldn't afford a felony—he could be disbarred.

He tapped *contacts* on the phone screen and slid through the options. Jamie. Something sour stirred in his stomach. They sure had it out after dinner the night before.

No, not Jamie. Wasn't going to ask her to pick him up from county jail, especially after that fight.

He blew out a breath, but his stomach wouldn't calm. Why did he feel sick?

His shoes echoed against the tiled hall as he rounded the corner into the front lobby of the court house.

"You're out." Ryan stood from a bench near a window.

Wait, Ryan? Andrew stopped. "Why are you here?"

"Figured you'd need a ride." Ryan turned for the exit. "And I need some answers."

Great. Walking home would be better.

No it wouldn't. Andrew followed him, quickening his steps to catch up. "Know where my car is?"

Ryan kept his pace and didn't look back. "Probably sitting next to Jamie's in the scrap metal pile."

Andrew stopped. That burning in his gut turned to hard core nausea. "Jamie's?"

Ryan glared from his spot beside his Jeep. "Yeah. Jamie's." His jaw moved hard and then he dropped into the vehicle.

Oh no. What had he done?

Andrew slipped into the passenger seat and blinked against the sunlight. His head pounded cruelly, but he forced his mind to retrace his steps from the night before. The images came fuzzy and scattered, and they made very little sense.

He'd gone to a bar in a part of town that was less than stellar. Panic erupted. His memory couldn't pull up much, but he knew beyond a doubt that he'd done something really stupid. Possibly devastating. He'd gone back to her house—there was a crash. He'd smashed her car.

Andrew dipped his head toward his knees and locked his fingers behind his neck. He'd driven drunk back to Jamie's and plowed into her car. Incredibly stupid.

And then a disturbing image flashed—one much worse than a wrecked car. Jamie's face filled his mind, but her expression wasn't one he'd ever seen.

Fear.

Absolute, paralyzing fear consumed her eyes, and they stared straight back at him.

His head snapped up, causing his brain to throb. *It didn't happen.* His heart twisted. *It couldn't have. I wouldn't do that to her.*

He felt the tremor of her hands as they pushed his away, the pounding of her heart as he pressed himself against her breasts. His ears echoed her cry as he'd covered her mouth with his own.

Andrew's face went into his hands, his heart throbbing unmercifully.

God, don't let it be true. I didn't do that—please don't let it be so.

But it was true. He knew it down in his sick gut.

She would hate him.

Ryan pulled up to his townhouse and parked. "Do you want some coffee?"

Yeah, coffee fixed everything. Andrew climbed out of the car, grumbling his thanks. How much did Ryan know? He battled guilt as Ryan led him into the house.

Ryan set Andrew's phone in front of him. "You left this at Jamie's."

Andrew stared at it. "Do you know of a decent rental company?"

Ryan shrugged. "Google it."

Right. After a search on his smartphone, he made the phone call. Ryan went about making a strong brew and a small breakfast until Andrew was finished.

Andrew set down his phone, and Ryan slapped a plate of toast in front of him. "You're in pretty deep."

Did he know how deep? The horrible images still flashed before Andrew's eyes, each one becoming more detailed. She had trusted him, and he had… Andrew couldn't even form the words. "Is Jamie all right?"

"She was pretty upset last night. I haven't talked to her this morning. Her house was still dark when I ran by."

Andrew tried to slouch away from the subtle accusations in Ryan's gaze. But he couldn't escape the truth, and he needed to know how Jamie really was.

"I think I really messed up."

Ryan smacked his coffee mug on the counter. "What do you mean?" His eyes narrowed as he gripped the counter top, and suddenly Andrew knew Ryan could take him. "Did you hurt her?"

Had he hurt her? He'd shredded her heart with one foolish act and, in a moment, killed a lifelong friendship. Andrew was pretty sure that hurt. But that wasn't what Ryan meant.

"Not like that," Andrew whispered. *I don't think…*

Ryan stood speechless. Andrew knew himself to be a coward, and part of him wished Ryan would use his fists on him. Maybe the bruises would make him feel better. Maybe it would help Jamie forgive him. But Ryan didn't move. A vein bulged near his forehead, and his knuckles turned white in his clenched fists, but he held his place.

Andrew sat in misery. He hated himself. He hated that there was part of himself that he couldn't cut off. A part that was uncontrollable, mean, and destructive. And he hated that he'd managed to wound the one person he cared about most.

Shoulders slumped, he turned on his stool to get up. "I need to talk to her."

"I'm not sure that's a good idea."

Andrew examined his host. Mad, but still in perfect control. The complete antithesis of himself. And everything Jamie deserved.

"Probably not." He stood in defeat. "But I have to apologize."

Andrew's stomach rolled as he walked to Jamie's. She would hate him. How could he have done that to her? What kind of man does that to any woman, let alone the one he loved?

Long before he was ready to face her, Andrew mounted the two steps to Jamie's front door. He stood for several moments, praying to a God who probably didn't care about any of it—if he was actually there at all—that somehow she would forgive him.

***

Ryan had called a half hour before. He'd offered to come, and the moment she heard the knock, Jamie wished she'd accepted. But she hadn't. She had every intention of opening the door, handing Andy his keys, and closing it in less than three seconds. She hadn't considered the possibility of finding a truly penitent man standing at the threshold.

She'd resolved not to allow him the intimacy of seeing her cry. But one look at his agonized expression, and the tears began to pool. With a trembling hand, she held out his keys, but she couldn't bring herself to shut the door.

"I don't think these will do me any good." Andy accepted them, careful not to touch her. He rubbed the back of his head with his free hand. "I have a rental company on the way. I'll take care of it, okay?"

Kind of like a giant cup of coffee. Way easier than an actual apology. Jamie sniffed and straightened her spine. "Money doesn't fix everything, Andrew."

He flinched.

She almost wanted to take it back. Almost. Until he moved toward her. She shivered, then hugged herself, leaning away. "Have a nice night in jail?"

His shoulders caved in. "Jamie, please..."

"No." She drew up straight. "Let's talk reality. What are you looking at? Drunk driving—that can't be good. What is it when you crash while intoxicated?"

He looked away. His Adam's apple bobbed, and he pushed a hand into his hair. "Possibly a felony. I don't know yet."

Jamie snorted. "Bet you've spent the morning figuring out how to get out of it, haven't you?"

Wow, she was being really nasty. He felt awful; every movement, every facial expression shouted regret. Why was she picking at it?

"I could lose my job, Jamie." His voice actually wavered. "Is that what you want?"

"I want you to do the right thing."

"I want to, but…" He tossed his head back and growled. "I'm not just talking about *this* job. Felonies don't look good on a lawyer."

Did they look good on anyone? "Well, I'm glad *something* in your life actually matters to you." Heat scorched her ears as she listened to her own voice. That was it, though—the real rub. He'd tossed their relationship to the gutter for a bottle, and the cut went deeper than she ever could have imagined.

"Jamie…" Misery weighed in his voice and he moved toward her.

Ache throbbed deep and hard in her chest. She held up a hand. "I can't do this. Just leave me alone. I can't deal with you right now." Without looking at him, she pivoted on her socked feet and headed to the kitchen.

Andy could let himself out.

***

God, please. Let her forgive me.

Andrew turned from the front door to the covered porch, a mocking voice laughing in the back of his head. An atheist praying. He was one messed up man.

No, desperate. Without Jamie, he was nothing. He had nothing— no hope, no inspiration to be better, no reason to reform. And he needed to reform. Last night…

A tremble passed over his limbs. How close had he come to devastating her completely?

A white sedan pulled up and a man in a green jacket popped out. The rental company. At least he could take care of that. Maybe it would be a step.

The car guy walked toward the house. "Are you Jamie Carson?"

"No." Andrew stepped down the porch to meet him. "But I'm the guy who called. Jamie's in the house. She'll...I'll get her when we're done here. Let's do the paperwork, and then you can take her to get a vehicle."

The guy squinted. "You paying?"

"Yeah."

"She you're wife?"

Andrew looked back to the house. "No. She's not my wife."

"No can do." He crossed his arms. "Spouses we can put on the same account, but—"

Andrew scowled. "Make it work. I wrecked her car and she needs a vehicle, so take my credit card, my birth certificate, and my left kidney if you have to. I don't care, just make it work."

"I'm going to have to call this in."

"Good idea." Andrew shoved his hands into his pockets. "I'll wait."

No can do switched to *sure* after a five minute discussion and a hold on his Visa account.

Green jacket guy tucked his paperwork under his arm. "What kind of car should I get?"

"Whatever she wants."

His eyebrows lifted. "Huh. Must have been a doosey."

Andrew ground his teeth. Not today. He was not sinking under this guy's insolence today. Ignoring the man, he turned back up the walk and pulled out his phone and typed a quick text to Ryan.

Jamie's going to get a rental. Go with her. Please.

Car guy called behind him. "Hey, you going to get a car or not?"

Andrew waved him off. "I'll get her. Just wait."

He peered through the screen door into her front room. Not there. Inside, everything was still. Should he knock? She wouldn't answer. He let himself in and found her in the kitchen, staring into her coffee mug.

"James?"

Her eyes darted up. The anger and mistrust in that glance nearly brought him to his knees, and it took an enormous amount of self-control not to wrap her in his arms.

"What?" Her tone was sharp.

Any hopes that his embrace would have been received vanished. He held her gaze for several breaths. *Please, please forgive me.* Sighing, he leaned against the counter. One stupid fight, one stupid decision.

You have to stop this. It will rob you of everything.

Everything could go, as far as he was concerned. Life held very little in the way of deep attachments. Save one.

"The rental guy is here. Ryan should be on his way."

Jamie's look softened. Her eyes wandered out the kitchen window. "Ryan?"

"I thought you'd rather have him go."

Jamie turned and he was amazed to see a glint of compassion. But when he pushed off the counter and took a step forward, she recoiled.

"James," he pleaded.

She shook her head and took another step back.

He would have rather she slapped him.

A rap on the front door ended the exchange. Andrew ran a hand over his face before he stepped away.

He was out the door before Jamie moved.

***

Jamie was numb the rest of the day. Aside from asking her again if she was okay, Ryan didn't push and Jamie didn't share. She simply shriveled away inside herself, not knowing what to do or even what she felt.

She went to church Sunday. If she could just keep doing the normal things, maybe the crumpled-up parts of her aching soul would iron themselves out and she could move on.

But by Sunday evening she was exhausted, and the pain she kept trying to push away didn't budge. She sought refuge in a warm shower, hoping the hot water would numb the stubborn pain. As steam clouded around her and water ran down her back, the dam inside broke, and a torrent of sobs raged through her. Soap and water would not wash away the ache.

When the water turned cold, Jamie wrapped in a towel and curled up on her bed, still shaking with the cries of her broken heart.

She hadn't heard Melissa come home, but suddenly her roommate was there, kneeling at her bedside and gently shaking her shoulder. "Jamie, what's wrong?"

Jamie didn't know the words.

Again Melissa asked.

By the third time, she sounded panicked. "You're scaring me, Jamie." She gripped her shoulder and shook a little harder. "Talk to me."

Where to begin?

"Andy and I had a fight..." Jamie sat up, clutching her towel and running a shaky hand through her wet hair. And then the story tumbled out. She cringed when she discovered the sound of metal crashing still echoed in her ears. She trembled, still smelling his drenched breath, still feeling his fingers curl around her arms.

"He kissed you?" Melissa's eyes moved with warning, her voice cautious.

It sounded so stupid. She was sobbing because Andy had kissed her.

Melissa grasped Jamie's hands as she leaned in closer. "Did he do more than kiss you?"

No. It was just a kiss. An uninvited, threatening, terrifying kiss. But she was overreacting. It was just a kiss.

"He didn't—" She couldn't say the words. "He only kissed me." Her voice wavered, and she bit her lip until she thought it was under control. "I didn't know if he would stop. Melissa, he was so drunk, and I was afraid. He's so much bigger than I am..."

Melissa wrapped her in her arms. She didn't let go until Jamie pulled away, and even then she stayed by her side.

"What happened?" she whispered when Jamie could speak again.

"Ryan came and took him home."

"Does Ryan know what happened?"

"No."

Melissa sat a little straighter. "Jamie, you need to tell him."

Absolutely not. Jamie shook her head and they sat in awkward silence. She studied her fingers, recalling the conversations she and Melissa had had about her friendship with Andy. Melissa had warned her—several times over. Clinging to an alcoholic was dangerous.

Melissa faced her, placing a hand on her arm. "What will you do?"

"Nothing," Jamie croaked. "What can I do?"

"I think Ryan should know. Someone should know who could intervene for you. Andrew respects Ryan."

"What would I say? That Andy kissed me? It sounds so silly. It's so humiliating, I just can't." Jamie drew a shuddered breath. "The horrible thing is that I can't hate him. I wanted to, but he was so ashamed. I can't help but hope that maybe the whole thing has opened his eyes, and maybe—"

"No." Melissa stood and crossed her arms. "Jamie, no. You *cannot* let Andrew off on this. I know he's your friend, and I know that it runs deep, but you can't let this one go. It's not good for you, and it's not good for Andrew."

The room went still. Melissa was right, but Jamie hated the thought of facing Ryan. She wanted to hope, to believe that this would wake Andy up, that it would end his path of destruction.

But he was a Jekyll and Hyde—it would happen again.

"What if I talk to Ryan?" Melissa's arms fell to her side and she sat again. "Perhaps together we could walk through this with you. Would you be okay with that?"

What would Andy do? As much as he'd hurt her, she couldn't stand the thought of losing his friendship. Could Ryan and Melissa really understand that? But if she rejected this—if she refused their help, what would happen the next time?

Chapter Nineteen

Andrew was putting on his tennis shoes when Ryan knocked on his door. It was a Monday, and they had a standing appointment at the racquetball court. So far they led in the club league, so he expected the man to be ready to play.

Ryan was not. Andrew opened the door to a definitive scowl and angry eyes.

"Hey," he spoke tentatively, wondering at Ryan's uncharacteristic mood. "What's going on?"

Ryan moved past the door in silence. He was boiling, and Andrew's mind jumped back to Saturday. He hadn't talked to Jamie again, giving her time, and he thought it was unnecessary to talk to Ryan about it because by all appearances, they were cool.

"What happened Friday?" Ryan growled.

"What do you mean?" Andrew snagged his racquet. Was Ryan trying to "help" him again? "You were there, you know the story."

Ryan lunged. One moment Andrew was standing in the middle of the room, and the next he was shoved against the steel door. "What did you do to Jamie?"

Andrew froze. Jamie told him? Why would she do that?

Ryan shook him. "What did you do?"

As quickly as Ryan had pinned him, he released him.

Andrew tugged his shirt straight and tried to think.

The silence didn't satisfy Ryan. "I want to hear you say it, Andrew. What did you do to her?"

"I kissed her." Andrew stared at his feet while heat poured through his veins.

Ryan stepped forward, his jaw still set in rage. "You kissed her? Really? Was that it?"

Was it? The images were vague. What else had he done? His gut began to coil painfully.

Ryan glared at him. "You tell me, then, why Melissa found her sobbing Sunday night."

Andrew searched his memory. What had he done? Every image was fuzzy and disjointed. All he really could recall was Jamie's fear. "I don't remember."

"No. You don't. You know why? You were drunk!"

God, please don't tell me I forced her into more. His stomach lurched. Andrew moved away, slumping into his chair. *Stop! Please just make it stop.*

Ryan followed with only his eyes, but he looked ready to pounce again.

"Did I hurt her?" His voice was pathetic. He didn't really want to know. But he had to know.

Ryan breathed deeply, and the tense muscles in his arms slowly relaxed. "No. But you scared her." He sat on the low table across from Andrew, his arms on his knees and his head bowed.

The relief was slight. He knew he'd scared her—he couldn't escape her terrified eyes. And she'd told Ryan. She'd confided in Ryan about him. She'd never done that, not even when she'd been dating the guy. Why would she do that?

He'd lost her. That's why. She couldn't trust him and she couldn't face him. Maybe Ryan was here to tell him to stay away. What would he do with that? "Does she hate me?"

Ryan's eyes held his.

Was that compassion replacing anger? How could that be?

"No. Jamie doesn't hate you." He rubbed his forehead. "I don't think that's possible."

"Is she afraid of me?" He wasn't sure he wanted to know.

"Yes." Ryan shifted. "Actually, that's not really true. She's afraid of you drunk."

"It won't happen again."

Ryan shook his head. "I've heard that one before."

And there it was. Ryan was going to fix it. Andrew's spine snapped straight. "What do you want from me?" He jumped up and paced away. "Do you really think you're going to fix me?"

Ryan didn't move, didn't flinch. "No."

"Then what do you expect me to do?"

"I don't know." Ryan drew a deep breath. "All I know is that Jamie's my friend, and you're my friend, and I don't know what to do. You're a mess, Andrew. If this doesn't prove it to you, then what will it take? How far will you go next time?"

"I told you, there won't be a next time!" Andrew slammed his racquet against the table.

Ryan jumped up, stepping into Andrew's space. "When are you going to understand? Self-reform doesn't work!"

Self reform doesn't work. He'd tried everything to drown that mantra. It saturated him. It infuriated him. He wanted to cover his ears and scream. "Get out!"

Ryan's gaze turned cool as he held a silent challenge.

How could he be so calculated, so self-possessed?

"Ask yourself, Andrew, how far you're willing to push." Ryan snagged his racquet and stepped toward the door. He stopped, his hand on the knob. "Jamie's strong and loyal to a fault. But she will break. What will you do then?"

***

That week was one of the worst in Jamie's adulthood. She slept very little, despite the fact that she was completely spent. Each day she struggled to put forth her best while she taught, and more often than not she was short with her students. Every night she confessed that she had not lived in the Spirit of God and asked not only for forgiveness, but for grace and strength for the next day.

But in each one following, she continued to fail.

Friday ended in both relief and regret. Frustrated and longing for an escape, Jamie packed up her laptop and the giant stack of exams. She should stay and grade those. But she just wanted to be in her sweats with a hot cup of cider.

Home it was. She could start fresh next week.

She was moving to the classroom door when it opened. Andrew walked in.

"Andrew." She sighed as the world seemed to crumble on top of her.

He winced."Hi, Jamie." He held out a Styrofoam cup.

She looked at his peace offering. A smoothie? That was going to fix this?

"Peach-raspberry." He pushed it a little closer. "Your favorite, right?"

He was trying. This was all he knew to do. But it wasn't good enough. Not this time.

Why, then, did she accept his offer?

Andrew reached for her school bag. "Can I help you with that?"

"No, I've got it."

He took her bag anyway.

Jamie sighed. She couldn't reject him, but things would never be the same. He could try to charm her, to buy her off. But their friendship couldn't be the same.

It took some time to locate her vehicle. Six days had gone by, but she was still looking for her blue Honda rather than the cherry-red 4runner. It wasn't until she finally spotted the SUV that she remembered Andy didn't have a car anymore, and he'd probably lost his license.

She stopped on the blacktop, her voice accusing. "How did you get here?"

"I rode." He jerked his head toward the building. She hadn't noticed his mountain bike leaning against the brick wall. "I can get here from downtown using the trails. It might actually be faster to pedal than to drive. I may never go back."

He might never have the option to go back.

Jamie tried unsuccessfully to return his smile, and Andrew's shoulders sagged. She unlocked the car with her remote and opened the passenger side, stepping back so he could place her work inside.

"Do you have plans tonight?"

Jamie looked at the man squarely.

All pretenses vanished, and once again remorse etched his expression.

She shook her head slightly.

"Will you let me buy you dinner?"

Her gaze drifted across the parking lot, but she wasn't seeing the cars or the school building. She missed him. Secretly during the week she'd hoped he would call—that he would beg for her forgiveness. Then she'd have a reason to hang on, to move on.

But he hadn't. He'd just shown up with gift in hand, expecting it to be good enough. She'd been such a pushover. Melissa was right; she needed to hold him responsible.

The wind picked up, tossing her hair across her face. She shifted her gaze back to Andy. "What are you doing?"

"I want to make things right." He looked like he might beg. "I want us to be all right."

Jamie's head began to ache. She went back to Monday, when Melissa and Ryan discussed the whole thing with her again. Ryan was furious. He'd warned her about this, and he'd broken up with her because of Andy. She'd been so afraid that he'd tell her to walk away. Afraid—because she didn't have a good reason to argue.

But his words had surprised her. *"Jamie, Andrew is our friend too. You're not the only one who prays for him. And the good man you still cling to—we see him. But you can't go it alone on this. His problems are too big."*

Not one of them could abandon a friend. But the addiction could no longer be ignored. How could they offer him sincere friendship, yet draw a clear boundary? Life was not simply black and white.

"Please, Jamie?" Andrew's pleading brought her back. "What can I do?"

Anger erupted. "You could apologize."

"I'm sorry, James. So very sorry."

Her anger simmered. She examined her smoothie, and Andy rested a hand on her shoulder. She didn't jerk away but stiffened at his touch.

He looked like he would be sick. "I swear, Jamie, I would never hurt you."

"Until last week, I believed that was true."

Andy withdrew his hand, running it through his hair and then over his face. "You're my best friend. Please don't give up on me."

Her throat constricted until she felt as though she couldn't breathe. A tear slid down Andy's cheek, and she lost the fight for control. Sobs shook her as she wrapped her arms around herself. "I don't know what to do."

"Do you want me to leave?"

The words were barely out of his mouth when the squeak of the school door startled them. Andy stepped to her side, shielding her face from view. She looked up at him as he discreetly wiped moisture from his face.

This was the man she clung to, the one who was thoughtful, who looked out for her and stood up for her. The one who never let the big kids pick on her on the bus, who made sure she made it home okay when her brothers left her behind. He always managed to resurface, and Jamie couldn't walk away from the friend of her childhood.

**

Andrew waited until the car cleared the parking lot before he cautiously put an arm around her shoulders. Relief didn't begin to describe how he felt when she leaned into his chest. He wouldn't let her down again.

Dinner began quietly and awkwardly. Jamie didn't try to pretend nothing was wrong. Andrew couldn't either. Recovering their friendship was going to take more than he'd ever given anyone. But he didn't have a choice. He needed her.

"I'm sorry I didn't call you earlier this week." His fingers rubbed against the table. He wished he could touch her, hold her hand and make her believe in him again.

Jamie set down the fork she'd been using to push her food around. Her straight-on look demanded an explanation.

She deserved one. He dropped his eyes to his plate. "I thought maybe you needed some time."

She didn't look satisfied, like she thought it was a cop-out. Maybe it was. He didn't want to face her angry. He didn't want to see her heartbroken.

"My court hearing was yesterday." He sagged against his chair. Honesty was all he had left, and even at that, it might not be enough. "I pleaded guilty to a DUI—a misdemeanor. I know…that's not what you wanted, but I need this job. I already blew it in California…" He leaned against his elbow, which rested on the table. Humiliation didn't do this moment justice. "Anyway, my driver's license is gone for a while, and I'll be busy for the next few weeks."

"Busy?"

She was listening. She still cared. "There's this program. It's a combination of a few things. There's mandatory community service and rehab with a DUI."

Her eyes lit up.

He was on the right track. "So this group puts the two together. I'll be going to some meetings and then cleaning gravestones."

"Gravestones?"

"Of accident victims." He held his breath. That was profound—or it should be. Andrew hoped for approval.

She looked at the table, her lips pressed between her teeth. "How long?"

"Six weeks."

"And then what?"

Andrew stared at her. What else did she want? "And then I'm done. I paid the fines. I'll have to wait three months for my license. But other than that, it's done." Because he'd fixed it. Negotiated out of the felony charges and made it all look like a one time slip-up so that if the State Bar looked into it, he'd probably come out all right.

Jaime tilted her head and held his look. "Will you be done drinking?"

She had to be kidding.

He should just tell her what she wanted to hear, but her implication was frustrating. "Jamie, give me a little credit here." He worked to keep the irritation out of his voice. "I'll do whatever it takes to earn your trust back, but I don't have the kind of problem you're implying."

"Andy." Her eyes came back to his, a sheen glossing over them. "You're a good friend, sober. It's the drunk Andrew that I'm afraid of. And, to be honest, you're that guy more often than you realize."

"I know." No, he didn't. But if she needed to hear it, fine. "But, Jamie, I am trying, I have been. I'll get past this. I just need to know that you'll be here."

"I can't do anything for you." She slumped against her chair and crossed her arms. "Friday should have made that clear. You've no boundaries when you're drunk, and I can't come for you anymore. I can't help you with this."

"I won't call you again, I promise."

"How can you say that? You lose all inhibitions." She sat forward, heat building in her voice. "You're mean and you don't have any regard for anyone but yourself when you drink. There's no way you can keep a promise like that."

His jaw tightened. "It won't happen again, James. I promise."

A long silence followed. She stared off at nothing, the sheen returning over those sad emeralds.

"I think you need help, Andy," she finally said. "Real help."

His fist balled against his leg. He needed her support, not a lecture. Why couldn't she understand that? "I can handle this."

Chapter Twenty

Jamie stared at her phone as it continued to ring. She'd wanted to talk to him. She'd actually wished he'd suggested a hike or something over the weekend. But he'd been busy. Scrubbing gravestones. Now she had nothing to say. Their friendship was broken.

Maybe it would help if she apologized. She hadn't told Melissa what had sparked their argument in the first place. She couldn't bring herself to own it. The whole explosion was her fault, though. She'd been in a bad mood that Friday night, and she'd fired all of her blackness at Andy. But he hadn't deserved it. He'd been right— she'd been a lousy friend. Maybe if she hadn't… Well, maybe they wouldn't be broken.

She needed to apologize.

She rescued the call just before it went to voicemail, arranging in the tiny space before Andy's hello the words she needed to say.

"How are you today, James?"

She swallowed, her nose stinging. "Okay." *Do it now. Say what you should have said before everything went wrong.*

"Did the insurance check come yet?"

"Insurance check?"

"For the car." He sounded concerned. "It should be there any day now."

"Oh." *Andy, I need to tell you…*

"I wanted to tell you not to be in a big hurry. Just keep the 4runner until you find what you want. I'll take care of it." Andy paused, and the silence felt odd. "Okay, James?"

"Yeah." Jamie swallowed again. *Now say it. Now tell him.*

"Do you know what you want?"

"What I want?"

"To replace your Honda with." He waited.

"Oh." Jamie tried to think. "Uh, no. I guess something like it. I haven't thought about it."

Again the line stayed quiet.

What was she going to say? How was she going to say it?

"Can I help you with it?"

Help? With what? Cars. They were talking about cars.

"James? Are you okay?"

"I'm fine." She spoke a little too quickly. "I'm grading a lab, so I'm not concentrating." *Liar.*

"Oh, I'm sorry. I should have asked if you were busy. Listen, just let me know, okay? I'm a car guy. I like to do the research, and I want to make sure you get a good deal. Okay?"

"Yeah." She pressed her lips together. *It starts with 'I'm sorry…'* Jamie gulped.

"I'll let you go then. Call you later?"

"Okay."

And her opportunity went dead.

***

Andy made good on his offer, and they went shopping Saturday morning. Jamie had prepped herself with a speech. It shouldn't be that hard to apologize to a friend.

She didn't have the chance, though. "Are you sure you don't want something different?" Andy asked as soon as Jamie picked him up. "Maybe an SUV so you can throw your bike in, or drive to the back country?"

Her speech was forgotten. "No, I don't want to pay the pump ticket for those. I got everywhere I needed in my Accord, and a bike rack is a pretty easy alternative."

"Do you want a roof rack?"

Jamie thought on that. Maybe. Suddenly she was overwhelmed, and very glad Andy had offered his help.

He hadn't been kidding about loving cars. He'd spent the week researching Consumer Best Buys, Kelly Blue Book, and the lemon lists. And he came alive at the dealership. All Jamie had to do was drive. Which would have been all she would have done anyway. It was a good thing he was looking out for her.

By late afternoon he'd found her a deal—a previously leased, low-mileage silver Camry that already had a roof rack installed. Jamie felt confident as she signed over the insurance check. Maybe everything would settle and wash away, now that the mess had been dealt with. Maybe she and Andy would be okay.

Andy grinned as she took the keys from the salesman. The transaction complete, they left the office to claim her new car when he stopped dead. Jamie had to retrace her steps, then laughed at the look on his face. It was like the one she'd make in the Rocky Mountain Chocolate Factory.

She followed his gaze across the lot and to the next dealership where it rested on a black Jaguar XK R.

It wasn't funny anymore.

"Andy, you don't have a license."

He grinned, undeterred. "I know. But I will eventually."

He set his stride toward the Jag, which was sitting prettily on its own. Jamie made herself follow.

"Just two years old, twenty thousand miles." Smitten, Andrew sucked air in through his teeth. "Perfect for me. Right?"

"You're not serious."

He ignored her. "You want to go for another test drive?"

"You can't drive."

Andy winked down at her. "You can."

"No."

"Come on, James. Haven't you ever wanted to drive a car like that?"

She shifted her attention back to the sports car. Sleek, shiny, and tempting. Well, actually…

A half smile peeked through before she could catch it.

Andy's grin went full blown. "I'll get the keys."

"No, wait—"

But he was gone. The test drive was on.

Jamie's hands shook when she gripped the steering wheel. How would she pay for the car if she wrecked it? The machine cost nearly three times her annual teacher's salary. But she pulled out into an open lane, and her cares blew by in the smooth ride of the sweet car.

This was fun.

Until Andy started negotiating.

What was he thinking? He couldn't even get the thing home. How would he resist the temptation to drive with keys in his possession and wheels in his parking spot?

Suddenly the day became long.

"Andy." She snagged him while the salesman went happily to the financing office. "This is not a good idea. You can't drive it for months. There'll be another one later."

"It's all right, James. I've got this." He winked at her again and smiled like a child under the Christmas tree. "I'll be good. I promise."

Jamie's heart sank. Andy had a knack for finding trouble. And no sense whatsoever to stay out of it.

***

"What's Memorial weekend looking like for you?" Andy asked on a Saturday morning in early May.

He'd brought bagels and coffee and was going to help her clean up the winter mess in her yard. He came around often. He was always good to her, always her friend. Maybe always a little more.

It's always been you and me.

Andy's slurred words stayed with her. What if he'd said them in another context? What if he felt them in truth?

What if she did?

She couldn't let herself. He would destroy her. The pain of that awful Friday night was a mere shadow of what she'd be in for if she truly opened her heart to him.

She needed to get away. His constant pursuit clouded her thinking.

Jamie didn't make eye contact. "I'm going to my dad's."

Andy stopped, his coffee mid-air. "For a three-day weekend?"

Jamie shrugged.

He stared at her, his face falling with each passing breath. "What about the Bolder Boulder?"

She moved to the deck rail. "I transferred my entry to Ryan. He's going with Melissa this year." Her heart pounded in the silence, and she prayed Andy wouldn't push for a reason. She couldn't give him one. Not an honest one.

"Why?"

She searched the wood planks under her feet. He confused her, taking her heart places she couldn't go. "I'm not up for it this year."

"No." Andy set his mug down, stood up, and moved closer. "Why are you going to your dad's? You never go that far for a weekend."

Jamie moved her gaze to his.

Big mistake. They pleaded, invited. Begged her to love him. And right now she…

Andy reached for her shoulder, and she nearly jumped away. Dropping her gaze, she tried to put herself back together.

"Jamie," Andy whispered, his heart in his voice, "please forgive me."

"I do forgive you." She forced herself to look at him. "I just need to see my dad."

His Adam's apple bobbed twice. "You're coming back, right?"

"Yes, I'm coming back." Jamie painted on a smile. "We're still friends."

Andy nodded and stepped away. Leaving his coffee on her table, he moved down the steps and to the sidewalk.

Jamie's yard work was left untouched.

***

The bus was warm and smelled of sweat. And alcohol. Exactly what he needed. Andrew slouched in a seat and put his nose in his shoulder.

How could he have misunderstood her so badly? He'd sworn it was there—the tenderness he'd ached to see had touched her eyes. He was sure of it.

But she'd retreated from his touch as though it burned.

A paper bag rustled across from him, drawing his attention. The gray man smirked as he lifted it to his lips. Andrew sniffed. Tequila. Cheap tequila. He turned away, his fists clenching. What had they said in group rehab? *Remember the reason you won't and then find something else to focus on.*

A distraction.

Andrew pulled out his cell. He couldn't call Jamie. Wouldn't help. He slid through his contacts.

Ryan.

Without giving himself a chance to change his mind, he hit send. Ryan answered.

"Hey, are you up for some racquetball?" Andrew asked.

He was. In one hour.

Surely Andrew could gut it out for one hour.

Ryan showed up as promised, to Andrew's relief. He'd made it. Sort of. One drink—that didn't really count. Everyone drank a little. Most everyone. Anyway, he was fine. Fully functional, completely in control.

He fell behind two sets and conceded. Ryan hadn't said much, but somehow Andrew knew he'd suspected something was up. What could he lose by talking about it? "Jamie's going to Iowa for Memorial Day."

Ryan nodded, looking calm as he slid against the wall to the floor. "She gave me her entry for the Boulder run."

Andrew looked at the floor.

"Does that bother you?"

Yeah, it bothered him. Jamie always ran to him, confided in him. Now she was running from him. He shrugged, though. "She never goes there unless she's going to stay for a while. It's a long drive."

Ryan nodded, and the pop-pop from the court next to them filled the silence.

Andrew slid to the floor. "I thought she was doing okay." Why was he confiding in Ryan? Given their history, wasn't that weird?

"She's okay, Andrew. She just needs to breathe."

He could understand that. But it still shook him. The last time he'd "needed to breathe," he'd moved halfway across the country. "She's not thinking of leaving, is she?"

Ryan's brows rose. "I haven't heard her talk that way." He cleared his throat and twirled his racquet against the pine floor. "You'd be the first to know, Andrew. Look, you scared her, but she still believes in you. You're still her best friend."

***

May moved slowly, despite the whirlwind of activity the end of the school year brought. Needing inspiration, Jamie caught up on her photography and updated her gallery, hoping it would give her fresh vision.

She stopped when she came to the spider's web.

Don't give up.

Andy believed in her dreams, as improbable as they seemed.

Ryan hadn't been interested. He hadn't been opposed to it, but it didn't seem important to him. Jamie hadn't realized how much that had discouraged her. Maybe she and Ryan hadn't been the perfect match.

Returning to her work, a small piece of her burden rolled away.

On a whim, she checked the school district's website, browsing the newly-posted job openings. It was pretty late in the hiring season, so there wasn't much available. She didn't search intently and was about to close out of the browser when a posting commanded her attention.

Curriculum Coordinator for Outdoor Lab School, Spring View Peak. BS in Education. Teaching experience in Science fields required. Masters preferred.

Outdoor Lab.

It was the perfect job. In the mountains, helping kids study nature. She opened the application section feeling almost foolish. Who was she to think that she'd even be considered? But she was qualified. It didn't hurt to apply.

Andy would approve.

Except that the job would require her to move. Spring View Peak was an hour into the hills.

But he would be proud of her for trying.

Andy. He wouldn't leave her thoughts. She was so mixed up about him. She knew the textbook answer—Andy wasn't a believer. He was in complete opposition, in fact, to what she believed. But at one point, his heart had been tender toward God. Was it foolish to keep hoping?

She prayed for him so much. It was risky, though. Every prayer tangled her heart up even further. But if it meant that someday, somehow, Andy would repent, the risk was worth it.

Even if it held the potential for searing heartache.

***

May sixteenth. Andrew didn't forget. He left work early to hop a bus, finding a greenhouse along the way. But Jamie wasn't home.

Mrs. Carson had been buried at Daniels Park, two miles from Jamie's house. A walk would do him good. He could leave the columbine at her graveside.

The park felt lonely. Cemeteries, Andrew had recently discovered, usually did. Daniels Park wasn't huge, but it would take some time to find the right plot. He had time, though, to wait and catch Jamie.

Turned out he didn't need it. She was there. Kneeling with her face in her hands. Crying.

She hadn't cried last year. This time she was shaking and mumbling to the ground.

Andrew picked up his pace until he could set a hand on her shoulder. "James?"

She jolted at his touch.

He dropped to his knees and pulled her close anyway.

"I didn't hear you."

"You were crying." Of course she was crying. She was at her mother's grave, and her life as of the past few months had dipped into the gutter. Largely because of him.

She sniffed and pulled away. But not like she was running. She sat pensive, as though trying to understand her own thoughts.

Andrew waited, wanting so much to hear her heart. Perhaps if she would open it to him, he could repair the damage—make her happy again.

"Sometimes I feel like time trips backward." She fingered a tear trailing down her cheek. "Like something in my life throws me back there."

She looked up, her eyes begging him to understand. Andrew settled on the grass, silently inviting her to continue.

"She didn't want to move." Her lips trembled. "I can remember hearing them talk about it. She didn't want me to transfer in the middle of my senior year. But Dad—he was so determined. He really thought if they were closer, she'd get more rest and the treatment would work."

Jamie paused, her jaw rigid. Andrew rubbed her shoulder and then her neck.

"She went into hospice three months after we moved and died two weeks later." Her gaze shifted to the hills. "I felt so alone."

He pulled her close, and she leaned against him, crying as though the pain was fresh.

"What happened to your family?"

"John was stationed in Utah. He flew back the day before she died. Cole was married by then and finishing up his first year in med school. They came back about the same time as John. And then they were gone again." She sniffed. "I hated Denver. But my dad—he sank into a black pit. I was afraid to leave him. So I enrolled at DU."

Guilt ate at him as he stroked her hair. He should have been there. "I'm so sorry, James."

She wiped at her tears, but they just kept coming.

What had propelled her back to such an awful time? He couldn't ask. It seemed mean to make the day worse. So they sat quietly—he with his arms locked around her shoulders, and she, leaning against his strength. As it should have been thirteen years before.

"Is that why you don't see much of your family?"

Her head turned so she could see the hills, and she settled back against him. "My mom's death kind of tore us apart. I can't even say why. It was like it ripped the glue out of us, and we all needed to move on with our lives."

That was really sad. The Carsons had been close. An ideal family. He remembered the fun things they had done together—both of their families. Days fishing on the ponds. Campfires and s'mores on cool summer nights. Snowball fights and sledding down the giant hill near their homes.

How could it all fall apart? "Your mom made amazing snow forts."

Jamie laughed—a teary, pathetic sort-of laugh. "She did, and she was always on the winning team in our epic battles."

His shoulders moved as he chuckled. "Yeah, our team."

"She loved snow ice cream. She always made it after our first big storm."

Andrew remembered. The cold milk-and-honey treat had been a favorite.

He let the quiet settle again before he whispered his thoughts. "She loved her little girl."

"I know." Her hands gripped his arms, still wrapped tight around her shoulders. "I just hate being alone."

"You're not alone, James." Tightening his hold, he pulled her head under his chin. "I'm right here."

Chapter Twenty-One

On the last Saturday in May, Jamie pulled up to the farmhouse early evening. Her drive had been long, and sorting through life had made her head throb.

Andy had upended her by being who she needed when she needed him. How was she supposed to fight it? He was good to her. So good.

When he wasn't drunk.

The gravel drive sent dust sputtering, but it hadn't settled before the screen door flung open, and John came bounding out.

What was he doing there? She hadn't seen him in over a year.

"Jamie!" Her big brother scooped her up and spun her around, laughing like a kid.

"Such a surprise." She found his enthusiasm infectious. "What are you doing off your base?"

John stepped back and grinned. She hadn't seen him so happy since he was a boy. "Dad said you were coming, and I wanted you to meet Emily. My fiancée."

So John was to be married at last. Jamie smiled.

Emily was a darling. Perfect in looks and temperament. And John was completely smitten. Jamie was happy for him—for them both. But she couldn't stop the sense of isolation and—heaven help her— jealousy when she was alone in bed.

Was she to be alone forever?

She tried to stop her mind from going back to Andy. Tried not to remember how comforting his arms had been. It would be so easy to run to him. He would fill that aching desire to be held. Comforted. Loved. And she wouldn't be alone anymore.

***

Andrew almost wished he were a praying man. He could pray for Jamie. For whatever was plaguing her heart right now. For her to love him. But he wasn't. He didn't even believe in God. Jamie did. But he'd been enlightened.

Hadn't he? Jamie was an intelligent, educated woman. She wasn't a fool. So which one of them was in the dark?

Self-reform doesn't work.

That incessant voice. Why would he hear it now? Completely out of the blue and totally unrelated. Not to mention nonsensical. What other kind of reform was there?

Such a diversion. He was thinking about Jamie, not imaginary friends. What had set her back twelve years?

She was lonely. But he was here. Couldn't she see that? Didn't she understand? If she would stop running, stop pushing him away, he could fill the loneliness in her heart.

There are places in the heart that man cannot touch.

What did she mean?

God.

But that wasn't working for her right now.

His muscles flexed as he remembered the way she felt in his arms. He'd never wanted a woman the way he wanted Jamie. Not for self-gratification, but to fill his whole life. Every day of it.

Somehow he had to make her see that she needed him. Because he needed her.

***

Home after the long weekend, Jamie still couldn't drown the overpowering desire to cross the boundaries of her friendship with Andy. God had brought him back into her life. Surely He had a reason. Maybe in time, and with the relationship she knew he wanted, he would turn back to the path he'd been on as a child. Could that be true? If she removed that line, would God use her to bring Andy to himself?

Clarity came with a blow.

The phone call came somewhere between one and two in the black of night.

"Andy?" She hadn't even checked the ID. No one else would call her at that time.

"No, ma'am." The woman cleared her voice. "Do you know Andrew Harris?"

Jamie jerked upright. "Yes." She gulped. "Who is this?"

"My name is Julie. I'm an ER nurse at Lutheran Medical Center. Mr. Harris has been brought in, and we have no contact information. You're listed in the 'in case of emergency' on his phone. Is there someone else I should be calling?"

Her throat began to close over. "What happened?"

"He's been in a car accident, but, ma'am, I need a contact number if—"

"His mother's name is Kathy—she should be in his contacts. But she's in California." Jamie drew another shaky breath. "Tell me where to go, and I'll be right there."

The woman was hesitant. Heart throbbing, Jamie tried to quell her exasperation as the nurse hammered on about HIPAA policies.

"He doesn't have anyone here." Patience broke. "I'm it. He's my best friend, and you called me, so tell me where to go."

Jamie arrived at the emergency room within ten minutes and was met by Nurse Julie. "He's going back to surgery," the nurse said, "and then he'll go to ICU."

"Can I see him first?"

She hesitated. "I could lose my job." Sympathy softened her eyes, but she shook her head; rules were going to bind her.

Jamie's heart sank.

She was ready to plead further when Melissa, dressed in scrubs and capped for surgery, appeared by her side. "I've got this, Julie."

"It against regulations." Julie bit her lip. "We both could lose our jobs."

Melissa jerked her head, silently telling Julie to disappear. "It's on me. You had nothing to do with it."

Jamie's thundering heart filled with gratitude.

Melissa slipped an arm through hers. "Come with me."

Jamie followed her through the ER hall. They halted at the security doors, and Melissa turned to her. "Jamie, it's bad."

She gulped, her ribs aching. "How bad?" He-was-going-to-die bad? He couldn't die! He wasn't ready to die.

"He's on life support right now—crushed chest and at least one of his lungs has collapsed. He wasn't wearing a seatbelt, and his vehicle rolled."

Of course he wasn't wearing a seatbelt. He didn't have a license either. Why bother with trivial stuff?

"I just wanted to warn you," Melissa continued. "He's really bad. I'll take you back, but you need to know that first."

Jamie nodded.

Melissa took her through the coded double doors. They entered a sheeted area buzzing with scrub-garbed people, beeping machines, and a hissing ventilator. In the middle of the flurry of activity, a long, dark-haired figure lay battered and motionless on a wheeled stretcher.

His nose hung off to one side, nearly completely torn from his face, and his blood-soaked shirt hung off his body, cut away by the first responders. Tubes disappeared into his mouth and down his throat, and defibrillator paddles lay bloody on the metal table at his side. He lay lifelessly still.

Her heart wrenched as she took in the barely recognizable man. "Andy."

Melissa's hand held her steady as Jamie stood in nauseated horror.

"What happened?"

Melissa drew a long breath. "He wrapped his car around a boulder in Clear Creek Canyon. No one seems to know much beyond that."

Jamie's eyes slid shut as she pictured his new Jag smashed against granite.

"Was he drunk?"

She didn't know why she asked.

***

Jamie sat in a dark cushioned chair in a deserted room. The walls had been painted a calming green, and a river-rocked wall complemented by potted bamboo lent an organic feel. Someone had tried to give the space a soothing ambiance, which at the moment seemed ludicrous. For anyone sitting in the ICU family-gathering room, paint and plants could do very little to impart peace.

Ryan showed up somewhere around seven. "Melissa called." He pulled Jamie into a strong hug. "I didn't get her message until now."

Jamie's legs trembled, and she leaned against him.

Ryan squeezed her shoulders. "How long have you been here?"

"I don't know. Since before two."

He stepped back, gripping her arms as he examined her face. "You look spent. Can you sleep?"

"I dozed." Sleep wasn't an option. Every time she'd drifted off, Andy's battered face resurfaced in her mind. "He hasn't come out yet. How long until he's out of surgery?"

Ryan squeezed her arm and stepped out of the room. Missing his strength, she hugged herself and dropped back into the chair.

Moments later, Ryan returned, bringing a short, strawberry-blonde woman with him.

"Miss Carson?"

Jamie stood.

"Mr. Harris will be coming out of surgery in about five minutes, but he'll not be awake."

"Can I see him?"

"You can, but we'll need a bit of time to get him situated."

"Is—is he okay?" She nearly choked on the question.

The nurse's lips drew a thin line. Not a good sign. "I'll let the doctor talk to you. Wait here. I'll get you when you can come in."

She left, and reality began to creep back. Would he look dead? Would she feel sick again? Jamie wrapped her arms around herself and tried to steady her tumultuous thoughts.

Only a week before, Andy had held her, promising that he'd always be there for her. He never was, though. Every black moment of her adult life she'd mustered through on her own.

Minutes ticked by, and the nurse came for her, leading her into a glass-paneled room.

Beeping buzzed in the back of her skull, and the humming of a ventilator settled in her ears. The room smelled like plastic and hospital linens and dried blood. It felt like death.

And there in the middle lay her friend.

Except for the sickening yellows and purples oozing through his skin, his face was ashen. A pouch of inflated flesh swallowed his left eye. Taped to his cheek, a tube disappeared down his mouth. Stitches ran from the middle of his forehead, down the length of his nose, and half-way through his cheek.

Jamie trembled. Every detail confirmed that this was indeed real, for nothing in her imagination would have made this up.

"Miss?"

She turned her body toward a man's voice, but she couldn't peel her eyes from Andy.

"Are you Jamie Carson?"

"I am." Her voice sounded foreign. She forced herself to look at the stranger. Certainly the middle-aged man was Andy's surgeon.

The doctor nodded. "His parents should be here around noon."

"Is he okay?"

"We'll see." He was all profession, no emotion, as if Andy were a plastic dummy in a life-size game of Operation. "I think we dealt with the internal injuries, but the swelling was so severe, it's hard to know for sure. We had to pump his stomach, but even at that, the alcohol is interfering. He's still not breathing well on his own— which could be the result of an injury, but again it's difficult to determine. Right now, we simply have to wait."

Jamie listened, trying to understand. "How long until he wakes up?"

The doctor shrugged, his eyes communicating softening. "The anesthesia should wear off any time, but—"

"The alcohol." Always the alcohol. But Andy could handle it, right? Yeah, clearly. He'd die before he saw how badly he needed help. Which could, in fact, be very soon. *God, please no. He's not ready...* She blinked, willing away the hot moisture in her eyes.

"We've given him everything we can to wash his system." The doctor drew a long breath and then exhaled slowly. "There's nothing more I can do right now."

Jamie nodded, her arms once again wrapping around her frame. "Thank you."

The doctor dipped his head and moved to the door.

"Will you..."

He stopped at her voice.

"Will you talk to his parents? I won't remember what you told me. Will you tell them?"

"I will." And then he was gone.

***

Andrew woke to an annoying beep in his ear and enormous pain pulsing through his body. He remembered nothing beyond the casino and couldn't comprehend where he was or why his mother was in a chair at his side.

When he stirred, she jolted to her feet, her motion making him woozy.

"Thank God." Tears leaked onto her cheeks as she moved closer to him.

His eye, the one that was not stuck shut, squinted in question, but he couldn't talk through his swollen, burning throat.

"You've had an accident," she explained as if she could read his thoughts. "You've been out for two days."

Two days? What happened?

He'd gotten himself hammered, that's what. He'd driven his new, unlicensed, uninsured car up to Black Hawk and drank himself stupid. Because he was mad. But everything in between that and the hospital was an empty question mark.

Mother grasped his hand, and leaned her forehead against his knuckles. "Andy we thought—" She choked on her tears.

He was going to die? That's what they thought? He tried to swallow, which was painful. Why did his throat feel like someone had been digging around in there with a wire brush?

Dad came through the door, looked at him, and rushed to the bedside, circling Mother's shoulders. "Andrew Harris—" He couldn't finish his sentence either.

If his parents were both this emotional, how was Jamie?

Where was Jamie? The beeping of his heart monitor skipped into a faster rhythm as panic overtook his confusion. Had she been with him? Come on, remember…. Dear God, what had he done now?

He raked a glance around the room. "Ja—" His voice wouldn't cooperate around the hot bulge in his neck. But he had to know. Now. He tried to push up on an elbow.

"Jamie?" His dad laid a hand on his shoulder. "Is that who you're looking for?"

Andrew stilled, begging in the silence for his father to be gracious. How would he live if…?

"She went to get some supper." Dad squeezed his arm. "She'll be back soon. Pretty much hasn't left your side since they called her."

Every muscle relaxed. Nothing else mattered for the moment. As long as she was okay, he'd be fine, even if he couldn't remember what happened.

***

"You really can't remember anything?" Jamie crossed her arms, her face drawn in disappointment. "Why do you keep doing this? Do you know how close you came to dying this time?"

Andrew stared at her, anger building in his muscles. He didn't die, so why bring it up? She'd been so relieved he was alive yesterday, but today he gets a lecture?

He drew a long breath, which pulsed an unbelievable amount of pain along his broken ribcage. Perhaps it was a good thing he was in too much agony to talk. Arguing with Jamie when she was so strung out on emotion probably wasn't a good idea.

"You need help, Andy."

He growled, focusing his stare into a glare. He needed compassion from her. Laid out in the ICU, still attached to machines that hissed and beeped and wouldn't let him sleep, and let's not even talk about the pain—there wasn't enough morphine running through the IV to deal with it—and she thought this was a good time to bring that up?

Didn't matter how much it hurt to talk. He wasn't letting that one go. "Look, Jamie—"

A rap at the door interrupted. "I hear we're awake." His doctor entered the semi-private room. Glancing between Andrew and Jamie, he settled his look on her. "Why don't you go find a cup of coffee, Ms. Carson?" He walked toward Andrew's bed, giving Jamie a sympathetic smile.

Great. What did that mean?

Jamie sighed and she wrapped her arms around herself before she turned and left the room.

The doctor wheeled a chair next to his bedside. "How are we today?"

"Terrific." Sarcasm dripped from Andrew's raspy voice.

"Yes, I can tell." The doctor tugged on the bandage secured across Andrew's nose and leaned in close to inspect his who-knows-how-many stitches. "She's right, you know. You definitely need some intervention."

"What do you know about it?"

"Your blood-alcohol content was the highest I've ever seen in anyone still living. You're lucky you weren't dead, even before you crashed."

Pompous jerk. "Do you know who I am?" Andrew hissed. "I'm a lawyer, a good one. And I wouldn't think twice about filing a suit against an unprofessional and abusive doctor."

The doctor raised his brows and sent him a steady gaze. "I was called out of my home at two in the morning. For you—because you couldn't put a bottle down when you should have. I've no fortitude for people whose injuries demand over five hours of my time and my best surgical skills to patch up their stupidity."

His glare burned hot, and he didn't let up. "That girl was here the entire night, crying her eyes out, because you couldn't exercise self-control. Your parents flew halfway across the country, wondering if you'd be alive when they got here, all because you passed out drunk going who knows how fast on a highway. I don't care who you are or what you do. In my book, you're an idiot. If you want to take me to court for telling you so, then do it. I'd be glad to share with a judge how drunken recklessness looks in real life. And you know what? I'll bet your career suffers for it more than mine."

He finished checking Andrew's nose, then replaced the bandage using ironic gentleness before he pushed away from the bedside. It took a half minute to update Andrew's chart before he turned and left the room.

Andrew's head pounded viciously against his damaged skull. How dare the man! He wouldn't let him get off with that. When he was out of this bed, his first order of business would be a trip to court.

Well, yeah, probably. But it would be to deal with his long list of legal trouble, not to sue a brazen doctor.

How could he have done something so stupid?

Chapter Twenty-Two

Andrew stayed three more days in ICU before they moved him down to a recovery room. Jamie spent every moment possible at his side.

He battled a mix of emotions. She had better things to do with her short summer break. He knew she'd had a conference scheduled sometime in early June and was fairly certain she'd missed it on his account. He'd talked her into showing her photography during the summer festival up in Winter Park. He'd paid for her booth fee, insisting that she do it. She'd skipped it to be with him. He was disappointed for her and felt enormously guilty because of it. But he also felt a strange twist of pleasure, knowing she skipped it for him.

When he'd been stabilized and relocated for four days, a uniformed man with a gleaming badge entered his room. Anthony Locke, a senior partner from Andrew's firm, tailed in three seconds later, closing the door behind him.

"Mr. Harris," the officer said, "I trust you're well enough to discuss what happened."

"Do I have a choice?" They had to do this now? As if the sweating, the shaking, the unquenchable thirst, and the constant throbbing in his head—not to mention the pain from the actual injuries—weren't enough for him to deal with?

"Harris." Locke spoke firmly. "Don't be difficult."

Andrew sank into the flimsy pillow.

Pulling out a small notepad, the officer took that as a go-ahead.

"I'm Jacob Randall, and I've been assigned to investigate your misadventure. I'd appreciate it if you'd make this easy by just telling me everything."

"I don't remember."

Randall sighed and scooted a chair uncomfortably close. "Tell me what you do remember."

"I was at a casino in Black Hawk. I gambled five dollars at the nickel slots and then headed to the bar."

"How long were you there?"

"I went up around seven. I don't know when I left."

Locke interrupted. "Why did you go there?"

Locke knew exactly why Andrew took off for the night. They'd had a lovely discussion that afternoon during which Locke had informed him he had *not* been recommended for junior partner. Andrew remembered that part of the day perfectly, and it still infuriated him. His mind went back over all of the rebuttals he'd laid out—the fact that he functioned perfectly in society and drinking never interfered with his work. Not to mention that he was good at his job. Very good. Locke hadn't addressed a single dispute. He eyed him sternly, much as he was doing at this very moment, and told him the decision had been made; he could work harder for next year's evaluation.

"I just went." Andrew snapped.

Randall took the conversation back in hand. "Had you been drinking before you left Denver?"

The air thickened. Pain sizzled through every muscle as his body tensed.

"Yes." The monosyllable came hissing through tight lips. Andrew glared first at Locke and then at Randall.

"And you don't remember leaving Fitzgerald's?"

"No." His gaze moved to his hands. "I don't remember anything but waking up in the hospital."

The air thickened. Locke cleared his throat, and Randall's head bowed.

Andrew felt like he'd been shoved underwater for much too long.

Randall broke the icy silence. "I've some other details to look into. I'll be back in a couple of days." Rising, he tucked his papers under his arm. "Mr. Harris, Mr. Locke." He nodded to each man and was gone.

Andrew held his tongue until his footsteps no longer echoed in the hall. He speared Locke with a scowl."Why are you here?"

"To hear what you had to say."

"Why?" His eyebrows pinched together. "I don't need your representation."

Locke hiked his brow. "That was never my intent. I am ascertaining whether or not we need yours. Good afternoon, Harris."

Andrew waited until Locke was out of sight, but the moment he was alone, he slumped heavily against his bed. He was fairly certain he'd just lost his job.

He didn't see Jacob Randall again. Three days passed before he heard anything regarding his case. He wasn't sure if that was good or bad. These things usually did take time.

A younger man appeared in his room as he was eating his rubber hospital eggs and let's-pretend-it's-meat bacon.

"My name's Tim." The man didn't wait for an invitation. "I'm from the DA's office."

Andrew eyed him.

"Here's the deal." Tim dove right in. "You're in deep. Real deep. Aside from the fact that you didn't take anyone else out with you, the only good thing you've got going is Anthony Locke."

"Locke?"

"Apparently he's got pull. I guess being a lawyer has its perks. Anyway, you've got two options: One: you can argue your case in court where you'll be charged with your second DUI in two years— aggravated DUI, to be exact. Not to mention driving an unregistered vehicle with a suspended license. I can guarantee you'll not be given any grace. Fines and jail time will be maxed, without any sort of bargain. And you can bet this won't go unnoticed by the Bar."

He pushed a big envelope toward Andrew. "Option two. You can accept the arrangement Locke negotiated for you. It's spelled out for you here. I'll stop by tomorrow afternoon, expecting a decision."

Andrew fingered the envelope. "How'd this get pushed through so fast?"

"Like I said, Locke's got some pretty tight connections." Tim paused, his eyes dark with contempt. "I was reviewing your case when this came in. Let's just say I'm not impressed. But I have to work under authority. I suggest you take the deal. You won't get another chance to bargain if I see you in court."

Andrew shifted so that he could open the packet, failing to acknowledge the man as he left. Locke negotiated it down to a misdemeanor. His driver's license would be suspended for one year. Much better than the five year max. No jail time. The fines were roughly half. Andrew nodded, satisfied. Until he reached the second paragraph.

Twenty eight days would be spent in a *rehab facility*. What? Those places were for serious addicts. People who always had a bottle in their hand, couldn't hold down a job, take care of personal necessities, function in society. Not him. Some twelve step program with meetings once a week, now that he would consider. But not four weeks in a center with a bunch of hard-core lushes.

It only got worse. He would be released only on the recommendation of the supervising staff and contingent on *Locke's* satisfaction. How was this even legal?

It wasn't. It couldn't possibly be legal.

Arguing the point wouldn't work in his favor. Aggravated DUI? What was that, a class four felony? His BAC was off the charts. And he'd driven with a suspended license, destroyed tax-payer property. Tim was right; if he were convicted of a felony, he'd likely be subjected to a professional inquiry by the State Bar. He could lose the privilege to practice law.

Andrew continued reading, his brain steaming. In lieu of a bar investigation, he'd be held on retainer with the firm, but his practice would be supervised by Locke, and he'd be demoted to a probationary status until he'd been completely dry for one year.

He'd be reduced to an undergrad intern, both in status and in pay. His clients would be informed that he could not practice without supervision, and they would be offered a transfer of representation if they preferred. He would be stripped of all he'd worked for in the past three years and held on a leash for the next twelve months.

Veins bulging, Andrew reached for the first thing in his line of vision. Two seconds later, his cell phone crashed against the opposite wall, but he received no satisfaction from the damage. And to top it off, the craving he claimed was not an addiction pressed into madness.

He lost every shred of self-control. His glass of orange juice and then his breakfast plate flew, making a mess on the wall and floor. His laptop was next, shattering against the bricks. He ripped the needle out from his wrist and flung the IV tree toward the television, crushing the screen.

Hospital staff rushed in. Two men held his shoulders down, and a nurse stuck his arm while he fought with blind rage.

Within a minute, his muscles would not respond and his tantrum came to a medicated end.

Jamie appeared in the doorway, her eyes huge. Andrew hated watching her face turn white with horror.

"Jamie," he mouthed.

She backed out of sight.

***

Jamie's heart pounded as she bit her bottom lip. Leaning against the hallway wall, she curled her fingers into her palms and willed the trembling to stop. Andy had been difficult before, but never violent—and he wasn't even drunk.

"Miss Carson?"

Jamie jumped. She'd not heard Andy's nurse approach.

Anne touched her arm. "He's still going through withdrawal."

Jamie's eyes widened and she looked back toward Andy's room.

The nurse stepped closer. "He's not had any alcohol in over two weeks—a first in who knows how long. Alcohol changes the balance in the brain. When it's suddenly removed, the brain reacts—sort-of like a knee-jerk. Uncharacteristic rage is expected in detox."

Still appalled, Jamie swallowed, trying to gain some sense of understanding. "Did he hurt anyone?"

"No." Anne assured her with a squeeze.

"They were holding him down."

"It's not uncommon."

Restraining a patient was normal? She was in way over her head. "How long will he be this way?"

Anne frowned, her eyes dropping. "It's hard to say—each patient is different. There are so many variables; how long he's been drinking, if and how many times he's tried to quit before, and even his heredity. The most severe will be in the next two to four weeks, but sometimes people struggle with related symptoms for a year or better."

There seemed to be no good news with this man. How could she walk with him through something so terrifying?

Don't.

What? That couldn't be right. Andy needed her, more now than ever. She cleared her throat and straightened her shoulders. "Can I see him now?"

The young woman examined her, but Jamie couldn't read the expression. After two breaths, Anne gave a small nod. "I'll check to make sure."

Jamie leaned against the brick wall, her head tilted back while she waited. That one word still whispered in her heart—*don't*.

Don't what? Don't be there for Andy? There's no way that's what God meant. Why would He put her in Andy's life if she wasn't supposed to walk with him through this?

Anne returned, touching Jamie's arm again. "He's settled again. You'll be okay."

She would? When? How was all of this going to be okay? *God, are you seeing this?*

She bit her bottom lip and pulled her posture straight. Andy was waiting.

In his room, Jamie balled the sweatshirt she'd brought, wrapping it around her fists while he stared at the lump created by his feet at the end of the bed. An eternity of silence crawled by. Her stomach hurt, and her hands still trembled. She sat slowly, wondering if she shouldn't just go. What on earth had she landed herself in?

"Jamie." Andy's husky voice beckoned her attention.

Her eyes slid shut. She knew that crack in his voice, the one that tugged at her heart and melted her anger.

"Jamie." His hand covered hers.

She lifted her gaze to pleading brown eyes. *God, he needs me. You know he needs me.*

"I'm sorry, Jamie."

An immediate and sincere apology. Surely that must be a sign. God didn't mean for her to walk away now.

"What happened?" she whispered.

Sighing, Andy examined the ceiling. His jaw hardened, and he reached to the table behind her to retrieve an envelope.

Jamie accepted it, but her eyes remained on him.

"Read it."

She complied, but it didn't explain anything. "What is this?"

"A plea bargain." His voice had gone hard. "Anthony Locke—a senior partner at work—arranged it."

"Is it good?"

"There's no felony charges, no jail time, and the fees are cut in half." He stared at the document as if it were a rat.

Jamie scowled. "What's the problem?"

His eyes went cold. "I don't need any more therapy," he snapped, "and I certainly don't belong in a rehab center."

Jamie's mouth dropped. "You don't think you need help?"

He turned away, his mouth rigid. The temperature in the room took a plunge.

"I don't need to be stuck in a center," Andy hissed. "And I'll lose my clients before the end of the year. Locke did this on purpose."

"Of course he did this on purpose." Jamie sat forward. "He's trying to help you."

Andy turned flashing eyes to her. "I'm fine, Jamie!"

She shrank back in her chair and held her breath.

Dropping against the pillows, he glared at her.

She gulped and in the next moment stood to leave.

His hand shot out, snagging the sweatshirt she carried. "Jamie." He tugged her back. "I'll do it. I'll take the deal."

Taking a quivering breath, Jamie chewed on her bottom lip. Dare she say it?

Things couldn't get much worse.

"You're not fine, Andy." She left before he could react.

Chapter Twenty-Three

"I need your help." Jamie dropped onto her couch after church, looking first at Melissa and then Ryan. They'd been bulwarks in her world, especially after Rick and Kathy Harris had gone back to California. From the long days at the hospital to Andy's transfer to the rehab facility, they were her lifeline. Maybe they could offer clarity.

Andy's first week in rehab had been rocky at best, and he made sure everyone around him knew he was not a willing resident. He was miserable, and visiting him made Jamie nearly as miserable. She hadn't gone today—visitations were limited. Anyway, Sundays were supposed to be a day of rest.

She squeezed her hands together, gripping her emotions before she continued. "What am I supposed to do?"

Melissa leaned forward in the overstuffed chair. "What do you mean?"

"I'm confused about what I'm supposed to do with Andy. I'm scared, and part of me feels—" Jamie gulped, afraid to say it out loud. She pressed her lips together and drew a long breath. "Am I supposed to leave?"

Melissa and Ryan exchanged a look.

"How long have you thought that?" Ryan asked.

Jamie stared at her hands. She hadn't told them about the day she'd seen him go ballistic at the hospital. She wouldn't. "Since Andy was moved out of ICU."

Melissa rested her hand on Jamie's. "On the front end, Jamie, know that whatever you decide, I'm here for you." She glanced at Ryan, who bobbed his head. "We're both here for you. But maybe it would help for you to know what I told Ryan last week."

They'd discussed this? How could they know she'd been thinking about leaving? Jamming the confusion back, Jamie bit her lip and nodded.

"Andrew sees you as his strength out of this." Melissa's grip on Jamie's hand increased. "He can't see Christ in you, because all he sees is you."

Jamie's chest caved. With all of her heart, she'd ached for Andy to see Jesus in her life—for him to remember everything they'd learned together as children.

But she'd failed. Attraction—that foolish emotion—had interfered, and she'd confused her heart for God's will. Her face went into her hands as a cry shook her shoulders.

Melissa moved next to her, and Ryan put a hand to her knee. "That's not to say you didn't do what you were supposed to," he said. "You've lived Jesus in front of him."

Her hands dropped back to her lap. "All this time I thought God was calling me away because I'm not strong enough to walk through this, but the truth is that I'm really too weak to walk away." She searched them both for wisdom, for strength. "What will I do?"

Nobody spoke for several breaths. Jamie sniffed back her tears and regained her composure.

Melissa hugged her from the side. "We'll pray for you, Jamie."

What else could they do? Jamie nodded, mumbled a half-hearted, thank you, and pushed herself up from the couch. Life went on—it always did—and she had a conference she needed to prepare for.

Monday finally slipped by. Did it matter? Life had become a Ferris wheel—an endless cycle of going through the motions whether Jamie felt like it or not. Mostly not.

She pulled into traffic and mindlessly drove toward Andy's rehab center. After sitting in the parking lot for ten minutes, she decided to go in and take whatever came.

Andy sat in the visiting lounge, engrossed with a laptop.

Her ever-optimistic heart dared to lift, and she sent him a small grin. "You've gained access."

His eyes moved to glare above the screen. "Very limited."

That cold stare said it all. She should have known by now—hope with Andy would always fall flat.

Andy scowled. "I don't know how anyone expects me to maintain any clientele under these conditions."

Jamie sighed and dropped into the chair across from him.

"Fine." He snapped the loaned computer shut and glared. "Yes, they've been so good as to allow me to do my job. Life is good. Everything's terrific. Is that better, Miss Carson?"

Jamie kept her stare blank. This roller coaster ride was old, and she wanted off. She folded her hands and pressed her thumbs against her mouth.

Anger sizzled in his eyes. "I don't belong here," he seethed.

Yes, you do.

His jaw jumped as if he'd heard her thoughts. Alarm pricked at her skin as she remembered the scene from the hospital. He wasn't safe. "I'm going to go."

"No." Andy jumped to his feet, his borrowed laptop sliding to the floor. "Don't."

Her teeth sank into her bottom lip. Balling her fists, she shut her eyes against his fierce look. He was fighting for control. What were the odds that he'd maintain it if she told him what she really thought?

Slim to none.

"Stay, Jamie." His voice came tight—hot with an explosive mix of resentment and desperation. "I need you to stay."

He can't see Christ, because all he sees is you.

She couldn't be his way out.

There are places in the heart man cannot touch.

A young man had said that to her when she'd been desperate for him to be her way out. Out of grief, out of loneliness. He'd been right. She had to throw herself on the cross, had to let God's love and strength fill the places of frailty and loneliness. Had to let Him do what she was too weak to do.

Like a timid child, she peeked at Andy. *God, please let him hear me.* "Andy, you don't need me."

"Yes, I do." He'd stepped closer, his voice still blistering. "I need you here. I need you to be on my side."

"I'm always on your side, Andy. It's not enough."

"It'll be enough!"

Why did he snap like that? Was it him, or the withdrawal? Who was Andy, really? A tear rolled onto her cheek. "You scare me."

Andy stepped back. Maybe it was the meekness in her voice. Or the fact that she actually said the words. Either way, he retreated.

This ride was over. It was time to go.

***

Andrew brooded as he paced the room with a fresh reminder of their precarious relationship. She wanted him to be okay, she wanted to hang on to their friendship. But she'd left.

He was losing her.

No. He couldn't allow it. She just needed to see, to understand. This wasn't him. This couldn't possibly be who he really was. Hadn't he always been around to rescue her? Wasn't he the only one encouraging her, cheering her on in her most cherished dreams? He was good to her. Usually. This thing right now—well, it was a flub. A small blip of darkness in an otherwise good life. He was a good man.

Would she call him a good man? He looked around the lounge. Bare, but for two hospital-style sofas and a low table. Otherwise there was nothing of consequence, nothing that could be thrown, nothing to be grabbed in a fit of rage.

An intentional omission.

He remembered his last outburst, just weeks ago in the hospital. Jamie had literally shook while she sat at his side. When he'd snapped at her, she had sunk back in fear. When he sat forward, she moved as though she were ready to duck for cover.

A good man didn't draw that kind of reaction from a woman. He wouldn't frighten her.

It was this place. He was all bound up here, and it was infuriating. He wasn't himself. Surely she would agree. She knew him best. He just wasn't himself here.

Yes, she would see it. She had to. Because he needed her.

***

Jamie came back on Friday afternoon, and though she looked distressed as she entered the visiting lounge, he was relieved. She'd come back. Andrew greeted her with a smile.

She didn't grin in return.

His heart quit working. "What's going on?"

Jamie stared at her feet for several breaths before she forced her eyes to his. Alarm blared in his head and he moved forward.

She stepped back. "I've come to tell you goodbye." Her voice was soft, but firm.

"Goodbye?" His pulse began to throb. She couldn't mean *that*. Not goodbye, goodbye. "Are you going to see your dad?"

"No."

Again he stepped toward her. This time she remained still. Resolutely still. She was saying goodbye, for real.

Not acceptable.

"I get out next week," he argued quietly. "What do you mean, goodbye? Where are you going?"

"I don't know." Moisture glistened in her green eyes.

Full-scale panic raced through his veins. "Jamie, what are you talking about?"

"I can't keep going like this, Andy."

"Like what?" He crammed a hand through his hair. "I've done what you wanted. I went through rehab. I'm fine. Don't do this."

Shaking her head, those tears spilled down her cheeks. "You're not fine. Andy, you're so lost. You don't know your right hand from your left. I can't save you."

The phrase sounded distantly familiar. Was she quoting the Bible? Alarm flipped to anger. Taking another step forward, he towered over her, and though she trembled, she didn't retreat.

"What are you saying?" he hissed.

"All this time I've prayed that my life would point you to Jesus. That I would live in a way that would make you see—would make you want His salvation." Jamie drew a quivering breath and wiped her wet face. "But I'm only standing in the way. I can't save you. You need Christ, not me. He's your only hope. I won't be the reason you never see it."

He needed Jesus? That was her reason for ending their friendship? "*This* is your Christian love?" Andrew's heart pounded. With both hands he gripped her upper arms, squeezing fiercely. "You're doing this because of God?"

She shrank in his hold. Her shoulders shook.

Let her go.

The calm, unfamiliar voice in his head pried open apprehension. The command demanded obedience, and he released her, but his anger didn't die.

"At a time I need you more than ever, you're just going to walk away?" With an unbridled curse, he turned away. He stepped back into her space, hunkering over her like a predator. "How could you? What kind of religion is that, Jamie?"

She drew up straight as she rubbed at the marks he'd left on her arms. "Goodbye, Andrew."

Andrew? He hated when she called him that. It felt like a slap. "Don't." He shot a hand to her elbow, pulling her back. Seeing her cringe killed his outrage, and he let her go, hating the sight of the bright red finger impressions he'd left.

Could she call him a good man? Desolation dumped over him. She couldn't. Because he wasn't.

"Don't call me Andrew." He took her hands and laid them flat on his chest. "Please, Jamie? Please don't do this."

For a moment he thought she'd cave. He could feel her body lean toward him, and he was ready to take her in his arms. He'd apologize, and she'd change her mind. They would be okay.

But she didn't come to him. Her eyes held his, and in that excruciating moment he could see her resolve. This was immutable.

But the killer? He'd just been given a clear view of the anguish in her heart—the imprint of his life on hers. No good man left that kind of mark.

Let her go.

He heeded the voice, and in the next instant she stepped away. The door closed, and he was left alone.

***

Curling up in a ball on her bed, Jamie let the ache take over. The phone rang, but she ignored it, allowing it to go to voice mail. She'd need a new number. A new life, far away from Andy. Maybe a new heart.

When her nose felt swollen and the tears stopped coming, she shuffled her way to the kitchen to brew some mint tea. She shouldn't check the message; he wasn't going to change her mind. Ignoring the logical warning to not even look, she pushed the home button on her phone and dialed voice mail.

"Miss Carson, this is Creighton Nelson."

Not Andy. She should be relieved.

"I'm the program director at Spring View Outdoor Lab School. I know it's late in the year to be hiring, but the position hasn't been filled. I'd like to set up an interview, so please call me if you're still interested."

With a hand on her forehead, Jamie leaned back against the doorframe. Any other day, she would have danced with excitement. She slid to the floor and pressed her head to her knees. God had shown her His path, and Andy was no longer to be part of her life. Instead, He'd granted her an escape by way of a dream job. Yet she couldn't find any part of her heart that could rejoice in the exchange.

Chapter Twenty-Four

Andrew prowled the visiting lounge like a caged beast. The pulse in his forehead pounded furiously while he clenched and unclenched his fist.

Ryan stepped through the doorway. "Another good day, I see."

Andrew stopped mid-stride and glared.

Ryan waited calmly, apparently unaffected by Andrew's mood.

For a moment, Andrew really considered Ryan Anderson. A man of conviction and consistency, he was also completely disarming. It seemed a paradox that such a tranquil person could actually put Andrew in his place without uttering a single word. His entire being radiated peace while at the same time challenging opposition. It didn't make sense.

Who cared? This was his life, not Ryan's. "Locke wouldn't sign off. I'm stuck for another week."

Ryan nodded.

His demeanor mocked Andrew, and anger erupted. "Where is she?" he growled. "I know you know. Tell me where she is."

Ryan remained still. Infuriating.

"Did you tell her to do this? How could she do this?"

Nothing. Slightly raised brows, but beyond that, Ryan did nothing.

Andrew couldn't stand it. Lunging forward, he took Ryan by the shirt and shoved him against the door. "I'm stuck here!" He pulled Ryan forward and slammed him back again. "I'm stuck, and it's her fault. How could she do this?"

Ryan didn't struggle, nor did his eyes show panic. When Andrew released him, he tugged his polo back in place and stepped toward the middle of the room. "This is Jamie's fault?"

"You know it is."

"It's her fault you put a hole in the wall?"

Andrew retreated behind the small sofa. He couldn't stop his glance from traveling to the knuckles he'd bloodied against the drywall in his room the day Jamie had left. Yeah, that was kind of her fault. If she hadn't said goodbye, he wouldn't have been irate.

His chest caved, and somehow he suddenly felt smaller.

"It's Jamie's fault you don't have any self-control?"

Andrew's eyes lifted as the smoldering rage cooled. Ryan's words were calm and even, a rational challenge to his irrational pandemonium. The air in the room held while the confrontation settled. Andrew's shoulders dropped, and Ryan took a seat.

"One more week," Ryan kept firm gaze fixed on him, "could mean that you'll be able to walk out of here truly free. You could take to heart what is being pounded into your head, and you wouldn't have to live life bound by addiction."

"I'm fine," Andrew countered, dropping in the seat opposite. "I'm not bound by anything."

Ryan stared, as if debating. He reached for the Bible that always accompanied him these days.

Andrew snapped his spine straight.

Ryan opened the front flap, removed an oversized envelope, and replaced the book at his feet. "I think you should take a look at these."

Andrew snatched the packet Ryan slid across the table between them. He ripped out the contents: three photographs telling an unpleasant story. An expensive sports car, lying on its side. The hood and the front two-thirds were wrapped around a boulder the size of a small pick-up. The back wheels hung precariously off the rocky embankment over Clear Creek.

He shuffled to the next photo. Same vehicle sitting atop a flatbed wrecker. The new angle gave a fresh view. The entire top had been crushed, every window shattered, and the metal guardrail was plastered to the passenger-side front. It was inconceivable that anyone inside would have survived.

And yet here he sat.

Which brought him to the last picture. The man he was looking at had to have been himself. His face was so swollen and covered in blood that if he hadn't known what he was looking at, he wouldn't have recognized it. The skin on his left cheek gaped, exposing the bone beneath, and his nose literally hung off to the side.

His lungs seemed to quit working. What if... "Did Jamie see me like this?"

Ryan settled against the sofa. "I have no idea what she saw, and that's not the point."

Andrew shifted, but his eyes remained glued to the photo. His stomach began to roll, and heat filled his face.

"You keep telling everyone that you're fine, that you don't have a problem." Ryan leaned his elbows against his knees and nodded toward the pictures. "You're a lawyer, Andrew. Tell me what the evidence says."

Oxygen, now.

But his lungs wouldn't fill. What if Jamie had been with him?

What if he hadn't survived? For the first time real fear seized him. Paralyzed him. What happened when you died? What if he'd been wrong all these years—what if there was a God?

If? Was that really the question he meant to ask?

You're a lawyer, Andrew. What does the evidence say?

Whose voice pushed into his mind in these kinds of moments? Was he crazy—maybe just a little cracked because of detox? But he'd heard that whisper before rehab, he couldn't blame it on detox.

What did the evidence say?

Ryan cleared his throat. "Jamie did what she had to do. I don't know if you'll ever understand, but to be blunt, it doesn't matter. You do need to understand that you need help. You're not okay, Andrew." He folded his hands together, squeezing until his knuckles turned white. "You should also know that you're not alone. But whether or not you choose to acknowledge either of those things is up to you. You know my number. My offer to help stands, but it's your call."

Ryan lifted his Bible and rose to his feet. "I mean it, Andrew. You can call me anytime."

***

Melissa squeezed Jamie's shoulder. "Will you be okay?"

With a quivering breath, Jamie straightened her posture. She'd survived before. When her mom died. When Dad dipped into a thick, inky depression. When he remarried suddenly and left everything they'd known with her mom behind. She'd survived.

But this? Andy had made the decision for her. She couldn't stay. Survival had been programmed into her, and she'd defaulted to that. What choice did she have?

"I'll be fine." She swallowed and forced a smile. "My dream job in the mountains—could be worse, right?"

Melissa looked like she'd cry—again. "Jamie…"

"Don't." Jamie held up her hand. "I'll be okay, I promise. Please, just don't cry." Tears stung her nose. *No more tears.* She blinked and cleared her throat.

After a long draw of breath, Melissa nodded and linked her arm through Jamie's. "You will call me, right?"

Jamie stepped off the front porch and toward her loaded car. "Every week, at least. I promise."

Melissa walked beside her, moving her arm so that she could side-hug Jamie. Jamie leaned her head against the smaller woman's and hugged her back. A small burst of anger warmed in her chest. Andy had no idea what he'd done. How much he'd ripped from her life because he couldn't face reality. Her home, her job, her friends… she was leaving everything because of him.

The heat cooled, quickly replaced by ache. Leaving him was like leaving everything, no matter how that played out. He'd been her solace, her best friend, and maybe so much more...

"Are you sure all this goes to the curb?" Ryan's voice shut down those thoughts as he bounced down the front porch steps behind them.

Thank God. "All of it."

He caught up to where the women had stopped and set the box on the grass. "I think you'd better double check. There were a few things... a box of old pictures and a frame of some flowers—"

Jamie's heart squeezed hard. Those were near the bottom of the box. What had Ryan been doing? "Digging through my stuff?"

He met her eyes without shame. "You're emotional right now, Jamie. Some of this you may want someday." Stepping back, he waved a hand over the used Amazon box she'd tossed the junk into earlier. "Give it one more pass to be sure. Some things can't be undone."

Exactly. So there was no going back, which meant it was stupid to hang on.

"I'm sure." She squatted to lift the box and hefted it to the curb by the garbage can. Letting it drop, her horded treasures slammed against the pavement and the sound of shattering glass punctuated her decision. "I don't want any of it."

Ryan and Melissa held a look between them. So, maybe she was acting a bit melodramatic. She sighed, crossed her arms, and walked back to where they waited.

Ryan pulled her to his side. "You can't let yourself hate him." He squeezed her close. "It'll ruin you, you know?"

Her eyes burned again. *Stop. No. More. Crying.* "I don't hate him."

Hating wasn't possible. Andy filled her thoughts—her heart—with a ton of tender, precious memories. But she couldn't walk away and take him with her at the same time. She barely had the strength to leave as it was.

Melissa wrapped her hand around Jamie's and held on. "This is the right thing to do. But, Jamie, you don't have to give up on him. God's redemption reaches past the things we think are impossible."

Jamie's lips began to quiver. It was time to go. She drew a long breath and pulled her posture straight. "I know you guys will look after him—and I'm so grateful. But I can't carry this anymore. Don't tell me—I don't want to know anything about him." She turned to make eye contact with both of them. "Please? Even if you don't understand, please leave me out of it."

***

Andrew tried Jamie's cell. Again.

The number you have reached...

Same drill—kind of insane that he'd hoped for a different result. This would change, though. He stepped from the gates of West Pines and climbed onto a westbound bus. Jamie wouldn't refuse a face-to-face talk.

Nobody answered the door. Andrew walked to the back and found the gate locked. He peeked in the garage window. No Camry. His hands pushed into his hair as he turned to scan the street, knowing even while he searched that there'd be nothing to give him hope.

But something caught his attention. Her trash had been set out by the curb, heaping full, and accompanied by a large box. Knowing the evidence would slice hope from reality, Andrew walked to inspect the things he didn't want to see.

Files marked as classes—first hour biology... fifth hour study hall. Trashed. He ran his hand over the large box sitting by the trash—a pair of torn jeans with paint splatters. Trashed. He flipped them to the side and his heart broke. He actually felt it tear apart as he examined what lay under those jeans.

An old, chintzy frame encased shattered glass. Beneath the shards, five papery blue flowers lay flat against yellowed wax paper. He picked up the broken frame and shook the glass into the box. Writing caught his attention as he turned it over.

Andy, 1986

Andrew's eyes slid shut. All these years, and she'd kept them safe. Until now. Hot tears flooded his vision as he examined the blue columbine beneath the broken glass. A picture of his life—and now hers. Beauty shattered. Memories broken. Lives ruined.

What had he done?

***

Sober. He could claim that, right? Three full months without a drop. And yet the impact of his habit continued to haunt him. Income squeezed. Mobility limited. Social life drained. And no Jamie Carson. Andrew stared across his loft as sorrow hit a hard ledge. Why did she think she had to leave completely? Look, he was sober. She didn't need to flip life upside down. She'd been dramatic with this—punishing him because she was mad.

Heart rate climbing with every breath, he pushed to his feet from his leather club chair. The room suddenly felt stuffy, and a raw emptiness began to claw deep in his gut. Glancing to the kitchen, he began to pace. His vision narrowed, and the throbbing of his pulse pounded a silent mantra for which he knew no words. He glanced again at the cabinet where it used to wait...

Get out.

A walk. Yeah, that's what he needed. Just to get out. He'd be fine outside these walls.

Warm evening air swirled around him as he wandered the streets of downtown. Traffic whirled by while Friday melted into weekend mode. The roar of a cheering crowd came from Coors Field nearby. He'd gone to the games often, but his tickets were perks that came from the office. Perks that had recently vanished.

Kind of like everything good in his life.

Financially, he was in trouble. His change in status at the firm resulted in a significant decrease in pay. City life wasn't cheap. Not to mention medical bills, legal fines, and a massive amount of debt he'd carelessly accumulated—they all made demands on his accounts that he simply couldn't meet.

Defeat pressed in as he ticked off the utter failures of his life. He'd been stripped down to nothing. As the sun lowered behind the Rockies, he slipped into despair.

And then suddenly he found himself in front of The Bull Pen.

Swallowing hard, Andrew reached deep. Three months without a drop. This shouldn't be that hard.

Just walk away.

But his feet did not heed, and worse, he was reaching for the door. Andrew literally grabbed his own hand, squeezing until he could feel pain. Why was this so hard?

You don't need it. Just go home.

But as he mentally went through the route, he pictured every bar between his location and the loft. There were six, not to mention the easily accessible liquor stores along the way. He couldn't even walk away from this one. Fear squeezed in his chest. He really couldn't do this. One foot in front of the other... impossible.

Addicted. Was this an addiction?

Hello, my name is Andrew, and I'm an alcoholic. He'd said those words—a couple of times in fact. Group expectations at rehab. But he hadn't believed them.

He looked at the man reflecting back at him in the dark tinted windows. *I'm an alcoholic.* The man stared back. *Yes, you are. What will you do?*

His hand quivered when he reached into his pocket for his cell.

Ryan answered on the third ring. "Hello?"

"Ryan?" Andrew's pulse thundered in his ears.

"Andrew—what's going on?"

Andrew's throat swelled. He swallowed, fighting for words. "I'm not okay." His voice trembled, and he hid his face with his hand. "I need help."

Chapter Twenty-Five

Jamie inhaled the cool, late September air. Snow had dusted the pines throughout the camp, but the sun peaked between the eastern hills. A token of a promising day. She pressed the bugle option on her bullhorn and waited for the commotion. One hundred twelve-year-olds were about to pour out of their cabins, sleepy-eyed and hungry, ready to start their week of adventure.

She was ready. She loved this job. Loved living in the mountains again. Loved her snug little cabin. Loved school days redefined. And yet…

Relocating hadn't given her any distance from Andy. He stubbornly lived with her, his memory making her exponentially lonelier than she'd ever been before. What was he doing now? Had he met with Locke's approval? Was he still angry with her?

Was he still drinking?

He haunted her, overshadowing what should have been the most exciting season of her life.

Moving had been surreal. She'd been offered an opportunity of a lifetime. It seemed something of a tragedy that she felt no joy in it.

After so many weeks, she'd thought it would get easier. It hadn't. Her new bosses had picked up on her gloom, though she'd tried with all her heart to stuff it out of sight.

"Jamie, there seems to be a sadness to you," Ellie Nelson had said. They'd been scrubbing the kitchen on Saturday, listening to Third Day while they worked.

Jamie focused on the stainless steel countertop she'd been cleaning. She'd been shocked to find that Creighton and Ellie Nelson were both believers. Amazing. It opened up an intimacy that would have been impossible otherwise.

What could she say now? She'd been too devastated to relay the events of the summer. Even saying his name would break open a dam of emotion. "I'm sorry, Ellie. It must be a bummer to work with me right now."

"That's not what I meant at all." Examining Jamie, Ellie set her rag and spray aside. "I'm a good listener, if you need to let it out."

Let it out? Wasn't possible. She could pour and pour and pour, and the hurt would just keep coming.

"I was just thinking about some memories." *Please leave it at that.*

Ellie continued to look at her, but she didn't push. They went back to work as "Love Song" filled the kitchen.

Jamie drove the replay to a distant corner of her heart. Monday. It was Monday. Time to stop living in the past.

***

Andrew swiped sweat off his forehead with the sleeve of his white tee shirt. Ryan's face also gleamed with perspiration, in spite of the cool November day. They were nearly done unloading the small U-Haul outside Ryan's duplex and soon they'd stop for a late lunch.

His loft had sold in an amazing amount of time. It had to have been the hand of God, because the Denver housing market had tanked the year before. But by selling his loft furnished, Andrew had broken even on the place, and the provisions in both the financial relief and in Ryan's offer were at once humbling and comforting.

Why had he never seen the consistent kindness of God? How had he overlooked the generosity of each new morning, the renewing promise of hope in a day yet unlived?

Two months and counting. He'd been set free, truly and wonderfully liberated from his own blind arrogance. Life had new meaning, a whole new purpose. It no longer began and ended with himself, and the abundance of life beyond his narcissism was unparalleled.

That didn't mean he'd left all of his struggles. He continued to battle the addiction he'd spent fifteen years cultivating. Which was another reason to move. New geography, new habits. A complete separation from the mire he'd buried himself under.

Jamie would be pleased. Not because he'd finally been successful in self-reform. Nothing could be further from the truth. He'd finally swum in the muck long enough to admit he couldn't fix himself. He needed a savior. He needed Christ.

The reflection stung at his nose. Setting the last of his boxes down, his mind settled on Jamie. Ryan and Melissa barely spoke of her, and he couldn't bring himself to ask. Sadly, she was part of a past he had ruined, the greatest casualty of his rebellion, and he felt too much regret to persist in finding her.

But he prayed for her. Every time she came to mind, which was many times every day. Whenever he felt the sting of shame, or the longing to see her smile, as he did at that moment, he lifted her in prayer.

Ryan passed through the doorway. Swallowing the lump of emotion, Andrew turned to his new housemate and smiled. "Hopefully this is not an offer you'll regret."

Ryan chuckled. "Seeing you transform is not anything I'll ever regret. I'm glad to help."

It didn't take much to imagine Jamie's smile. It would animate her eyes and make his heart swim in pleasure. If only...

"She'd be so proud of you." Ryan spoke as if he could read his thoughts.

"I wish she could be there Sunday." Wish wasn't the right word. He desperately *wanted* her there. So she would know, see it firsthand.

Silence followed. Ryan didn't force a comment, and Andrew let it lie. Had Ryan loved her? Had he lost her because of him? Fresh shame stirred in his gut. Was there no limit to this man's grace?

It appeared, though, that Ryan was at peace with every aspect of their situation. And more recently, he seemed to have developed an unexpected attachment elsewhere.

Ryan put a hand to Andrew's shoulder. Nothing more was said about it, nothing more could be. Both moved on with the day; there was still much to be done.

***

"How are you?"

Jamie sat with Melissa over mugs of warm cider. It'd been only a few months, but sitting at her old table felt odd somehow. Like she was trying to pull on an old pair of jeans. The wrong fit, the wrong style. Remnants of a life gone by.

But it was good to be with Melissa.

"I'm okay." She'd spent the last three months smiling, whether she felt like it or not. Answering with the standard "I'm good," whenever asked. But Melissa knew the whole messy tale. She wasn't obligated to pretend.

"Do you like the job?"

"It suits me perfectly." It was true. Outdoor Lab was an ideal fit for her. She taught hands-on science, taking kids on daily hikes, getting her hands wet and dirty, and loving the wonder in her students' eyes.

"Tell me about it."

"Teaching up there is different. Way different. There's not really a classroom, although we have several labs. The kids just come alive. It blends everything I love together in one package. I can't believe I get to work there."

Melissa laughed. "I recall you telling me you'd never be considered. Just goes to show you—"

"You never know." Jamie finished for her. "The craziest part is that I wasn't at first. Creighton, the director, pulled my file as his top pick, but the board overruled him. They hired another candidate, but he only stayed for two months. The decision became last minute, and Creighton was told to do what he felt was best."

"And now you're there."

"And now I'm there." Jamie bit her lip. How she needed the reminder of God's goodness. It'd been hard to see lately.

Melissa took a swig and circled the rim of her mug with her finger. "Jamie, I need to talk to you about a couple of things."

Jamie could guess who one of those things was.

"Andrew is—"

"I don't want to know." It was rude. Jamie hated cutting Melissa off, but she couldn't handle it. "I'm sorry, Melissa. I just don't want to know. It still hurts too much."

Melissa dropped her stare, her fingers tracing the wood grain of the table. Her nod came slowly, but she looked like she wanted to argue.

Jamie looked at the floor. Everything was broken. Even her friendship with Melissa.

"There's something else." Melissa reached across the table, grabbing Jamie's arm. "I *have* to tell you something."

Picking up her head, Jamie caught foreboding in Melissa's eyes. He was dead. Or incarcerated. She held her breath, fear billowing inside.

"There's something between Ryan and me."

Huh? Jamie's head snapped back. She recited Melissa's last sentence in her head and then suddenly laughed. So, the world didn't revolve around Andy and her. Melissa had a life all her own. She saw herself sitting there, completely narcissistic, sulking about her life. Never once asking Melissa about hers. It was funny. Laughter burst from her chest. Pure, tickled silly laughter.

Melissa looked more frightened than amused. Jamie could hear her silently wondering if she'd snapped. If life had sent her over the edge and she'd just snapped.

It was so funny.

"Jamie?" She was *really* worried.

"I'm fine." Jamie wiped her eyes, still not able to stop the giggles. She cleared her throat and straightened her spine. "I'm sorry."

"Ryan and me together is funny?"

"Not at all. I just had this out-of-body experience... I see you trying to tell me something wonderful in your life, and me, too consumed with myself to hear you. I guess it's not that funny, but it seemed funny."

Melissa looked at her wide-eyed, then breathed a soft chuckle. "So, let's try this again. I've been seeing Ryan."

"Really?" Jamie tamed her reckless giggles. "How long?"

"Officially, since August."

Jamie settled into a more serious frame of mind. August, when she left. Seems that her leaving had been ordained for more than one reason. "What happened?"

"I wasn't trying to hide it from you, but I wanted to tell you in person." Melissa squirmed in her chair. "And I promise, there was nothing, *nothing*, between us before..."

"I know." Jamie grinned, and another laugh escaped. "Actually, now that I'm really thinking about it, you're perfect together. You both walked with me through some pretty tough times, and you made a great team of it. Plus, you can spice up his predictability with your spunk. You're a good match."

Melissa blushed. Her little smile looked... dreamy. Dreamy!

"Is it serious?"

She nodded, glowing. "He's coming home with me this week, for Thanksgiving." She paused, gulped, and then forced eye-contact. "I love him."

Well, someone should.

It was good to know love really could be dreamy. All the whimsical stories captured in paperback books had, as of late, seemed to be outright lies. For Jamie, love felt more like agony than anything else.

Humor vanished. Sincerely happy for Melissa and Ryan, Jamie abruptly found herself numbered among the disenchanted.

So, maybe she was obligated to pretend.

***

Tennis shoes squeaked against the wood floor as the pop-pop of the ball echoed off the walls. One more volley and Andrew had him. Ryan was good, and a win against him was rare, but Andrew felt in rare form.

A high floater to the back wall set his opponent on his heels, and Andrew was able to return the scrambled lob with a kill shot. Set. Game.

"Nice shot." Ryan grinned, still a little out of breath.

He just really never got upset. Not over stuff that didn't matter. That wasn't to say he wasn't an intense person, but he wasn't uptight. He was a good friend—and a good fit for Melissa.

Andrew had known about them long before Ryan spoke up. But he didn't feel like he was in a position to ask. Not until Ryan broached the topic the week before.

"I'm going to Melissa's parents." He had stated it as though it were a common arrangement. Andrew had mentioned his own plans for Thanksgiving—his parents were flying in again. Ryan had answered the implied question with an implication of his own. Andrew had nodded, wondering if he should just come out and ask, but the subject changed.

"I'll be here Sunday, though," Ryan continued. "Melissa and I both will."

That closed the subject. They had begun talking about those particular plans, and Andrew had let the other keep for another day. This day.

Andrew used the hem of his tee shirt to wipe the sweat from his eyes as he dropped against the back wall. Ryan snagged a water bottle from the wall shelf and joined him.

"So." Andrew tapped his racquet against the floor. "What happened with you and Melissa?"

Ryan eyed him as a slow grin crawled over his face. A silly, lovesick-boy kind of grin.

Andrew laughed.

"It's been killing you for weeks, hasn't it?"

Andrew laughed again. "Not killing me, but I've been curious."

Ryan nodded, still looking smitten. "I just saw her."

What did that mean?

"One day she was Jamie's roommate." Ryan settled against the wall. "And the next I realized she was the woman I love."

Andrew pushed an eyebrow up. "Just like that?"

"Well, yes, but I guess there was more to it than that."

Suddenly, the court went still. Ryan's expression turned serious, as though he were gauging Andrew. "We were together often last summer, for Jamie." Ryan twirled his racquet and smacked the ball against the front wall. It bounced once and he caught it before he looked back at Andrew.

He was calculating. How much could Andrew handle, how much did he really want to hear? "That set a romance in motion?"

Ryan shrugged. "I'm not sure I'd say that. But it allowed me to really see her. She's a tremendously caring, selfless woman, and very loyal. Not to mention beautiful and funny and the woman I can't wait to see every day."

"So, one day you woke up and realized you wanted to be with her. The end?"

"You're kind of acting like a girl, being all nosey."

Andrew joined his laughter but didn't rescind the question.

Ryan measured him once more. "We were both there the day Jamie moved." His tone turned serious again. "We both helped her. They cried and hugged, then Jamie drove away. Melissa walked into the house without a word. She never does that. She's the kind of person who always wants to make sure you're okay, you know? So I knew she wasn't. I followed her in and found her sobbing. When I hugged her, she clung to me, and I just wanted to make it all better. I don't know if that makes sense. I just wanted to make her heart okay."

Andrew chewed on that. He could relate.

Quiet settled between them. It seemed like such an odd twist that Ryan would end up with Jamie's roommate. Stranger still, that his drama with Jamie would be instrumental in bringing Ryan and Melissa together. Strange, but somehow comforting. Like something good came out of it all. Like God really could work all things for good.

He hoped so. He needed to believe so. The alternative was a vast bleakness. Something he'd lived with for too long.

"Does Jamie know?" This was his heart in the matter. Not that he didn't care about Ryan and Melissa. But if he had to speak bluntly, she was what mattered most to him.

"She does. Melissa talked to her last week."

"You didn't?"

"She was only in town for one night. I was helping you move."

She'd been in town. Something twisted cruelly near his heart. He didn't have any right to expect her to check on him, but knowing for a fact that she didn't was a bitter reality.

"Was she okay?" That question could have so many answers. Was she okay with Ryan and Melissa? Was she okay with life?

"She was."

Andrew's hand slid over his hair as his head bobbed forward. Jamie had been home. So close he could have walked down the street to see her. Did she know what had happened the past few months? Did she know he finally saw what she'd been begging him to see? That he'd been saved?

Surely Melissa would have told her.

"Why didn't she come…?"

Ryan shook his head. "She didn't know, Andrew. Melissa started to tell her, but she said she didn't want to know. Melissa didn't know how hard to push, so she didn't push at all."

Andrew pulled in a long breath. A harsh blow, but he couldn't blame her. But her knowing—having her there to see his baptism— would have been a step toward making sure her heart was okay. That was what he really wanted.

Chapter Twenty-Six

Jamie bounced out of her cabin when the sound of a vehicle rumbled through her wall. It'd been months since she'd last seen Melissa. Now she and Ryan were both at the camp, and Jamie was thrilled.

"I was afraid you wouldn't make it." She gathered their coats after they'd scooted to her cabin. "It's been snowing all night. Is it snowing in town?"

"Yes." Melissa removed her boots. "But not as much. By the looks of it, you might be stuck with us the whole weekend."

"Perfect."

Ryan and Melissa both laughed as they moved toward the small table in Jamie's tiny kitchen.

"What's new, Jamie?" Ryan stretched back, looking like the consistent guy she knew him to be.

"Nothing." Jamie gathered three mugs for coffee. "I think I might miss living at a lower elevation in about three weeks, though. I forgot that winter lasts so long up here."

Melissa nudged Jamie's arm with her elbow as she took one of the mugs. "You could come down more."

Jamie smiled. She missed visiting them. Friday nights, hanging out and finding something fun to do, running with Melissa, her church home. She missed all of it. She could visit more often—they weren't that far away. But she might run into Andy. It wasn't a risk she was ready to take.

"Maybe during the summer." Jamie settled at the table, inhaling the subtle butterscotch undertones of her favorite brew. "What's new with you guys?"

Ryan grinned. "I asked Melissa to marry me."

Jamie snickered. "I assume she said yes."

"I said I'd think about it." Melissa winked, her eyes like glitter. "And I did for about half a second."

Pulling out her left hand, she let Jamie inspect the diamond, and then they were wrapped together in celebration.

"That is the best news." Jamie hugged Ryan. "Details?"

"He totally took me by surprise." Melissa's eyes sparkled like the diamond on her finger. "I'd wondered if maybe Valentine's Day would be it, but he took me out to the Landing and that was it. No flowers, no chocolate, no diamond." Melissa eyed Ryan as if she were annoyed. "But the following Friday six roses arrived at work with only my name on them. I found a large Hershey's kiss on my front seat when I left for the day, and a diamond after we'd gone for a four-mile run. He'd tied it to a new pair of running shoes. I was trying them on before I found it."

Ryan smirked, obviously quite pleased with himself. "I can't always be predictable."

Both women laughed.

The day flew by. Melissa's prediction turned out to be more accurate than expected. The snow fell heavy all day, and around four Creighton came over to share the latest news: I-70 was closed. A rig had jack-knifed just before Genesee, and the pileup behind it was ugly.

"No worries, though," Creighton added. "The cabins all have heat. You can have your pick."

Melissa bunked with Jamie, and Ryan stayed in the teacher's quarters beside the kitchen. Creighton and Ellie invited the small group over for brownies and hot cocoa, and they played several rounds of Scrabble before calling it a night.

Sometime after ten, Melissa stretched out on her cot, wearing the flannel pants and a waffled Henley she'd borrowed from Jamie.

"You're happy." Jamie grinned at Melissa, who was glowing. "I can see it seeping through your pores."

"I am." Melissa shot her a dreamy smile. "I want you to stand up with me. Will you?"

Jamie loved having a reason to laugh again. She'd been starving for her friend. "I'll have to think about it." She crossed her eyes and stuck out her tongue. "Of course I will."

Melissa looked pleased. And then not so much. "You might need to think about it. Andrew will be there."

Jamie felt her face fall as all the joy was sucked out of the room. Why did every moment have to be tainted? Accepting Ryan and Melissa as a couple was easy. She hadn't been in love with him, and Melissa obviously was. Being asked to be part of their wedding was an honor. But Andy? How could she heal like this?

"He and Ryan have become pretty close." Melissa rested her hand on Jamie's arm. "Oh, Jamie, so much has happened. I'll tell you if you want."

She didn't want to talk about him. Her heart still hurt too much. She couldn't snag onto hope only to have it ripped away again.

"He'll be in the wedding." Melissa's shoulders drooped. "I know that must feel like a slap in the face, but as things are…" She drew a long breath. "I wish I could explain. But Jamie, Ryan and I both want you there. With all our hearts, we want you up there with us."

Jamie studied her hands. It didn't feel like a slap. She'd no intention of making anyone choose between Andy and her. But it felt like… agony.

But for Melissa, for Ryan, she would suck it up. "You know I wouldn't miss it."

***

Andrew slid his phone onto his side table and reached for his Bible. The early March storm had already dumped more than had been expected, and the snow was still falling. Which was why Ryan had called. He and Melissa had gone up somewhere toward Idaho Springs to meet an old friend of hers and were snowed in. They were fine—it gave Melissa a chance to spend more time with her friend. Ryan just didn't want Andrew to worry.

He did, though. Not about Ryan or the storm. Ryan and Melissa were engaged. Andrew had no doubt they would tell Jamie sooner than later, and he was certain of her reaction.

She'd be glad for their joy. And since he was sure Jamie hadn't been in love with Ryan, he was certain her reaction would be heartfelt. But the news might hurt just a little. Way down deep, in the place that was rarely seen, would she feel the ache of loneliness?

He did. Not a general solitude, but one for her alone. He missed her, and once again he wouldn't be there at a time when she'd need a shoulder. Would she forever have to walk through difficulty alone?

Andrew's eyes fell to the printed page of God's Word, opened to First Peter.

Cast all your cares upon Him, for He cares for you.

***

Spring was blooming in a colorful array when Jamie made it down for a visit. She and Melissa had a full-fledged wedding planning weekend ahead of them.

She arrived shortly after four. Melissa had scouted a couple of dresses and pinpointed locations that had the correct sizes in stock, so without much of a pause, they dove into the satin, lace, and tulle at several boutiques. It was dark before Melissa narrowed her picks down to two, and Jamie suggested she sleep on it before she made her final choice.

Leaving behind the rich fabrics and the clichéd flowers and hearts of the shop, both were ready for some sustenance. They landed at their favorite Mexican restaurant.

"What do your parents think of Ryan?" Jamie asked in between bites of smothered enchiladas.

Melissa laughed. "They adore him."

"Well, who wouldn't?"

Melissa's grin faded. "In all honesty, Jamie, does it bother you?"

"Not even a little." Jamie reached for Melissa's hand. "I think it's wonderful. He's such a good man, and you're perfect together. I'm not even remotely upset."

Melissa nodded, looking unconvinced. "There's something sad in your eyes."

Jamie sighed. Hadn't she heard that before? She'd tried to hide her reluctance. But it would be better to be honest than to have Melissa think she was jealous of Ryan.

"I live on a roller coaster." She smoothed her napkin, then refolded it. "I'm so tired of it."

"I'm not sure what you mean."

"I'll have nightmares. Andy is lying, mangled and lifeless, on one of those cold steel tables." Jamie forced back a shudder. "I pray. Oh, Melissa, how I pray for God's peace. For Him to release me. And it'll get better. I'll think I'm finally moving on. Then I'll remember the warmth of his hand on my cheek, the tenderness in his voice telling me not to give up on my dreams. I'll remember how he was at my mom's grave, how he held me while I cried. I think maybe he's okay. Maybe..." She shook her head. "Then the nightmares will come back. He'll be drunk, and I'm afraid."

Melissa shook her head, her face drawn with concern. "Has this been going on all year?"

Had it? Jamie balled her napkin. She'd been down for sure. But the worst of it was more recent. "Mostly since you and Ryan got engaged."

"Why?"

"Because I know I'll see him again." She pushed her plate away. "He'll either hate me, or he'll want everything to go back the way it was." She ground her teeth and drew in a long breath. "I can't go there again."

Melissa examined her for two long breaths. "He's dry, Jamie."

Jamie's eyes darted back to hers.

"It's been almost a year." Melissa held a steady look. "He hasn't had a drop since the accident."

Jamie chewed on that. She wanted it to be true, but it didn't seem possible. Andy had hidden stashes and a life that he carefully kept unseen. He was pretty good at deceiving people, keeping them at arm's length.

"That you know of." When exactly had she become a cynic?

Melissa shook her head. "He lives with Ryan. He's completely sober."

"What?"

"He sold his loft and moved in November."

Jamie's lips parted. It should have been good news. But somehow it stung.

"Oh, Jamie, he's so different now. Wouldn't it be okay to call him? Wouldn't it be okay to see for yourself?"

Call him? Jamie pressed her lips together as she examined the place setting in front of her. What would she say?

Are you all better yet?

What would *he* say? There was a disheartening prospect. He'd be angry. She'd left him. At the lowest point in his life, she'd walked away, and he'd never understand why.

Jamie gulped, shaking her head. "I don't know. Part of me wants to, but—" Her breath quivered as she drew it in deeply.

How had this day spun in this direction? Melissa was getting married—this whole weekend was about love and happiness. And here Jamie sat, ruining all the fun. She sat up straight. "This is your time, Melissa. It's not about the Andy-and-Jamie saga. So I'm not going to sit here and cry into my soda, and you're not going to worry about anything but wedding cake and pretty dresses."

Melissa held her eyes. She looked like she'd argue, that she'd push the issue. But after a slow breath, a weak smile crossed her lips and the subject was dropped.

They left shortly after and stopped at a Redbox for a movie. Jamie spent the rest of the night trying to drown the curiosity Melissa had sparked. Didn't matter what happened. Short of his salvation, she didn't want to know.

After a not-so-restful night peppered with memories, Saturday started with an elegant breakfast downtown. From there, Jamie and Melissa went to a lengthy meeting with Melissa's wedding planner and returned to the dress shops. Melissa made her final selection, and the fittings were scheduled.

For Jamie, Melissa picked a shimmering green. "It suits you."

Jamie smiled in the mirror. The color was perfect. She wasn't sure, however, that a fancy dress of any kind suited her.

By nightfall they were both happily exhausted. On the way back to Melissa's, they stopped for take-out pizza and another chick flick. It was after midnight before Jamie pushed herself off the couch and said goodnight.

"Jamie, wait." Melissa caught her before she headed to her room. "I assume you're going to church tomorrow?"

Jamie smiled. She'd been looking forward to a Sunday at her home church. "Yep."

Melissa's mouth twisted. "I think maybe I should give you heads-up. Andrew will probably be there."

Andy in church? "Does he know that I'm in town?"

"No, Ryan and I didn't say anything. But he usually goes these days."

What? He hated church. He only ever went out of guilt.

Melissa cut the tense silence."I just thought maybe you'd like to know beforehand."

Jamie gathered her scrambling thoughts and tried to push them away. Maybe things had really changed. Maybe... no. An atheistic alcoholic? Not happening.

Knowing he'd be there didn't help. Maybe she just wouldn't go.

***

Andrew blew his nose before he gulped back an aspirin. His full head ached, but he really didn't feel awful. Just a spring cold. He probably should have gone to church.

Perhaps a Sunday walk would clear the congestion. In old blue jeans and a worn sweatshirt, he walked in the direction of Clear Creek. He wasn't sure he'd make it that far, as his heart pounded unusually strong, and he felt more chilled than he should in the spring sunshine, but he went until he felt he needed to turn around.

That distance measured exactly to Melissa's house.

He glanced up as he came to the intersection. Her place was three houses to the left from the stop sign, and parked in front was a silver Camry. With a roof rack.

Jamie.

Andrew's steps halted. A dozen questions went off in his head, but all of them ceased with one thought. If she'd wanted to see him, it would have happened.

With his head still stuffy and now a sick heart, Andrew turned his steps around and took himself home.

***

Lilacs bloomed along the iron fence line as Jamie pulled into a mostly deserted parking lot. Children scattered over the softball fields below, but Jamie's visit to Daniel's Park didn't include a game. Turning her back on the field chatter, she wandered through the iron gate. Two blocks up, three sections over, her feet moved automatically until she stood on the grass before the familiar headstone.

Stacey Evelyn Carson.

Jamie's eyes moved from the chiseled marble to a swirl of blue. Settled next to her mother's grave, a small cluster of columbine danced in the breeze. Jamie dropped to her knees and pulled the small potted plant into her lap. Her lungs expanded as if she'd been given a breath of fresh air. Andy had remembered.

She'd loved him. It had taken her all these months to come to terms with it. Whether she hadn't wanted to admit it or she'd known deep down that it was too dangerous to own, the aching reality was that she'd loved him.

How had life turned out this way? She'd known better than to tangle with Andy. She'd done everything she could to guard against it. And yet here she sat, crushed and alone.

Oh God, help me. I am so broken.

Chapter Twenty-Seven

"She's not going to come." Andrew looked up from the floor.

Ryan leaned against the wall, kicking one foot across the other. "She'll be here."

"Jamie hates being late."

Melissa lifted a small smile. "She is not going to ditch us right before our wedding, Andrew."

As if on cue, Melissa's phone rang, and she stepped away. Andrew strained to hear, but the only thing he could determine for certain was that it was Jamie. He clenched his fists and held his breath.

"Andrew, she'll be here." Ryan stepped closer and squeezed his shoulder. "It'll be all right."

"I told you this wasn't a good idea." Andrew crossed his arms. "Look, you know I want to be here, but if she can't do this—"

Melissa stepped back to Ryan's side before Andrew could finish his thought. "She's stuck on the interstate. There was a pileup about two miles before she got to town." She smiled back to Andrew. "She'll get here as soon as she can. Let's do the first walk though. She'll catch up."

Ryan nodded, and arm-in-arm they moved toward the rest of the wedding party. Andrew stood rooted, praying for wisdom, for a calm heart, and for the woman he longed to see.

It took nearly twenty minutes for the wedding planner to give her instructions, and another ten for their pastor to speak his prelude, and then the small wedding party lined up for the first walk through. Andrew's responsibilities as one of two ushers was minimal, so he remained outside the large double doors after the party marched down the aisle.

The glass door in the foyer squeaked before she rushed through the entry. The warning didn't do much to prepare him, though. She stopped to replace her ballet flats, and then she looked up. His heart pounded near his throat, and he struggled to breathe.

He caught her green eyes as time seemed to stop.

She straightened slowly.

He couldn't move.

"Andy." Her lips moved, but his name wasn't audible.

"Hi, Jamie."

She looked so timid, so vulnerable. Would she reject him if he took her in his arms? His mind jolted back a year. He'd wondered that very thing in her kitchen the day after he'd come to her home, drunk. She had shrunk away from him, afraid.

The memory sizzled through his core. He held his place.

"I'm really late," she whispered.

His brain wouldn't work. He couldn't find any words.

After another uneasy moment, she stepped toward the door, and Andrew mechanically reached for the handle, pulling it back a crack. Jamie stopped, waiting for the opening to allow her passage, and his gaze locked onto her face.

She slowly shifted her eyes back to him.

"It's good to see you, James."

She blinked twice. "You too."

He tried to fill his lungs as he swept the door open. With a quick pace, Jamie scurried down the aisle toward the rest of the wedding party. Andrew stayed planted, his hands trembling.

She came—she was there. And she'd called him Andy.

***

Jamie reached the small group on the stage and was greeted with a round of hugs.

"I'm so sorry," she puffed, hoping they didn't figure it was Andy and not her run from the parking lot that left her struggling for air.

She hadn't been ready to see him. And then she wasn't ready to leave. Andy's voice had come to her softly, and for a moment she dared to hope he'd embrace her. It died quickly when a cloud moved over his eyes. She tucked her bottom lip under her teeth, commanding her emotions to stay buried. Alone in bed later that night, she could cry all she wanted. Not here.

Nate, Ryan's younger brother, came to her side, and she turned to say hello. Built like his older brother, he stood about six foot and had broad shoulders. With blue eyes instead of Ryan's brown, Nate would be an attractive escort. But he wasn't Andrew.

His well-toned arms drew her in and then held.

Wait. Was this a hello hug? Lasted way longer than your typical hey, *it's been awhile* embrace.

"How you doing, Jamie?" His voice, feather soft, drifted the short distance to her ear.

Awkward. Heat crept up her neck. She pushed back and stood a little distance away. "I'm good, Nate. How are you?"

He stared at her. Too long.

So weird.

"I'm glad to see you." With one stride he closed the space she'd put between them, and his shoulder brushed hers as he turned to stand next to her, facing the rest of the group. His head dipped toward her, and again he whispered near her hair. "I'm your wedding partner. Just stick with me, okay?"

Bizarre. Did he mean to be funny? Maybe she should laugh. She glanced to see his face. Serious. Didn't comedians keep a poker face, though? Surly he was fishing for a chuckle. She forced one, but didn't know what to say.

"Let's take our positions for the service so Jamie can see where to stand, and then we'll do another walk-through."

Saved by the preacher. Jamie exhaled slowly and moved toward Melissa. Within moments she was positioned to the bride's left, and she tried to concentrate on what was being said. Didn't work. She peeked over her shoulder, back to the double doors she'd swept through. Andy wasn't there, or anywhere else in the sanctuary. Being in the same room apparently wasn't an option.

Her stomach twisted. He despised her.

***

Ryan's brother Nate was to escort Jamie down the aisle. No one had given that a second thought, but watching from the shadows at the back of the church, Andrew fought a surge of jealousy as they moved painfully slowly toward the front. Maybe he wouldn't have an irrational suspicion if he hadn't watched people welcoming her. While everyone's greeting was warm, it seemed that Nate's was overly friendly.

He tried to purge the ridiculous notion from his mind. Nate was six years her junior. Not that anyone would be able to tell—and they were both grown adults, so that hardly would matter.

He slid into a pew and bowed his head, resting it on clutched hands. His pulse raced, and he prayed for clear thought as the music reached its final chord. *You're imagining things. It wouldn't be the first time you reacted poorly to another man's notice of her.*

His eyes scanned the scene down front, taking in all of the characters before settling on Jamie. She'd cut her hair off. It lay stacked at the back of her head in an asymmetrical bob, leaving her neck exposed. Her form looked smaller than he'd remembered, and her skin was several shades paler than he'd ever seen on her in July.

His gaze darted back to Nate. Lean, tan, and still looking like a kid. Andrew's unreasonable notion began to subside. Besides, if there had been something between his brother and Jamie, Ryan would have warned him.

Andrew leaned back. Perhaps Nate had an interest. Frankly, Andrew couldn't fault him, but it couldn't be mutual. Furthermore, he was sure Jamie lived in Iowa now. The entire scenario was as impractical as it was improbable.

The rehearsal concluded, but the participants retreated past him and into the church entry before he moved. When he finally regained his whereabouts, Andrew discovered himself seated in the sanctuary with only Ryan and Melissa remaining.

"Are you all right?" Ryan asked when they were near enough for a discreet conversation.

Andrew forced a smile. "Fine."

Melissa's eyebrows rose. "You looked… perplexed."

"It's nothing."

Ryan released his fiancée's hand. "I'll catch up."

Melissa squeezed Andrew's elbow as she passed.

Ryan watched her glide up the aisle and out the door before he turned back to Andrew. "Did you talk to her?"

"I managed a couple of inane sentences." Andrew pushed his fingers through his short hair.

"What'd she do?"

"Said hi, then ran away."

"And that upset you?"

Andrew's brows dropped. "No, I'm not upset."

Ryan leaned against the pew opposite him. "You're brooding."

Brooding? Great. He chuckled, shaking his head. "Ryan, you really don't want to know half the things that spin in my head. You're getting married tomorrow. Don't worry about me."

Ryan looked like he wanted to argue.

"My troubles will keep for another day." Andrew stepped forward and clapped him on the shoulder. "This one is yours."

No more brooding. Smile, be happy, and move forward. Shouldn't be that hard, right?

Both men walked outside just in time to see Nate shutting Jamie's car door.

Andrew couldn't force a smile past his jealous heart.

***

"Jamie."

Ryan's voice snagged her in the church hall as she whisked by. She stopped and spun around with a full smile.

He stood with his head poked out of the classroom-turned-men's dressing room, the brightest grin she'd ever seen plastered on his face.

She laughed. "Hey, Ryan."

He jerked his head toward the room, and she followed the implied instruction. Stepping through the door, she joined Ryan along with Nate, Andy, and Ryan's former roommate from Ohio. Dark-suited and appropriately groomed, the panel made up a handsome group, but Jamie's eyes rested on only one face before she turned back to Ryan.

"How is she?" He rubbed his hands together.

Jamie's laugh bubbled, despite her sudden self-consciousness. "She's been singing since she woke up this morning."

Although it didn't seem possible, Ryan's smile grew. "I have to see her."

Tipping her head, Jamie tapped her lips with her finger. "Give me five minutes."

She hustled down the hall and through the foyer, circling the sanctuary to where a separate hall housed more classrooms, one of which had become the bride's chambers. It took all of two seconds for Melissa to agree, as Jamie knew she would, and she headed back to get the groom.

She didn't have to go far before she met both Ryan and Andy en route.

Jamie dropped back, allowing Ryan to pass unaccompanied. She stopped, not knowing what to do next, only to discover that Andy had halted beside her. Her eyes reached his chin before they fell to the floor. Her ears burned. No doubt she was crimson from the neck up. What was he thinking? Would he say anything?

"You look beautiful, James."

Her eyes darted back to his. Had he really just said that? Did she only imagine the tenderness in his voice? He studied her and was uncomfortable to be sure, but nothing in those amber drops hinted anger.

She took in the face she'd known by heart, one she'd seen often in dreams—some good and some horrible. The picture was different now. A fierce and jagged scar dominated his handsome features, beginning between his eyes, running down his nose and fading into his cheekbone. It was startling. Not because it was ugly, but because it was a sharp reminder of why they were now strangers.

She stood in silent regard for way too long. Realizing she was staring, she was anxious all over again. *Stop acting like an awkward teenager!* "Thank you."

Silence. Loud and unnerving silence. Neither had anything to say. Nothing could salvage their relationship.

They were rescued by a woman dressed in a dark -gray business suit, cut with feminine lines. Motioning down the hall, she asked if the bride was ready for pictures.

"In a minute," Andy answered. His attention went back to Jamie and settled, a small smile tilting his mouth. After a few breaths, he started toward the door. A simple knock, a duo of laughter, and then Ryan appeared in the doorway.

Andy crossed his arms and rocked back on his heels. "Your photographer's here."

"Good." Ryan beamed, looking back at his bride. "Then you can hurry up and marry me."

Jamie could imagine Melissa's smile. Beyond a doubt, the sentiment was mutual.

***

Andrew walked beside Ryan as they made their way back. *Hurry up and marry me.* The words slithered around his heart and squeezed.

"I'm sorry I couldn't have you stand up front with me, Andrew." Ryan's comment came out of the blue.

Andrew turned off the line running through his mind. "I never expected you to. In fact, I thought it was generous of you to have me in your party at all."

Ryan stopped. "You're a friend I value greatly. Melissa also. We're both proud of you." He paused, his eyes pinching a little. "Jamie would be too, if you two could find a way to break the ice."

Andrew stood in silence. He would like nothing better than to see her smile. But he'd done too much. Surely he had carved out every part of her that could possibly care.

"I think it would have been too difficult for Jamie if I were up there with you." Andrew pushed his hands in his pockets. "It's hard enough as it is."

Ryan's nod was slow in coming. "I have a suspicion that having my brother as her escort is going to get old fast."

So Ryan had picked up on Nate's attention. He wasn't imagining things. "Why is that?"

"He's convinced that this whole thing is mean—having Jamie in the wedding."

Of course. How many others would assume… that? Andrew rolled his eyes.

They let the subject go. The whole party was due in the sanctuary for pictures. They finished the trek back to fetch the other tuxedoed men.

The ceremony went beautifully. In keeping with both Ryan and Melissa's commitment to Christ, the service clearly communicated that the bride and groom both loved Jesus, and their vows were taken in His name and dedicated to His glory.

Andrew had attended a few weddings, but only his brother's had been so plainly devoted to God's honor. Sadly, Andrew had been fuzzy long before that ceremony began. Unavoidable shame made his ears burn. He'd apologized to his brother at Christmas, and Devon forgave him. But what man should have to deal with his inebriated little brother on his wedding day?

Andrew's jaw clenched. *Forgive me, Father.*

Mr. and Mrs. Ryan Anderson neared his position at the back of the church. Ryan moved his way and Andrew stepped forward with an outstretched hand. Ryan clasped it and the newly married couple finished their recessional walk.

Jamie followed, Nate at her elbow. She moved gracefully, the scooped neckline of her pistachio dress perfectly framing her slightly freckled face and highlighting those green eyes. Andrew pushed away the image of her escort and allowed pleasure to wash over him.

Her eyes met his and she seemed to freeze. Her feet kept moving, but her breathing stopped, and her face changed. Her smile faded, and her eyes moved in startled question. But as she came nearer, the curve of her lips tipped up, and a familiar light flickered behind those emeralds.

She'd smiled. A real smile—the kind that reached her eyes and transformed her face. And it had been for him.

Chapter Twenty-Eight

The view from the Stone Bridge Clubhouse was breathtaking. The sun still kissed the tops of the mountain peaks across the Denver valley, but after it sank, a million city lights would twinkle in its place.

Jamie stood at the ceiling-to-floor windows overlooking the stone patio. To the south, skyscrapers poked straight and tall into the skyline, sunlight gleaming off the towering steel and glass. Looking west, the Rockies held their ancient place, a barrier of immovable beauty and challenge.

She scanned the panorama, taking in the accomplishments of man's ambition and the incomparable beauty of God's creation. The sky turned a pale blue as electric oranges and intense pinks colored the scattered clouds.

Exhaling, Jamie closed her eyes and squeezed her fists. She'd survived thus far. Halfway to done, she'd be okay. The reception dinner was what she had been dreading most, though.

Suck it up and smile.

Jamie glanced around the large room. White-clothed tables with small bouquets of cream calla lilies were scattered across deep-brown carpet. Light green and shimmering silver splashed color over the elegant room, and lights strung overhead created a tent of glowing ambiance. After scanning the guests, her shoulders drooped. Andy was not among them.

Shouldn't that be a relief?

She redirected her attention outside. A white limo pulled up the long, inclined drive. Ryan and Melissa would make their entrance in moments. A small, genuine smile touched Jamie's mouth. Love was beautiful.

"Jamie, there you are."

Her back stiffened. Nate. Why did the guy keep hovering? "Here I am."

"I found our table." He stepped a little too close. Again. "I thought perhaps you would join me."

She slid a half step away, and her gaze moved back to the window. Oh, for an excuse to say no.

Sighing, she turned back to Nate, but as she moved, she found the man she'd sought before. Standing near the entrance where Ryan and Melissa were expected, Andy stood next to a red-haired woman. Jamie couldn't stop her stare or the hitch in her breath. He had a date.

Andy caught her eyes, and her glance darted to the floor. Heat crawled up her neck. Why hadn't she considered that he would have a date?

Ryan and Melissa swept through the double doors, and Jamie pasted on a smile. Dinner was served as music floated above the humming room. A few couples swayed to the music, and others mingled about.

Without request, Nate sought her hand and pulled her toward the floor. Her muscles bunched. What was with him? Didn't he know it was polite to ask a woman to dance before you dragged her out?

He spun her toward him and pulled her near. Did he expect her to lean against him?

"I know this must be a hard day," he whispered. "You don't have to pretend with me."

What? Jamie pulled away, scowling. Had Ryan told Nate what had happened between her and Andy? Heat poured through her veins. She'd trusted Ryan. Why would he do that?

"I couldn't believe it when Ryan told me you were in the wedding." Nate tried to cuddle her. "As if it weren't bad enough that he was marrying your best friend."

Oh. She relaxed and even laughed softly. "Nate." She patted his arm. "I have no problem with your brother's marriage. Honest."

Nate shook his head and tried to pull her closer.

Oh, for goodness' sake. Jamie put a hand against his chest and gave him her stern teacher look. The one that said, *That's enough.* She'd endured pathetic glances and sympathetic hugs the entire night. Now this. She was encased in a room full of people who believed her to be watching the man she loved give his name to another. Definitely enough. "Look, I—"

"May I steal a dance with my new brother-in-law?"

Jamie turned to find Melissa and Ryan, both looking as though they shared a scheme.

"Of course." Jamie stepped aside, not even trying to hide her relief.

Melissa stepped in her place, and Ryan waited only a moment before he held his hand out to her.

See? Gentlemen asked—even if without words. *Nate.*

Ryan waited until the rhythm settled between them. "How are you holding up?"

Jamie snorted and rolled her eyes. "Apparently I'm a pathetic, heartbroken girl."

"I'm sorry about my brother. Is he smothering you?"

"I'm fine." She drew a long breath, letting her irritation drain away, and then tilted her head. "I'm sorry people think… what they think."

Ryan shrugged as if it really didn't matter.

Well, then, it didn't.

"Have you spoken with Andrew?"

From bad to worse. Why would she speak to Andy? She was going to survive this day and move on. Maybe Ryan didn't understand the plan. Jamie stared at him, scowling.

He wasn't even a little repentant. He expected an answer.

"Who's the redhead?" she snapped.

Ryan looked around, squinting before he looked back at Jamie with a raised eyebrow.

"He came in with a redhead." Maybe she should stamp her foot, cross her arms, and poke out her bottom lip. *Sheesh. Act like a grown-up.*

"Andy doesn't have a date tonight."

"Andy?" No one called him Andy. Only her. Usually. She pulled back, her eyebrows arching into her forehead.

Ryan's face hardened.

Her cheeks warmed—she'd behaved badly. If only this wasn't so… humiliating. And painful. "No." She looked at the floor. "I haven't talked with him."

His mouth twisted as though he were silently rebuking her cowardice. The song ended, but he subtly held her elbow, stopping her escape. "You'll regret it if you don't."

Defeated, Jamie met his eyes. Couldn't he understand how hard this was?

Nate and Melissa drew beside them before she could detangle her thoughts. Melissa slid next to Ryan. "It's time for the bouquet."

Ryan nodded, and Melissa latched arms with Jamie, moving toward the head table.

Jamie leaned into her friend. "Will you mind if I skip this?"

"Not at all." Melissa winked and squeezed her hand. "We'll be taking off shortly."

The women stopped, facing one another.

"I'm so glad for you both." Jamie hugged her. "You do know that, right?"

"Yes." Melissa returned her tight embrace. "God hasn't forgotten you, Jamie. Ryan and I won't either. You're always welcome in our home."

Jamie forced a smile. "You have a good trip."

While several single women laughed and giggled, playfully elbowing for position, Jamie slid into the shadows and escaped through the patio doors.

The cool Colorado evening pricked at her skin. She wasn't used to bare shoulders. Or dresses. With all her hiking cargos, thermal Henleys and polar fleece vests, she was probably a candidate for *What Not To Wear*.

With her life experience, she could come up with her own show: *Who Not To Love*.

Rule 1: If he makes fun of your job, don't go riding with him.

Rule 2: If he mocks your beliefs, don't let him buy you treats.

Rule 3: If he's an alcoholic, *run*.

Sounded like good advice. Except Andy wasn't one-dimensional. He was so much more than all the things that made him wrong.

Her heels clicked to the edge of the patio where she stood with her arms wrapped around her shoulders. Urban sprawl flickered against the early night sky. A water hazard on the golf course reflected the twinkling lights of the grand clubhouse. Beyond the stretch of fairway, thousands of headlights blazed on the I-25 corridor. The buzz of the gathering fell on her ears, conversation and laughter wafting on the breeze. Evidence of people surrounded her, but perched on that grand crest, Jamie had never felt so alone. Hot tears escaped, and she simply let them roll.

Uproarious laughter culminated inside, and then the crescendo died. The music began again, and Josh Groban's rich baritone floated on a cool breeze.

"Always looking to the mountains."

Startled, she sniffed, dashing away her tears. Her nerves rippled as he neared. He dropped his suit coat over her shoulders, sliding to her side.

"Are you okay, James?"

That voice. The tender voice of her dearest friend.

She couldn't help but sniff again. "I'm fine."

Amber eyes examined her, and she couldn't bear to have him believe...

"It's not what you think." She straightened her shoulders. "I'm very happy for Ryan and Melissa and wish them the best, with all of my heart. I—"

"I know, Jamie." Andy's fingers curled around her arm.

He held her eyes, and fear and hope tumbled together. What were those rules again? Did they apply to *this* man?

"I know what you're thinking." His thumb brushed over her cheek. "And it's not true."

Jamie searched his face, wondering if he really did know all that she thought, how much she felt.

"You're not alone."

Another tear escaped.

He quietly wiped it away. "I don't want to know about Ryan and Melissa." He cupped her chin, bringing her eyes back to his. "I want to know if you're okay."

A small smile tickled her mouth. Oh, how she missed her friend. Andy always saw what was hidden from all other eyes, because he cared enough to look.

"My head hurts." She rubbed her temple and drew a shuddered breath. "And Nate is driving me crazy. But I'm okay."

Andy nodded.

She could get lost in the tender warmth of his gaze.

He held out a hand. "Will you dance with me?"

A gentleman. She stared at his offer while her heart puddled. She slipped her hand in his and he slid his arm around her. The music set them in motion, and she inhaled the familiar undertones of Irish Spring and Old Spice. She hadn't realized how much she'd liked the scent. Missed it.

Why, God? You had to know I'd fall in love with him. Why did You do this?

The rhythm of the music and the sturdy feel of his arms took her captive, and she was only vaguely conscious of him pulling her closer. Indeed, as they swayed in the dimly lit night, she lost almost all awareness. Tucked close against him, she buried her face in his chest.

Lyrics about love, lasting love that endures time and trials, drifted into her consciousness. The words were not sung by Groban alone; Andy sang them softly against her hair. Her breath caught in her chest as reality broke through. Andy held her, cradled her as if she were beloved.

She'd leaned into him. Wrapped her hungry arms around him, held him as if he were beloved.

The ballad continued, but Jamie pulled away. Andy's arms loosened, though his fingers trailed down the jacket she'd slipped her arms through, stopping to linger on her hands. He waited, looking uncertain, while she wandered through a labyrinth of emotions.

"I got mascara on your shirt," she whispered, her voice painfully forced.

"It's fine."

"Is it a rental?"

"It will be fine." He traced her tears with his thumb. "Don't worry about it."

She ached to return to his arms. To hear his heart next to her ear, to feel his breath dance over her skin.

To hear him repeat the words that he'd sung.

What had she been thinking? She hadn't been. At all."I should go."

"Don't leave because of me." Andy took her hand. "Please, if I've upset you—"

Too tempting. She slipped her hand away, looked up, and shook her head. "Ryan and Melissa have gone. I just want to find some Advil and a bed."

His Adam's apple bobbed. "Where are you staying?"

"I'm house-sitting for Melissa and Ryan." Oh dear. Too much information. Survive. Leave. Move on with life. Remember that?

"Can I give you a ride?"

She looked at the ground, feeling limp inside. He was the same old Andy. His eyes had looked soft, inviting, and yet uncertain.

Not the same old Andy, actually. The old Andy would have bullied her into whatever he wanted. Insisted she stay, or let him take her home. He would have manipulated every angle until he won.

Was he manipulating her again?

Her gaze traveled back to his face, settling on the jagged scar across his nose. She was on dangerous ground.

"No," she whispered. "I have my car, and I'd hate to leave it here overnight."

Andy nodded. "I'll walk you out."

She moved toward the patio doors, but he tugged her back, redirecting her to an alternative exit.

She pointed toward the room. "I left my things at the table."

"I'll get them." He guided her through a side door leading into the hall. "You've been crying, and everyone will assume they know why."

Heat poured into her cheeks.

He passed through the main double-door entry, leaving her to dab at her running makeup. The table at the end of the hall caught her attention, and Jamie sighed. She moved to size up the mound of gifts and began to gather what she could.

Andy came toward her, her purse in hand. "What are you doing?"

"Nate and I are supposed to take these back to their house. I completely forgot."

"I'll help."

In the parking lot, Jamie popped the trunk with her remote, and they stowed the packages before Andy shut it. Jamie stepped to the driver's door.

"You still have Colorado plates."

She spun from the handle she'd reached for and stared at him.

Andy watched her reaction, slowly closing the gap between them. "All this time I thought you'd moved to Iowa."

She shook her head, considering her words. "I'm up at Spring View, just beyond Genesee Park. I teach at the Outdoor Lab School."

Andy processed, his look steady.

Jamie prepared for his outrage.

But he didn't even scowl. A faint smile touched his mouth. "That sounds like you."

Of all the versions she knew of this man, this was the one for which she was least prepared. Music hummed in her ears, and her mind began to numb. If she continued to stand, warm and defenseless under the caress of his gaze, she'd dissolve into a puddle.

What would it be like to melt in his arms? To feel his strength seep through her, to have his love pour over her?

Wonderful.

No. Disastrous. She was heading for ruin. Removing his jacket, she pushed away longing. "Thank you." Handing over the coat, she hoped he couldn't see the heat on her face.

His fingers brushed hers as he took it, and she ducked into her car.

"Jamie." He caught her door, bending over to meet her eyes. "Can I see you again?"

Turn away. Ignore the pleading in his beautiful eyes. But his soft singing voice still echoed in her ears, the warmth of his embrace still lingered on her skin.

She agreed and he shut her car door.

Chapter Twenty-Nine

Andrew inhaled deeply, his nose buried in the suit coat. It smelled like the lotion Jamie used to smear all over her hands after a day of skiing. Maybe he'd just keep it.

He'd held her, and she'd leaned into him. For more than a minute, life had felt like the way it should have always been. And then she'd remembered. Everything. He had unequivocally broken her heart. A woman didn't just forget.

Letting her go had taken an exertion of discipline. How could he let her walk out of his life again?

He couldn't—at least not without an honest baring of his soul. Then if she chose to walk away… His eyes slid shut.

Gathering the pile of rented tuxes, Andrew let himself out of his vehicle and covered the five steps to the store front. He had to make another trip for the three pairs of shoes in his back seat, and then he was finished with his wedding role. He was free to see to personal matters.

Jamie's car sat in front of Melissa's—Ryan and Melissa's house, but she didn't answer the doorbell. He rang it again, but nothing happened. Andrew stood on the front porch, glancing toward her parked car. Was she ignoring him?

Unlikely. She could be out jogging or riding, or sleeping, or visiting with friends. Jamie didn't ignore people—it was rude.

He turned from the door and stepped down both risers, pausing on the sidewalk. On a whim he crossed the narrow strip of grass between the front walk and the driveway, making his way around back.

Success. With a ball cap shading her eyes, she lay stretched out in the sunshine. He paused, trying to calm his racing heart.

He started up the steps to her porch, but she didn't move. "Jamie," he called softly.

She jolted upright.

"I'm sorry, James." Chuckling, he came closer. "You were really out."

She blocked the sun with the worn cap, looking dazed as she stared at his face.

Andrew cocked his head. "Are you okay?"

She blinked twice and then rubbed her eyes. "Am I awake?"

He grinned. "I'm not sure." Turning, he snagged a chair and set it at the foot of her chaise. "Are you okay now?"

"Yes, I'm sorry." Her eyes cleared. "I couldn't remember where I was."

Andrew smiled, and her expression turned timid. The air wrapped in slight tension, but she didn't retreat from his gaze.

Heaviness pressed against his lungs. What was she thinking about? He hoped she wasn't revisiting the ugly scenes from their past. When the green in her eyes didn't spark in anger, the weight in his chest began to drain. He had nothing left to lose. She could walk away again and that would be the end of it. But he had to take the chance—for both of them. What he needed to tell her could change everything.

"James, I wanted to ask you something, and I need you to be a straight shooter with me."

She stayed quiet, her look slightly fearful.

Swallowing, he finished the plunge. "Do you hate me?"

Her eyes widened. Surprise faded into a guarded hesitancy, and then her expression began to crumble. "Sometimes I'm still really mad at you." She paused, her attention dropping to her hands. "But mostly I miss you so much it hurts."

Andrew exhaled, and the muscles in his arms tensed, longing to hold her. Prudence held him off. She would push him away. However, he couldn't resist some kind of contact. He dropped a hand to her bare foot and squeezed.

"Have dinner with me," he whispered around the lump in his throat.

Her eyes slid closed, and she remained still for many heartbeats. Moisture darkened her eyelashes, and Andrew's fingers twitched to wipe it away.

She answered with only a nod, and Andrew slid to a knee. Still wary of her rejection, he lifted a hand to her cheek.

She didn't shrink from his touch.

"I'll come back in an hour."

***

Jamie remained still, sorting through her fears. The loneliness of the past year had worn her defenses down to nothing, and she was terrified of her own weakness.

He was different, though. But not really. In many ways, in fact, he was more like the Andy of her childhood than he'd ever been.

He was the man she could fall in love with.

Panic stirred. He couldn't change, though. Not by himself. Deep down, the monster would lie in wait, and when Andy couldn't suppress him anymore, she would be in the epicenter of disaster. She couldn't put herself there.

He would break her heart. As tender and kind and wonderful as he could be, he could be equally hard, selfish, and destructive. He would shred her world, and she couldn't start over again.

But what if he had changed? What if God had poured His mercy on him—and he'd received it?

What if they could be happy?

***

Their meals were consumed in a quietness born of awkward unfamiliarity—something that made Jamie's heart twist.

When his plate was nearly clean, Andy turned in the rounded booth, his arm stretching across the back. He laughed quietly, a sound of nervous defeat. "I can't tell you how many times I've prayed to see you again. For a chance to talk to you." His thumb brushed over her shoulder. "Now you're here, and I don't know where to begin."

For the first time since they were seated, Jamie's eyes met his. "You pray for me?"

"Every day."

He prayed? The wall around her heart weakened as she stared at this familiar stranger. "What happened to you?"

A half-smile tipped his mouth. "Can I tell you the long version?"

She nodded.

His smile grew. "You were right. I really believed that as long as you stuck by me, I was okay. I couldn't see how hopeless my life really was. When I was released from White Pines, I was so angry that I determined I would quit drinking to prove you wrong. Anger carried me for a month, and then one night I found myself in front of a bar. I couldn't walk away. I just couldn't do it. It was the scariest moment I've ever known in my life." His fist slowly squeezed while his jaw tightened, turning his scar white.

Jamie waited, dread lingering in the background. In her head, there was only one path this story was going to take, and she hated to think about him back in rehab—or worse. "What did you do?"

"I called Ryan."

He did what?

"From that night on for several months, Ryan and Melissa made sure I didn't spend an evening alone." Andy ducked, his complexion coloring. "Their lives completely shifted for me. While my pride balked at it, I finally understood that I needed help—and not just a little.

"One day in September Ryan picked me up at work and said we were going to see a comedian. Next thing I know, we pull into the church parking lot. A comedian at church? So not my thing, right? But I was trapped." Andy chuckled. "Turned out I had some good laughs. I figured it was a night. But then Pastor Bartley called the guy back on stage to 'share his testimony.' I was ready to tune the whole deal out, but his story sounded familiar."

He shook his head. "He'd been an atheistic alcoholic. Arrogant, ignorant, and a total mess. The details of his life were different, but our stories were the same."

Jamie's heart melted.

He cleared his throat. "I finally admitted I'm an alcoholic. All those years, I couldn't believe it was true of me. Alcoholics were poor, uneducated, and unattractive. I wasn't any of those things. Listening to this guy describe how his life fell apart, I could see scenes of my own life. It resonated with me, James. I had nothing. My career had tanked, I was in deep financial trouble, and you were gone. I'd been stripped down to nothing. *Nothing.*"

Jamie felt as if she were there. The emptiness of that moment clawed at her soul. He must have seen it.

Andy reached across the table, taking her hand as though he might stop her from going into that abyss. "But an amazing thing happened. I saw my life for what it really was. For the total failure that it was." He bit his lip, clearing his throat. "Suddenly, the things we were taught as kids—the verses in AWANA and the Romans Road from Sunday school—they filled my mind. I could see the words, hear my ten-year-old voice reciting them. It was as if the barrier had crumbled and I could finally hear, finally see.

"I repented where I sat." Raw emotion interrupted his story, and it took a minute for him to swallow it. He finished with his voice low and wobbly. "Can you imagine, James? Me, a total rebel who had thrown God out of his life, forgiven. Saved."

Jamie's shoulders began to shake. "I can imagine." Tears dripped from her eyelids. "I wish I'd been there."

Tenderness crossed his face as one large hand cradled the back of her head. "James, you did the right thing. I can only imagine how much it hurt to do it, but you were right. Since that night, I've prayed that God would redeem my disaster of a life, and that He would give you comfort where I had left pain." He stopped, framing her face with his free hand. "I'm so sorry. I'm sorry our friendship cost you so much."

Jamie swiped at the current of tears, but they flowed more quickly than she could remove them. Andy pulled her to his shoulder, and she buried her face in the starched cotton, unable to speak.

The world left them alone. Andy got the check and walked her to the car, shielding her from curious stares.

The pale darkness of the summer's night had descended by the time he escorted her to the front door of her former home. She stood in uncertainty, feeling his watchful gaze. It was getting late and she assumed he still had a job, but their conversation didn't feel complete.

Inviting him in, however, was out of the question. Her guard was not completely lost.

"Have you told your family?" she asked.

"Yes." Andy smiled. "Dad and Mom were here when I was baptized."

Wonder lightened her chest. He was really serious. "When?"

"The Sunday after Thanksgiving."

I need to tell you something… Jamie swallowed regret. "Melissa tried to tell me. I wouldn't let her." Her eyes dropped to the handbag she clutched. "I'm sorry, Andy."

She forced eye contact so he'd know her sincerity. He had wanted her there—she could see it. But he wasn't angry. Instead he wrapped both arms around her shoulders.

The movement of the city sounded all around them, part of suburban life that Jamie didn't miss. But it wasn't long before the sound of traffic and the buzz of electrical boxes were lost in the rhythm of his heartbeat.

She could call his embrace home.

For how long? A fearful alarm went off in her head—the same one that had sounded when they'd run into each other two years before. Her spine stiffened.

He responded immediately, taking a half step back, and examined her, his expression gentle. "Goodnight, Jamie." His knuckles trailed down one cheek, and then he stepped away into the falling darkness.

His whisper stayed with her as she readied for bed, the tingle of his touch remaining on her skin. Confusion consumed her as she crawled into bed. What was she to make of it all? What was she supposed to do with him?

Be still, and know that I am God.

Jamie flipped on the light beside the bed and pulled her Bible into her lap. Opening it, she read the entirety of Psalm 46. God was a proven and present help. Whatever happened, He was God. He was her refuge, her security, her deliverance, and her peace.

Two years ago she'd been sure that her reunion with Andy had purpose—that it'd been ordained by God himself. After everything went yucky and hard, she'd stopped believing. But maybe… maybe it had. Maybe God's design looked different than anything she'd imagined. Maybe the cost had just been more than she ever dreamed. Maybe it would still be worth it in the end.

Not maybe. It was. Andy was saved. That alone meant all of eternity.

But there was still life on earth. Where was she supposed to lead her heart?

Chapter Thirty

Andrew pounded his pillow. The compulsion that had landed him in bondage had subsided significantly, but anxiety had always been a trigger. It was what had driven him to the bottle in the beginning.

Alone in the lateness of the night, he replayed the memories of those misdirected steps. He'd been angry at his mother, but more than that, he was scared to death. Nearly sixteen, he was to start his sophomore year at a high school that was triple the size of the entire school district he'd been part of his whole life. And worse, Devon had graduated and would not be with him.

As a kid, Andrew hadn't thought of himself as much, and that was fine. Had anyone asked him his future plans, his answer would have been simple. He would marry Jamie Carson and together they'd figure out life.

Thomas Jefferson High had been a monster that kept him up at night. The first day of school he'd approached the giant of a structure on trembling legs, dizzied by the amount of peers moving in every direction. He hoped desperately that nobody would notice him. Ever.

It didn't work out that way. He was noticed immediately.

Andrew hadn't realized his looks were anything outstanding until that day. The sudden attention was intoxicating, and it made a good cover for the cowering boy inside. When a junior cheerleader invited him to a "gathering" at the end of the week, he had decided that fitting in was a much better plan.

That Friday night was the first time alcohol crossed his lips. It was also the first time his parents were confronted with a drunken child. Nothing was ever the same.

Reflecting on the past, Andrew was startled to discover how quickly he'd been hooked. He became really good at being sneaky, purposefully excelling at school in an effort to cover his tracks. Instead of succumbing to guilt, he became calloused. When his science class offered him an escape from the last ties of accountability, he embraced it readily. Without a God to whom he would answer, every other source of moral reasoning became relative and therefore easily written off.

He did think on Jamie, though. Secretly, he'd hoped she hadn't taken the same path in life. That she wouldn't ever change.

He wasn't the best choice for her. He came with a myriad of regrets, the burden of an ugly past. Things a woman like her should go without. But his repentance had been sincere, and with the encouragement of both Ryan and Melissa, Andrew was willing to come to her, scars and all, to humbly seek her heart.

Therein lay the source of anxiety. If she'd turned aside at the wedding or shut him down earlier in the evening, he would have had a definitive answer. It would hurt, but it would be clear.

But she hadn't turned him away—in fact, he'd witnessed the battle of her heart. The same battle he thought he'd seen in the months before the car wreck. Her heart was leading her places her head couldn't allow.

Fretfulness robbed him of sleep and teased the old self. He needed a distraction. Snapping on the light, Andrew swung his feet to the floor and slid to his knees. His Bible, the Sword of the Spirit, was never far from reach, and he took it in hand.

Not knowing exactly where to go, Andrew flipped to the middle of the Word and found the chapter in Proverbs that would correspond with the date. *June 23.* Half way through, the words drew him in and took him captive.

Who has needless bruises? Who has blood shot eyes? Those who linger over wine, who go to sample bowls of mixed wine. Do not gaze at wine when it is red, when it sparkles in the cup, when it goes down smoothly! In the end it bites like a snake and poisons like a viper. Your eyes will see strange sights and your mind imagine confusing things. You will be like one sleeping on the high seas, lying on top of the rigging. "They hit me," you will say, "but I'm not hurt! They beat me, but I don't feel it! When will I wake up so I can find another drink?

Images Andrew was ashamed to be intimately familiar with took over his sight. He could feel the rolling seas of the inebriated as his mind remembered distinctly the strange imaginings of his many drunken stupors. Though healed and gone, he could readily see bruises, dark and ugly, for which he had no explanation. His skin prickled as though fangs had sunk in, delivering the viper's poison. What kind of life had he indentured himself to? And yet his mantra, unpracticed but still branded, had remained.

When will I wake up so I can find another drink?

"God, don't let it be so!" His voice pierced the dark solitude. "If I am to be bound, let it be to you!"

Andrew slid facedown on the floor. "Jesus, help! Break these chains, I'm begging You. I cannot, but You can."

Over and over his cries filled the still house until promises recently learned began to replace the taunting.

Whoever drinks the water I give will never thirst. Indeed, the water I give them will become in them a spring of water welling up to eternal life.

Life. Real life.

I am the bread of life. He who comes to me will never go hungry, and he who believes in me will never be thirsty.

Wake up and drink. I give you life.

Life. Boundless, unchained, free.

"Lord, if you are willing, you can make me clean."

"I am willing. Be clean!"

Redeemed, eternal life.

I am willing. Be clean!

The battle raged, but for every compulsive demand, His promises struck their defending blows. Though not audibly, Andrew heard the Spirit of God stake His claim.

This one is mine.

When morning broke, Andrew had slept a negligible amount, but he readied for the day in victory. He had found refuge—he had risen to another day of freedom.

***

Jamie stepped through the sliding back door as the phone rang. Out of habit, she stepped to the cordless in the hall before remembering this was not her home. Her eyes dropped to the digital display anyway, and she was startled to see Andy's name.

The jingle sounded two more times before she pushed the on button. "Hello?"

"Hey, James, I was hoping I'd catch you. Were you busy?"

She slid against the wall to the carpet. "Not really. I just got done with a run."

"Yeah? Where did you go?" Andy sounded as if he hadn't a care in the world, and all his time was at her disposal.

"Up to Ulysses Park. I don't run as much as I used to, so that was enough."

"Have you had an injury?"

"No, but trail running up where I live is a little too risky for me. I can't really do my job with a twisted ankle, and the Jeep trail is hardly worth lacing up my tennis shoes."

Andy chuckled, and the tension in Jamie's shoulders began to relax. Without thinking about it, she slid into familiarity with her old friend.

"So why start running now, then?" he asked.

"Bored, I guess. I don't know what to do with myself anymore."

"Bored? I've never known you to be bored."

Jamie pulled herself to her feet and moved to the kitchen for water. "I don't have the summer off anymore, so I don't know what to do with the time."

"I thought you said you were still teaching."

"I am. But it's really different up there."

Their conversation paused.

What was he thinking? Was he scowling or smiling?

"Hey, James." He sounded hesitant. "I really want to hear more about it, but I've got a few things to wrap up here. I was hoping you'd be up for pizza and Xbox Wipeout tonight. Are you game?"

Jamie agreed without a second thought and smiled as she hung up.

She was in the shower when the past collided with the present and fear began to rise. Andy's salvation, his total one-eighty was almost unbelievable. Which was the problem. How could she know if she could trust it? She replayed the phone conversation they'd just had, wondering how he'd managed to disarm her so easily. Pictures of past days when he had exercised his charming manipulation began to flash.

Once again she fortified her wall.

**

Andrew had to make a real effort to focus on his paperwork. He wasn't working on anything overly complicated, but if he misfiled the counterclaim, his case would be tossed on technicalities.

After a second run-through and a few corrections, he secured the documents and left them with the legal assistant. He changed clothes, hopped on his bike—which he kept in a locked maintenance closet—and pedaled the streets of downtown to the bike path.

Clear Creek wasn't exactly secluded. It was a common thoroughfare for two-wheeled commuters, and I-70 paralleled most of its banks. But it was so much less stressful than driving Denver's rush hour, and it afforded Andrew time of uninterrupted reflection.

Jamie easily became priority in his thoughts. She looked so weary. Every time he saw her she looked tired. She needed to laugh. They both did. Tonight would be about fun. A throwback to good times. The plan brought peace as he pedaled steadily along.

When Jamie knocked on his front door, Andrew had showered and was waiting for the pizza to arrive. She forced a nervous smile as he stepped back to let her through, which confirmed the need to simply have fun.

She stopped in his front room, taking in what she'd known as Ryan's home. Her eyes flitted from a small recliner to a midgrade, used sofa and a simple straight-backed chair. Andrew could feel her surprise and guessed her thoughts. "It must be strange."

Her head swiveled back to him, her look telling him she felt caught. He smiled, hoping it would ease her discomfort. She watched his eyes and then looked about the room again, pushing back the hair that had fallen across her face.

"Yeah." Her nose wrinkled. "Everything the past few days has felt strange, though. My old room has Ryan's furniture in it, and wedding gifts are piled all over the front room. It's really weird thinking of him living in what was my home, and I can't seem to wrap my head around this being yours. Melissa told me you'd moved, but I guess I still pictured you in the loft."

His head bobbed. "Life is definitely different."

"I feel like I was in a time warp or something. Like everyone's life moved on and I'm behind."

He was sure she hadn't meant to tug at his heart, but he felt the pull anyway. "Life is different, James." He squeezed her shoulder. "But it hasn't moved on. You've been missed."

Jamie blushed, but they were saved from going deeper by the delivery kid at the door. Andrew returned with a steaming meat lover's pie, and after a prayer, their evening moved forward.

Wipeout turned into tennis and then boxing. They were tied at two KOs when he realized she'd let down her guard. She laughed and shouted without reserve and didn't watch him through anxious eyes.

His reflection cost him. Her avatar threw a jab right between his eyes. The character on the screen went down. Jamie threw her hands up, shouting in victory.

He tamed the urge to laugh and pushed at her shoulder. "I demand a rematch."

"On what grounds?"

"You distracted me."

Jamie's face scrunched.

With a grin, he headed to the kitchen for some water, messing her hair as he passed. She pushed his hand away, flashing a daring look he'd seen when she was a girl—one that had incited several games of chase in the open meadow. Tempted as he was, Andrew made his feet continue to the faucet. Her wall was down, and he was fairly certain she hadn't intended to flirt.

Jamie followed him to find her own glass. Stillness settled as they both regained a normal heart rate until her eyes caught the green digital numbers on the microwave.

"Is it really eleven thirty?"

Andrew glanced behind him. "Yep."

"Goodness, I didn't know it was that late." Jamie reached across him to set her glass in the sink. "I should go."

She was near enough that he could feel the heat rising from her body. Inhaling her scent, a feminine mixture of hair product and sweet sweat, Andrew's fingers curled around the counter top, staying the longing to touch her skin. Her nearness was brief, and she moved toward the door without knowing the difference, but he remained planted.

"I'm sorry it's so late." She grabbed her keys from the table. "I know you have to work in the morning."

"I'll be fine." His heart pounded, and heat washed over him as his vision narrowed on her lips. What would she do if…

She looked at his face, and her eyes became puzzled. "Thanks for the pizza."

Andrew mentally shook himself. She was not ready for that, and he was giving her the wrong impression. He caught up with her as she headed for the front door, smiling so she wouldn't leave upset. "Thanks for letting me win a couple of rounds before you humiliated me."

Her laughter returned.

Relief spiraled through him. "So if I call Melissa's house tomorrow, are you going to answer?"

She studied him, her expression growing serious. Her bottom lip went under her teeth before she pulled her cell from her back pocket. She dialed from memory, and Andrew nearly jumped when across the room his phone began buzzing. She pushed end, and his phone went still.

With eyes that were once again anxious, she held his. "Now you have my number."

Chapter Thirty-One

The week picked up after Monday night. Andy called during his lunch break, and they made plans to ride Dakota Ridge. As Jamie loaded her bike, she felt a good version of anticipation. Hanging out the night before had been fun. He'd been weird for a moment, and she'd wondered why he looked so serious right before she left, but overall they'd had a good time.

He made her laugh. She loved that about him—always had. She could tell him anything. He was her biggest fan. But what she liked most, what she had missed most, was that he made her laugh.

How could it be possible that her darkest moments were with the same man? Ryan had once told her that her friendship with Andy was unique. What exactly were they, though? He had been her buddy last night, and she was comfortable with it. But the night before he had been revealing and tender, like—like something so much more than a buddy.

Involuntarily, she revisited the sensation of his hand cradling her head, pulling her close. His arms wrapped around her, making her feel secure, cherished.

And then alarmed.

Who would he be tonight? If he was more than a friend, would she drink it in, or would she wall up her heart?

***

Andrew spared Jamie the dreaded hill. There was a spot on the trail where the foothills separated narrowly and the city view was spectacular. Without discussion, they dismounted to watch the flickering lights appear as darkness crawled in from the east.

Jamie stared at the panorama below them. "I miss this."

He studied her. "The view?"

"Well, yes, that. I didn't think I'd miss the city, but it really is remarkable." She tossed a rock, keeping her focus on the urban sprawl. "But I miss hanging out with you too."

Andrew swallowed. Oh, how much he missed her. Would it help if she knew? If he told her everything—that he ached to see her, to hear her voice, to be near her. Would it begin to heal the wounds between them?

"You were my best friend, and I hated leaving you." Her wide, green eyes settled on him. "Especially not knowing if I'd ever see you in eternity if you didn't manage to cheat death twice."

Andrew remained still, wondering if this was the door he was waiting for.

It wasn't.

Somehow, he knew it wasn't. Maybe it was the subtle guard she still kept between them, or the fear he could still read in those lovely eyes. Praying for wisdom, he squeezed the shoulder closest to him. "I know, James. I'll be there. By the promise that is in God's Word, I'll be there."

She didn't stiffen at his touch or try to shut away the intense moment, and Andrew was reassured that he was taking the right course. He would be her friend, the one that she depended on, the one she had remembered from her childhood.

The one that she could maybe come to love.

***

Friday night arrived, and Jamie knew it was time to head back to Spring View. She would help with the brunch for the new Mr. and Mrs. Anderson and stay while they opened gifts. But she had a ton of work to do at school with a group of teachers and high school kids coming at the end of the following week.

Ultimately, though, she needed to separate herself from Andy before it became too difficult.

The day had been hot, nearing one hundred, but a cool wind came down off the mountains. It was hardly surprising when billowing clouds of various grays crawled over the peaks, bringing in them a show of lightning. Andy's late nineties Camry pulled alongside the curb about the same time thunder began to roll through the skies.

Jamie had been busy cleaning, getting ready for the arrival of Ryan and Melissa's families. Andy had come to help. When the gathering areas were met with her satisfaction, they washed and chopped fruit, working side by side while rain watered the streets.

When the prep work was completed, Jamie filled two glasses with cold tea, and they made their way to the covered front porch. Using an old towel, she wiped down the hanging porch swing. The air smelled of wet grass, and an occasional rumble coursed through the heavy black sky. Rain sputtered, colliding with the roof and splashing against tiny puddles in the street. They listened to the dialog of nature while swaying to a lazy rhythm.

"Do you leave tomorrow?" Andy asked.

"Yes."

"Will you be glad to go back?"

"Yes." Jamie leaned forward to set her glass on the window sill. "I have a lot of work to catch up on and a group coming in. And to be honest, this isn't home anymore."

The swing stopped.

"Is it home up there?"

No, it wasn't. Spring View was a wonderful place to live and work, but her heart felt like a lonely wanderer—a misfit.

His question hung between them, unanswerable.

She stared at her hands, heat filling her face. "I'll miss you."

Andy turned in the swing, and one long arm draped behind her as his hand went to her neck. She didn't pull away while his fingers moved ever so softly along her hairline. His touch set her skin tingling and her heart pounding.

She could lean into him. He would wrap her in his arms, and it would be home. They could be happy together.

But what if everything fell apart? What if he went backwards? She would be crushed.

"James." His voice was low and tender. "I told you that you were right about almost everything. But you were wrong about what your life said to me."

Her eyes slowly turned to his.

"You lived Christ in front of me every day. I didn't understand, but it was what I loved most about you."

Her eyes widened. Had he just said—again?

"The dance at the wedding… Those words, they were more than just lyrics to a song. I'm not sure how long I've loved you—maybe for forever, but I was incapable of loving you unselfishly."

He paused, and she remained still under his affection. One hand slid against her cheek, and she leaned into his touch.

"I still love you, Jamie. I'm completely unworthy, and I know all of the very genuine reasons you should not love me, but I can't help but ask if I can seek your heart."

Thunder rumbled in the background and the rain began to pour, but Jamie couldn't move. She tucked her bottom lip in her teeth while tears slipped down her cheeks. He wiped at a few and then his hand drifted from her face. Her eyelids slid shut and she leaned her elbows against her knees. Andy's hand followed the curve of her back and rested just below her shoulder blades.

She didn't want to reject him. But she couldn't say yes, either. "I don't know what to say," she whispered, looking sideways. "I don't know what's right."

Andy pulled her close, the touch of his embrace a mix of a faithful friend and loving companion.

"Jamie, I'm always your friend." He spoke against her temple. "If that's what you want from me, if that is all you can accept from me, then that's where we'll stay. I promise. You can answer me honestly. I'm not asking for all or nothing."

Sniffing, she pulled away, shaking her head. "I really don't know, Andy." She needed him as her friend. Wanted him as so much more. But… "I've missed you, but I'm not sure—" Her throat closed, and she couldn't finish.

A small smile smoothed over his lips as he pushed her hair away from her face. "Promise we'll always be friends."

The warmth of his breath skimmed across her skin, and his lips brushed her temple.

Her eyes slid shut. She felt his weight leave the swing.

"Goodnight, Jamie."

She watched his back as he ducked into the rain.

***

The sun showed triumphantly the following morning, its light setting the wet leaves to sparkle as birds chattered away. Jamie lay in bed, propped against the headboard, drowsily watching the outside world come alive.

It was time to go. If, for nothing else, to gain a full night's rest. She didn't need an abundance of sleep, but more than two or three hours a night was generally required.

Andy. He was part of her. He had always been part of her, and he had promised he always would be. But she felt so divided. She had loved being in his arms, and the spot near her right eye still tingled where his lips had touched. But the moment she nearly voiced her heart, a horrible flash from the past blazed through her mind. What would happen to her if Andy slipped back into the grip of alcoholism? Surely she would not survive the heartache.

She could avoid it. She could fight forever and hold Andy at a safe distance. Just in case. He'd said he would accept her choice. But it meant killing something in her that she'd not yet managed to destroy, something she wasn't sure she wanted to destroy.

Jamie agonized over the consequences of either direction.

Be still.

If only she could make her whirling mind obey. It wouldn't. Oh well, time to get up anyway. She had work to do.

Andy showed up just after seven thirty. Ryan and Melissa arrived a few minutes after eight, and the four friends gathered on the deck with a fresh brew. The Andersons' families began to arrive around nine and cinnamon rolls, egg dishes, and fruit were put out buffet style.

Jamie was content to serve the crowd, making sure that the juice pitchers remained full, and the coffee pot didn't go empty. Andy worked alongside her, his countenance relaxed. She felt his presence, but oddly, it was comforting. Especially with Nate in company.

The gifts were opened and the mass of wrapping paper and gift bags taken care of by early afternoon. While others cleaned the kitchen, Jamie told Ryan and Melissa goodbye, promising to be their guest often. Then she shouldered her single bag and slipped quietly out the door.

***

It was time. Jamie was leaving.

Andrew had laid out all his cards. His heart had pounded recklessly the night before, knowing she had every rational reason to reject him, but he'd determined not to let her leave without having said what he felt.

She hadn't rejected him, though. She didn't give him an answer at all. That was okay—if she needed time, he could give her time. But he didn't know where to go from there. She didn't live in another state, which made things less complicated, but she wasn't the girl next door anymore, either. Pursuing her was so much easier when she'd lived nearby.

Andrew waited on the front porch while Jamie said her goodbyes. He would have to push her a little to know what to do next. That felt almost as intimidating as his confession had been the night before. She might tell him she just couldn't do it. She might end all hope.

But she didn't act like that was her conviction. Actually, she'd been subtly seeking him out. He'd found significant pleasure when she began drifting toward him during the late morning. He knew her behavior had more to do with Nate's hovering than anything else, but he was glad to be her shelter, in whatever measure. Glad that she still turned to him.

Perhaps that meant she would not turn him away.

Jamie came out of the house, and before she hit the first step Andrew matched her stride, relieving her of the bag she carried. In silence, they walked to her car. He had her luggage in the trunk and her driver's door open before he stretched a single arm across her shoulders. It took a moment, but she leaned his way, and he used his free hand to cradle her head against him.

The moment had come. How would she answer this wordless question?

Timidly she slid her hands to his shoulders. And stayed put.

Unconsciously, the muscles in his arms flexed, pulling her closer.

Her spine went rigid.

His heart begged her not to run away as he softened his hold. If nothing else, he wanted her to know that she was precious to his heart. Not a conquest to be won, not a regret to put down, but a woman greatly valued.

Loved.

"Will I see you again, Jamie Carson?" he asked, still cradling her close.

She pulled back only enough to examine his face, which gave him opportunity to study hers. Indecision. Yearning and fear.

"Yes."

Andrew's mouth turned up as warmth rushed through his limbs. She looked alarmed when his eyes dropped to her lips. That was the last thing he wanted her to feel. He tucked her hair behind her ear and drew her head back to his chest. "Next weekend?"

"I have a group coming up on Friday. They'll be there until Saturday afternoon."

Andrew stepped back, realizing he still knew next to nothing about her job. "You mentioned that. What kind of group?"

"Teachers and high school students. They'll come up with the sixth graders later during the school year. I have to train them."

"So you don't have a full-time staff?"

"Just the directors and me."

Chancing contact, he reached for her hands. "What if I came up Saturday? Would I be in the way?"

Jamie hesitated, staring at her feet. "That would be nice." A soft pink crept up her face. Looking uncertain again, she stepped away and slid into her car.

"Do me a favor, James?" He bent to see her face, waiting until she looked at him. "Call me when you get up there?"

She managed a small smile. "Okay."

Andrew let that be enough.

Chapter Thirty-Two

"When will your friend be up, Jamie?" Ellie asked.

Jamie's shoulders tightened, and her skin grew warm. Hoping her fluster didn't show, she slid the tray of dishes across the stainless steel counter.

Creighton caught it and pushed it into the industrial washer.

"He was going to leave after work, around five I think. But he works downtown, so it could be a while." She swallowed, loading another tray. "Are you sure this is okay?"

"Of course." Creighton chuckled, sounding fatherly. "You're not in a prison camp here."

Jamie did her best to ignore the heat on her ears. The final tray of dishes came out steaming hot, and they shelved the last of the glasses before she headed to the lodge. She had about fifteen minutes before the evening session, and she needed the time to gather her thoughts.

What am I doing?

She'd called Andy as he'd requested that Saturday night. He'd managed to coax a laugh or two from her, but she went to bed with a headache and an anxious heart. She was not at all sure about the impression she'd left him that day.

She'd expected Andy to call Sunday and discovered acute disappointment when he didn't. When his number flashed on her phone Monday night, her heart squeezed with an unfamiliar pleasure, and she'd surprised herself by suggesting he come up Friday night. Andy had agreed immediately, and now the time was nearly upon her.

The tension between anticipation and doubt tugged at Jamie. Andy would be pulling into camp any minute, and somehow she needed to behave normally.

She felt anything but normal.

***

Traffic had been horrible. What should have been a forty-five minute drive proved to be an hour and a half. Andrew was more than ready to be done when he parked next to a school bus on the dirt-packed lot.

Walking up the steep hill, Andrew took in the cluster of cabins and two long buildings nestled on top of the incline. Each of the twelve small shelters was tucked into the native trees, making them seem random and autonomous. Perched near the edge of the overlook, both of the larger buildings were long and narrow. Together they formed a broken *L* that hemmed in the grouping.

Andrew inhaled the piney mountain air as he scaled the rocky Jeep path. A shorter man with a head of thick, pure-white hair appeared from the long building. With a welcoming smile, the man approached him, offering a friendly hand as they met near the flagpole. "You are Andy, I suspect."

"I am." Andrew smiled as he gripped the older man's hand.

"I'm Creighton Nelson, camp director."

Andrew nodded. "Jamie's boss. It's good to meet you."

"Jamie's teaching the last session in the lodge." Creighton motioned to the building on Andrew's right. "She should be done in about forty minutes. I can show you where you'll be staying, if you'd like, and then we can sneak in."

"Very good." He adjusted the hiking pack he'd slung over his shoulder.

"We enjoy having Jamie up here." Creighton led Andy across the fifty yards of dirt to the building. "She has the perfect blend of science and instruction for what we want to accomplish. Her love for the outdoors and for kids are real assets for us."

"I could see that. Jamie has a passion for all of creation."

Creighton looked surprised. "Have you known her a long time?"

"All my life." Andrew smiled, knowing the man had assumed they'd only recently met. "She was the girl next door."

Creighton held the door open, a puzzled expression on his face. "Your room is down the hall, second door on the left. The bathroom is shared. There are five teachers up here right now, and they are all rooming in this building, so you might plan accordingly." Creighton pointed to the door directly in front of them. "This is the staff lounge. It's stocked with coffee and muffins. Feel free to help yourself anytime. The door to the left leads directly into the kitchen, which is where I'll be."

"Can I help?"

Surprise again. "We're just cleaning up. It shouldn't take us but another ten minutes."

"Perfect." Andrew nodded. "I'll just throw my bag in the room and join you."

Creighton's silent inspection hinted approval. They parted briefly, but within three minutes Andrew found his way into the kitchen where he was introduced to Ellie Nelson.

They had very little left to do. Ellie offered Andrew coffee, and they covered the surface stuff of "Where are you from? " and "What do you do?" before Creighton suggested they head to the lodge. Coffee cups were drained quickly, and both Ellie and Creighton accompanied Andrew as they slipped in the back for the last of Jamie's presentation. Although she noticed their arrival, she remained focused as she finished the class.

She invited questions before dismissing the group. A small collection of adolescent girls circled her briefly, followed by three of the five teachers. Jamie conversed with all of them, looking completely at ease.

Andrew watched, resting against the back wall. Beside him, Creighton leaned toward him.

Andrew bent down to hear.

"It's always the same, and she never notices." His whisper held a conspirator's tone.

"That they're men?"

Creighton nodded, his eyes still on Jamie. "At first I thought she was just extremely professional, but as Ellie recently pointed out, she honestly doesn't know."

Remembering when she'd first met Ryan, Andrew laughed under his breath. A guy couldn't be understated with Jamie. They'd need an I-like-you sign to get anywhere with her. Good thing, for him. By all appearances, she had plenty of fans.

"She wouldn't notice. Growing up, it was Jamie and the four of us boys. She's always figured she was one of the guys."

The corners of Creighton's mouth lifted, and Andrew felt again that he'd gained approval.

Jamie chose that moment to glance his way, and he took the look as an invitation. The group parted as he stepped to her side, and she introduced him to the three Mr. Somebodies gathered round. The circle seemed to loosen, and although the others didn't retreat entirely, Andrew didn't miss the mild disappointment passing over them.

Jamie was oblivious.

Night fell fast in the hills, and the shadows melted into darkness. People left in groups as Jamie tidied the lodge. Andrew snagged a few gum wrappers, meeting her at the back door.

"I was hoping I'd have time to show you around." Jamie flipped off the lights. Once the doors were secured, they fell into step, strolling down the dirt path.

"Creighton showed me where I'm staying. The rest will keep for another day, right?"

Jamie smiled. She shifted their path toward a large gazebo at the west end of camp.

He glanced around as she settled on the top of the two steps. "This is some office, James."

"It is. I'm a pretty lucky girl."

He smiled, holding her eyes.

She studied him, and he absorbed the warmth of her gaze.

But when it stopped on the line running down his nose, she froze. The tenderness faded, and her attention fell to her hands.

Was it hideous to her?

He didn't love it. His scar was the first thing he saw every time he looked in the mirror, a daily reminder of the disaster his life had become. But he could live with it.

Did it repulse her?

"Tell me about tomorrow." He sat, stretching his legs beyond the two steps. He needed to keep her talking, to draw her back out. "What are the two hikes?"

"I'll lead one group on our new hydro-ecology trail, and Creighton will take the other group on the forest-ecology trail. They each last a couple of hours. We'll meet back at the lodge and then switch groups after a snack. When we're done with the second round, we'll meet down by the ponds for a sack lunch and then we'll be done. The group will pack up and head down the mountain."

He listened, nodding occasionally. "Will you switch trails, or will you teach the same one twice?"

"I'll teach the same one twice. I put the trail together, and I don't have the post markers up yet, so it makes more sense for me to take it."

"Do I get to come?"

Jamie gave a small laugh. "Of course."

"Would you mind if I do both?"

"Not at all."

Silence settled in the soft blackness. Tall lodgepole pines rustled against a breeze. Below, the water rippled and splashed as the brook trout nipped at the evening insects.

Was she enjoying the moment, or did she feel trapped?

Once upon a time he'd known what she was thinking. Now he felt like he was blindly grasping at a heart she'd determined to tuck away.

"What time do you get up to put breakfast out?" Andrew hoped he didn't sound dejected. It wasn't her fault.

"We get going about six thirty."

He nodded, pushing himself up. Reaching a hand down to Jamie, he pulled her to her feet, and as they began walking in the direction of the camp, her hand stayed in his. A thrill of pleasure shot from his fingertips to his shoulder, and a slender cord of confidence lifted his spirits.

"This is me." Jamie stopped in front of a cabin tucked behind a stand of trees. It sat apart from the others, unnoticeable from the center of camp. Andrew inspected it. It was small. Very small. Room for one tiny bedroom, a half bath and a scrunched up front room/kitchen combo.

"I'm sorry there's nothing much by way of entertainment here." She interrupted his inspection. "I hope you're not bored."

She'd misunderstood his silence. He ran his thumb over her knuckles, wanting her to feel his heart. "I came to see you."

A shy smile tipped her mouth, and he released her hand to run a single knuckle down the side of her face. She held his gaze, her expression soft, innocent, and captivating. His fingers fanned against her cheek as his heart kicked against his ribs.

Her eyes dropped. Taking a half step back, she moved from his touch.

Time. She needed time.

He needed patience.

***

Jamie stepped through the dining room door, heading straight for the large coffee dispenser. It would be a three-cup morning, at least.

She had stood out in the night long after Andy disappeared behind the evergreens, still warm from his touch. When she'd finally forced herself to bed, she'd fidgeted in the darkness, arguing with herself for hours.

He was going to kiss her. She'd seen it coming, and she'd retreated. Then when he hadn't kissed her, she'd found herself more disappointed than relieved.

What am I doing?

She honestly didn't know. The possibility of great pain lay on either path. Which direction was worth the risk? As soon as her mind settled one way, her heart insisted on the other.

But a new day was at hand, and she had a job to do.

She took the first sip as she stepped through the kitchen and stopped, literally looking into her mug. "Ellie, this is *good* coffee."

"It is," Ellie agreed with a smile. "*And* I didn't have to make it."

"You didn't?"

"Nope. It was brewed and simmerin' when I came in. He used that fancy stuff too. A whole bag, at least."

"He?"

The woman nodded and winked.

Jamie did an about-face, walking back to the coffee server. There in the trash lay a large bag of her favorite blend, completely empty. Jamie inhaled the aroma. Oh so good.

She moved to the back of the dining hall where a screen door led to the back observation deck. There, in jeans and his old, red Stanford sweatshirt, Andy sat on a bench reading.

Jamie stepped onto the deck. "Good coffee."

He looked up with a smile. "It is."

She gave him a knowing look, but he said nothing. She reached his place, dropping beside him. A morning choir of birds called through the evergreens as Jamie took in the overlook. Pines sloped down, transitioning to aspens and then an open glen. She didn't spend enough time here.

Andy stayed quiet, and she glanced back at him. His eyes had returned to the page.

"What are you reading?"

He shifted his Bible so she could see. "I'm in Matthew right now."

"Are you in a group study or reading through on your own?"

"A little of both," he answered. "I've been meeting with Pastor Bartley. I didn't know where to begin, so he suggested I start with the gospels. We've gone through John and Luke, and now I'm in Matthew."

Who'd have dreamed it? "Is that the Bible you earned in AWANA?"

He chuckled. "It is. Unbelievable, right?"

She nodded.

"Whenever I moved, I threw it in a box of stuff to get rid of, but every time, it managed to move with me. I just couldn't do it."

A soft smile lit her eyes as she marveled over it. God was irrepressible.

"Do you still have yours?"

Her head dipped again. "It's on a shelf. The pages are falling out and the front cover came off."

Andy chuckled. "That doesn't surprise me."

Jamie reached to turn the pages of his Bible. On the first leaf under the cover, *Andy Harris* was sprawled out in a ten-year-old's hand. Jamie ran a finger over the ink, then searched those amber eyes. "That's amazing," she whispered.

His hand covered hers and squeezed. They remained still for several breaths before he shifted to close his Bible. Jamie wondered if he would pull her close. She would lean into him, if he did. She could love this man.

"Is that Ellie working by herself?" he asked.

Mildly disappointed, she shifted away. But his restraint bumped up the level of respect she'd held him in. Had that been intentional? "She is. I'd better get to it."

He held her eyes for a breath. Maybe he could read her. He knew her better than anyone. Maybe he knew she longed to be loved by a godly man. Maybe he knew, and he was playing her.

But what if he wasn't? What if this Saul-turned-Paul conversion was genuine?

How could she know for sure?

***

The morning passed quickly. Andrew stayed with Jamie's group, though near the back, as she led them to a small cascade about a mile from the pond. The hike was different from any he'd ever done with her. They stopped often, and Jamie explained different aspects of the ecosystem. Andrew wondered if she'd always seen the complexity of the interconnected systems, if that was one of the reasons she loved hiking. He'd never paid attention before.

Two hours passed before they met up with the other group. Andrew stayed in the background, watching while Jamie interacted with her class. Seeing her teach was fascinating. It was like seeing the best of her blend together and pour out right in front of him. She was gifted in it, and doing her job was clearly a joy.

Andrew grinned. This life was so Jamie, and he was glad God had put her there.

Creighton caught him smiling. "She's a gem."

Heat brushed his ears, but Andrew chuckled. "That she is. I've never seen her teach."

"She's a rare one." Creighton let his pack drop to his feet. "She hasn't been pushed into cynicism. She puts so much devotion and energy into what she's doing here, believing that it matters, that her work makes a difference. We don't always see that in a seasoned teacher."

Andrew could appreciate that. "She's definitely the kind who pours herself out for others."

"That," Creighton nodded firmly, "is very true. I am thankful she was sent our way. To be honest, I was amazed her application even made it to my desk."

Andrew's brow furrowed. "Why is that?"

"She taught at Applewood Academy. Those applicants are usually weeded out before I get a look."

"Why?"

Creighton raised his eyebrows.

Suddenly Andrew understood. "Because it's assumed she promotes intelligent design?"

The older man's lips pressed together, and his eyes confirmed Andrew's guess.

"Surely that can't be legal. Isn't the district an equal opportunity employer?"

"The field of science education can be a pretty explosive firestorm. Discrimination can be justified by labeling Darwin opposition as unqualified, regardless of credentials. The screening panel is pretty vigilant, but Jamie slipped through the cracks — which, to be blunt, was the hand of God."

Andrew chewed on the information.

"She's a blessing to both Ellie and me," Creighton continued. "We love watching her highlight the intricacies of life as if she were silently pointing to the work of a master craftsman."

"Does it ever come up?"

"What's that?"

He glanced over to Creighton, catching his bewilderment. "Evolution. Does it come up?"

"Every now and then."

Andrew swallowed, remembering their first argument. Jamie wouldn't back down from him. He was fairly certain she wouldn't back down from anyone. "What happens?"

Creighton shrugged, mostly unconcerned. "She acknowledges the theory, but she also suggests questions that may indicate problems with it. Ultimately, Jamie tells her students to study carefully, diligently, and let the evidence guide their decisions."

Andrew could imagine how well that could be received. "Could she lose her job?"

Creighton eyed him. "Thus far it hasn't been a problem."

Jamie slipped beside Andrew, and the conversation dropped. They talked with Creighton for the last few minutes of the break and then hit the trails again. Andrew switched hikes, tagging along with Creighton this round.

Not knowing anyone provided him a solace in which to think.

And to worry.

He'd been one of them. If he hadn't known Jamie personally, he would have written her off as a brainwashed religious freak who practiced bad science. He would have said she didn't deserve the job. Her education, ability to teach, inquisitive mind, and careful study wouldn't have mattered. She would have simply been disqualified because of what she believed.

Andrew suddenly saw the injustice, and it made his blood run hot. He stayed to himself, lost in the whirlwind of emotion and thought while they finished the hike. What would he do if someone cornered her the way he had that day in Waterton? She'd stand her ground and probably lose her job—and part of herself. Even the thought of it tore his heart.

Lunch was served after the second hike, and not long after, the buses were loaded and rumbling down the dirt road. Creighton and Ellie disappeared, leaving Andrew and Jamie alone beside the pond.

Andrew took in the baby-blue Colorado sky reflecting off the water. The pond slapped against the wood of the dock while the serenity of the hills seeped through him. He remembered reading *The Secret Garden* as a kid. Colin and Mary believed in the healing power of the garden—they called it magic. Had they known to whom the magic of nature belonged?

Not magic. Miracles.

His gaze moved from the water to Jamie. She'd asked for miracles. He knew she did. Even after she'd left him, he was positive she'd begged God on his behalf.

And now here he was. A miracle.

But she didn't know if she could trust it.

Jamie's attention had been on the peaks, and several heartbeats passed before she realized his gaze had locked on her. Heat crawled over her neck. "I need to place those markers on the new trail." She tucked her hair behind one ear. Her eyes wandered down the Jeep path and up the evergreen rise before finally coming back to him. "Do you want to help me?"

He smiled, hoping she would relax.

She chewed on her lip.

"Tell me what to do, Teach."

Finally, a grin. She explained the project and within thirty minutes they were both loaded down with engraved plates, short wood posts, and tools. They spent the remainder of the afternoon in real work, but Jamie became Jamie again.

After he'd pounded the last of the posts into the stubborn earth, Andrew sank onto the ground, leaning back on his hands. "You didn't bring your camera."

Jamie shrugged as she straightened the information plate. "We have other things to do."

Andrew pushed his lips together, watching her avert her face. He'd touched something she'd wanted left alone. But it had been her dream.

Maybe now was not the time to dive into that one. "It's just weird seeing you on a trail without it."

She rewarded his lightness with a half smile. He'd bring it up again some other time.

It was after five by the time he had his pack restuffed. He made a point to say goodbye to the Nelsons before Jamie walked him to the parking area. He tossed his backpack into the backseat of his car, and then the pair stood in mild unease.

"Do you have a church up here, James?"

"I do."

He tried not to be disappointed. "I don't suppose I can get you to go with me in town?"

"Sometime." She kept her face pointed toward their feet.

Andrew shuffled in the dirt, putting a hand to her shoulder.

Jamie hesitated, then stepped into his embrace.

"Next weekend?" he whispered against her hair.

"I have another group, but you could come up again."

"I was hoping."

She stayed silent and still, and he was content to hold her for as long as she was willing.

Chapter Thirty-Three

Jamie's heart was still warm as she crawled into bed. She relished the sensation of Andy's arms surrounding her, of his breath brushing her neck. She'd stepped away before she really wanted to. His loving smile made her heart flop, and she'd been tempted to pull him close again. When he ducked into the Camry and pulled away, she wished she'd done exactly that.

Perhaps their relationship wouldn't be complicated after all. Maybe she could simply step beyond the hurtful memories and fully embrace the man he'd become. She drifted to sleep, hope burgeoning in her heart.

A cry woke her.

There was not a single hint of light as she lay trembling in the darkness. Swiping at her wet face, she sat up suddenly, sobbing and trying frantically to gain her bearings. With shaking hands she fumbled around with the bedding before she finally gained enough sense to reach for the bedside lamp.

The images in her head didn't match the reality of her room. She was alone. Safe. Her mind had taken her to an unfamiliar place—a bar perhaps, but the scene that had unfolded was too familiar. She hated that it replayed over and over. The hand that gripped her arm was unyielding. Acrid breath had heated her face. And his frame pushed against hers in a way that had terrified.

The face of her friend turned into the cruel image of the one who held her heart captive in fear.

Her pulse throbbed wildly as she drew her knees to her chest. She glanced at the red numbers on her clock. Only two in the morning. Clutching her comforter, she shivered against the chill that came from inside.

"It was a dream," she whispered to the quiet room. "It wasn't him. He didn't have a scar. It's not him anymore."

A fresh crop of shivers rippled through her body as she continued to repeat reality to herself. While the words were true, they did little to remove the chains that held her tight. It had been simplistic to think the past would slide away. Nothing between them would be uncomplicated.

***

Andrew called Jamie on the way home from church, anxious to talk to her. Concentrating during the service that morning had proved next to impossible, and he'd mentally wandered away long before the benediction. He couldn't help but ponder the possibilities of a life with Jamie and hope that they would be reality someday.

Thinking on that future, he began to compare his vision now to what it had been. He had lived unashamedly with the sole intent of self-gratification. Had even been so bold as to tell Jamie that very fact without a trace of guilt.

He often heard those words ringing in his ears. How many things replayed in Jamie's mind? She'd been subjected to the worst that was in him. It was not pessimism to say that a future with her would take a miracle. Not that he didn't believe it couldn't happen, but there were wounds they would struggle with—wounds she would struggle with, and the greater of that would be on her.

"Hello?" Her voice sounded hushed, strained, and he was set on alert.

"Hey, James. Are you done with church?"

"Yes." Something in her husky tone seemed off. "I only went to the service and didn't stay for class."

"Do you usually stay?"

"I have before."

Why was she being vague? His brows pinched. "Are you okay?"

"Yeah." She answered too quickly. "I'm fine."

"James?"

He didn't miss her small sigh and imagined her eyes dropping to the ground. Something was wrong.

"I'm just tired." Her voice didn't invite further inquiry. "I didn't sleep well last night."

Another space hung between them. He wished she was with him, that he could see her eyes. In fact, he considered setting his car westward rather than driving home. "Was something bothering you?"

"I'm fine, Andy." Now she was almost snappy. "Please don't worry about it."

He swallowed, on the verge of telling her he was coming up.

"How was church?" she asked.

Andrew told her about the new series they were beginning. Her interested response eased his fears, and he began to relax. He was home and had a sandwich made before they wrapped up the call, and it wasn't until then that he brought it up again.

"Are you sure you're okay, James?"

"I'm okay. Maybe I'll squeeze in a nap this afternoon, and I'll be back to normal."

He hoped she was being honest. "I'll call you later then."

Andrew spent a very long time in prayer before he finally got to his sandwich.

***

Jamie slept for two hours after lunch but still didn't feel rested. She had some paperwork to set straight and some laundry to work on, but her mind and body dragged about the rest of the afternoon, and she accomplished very little.

Talking to Andy had helped. His voice was kind, honestly concerned. It wasn't at all the slurred and menacing voice that haunted her dreams. In fact, what she'd heard and seen during that nightmare was distorted. Her dreams were much worse than what had really happened.

She considered telling him. It was obvious she couldn't hide her distress, even over the phone, and it could be that finally talking about it would bring resolution. But bringing it up again seemed mean. He'd been drunk, and he'd apologized. More than that, she knew he felt terrible about it. She also thought she'd forgiven him. Why did it still torment her?

The week passed slowly. Her Sunday afternoon nap turned out to be the only real rest Jamie was able to find. Each time she talked to Andy, which was every evening, she felt calmed. But every night her sleep was disturbed by exaggerated and frightening intrusions from the past.

By Friday Jamie was exhausted and frustrated. Added to her lack of sleep, or perhaps as a consequence, she felt a stinging in the back of her throat, and her head throbbed straight out of bed. She probably should call Andy and tell him not to come. Probably.

***

Andrew arrived a few minutes after six and found the Nelsons halfway through the kitchen cleanup routine. The week had crawled by, and he could sense in every conversation that Jamie was not quite right. To finally be where she was brought a feeling of relief, so his smile was genuine when he greeted Jamie's boss. "How's the week been?" he asked.

"Busy." Creighton put the last of the clean glasses on a long, open shelf. "We have one more left before the school year begins, and we're all trying to get the paperwork and schedules in order before the board meets on Thursday."

Ah. The inescapable drudgery of paperwork. "Is there anything special you have to prepare?" Andrew worked on the stack of steaming plates, fresh from the industrial washer, while they talked.

"Summer reports, as well as the schedule for each school and any revisions we have for the lab's policies and procedures. Everything has to be approved by the board before the school year begins."

"So that's why Jamie's been so distracted." He wiped his damp hands on a towel.

Ellie gave him a sideways glance."I don't think she's felt well." She poured a fresh mug of coffee and passed it to him. "She's been dragging all week. She's so hoarse tonight that she opted to use the mic. Creighton offered to cover her class, but she insisted she could do it."

Andrew's brows puckered. She'd said she hadn't slept well, but beyond that Jamie hadn't complained. The group finished the morning's preparations and headed over to the meeting lodge. It felt like a more comfortable rerun from the week before, and Andrew found a great measure of comfort when Jamie directed a smile his way. She did look pale, though, and her voice sounded horrible.

After her presentation, Creighton suggested a bonfire at the gazebo, and the group was eager to join him. Jamie and Andrew stayed behind in the deserted lodge. They remained near the stage, and she actually slipped her hand into his after the door closed.

"Long week?" He pulled her close.

She sighed, resting against his shoulder.

"Jamie, you're warm." He leaned a cheek against her forehead, alarmed by the heat. "You have a fever."

"I know." She didn't move. "It's just a cold. I'll be fine."

Her stillness set off another wave of alarms. Andrew ran his free hand over her shoulder as he considered what to do. He'd ached to see her all week. She hadn't said anything about feeling poorly. Even if she had, he'd have made the trip, if only to hold her hand while she rested. But he didn't want her to feel obligated to entertain him.

"You should go to bed." He fingered her soft hair, tucking it behind her ear. "Do you *have* to work in the morning?"

"Yes." Her raspy voice cracked. "No one but Creighton and I know both trails." She swallowed, her face reflecting pain. "What if we just go watch a movie? Would that be okay?"

Andrew chuckled. "Yes, that would be okay."

The inside of Jamie's home was as simple as the outside, but it was comfortable. Andrew noted that only two of her photographs hung on the walls. One of an aspen grove that stood behind their childhood homes, brilliantly lit up in the oranges and yellows of fall. The other a distant shot of her father, standing on the ridge line near the summit of a peak. Her dad and the mountains. The two things that had remained consistent in her life.

Pain squeezed in his chest.

The television in the corner of her small front room was archaic, but it probably wasn't put to much use. Aluminum rabbit ears stuck out from the top and a dial knob protruded right above the power button. He smiled at the late eighties set up, wondering how she'd managed to hook a DVD player up to the relic.

"It's not much." Jamie watched his inspection. "I'm not in here very often."

"It's perfect for you, James."

She smiled, and his heart flipped.

"What shall we watch?"

Andrew slid a hand to her face. Her eyes looked dull with pain, and he could feel her pulse pounding at her temples. She'd be out in five minutes. He should probably go. "Are you sure you're up for this? I can go to the bonfire and be perfectly fine if you just want to go to bed."

She kept his gaze for a moment, then leaned against his shoulder. There it was again—that cautious withdrawal that he'd sensed all week. There was something she wasn't saying.

"I'll fall asleep," she croaked, "but if you don't mind, and if you promise to wake me when it's over so I can go to bed, I'd rather spend the time with you."

"I promise."

Jamie leaned into his arms, and heat from her feverish body radiated through him. He should order her to bed. But she seemed to need him there. Not just want, which was thrilling, but need.

***

Saturday morning began slowly. Jamie had hoped she would sleep off whatever had her feeling yucky, but she woke up achy and still quite hot. But she'd slept. Deep, undisturbed, peaceful sleep. That alone provided enough relief to make it through the day.

Andy had made coffee, the expensive kind, and she found him reading on the back deck before the campers were about.

"Hey, sleepy girl."

"Good morning." She still sounded horrible. Getting through the day might be a stretch.

"Not any better, huh?"

"A bit, actually." She smiled as she dropped into the spot next to him.

His hand covered her forehead. "You still have a fever."

"I know." The fever, really, was the least of her concerns. "I slept well, though, and I only need to make it until noon."

Andy's mouth pressed into a line. Clearly he wasn't thrilled, but she ignored it. She was, after all, a big girl, and had been taking care of herself for a long time. Time to talk about something other than her. "Did you sleep well?"

"I did." He leaned back and quit inspecting her like she was a lab specimen. "Creighton and Ellie were still up, and we visited while the fire died. I went to bed around ten or so."

"Really? What'd you talk about?"

"I have a new client." Lines appeared on his forehead as his tone became more serious. "I can't give you details, but she's a would-be teacher, except her cooperating school wouldn't sign off on her student teaching, so the university wouldn't award her a degree."

Weird. Didn't he specialize in criminal law? "Was there a legitimate reason?"

"That depends on your perspective."

"What does that mean?"

"It depends on if you view evolution as science or philosophy."

Jamie gulped, and her heart stopped. What was he doing? Jumping into the ID/evolution debate? He had no idea how hot those fires burned. "Andy, did you seek this woman out?"

"Not at all." He faced her. "Believe me, I was a little freaked by the coincidence too. Turns out, though, that she was referred to me by someone who knows us both."

"Who?"

"Pastor Bartley."

He paused and then squeezed her shoulder. "I wanted to know the Nelsons' story—how they landed this position with the district while believing as they do."

"Was it helpful?"

Andy shrugged, and Jamie could see a hint of discouragement. "A little."

Anxiety began to swirl inside as she watched him. "I thought you were a trial lawyer—like criminal cases."

"I am." He shoved his hand through his hair, a sure sign that he wasn't comfortable. "But this girl came to my office last week, not knowing where else to go. I couldn't turn her out."

Jamie scowled. He shouldn't be in the middle of a case like this. It wasn't good for him, or for whoever this new client was. "This is a blow-out kind of deal, Andy. This war has been raging a long time, and it's pretty dicey."

"I know, Jamie." His tone edged toward the lawyer kind—the one that said, *Don't argue with me.*

Her stomach tied itself into a mess.

Voices floated from inside the cafeteria, a reminder that she was supposed to be working. She held Andy's eyes before she stood. "I need to get busy."

He nodded and followed her, still carrying his Bible. They made it to the door, but he stopped her hand as she reached for the handle. "James, I don't want you worrying about it."

Not worry about it? Sure. It wasn't anything big. Just that every other related case she'd heard of ended badly. Not just in the *good try, better luck next time* kind of way. Careers could be destroyed, lives changed. The Andy she knew didn't take that kind of a thing in stride.

"I mean it." He tipped her chin so she'd look at him. "You're not feeling well, and you have a job to do. I shouldn't have told you this morning. I'm sorry. I should have known it would upset you. Just don't stew about it, okay?"

Right. Like that was even possible. Looks like she had another long, sleepless week ahead of her.

**

Andrew walked beside Jamie as they moved toward her cabin, growing more concerned as he listened to her wheeze. She'd made it through her day, but she looked worse with each passing hour. She was not getting better.

Once she had the door opened he guided her to her small sofa and gently pushed her to it. "Do you have anything for the flu?"

"No, just Advil."

It didn't take much searching for him to locate the pain killer. With a glass of orange juice and a cool cloth, he lowered himself beside her. "I don't remember the last time I saw you sick."

Jamie leaned against his shoulder, looking perfectly miserable. Her skin felt terribly hot through his wicking shirt, but her limbs seemed to tremble. He pulled the crocheted afghan off the back of the sofa, settling it over her frame and shifting her lightly so she could snuggle against him.

Within minutes she was out.

Jamie had the full-blown flu, the kind that landed people in the hospital. She was miserable the rest of Saturday, so Andrew stayed through Sunday.

He wanted her to see a doctor. She wouldn't, mostly because she could hardly stand, let alone endure a drive down the mountain. It frustrated him because he couldn't fix it, and he couldn't be around to make sure she was okay. Not to mention the tension he'd caused by bringing up his new client.

Of all weeks, this would come up—when he really couldn't stay. He had a meeting early Monday morning.

Chapter Thirty-Four

Anthony Locke met Andrew before he entered the conference room Monday morning, concern shadowing his eyes. "We need to talk."

Andrew scowled—which he shouldn't do, considering this man was the reason he was able to still practice law. "What about?"

"Gary Matthison saw Lacey Stewart leaving your office Friday morning. He's concerned. That's what this meeting is about."

"I assumed I was free to choose my own clients." How did anyone know who Lacey was, anyway? "My probation has been lifted, has it not?"

"This has nothing to do with that, but on a personal note, I'm very pleased with the progress you've made."

Locke's genuine appreciation unfurled some of Andrew's irritation, and he lowered his head. "I'm sorry you were ever put in that position to begin with. Thank you for taking a risk on me."

"You're a good lawyer—and under all the mess, a good man. But this deal with Ms. Stewart is a ticking bomb. As your senior adviser, I'm suggesting you let this case go."

"How do you know anything about it?"

Locke frowned, looking almost guilty. "I didn't, but Matthison keeps a broad circle. The bottom line is that you're working against precedent. There is nothing in any state that would give you a backbone for her suit."

"She hasn't filed a lawsuit. She's appealing to the board of governors."

"Matthison seems to know how that one's going to go down." Locke's shoulders dropped. "When she's denied, what are you going to do?"

Andrew rubbed his bottom lip. How could Matthison know this? It teetered on a breech, but saying something would certainly get him fired.

What was he doing in the middle of this case? He practiced criminal law. All he'd intended to do was point Lacey in the right direction. He understood legal protocol and procedure, but he didn't have any experience in this kind of case.

So what would he do? The Nelsons had asked him that very question Saturday night. He'd opened up a little more to them to gain their perspective, sharing details he knew would be safe.

"Chances are pretty high that she'll be denied again," Creighton had said. "What will you say to her then?"

"She's young, barely married, and her husband's still in school." Andrew had gone over all the what-ifs in his head. "Suing is pretty risky. But I'm inclined to say that's the course I would push, because I think it's the right thing to do."

Ellie had watched him carefully. "You see Jamie in this, don't you?"

He had, and he couldn't let it go. Emotion was dangerous in this line of work. A good argument was passionate and full of conviction, but raw emotion opened a door to blind folly.

So the question remained. What would he do?

Andrew squared himself to Locke, pulling his shoulders straight. "I'll recommend legal action."

"I thought so." Locked rubbed the back of his neck, suddenly looking old. "Again, as your senior adviser, I'm forced to ask you to reconsider."

Didn't sound like something Locke really believed. "Coming from you, I have to say I'm surprised. Considering what you did for me, I'd suspected you were a more honorable man."

Locke sighed. "Andrew, I know where you're coming from. Please try to see Matthison's point of view. If you take this to court, the university *and* the school district will put it on a national level. The education association, the ACLU, and the National Council for Science Education will get involved. You're attached to this office, and this case is a potential media nightmare."

Andrew stared with a stony expression. This *was* the right thing to do. He knew it, and Locke did too.

Locke understood his silence. "Take a minute before you come in. Set your mind straight so you're sure. Matthison is expecting you."

He opened the door and disappeared, leaving Andrew alone in the deserted hall. Closing his eyes, Andrew prayed. He'd done a lot of foolish things in his life. How he handled this case couldn't be one of them.

Swallowing, he put a hand to the door, not sure he really wanted to know what was about to happen.

Matthison didn't make him wait. Barely a hello, and he went straight to the point.

"Lacey Stewart isn't a client you should be representing. Pursuing this end will put you in a precarious position with the firm." Matthison's grim eyes glared over his glasses. "Take note of that as the events play out this week. Filing a legal course of action will terminate your association with us."

"I've been so advised." He held the other man's gaze. "I'm not leaving this girl to fight on her own. It isn't right. None of it is right."

Matthison speared him with disapproval before he pushed his way from the table. "Waste of time." He turned to Locke. "I told you last year, didn't I? You stuck your neck out for nothing."

With a poker face set in place, Locke waited until he left the room, then turned to Andrew. "Don't file the papers on our letterhead. Work in your own name. I can't promise you anything, but I'll see what I can do." He stood to leave, then paused. "Bank on a brutal assault, Andrew. You're taking on Goliath."

Locke left, and Andrew was alone in the conference room, contemplating the irony. It would be conviction, not addiction, that would cost him his job.

***

Jamie couldn't remember the last time she'd been so miserable. Two days had gone by, and nothing got done.

Not good. She finally felt on the rebound Wednesday and worked like crazy to get her paperwork done. Her final revision for the trail description and a few other new activities were completed by three. Relief sagged through her body. Her electronic submission would make it downtown before the four o'clock deadline.

Sick of being inside, Jamie changed into hiking gear and started down a light trail not used with the school kids. She had just passed the lower ponds and was about twenty yards from the trail head when her phone buzzed in her vest pocket.

"Hi, Jamie." Andy sounded both rushed and a little disappointed. "How are you feeling today?"

"Much better, thank you." They'd talked over the past few days, but not much. "I was just about to start a short hike. The trail goes back to the remains of an old homestead. I'll have to show you this weekend."

"Yeah." He sighed. "That's why I'm calling. I can't come. I'm getting on a plane tonight, and I'm not sure when I'll be back."

Jamie stopped and turned back toward the camp. "Where are you going?"

"Texas. That case I told you about last Saturday?"

That again. "Yeah…"

"I've been running into one dead end after another. I found a legal group down in Texas that specializes in this kind of thing. I'm out of my league here, and if this goes to court, it'll need the best I can give, so I'm going down there for the rest of the week."

"Oh." Something heavy and hard lodged in her chest.

"James, you know I'm not blowing you off, right?"

"I know that." Swallowing, she tried to push away anxiety. "I'm worried about you, though."

"Pray, Jamie. Don't worry. Pray. And not just for me. This girl and her husband have put everything on the line to stand firm. Now she's in a legal battle, unemployed, and without a degree. I think their lives look a little more frightening than mine."

"I'll pray, Andy." Starting right now with, *God what are you doing? He can't handle this right now.*

The digital air hung quiet. What was she supposed to do? Couldn't tell him not to go—not to pursue the case at all. Then she'd have to tell him why. She didn't even want to admit to herself why.

"Jamie?"

Enough. She was being selfish. She pulled her head up straight. "When does your flight leave?"

"Eight."

She needed to see him. If she studied his face, saw the peace in his eyes, and burned into her memory the scar on his face that had changed his life, maybe she could kill these fears. "What if I come down? We could grab a quick bite to eat, and I'd take you to the airport."

"Really?"

"If I leave now, I should get there by five. Would that work?"

"Perfectly." He sounded shocked. "But are you sure you're up for it?"

Jamie started back to her cabin. "I'll be down in an hour."

Chapter Thirty-Five

Jamie wanted to sink into the white marble tiles as she walked through the office building. She hadn't thought about her hiking grunge and how out of place she'd look until she stepped through the high glass doors of the downtown business complex. Men and women in business suits surrounded her, their purposeful strides echoing rhythmically through the vaulted entry.

She took the elevator to the legal offices of Matthison, Locke, and Associates. A pretty, twenty-something woman wearing a silver silk blouse and black dress pants greeted Jamie, her eyes hinting disapproval. Jamie was certain it had everything to do with what Andy had once termed her "wild Jane" outfit. She should have known better.

Feeling like an ignorant teenager, she stepped to the granite-topped desk. "Is Andrew Harris available?"

"I'm sorry, ma'am." The young woman tried to sound sweet. "All our attorneys are seen by appointment, and Mr. Harris is booked for the rest of the week."

"Oh." Heat bloomed in her cheeks. "Um, forgive me, but I think…"

The door behind the desk opened, and Andy came through with his nose in a file. "Amanda, I'm expecting—" He looked up and smiled. "Never mind. She's here."

Jamie glanced to Amanda, who tried to hide her disapproval. "Thank you."

Andy came around the desk and slid a hand to the small of her back. "Hi."

"Hey." How could one word wash heat over her whole body?

He turned again to Amanda. "Would you make a copy of this file?"

"Sure." Amanda's speculative eyes grazed over Jamie before she turned away.

Cheryl's face suddenly flashed through Jamie's mind. She'd been stunning in face and form. The elegant woman wouldn't have been seen anywhere in the outfit Jamie was wearing. No wonder an onlooker would be shocked to see Andrew Harris with a plain tomboy such as herself.

Andy's hand stayed where it was as he escorted Jamie through the door and down a hallway. Opening his office, he allowed her to pass through first, and Jamie stopped somewhere between his desk and the door.

"I'm sorry, Andy." She turned to face him. "I didn't think about the fact that I'd be coming into your office."

"What are you talking about?"

Jamie gestured to her clothing. "I didn't even bother to take my hat off."

A slow smile spread over his face as he removed her ball cap. Her face burned as he pushed his fingers through the mess. "You're always beautiful, silly girl."

She leaned against him, letting the warmth of his arms chase away inadequacy. Andy exhaled, leaning his head down on hers.

"Have you had a long week already?" she asked.

"Very, but we can talk about it later." He took a half step back to examine her. "Are you really feeling better?"

"Finally." From the flu, at least. She didn't want to talk about the other.

He tugged her close again and rubbed her shoulder. Closing her eyes, she inhaled the starch of his dress shirt. *Home.*

Maybe.

If only she could be sure. Pulling away, she distracted her tumbling heart by inspecting his décor.

Actually, most of it was hers. Three large prints of her work hung to the left of his desk. On the wall opposite, he'd hung one of her favorites: a clump of columbine tucked against a rounded boulder. The background was slightly blurred, and she'd set it in black and white, but the columbine, which rested in the lower right third of the frame, retained their soft blue color.

"I didn't know I had a live gallery."

He smiled, but then his brow drew down. "I haven't seen anything new on your website for quite a while."

Looking away, Jamie shrugged. "I haven't done much."

Concern etched in his eyes. "Don't give up, James."

She wanted to cry. He always saw deeper, probed deeper. Did he know, then, how awful the past year had been? She couldn't continue feeding a dream when her everyday reality had crumbled so painfully.

"I know it's been a tough year." His hand curled around hers. "But don't quit."

Feeling his breath wisp over her hair, Jamie squeezed his hand, forcing half a smile. Having nothing to say, she studied one of the prints to her left. Aspen leaves danced in the sunlight, and she recalled the moment vividly.

Are you seeing anyone?

That day seemed like another lifetime. Had she known what would happen between them, would she have agreed to that first hike? Jamie looked back at the man who stood silently studying her.

"Can I show you my favorite?" Her hand in his, he led her to his desk. "It's not a Jamie Carson, but it has sentimental value."

He passed a four by six acrylic frame to her. Their faces were swathed in snow gear, and their eyes were hidden behind sunglasses, but the smiles were perfect.

You'll make some lucky man a fine wife.

Did he remember that conversation? She studied the picture. Her smile had been genuine. Innocent. She'd no idea the twists their relationship would take. No idea how much pain she was in for.

His smile in the photo wasn't as authentic. Really examining it, he looked… he looked lost. Unhappy. She hadn't noticed then. Not really. She'd known he was a mess, but she'd assumed that he was content in his disaster. Proud of it.

What did that verse in Ecclesiastes say? *God has set eternity in the hearts of men.* Something like that. His smile ached for eternity.

Did it still?

Jamie searched him. He smiled warmly. She needed her camera so she could capture it. Study it. Because it looked peaceful.

But maybe that was what she wanted to see.

Andy tapped the frame. "I call it *The Woman Who Saw More in Me Than I Saw in Myself.*"

Jamie's attention fell to the floor. He'd tried so hard to be what she wanted him to be. In the months before his wreck, he'd worked at self-reform with resolute determination. And he almost had her. Well, he did actually, she just hadn't acted on it. "Andy, I never wanted you to change for me."

He took the frame from her fingers, replacing it where he would see it from his chair. "I think I proved abundantly that I couldn't change for you, no matter how much I wanted to."

Hope sparked. She examined his eyes, searching for proof. He held her gaze openly, as if he knew. As if he *wanted* her to see inside.

A knock at his door severed the moment. Disappointment crossed his expression before he answered. Amanda handed him two files, and he thanked her, bidding her a good night.

Looking through both, he sighed, then searched through a short pile sitting on the corner of his desk. He pulled one out from near the bottom. "I forgot to give her a file. I need to go make some copies. Can you give me a few minutes?"

"Sure." Jamie dipped her head, and Andy left the office.

Alone in the space, she wandered to the wide window overlooking the busy one-way street. She'd been down that street several times, some of them at ungodly hours to pull her best friend out of a bar.

She looked around, suddenly suspicious.

A low refrigerator had been built into the wall to the left of Andy's desk. She glanced at the office door, then opened the refrigerator. Water bottles. Two dozen water bottles. Why would he need twenty-four bottles of water? Jamie searched through them, looking for broken seals.

The door knob clicked, and Andy stepped back in. She nearly jumped away, guilt coursing through her body. When had she become such an insecure woman?

Andy's attention stayed on his files. "Did you find what you wanted?"

"No." She spoke way too quickly. "I was just—" *Looking for failure.*

"If you want a soda, there's a machine in the main hall." He looked up, finally examining her.

She'd always been a terrible actress and a worse liar.

Andy set his papers on his desk and moved her direction. Her heart pounded as he took her hand and walked her back to the spot she'd just abandoned. Squatting where she had, his hand moved to a panel below the fridge. He pounded on it with the side of his fist. The hardboard fell away, and Andy looked up at her. "I kept it in here."

Heat spilled into her face. She closed her eyes. "I'm sorry, Andy."

He rose and reclaimed her hand. "It's fine, James."

Her nose stung, and she couldn't make eye contact.

"Jamie." He tipped her chin, forcing her gaze to his. "I didn't think that I would just walk back into your life, tell you I'm all better, and we'd move on."

Her vision went blurry. Just move on—why couldn't they? She wanted to be happy with him. Why did she let the past torture them both?

"Don't be afraid to talk about it, James." Both hands framed her face, and he leaned in close. "Yell at me if you need to. We may cry, we may feel bad, but I don't want you to bury this deep in your heart and let it fester."

Sniffing, Jamie nodded. But he was too close, his gaze was too intense. She couldn't do this now. Maybe not ever. She just needed to let it go. They would be okay if she could just let it all go.

"It's already five thirty." She stepped back, avoiding his invitation. "You won't have time to eat if we don't get going."

Andy gave her a long look.

He wasn't willing to leave it alone—which was probably wise, but she couldn't go there now. "Andy, you're getting on a plane. We don't have time for this."

"Please don't avoid me, don't avoid this. If we're just friends, then you can keep me at a safe distance and I'll leave it at that. But I really want your whole heart." He closed the space between them again, depths of emotion glossing his brown eyes. "If you haven't decided, that's okay, but I don't really know what to do because I'm not sure where I stand."

Locked in his gaze, she swallowed. Her hands trembled as emotion welled up inside. Confusing, overwhelming emotion. Love and anger pulled hard, tearing at a heart that hadn't healed. He couldn't be just a friend, and there wasn't a safe distance.

Why couldn't she forgive him and move on? Wasn't that the Christian thing to do?

"Jamie?" His voice cracked.

She swallowed again, looking at her hands. "You've always been more than a friend, Andy."

He reached to frame her face, but she caught his hands before he could. "Can we leave it at that for tonight?"

His thumb slid down her nose and across her lips. "For now," he whispered.

If she tilted her face to him, he'd kiss her. She wanted him to. She wanted him to be *this* man. Now, and fifty years down the road. But what if he wasn't?

She pulled away from his touch.

Andy dropped his hand, forcing a smile that didn't reach his eyes. Stepping away, he picked up the copied files and put them in his messenger bag. They left his office in silence.

He recovered by the time they reached her car, though it seemed like he was forcing a conversation he really didn't feel.

Jamie ached. She was confusing him, which wasn't fair. But she needed to wrestle down the past and be done with it, without dragging him through it. If she started pouring everything out to him, there'd be no holding back.

And it would hurt them both.

***

Dinner was hurried, and Andy filled in a few more details of his trip between mouthfuls of rotisserie chicken. He was hoping to gain some tactical ideas, as well as a better understanding of what exactly he'd be up against.

"What do your partners think of this?" Jamie asked as they sped down I-70 toward Pena Boulevard.

"I'm not a partner, James." Andy shifted in the passenger's seat. "Those who are aren't very pleased."

She knew that. Stupid. "What about Locke?"

"He went to bat for me, but it's not looking good. I haven't had to file her claim yet; the university is still in deliberation. I'll know more when I get back."

"But you think she'll be denied?"

Andy sighed. "Yeah. Everyone I've talked to seems to indicate that's what will happen."

"What happens if your firm tells you not to proceed?"

"They already have." Andy stared through the windshield. "I meant that I'll know if I need to clean out my office when I get back."

Jamie bit her lip. "Andy, I know this is really presumptuous, but you're not doing this for me, are you?"

"Does that sound like something I would do?"

"I don't know." She shrugged, feeling turned around. The whole evening had been emotionally exhausting. "It's not something you would have done before, but then again, this is a case that you would have literally laughed at. The change is good, but I don't want you to throw your job away for me."

"Honestly, Jamie, knowing you has given me a better understanding of what this girl is probably going through, and she's snagged a little bit of my emotion because she reminds me of you. But I'm not doing this for you. I think God put her in my office on purpose."

"This isn't your kind of case, though." Jamie tightened her grip on the steering wheel. Arguing about this now was a dumb idea. And yet she kept talking. "Why do you think God wants you involved?"

"Because of us." He brushed a knuckle against her cheek. "Because I was the university and you are you. I know how they think, and now I understand where you're coming from. I can pull the information apart with a lens from both biases."

Jamie pulled to the curb at the passenger drop-off. She set the car in park and faced him. "What happens if this doesn't work out?"

He met her eyes; measured, resolved. "It's the right thing to do. Even if I lose, which is highly probable, it will still be right. I can find another job. I can practice on my own. I can mow lawns, if it comes down to it. But I can't ignore this."

Such selflessness should have made her heart swell, and in some measure it did. But Andy didn't handle failure well. At all.

He searched her, his silence begging for her approval. He deserved her approval. But she couldn't bring herself to give it.

Disappointment shadowed his eyes as he reached for the door handle. Setting one foot on the sidewalk, he paused. Typically confident, she was amazed to see hesitancy cross his face. He reached for her anyway, his thumb brushing her cheek while his fingers cradled her neck.

"Thanks for coming down, Jamie." His lips brushed near her hair, and then he was gone.

Chapter Thirty-Six

Dressed in gym shorts and a white tee shirt, Andrew leaned against the foot of the hotel bed. Two days felt more like two weeks. One more morning and he could fly home, but Jamie would have a group when he landed. He wouldn't see her again until the following weekend.

He hated it.

Waiting for her to pick up his call, he replayed the day he'd left. The woman he'd known had been confident, but as of late, Jamie was timid. Because of him. Maybe he needed to start considering what was best for her. Even if that meant...

"Hey, Andy."

Just hearing her voice over the phone made him melt. "James, how are you?"

"I'm good."

He leaned his head against the bed while she told him about the rest of her week. She sounded better. Actually, a smile floated in her voice. "How's Texas?" she asked.

"Hot." His heart uncurled as he closed his eyes to picture her face. Sweet, innocent, and lovely. Just like always.

"Do you feel like you've gained some ground?"

"Some." Yeah. That. He pushed a hand through his hair. "I'm going to need to take a different angle. I thought to focus on the problems with evolution, the things that you pointed out to me when we were in Waterton, but from what I see, it's been done over and over again. The problem is that if you're looking from a staunchly evolutionary point of view, the information is interpreted differently. If you're looking at rock layers, for instance, you see millions and millions of years."

"That's true." Something happened — the smile left. She sounded defensive, or annoyed. "Or you could see a massive catastrophe, the work of a flood."

"Exactly." Andrew hoped she didn't think he was trying to provoke her. He had a lousy record in that department. "Two points of view. They both look at the same evidence, but the conclusions are very different."

"But there's really no way to prove one right and the other wrong. The only way to know what happened is to go back in time to observe it."

He pushed up from the floor and began pacing the room. "So that's the angle I need to take."

Silence. She didn't agree, didn't approve.

"You lost me," Jamie blurted.

"Both points of view begin with a philosophy. One comes from a pretext of naturalism, the other from theism. The conclusions you draw are impacted by what you believe to be true about the past, about the origin of life. If both intelligent design and evolution are philosophical, then mandating one idea in our educational system at the exclusion of the other would seem to be discriminatory. Unconstitutional."

Andrew waited, wanting to hear her smile again. Jamie remained quiet. It felt like when she'd told him he was more than a friend and then pushed him away in the next moment. He hated uncertainty, hated feeling confused and vulnerable.

"Everything else has been done, James." Failure dropped like a rock in his chest, pulling him down. "Every other attempt to prove the theory of evolution wrong or design right has been struck down. While no one can prove its certainty, there hasn't been a single panel or judge since the Scopes trial to accept that evolution isn't valid enough to teach. Worse, there have been cases that have closed the door to ID entirely. If I can trigger any change, I really think it will be through the avenue of our government endorsing, even unwittingly, a particular philosophy that can be seen as a system of beliefs."

"A government-endorsed religion?" She sounded puzzled. "But an evolutionist, an atheistic evolutionist, would claim that their beliefs are absolutely non-religious."

Her criticism felt like rejection. But he needed to listen. Honest judgment would give him a stronger argument. Andrew crossed the room to check his notes scattered across the bed. "Actually, humanism is a recognized religion in the United States, and it's a huge proponent of evolution. Naturalism, the pretext of evolution, is defined as a philosophy. And in any case, religion or 'non-religion' still propagates a worldview."

He scribbled a quick note in the margin of his research. *Define naturalism and philosophy.* As he shifted into work mode, the lawyer in him took over. "Not believing in God or eternity or anything beyond ourselves is still a system of beliefs, and it determines how a person sees the world, what value they put on mankind, what role government should play, and countless other aspects of life. It affects everything. If teaching evolution—a theory unproven and steeped with assumptions and unobservable hypotheses—if teaching it exclusively strips away a person's belief in God, whether we're talking about a Christian, Muslim, Mormon, or anything else, then isn't that the same thing on the opposite spectrum as a Christian teacher using the classroom as a pulpit?"

The line held in silence.

He'd hoped she'd be impressed, or at least encouraging. She was completely still. Was she disappointed in him? She hadn't wanted him to take this on from the beginning. Maybe she thought he wouldn't handle the material well. Maybe he'd just proven her right.

"Andy, do you really think you can prove that?" Her words came measured, like she was carefully examining all he'd said. "I mean, it sounds like you've got a good argument, but I'm on your side. Do you really think this will go?"

Relief sank through him. "I think it's the best way to take it on."

She was quiet again. She'd been too quiet. He couldn't take it anymore. "James, you don't really want me to do this, do you?"

She sighed.

He dropped onto the bed in defeat.

"No, that's not it," she spoke softly. "I'm just afraid for you."

"Because you see this failing?"

"No... I just—"

She didn't finish, she didn't need to.

"You see *me* failing, landing back in a bar."

He could hear her sniff and could imagine her biting her bottom lip. He wished he'd waited until they weren't hundreds of miles apart.

"Andy, I'm sorry." Her voice wavered.

He should have waited—except she was listening. She couldn't run away from him without hanging up, which she definitely wouldn't do.

Now might be a good time to get some things said.

"Listen, Jamie." He dropped the lawyer tone. "I hear you. I know you're not without grounds. But I need you to hear me. I don't ever want to go back. I don't ever want to be that man again. Ever. But that can't mean I'm not willing to take a risk for something I know is right."

Her words were soft. "I know."

What could he do? So much of his life had been wasted. He couldn't squander this opportunity. But Jamie's disapproval felt like failing before he'd even begun. He fingered the scar running down his nose. *God, I can't fail. Not again.*

***

Jamie flipped her phone over and leaned against the post. The gazebo belonged to her as she sat alone under a pristine night sky. Brilliant stars winked at her, each so bright that she felt sure she could see the entirety of the heavens. Such a view should have made her smile.

Andy's work should have made her smile too. If he could get a judge to see the philosophical angle, it could change everything. What if he could upend the status quo by setting a new precedent?

He could also provoke tremendous ridicule. As a teacher caught in the crossfire, she was used to disapproval and criticism. Andy wasn't. He'd been successful at every point in his life, professionally speaking. Did he really understand the mass of condemnation he was about to subject himself to?

You see me failing and landing back in a bar.

He was right. That was exactly what she saw, and shame spiraled through her core. But wasn't it a valid concern?

Turning her phone back to the screen side, she called Melissa.

Her friend wasted little time with chit-chat. "What's going on?"

"I was just talking with Andy."

"You sound like that's a bad thing."

Jamie took a deep breath and gave her a quick rundown.

"He really has changed, Jamie. He's not the guy you left in rehab."

"I know. I really do. I see it in everything he does." Jamie pushed her fingers through her hair. "But everything from before stays with me. I feel like this is too close to the past for either of us to deal with."

Melissa hesitated, leaving Jamie time to replay what she'd just said. Andy was dealing with it just fine. She wasn't.

"He *has* to do this. Andrew needs your encouragement."

She knew that. But she had yet to really give it. It shouldn't be that hard. He was fighting for something she believed in. He was fighting for her.

Melissa cut into her thoughts. "Have you really talked to him?"

"I talk to him almost every day."

"Does he know about your nightmares?"

Melissa never soft-footed anything, which was one of the reasons Jamie loved her. But at the moment, she wished it were otherwise.

"Jamie, you're going to have to get it all out."

What for? It was done, in the past. Why should she drag him through it all over again?

"He can handle it." Melissa spoke as if she could hear Jamie's thoughts. "He's waiting for you to open up, to trust him again."

She trusted him, didn't she?

Not hardly. She expected him to fail.

"Listen, this is hard. I know it is, and so does Andrew. He loves you, Jamie. You need to decide if you're going to take the risk. If you can't, then you'd better tell him. If you're willing, then you need to go all in. You can't expect to keep part of your heart shut away from him and have him be okay with it."

As usual, Melissa was right. But it didn't make Jamie feel any better.

***

"How's Jamie?"

Andrew leaned back against the booth, wondering if he looked as rundown as he felt. Ryan had picked him up from the airport, and they'd stopped for dinner. "I thought she and Melissa talked often."

"At least once a week, but that's not what I meant and you know it."

Andrew gave half a smile. "She's still hesitant." Ryan would be about the only person with whom he would share such a thing. "I'm not sure about this at all, to be honest."

"You're not sure about how you feel?"

"No." A single, defeated laugh left his chest. "I know perfectly well how I feel, and so does she. I'm not sure she can ever get past who I was, the things I did."

Ryan nodded. He took a swallow of his soda, looking thoughtful. "Give her time; she'll come around."

Andrew examined his sandwich, his shoulders sagging. "The wounds are pretty deep. What makes you so sure?"

"I guess I can't be sure." He paused and cleared his throat. "But I do know this: she loved you long before she realized it."

Andrew mulled that over. What exactly did that mean? Love, forgiveness—he could see both when he looked into Jamie's eyes, even when she was guarded. But trust? An entirely different issue. He'd done a lot of damage, and the trust he'd broken could be ruined. Forever.

Ryan leaned on the table. "Leaving you was probably the hardest choice Jamie's ever had to make. That year was awful for her. Melissa and I think there's a lingering fear that she'll have to go through it all over again. You're just going to have to give her time. Time to see the saved Andrew, time to be certain it's for real."

Andrew pushed away his half-eaten food. "She's changed." He stopped to clear emotion from his voice. "Sometimes it kills me to see it."

Ryan leaned back. "What do you mean?"

"In many ways, she's become fragile. And it's my fault. Watching her crumble in fear kills me. While she never liked confrontation, she was never frail. I broke her."

Ryan sighed. "I don't know what God has for you or Jamie. But I know He won't waste your life, and He won't waste hers. Your pasts won't be a waste—your wounds or your trials. None of it will slip through His hands. If Jamie is fragile right now, then God has a use for it."

Andrew's gaze dropped to his lap. He thought of Paul in the Bible. Another man who'd done some really awful things in life. God hadn't wasted any of it. He'd redeemed it.

Please, please redeem mine.

"Jamie is still Jamie." Ryan filled the silence. "You see the deepest part of her because your relationship is and always has been close, and right now that part is still healing. But I really believe you'll walk through these struggles together, and you'll never doubt in the end that it was worth it."

Chapter Thirty-Seven

Dinner was well under way when Jamie heard the moan of the screen door springs. Sandwiched in between a group of teachers, she looked up as Andy stepped in the dining hall, still dressed in his work suit. Excitement tickled her chest. She hadn't expected him until nearly dark.

Their weeks had been busy. The school year had officially begun, although she wouldn't have sixth grade students under her charge for three more weeks. Until then, they had maintenance chores, supply restocks, and two more groups to prepare, not including the one that she was currently training.

Andy had also been hard at it as he began to write his argument and perfect the parameters of the claim he would submit the following week. Every day during their phone conversations his voice had been weighed with exhaustion.

He walked into the cafeteria, scanning the crowded tables.

So handsome, and he was looking for her.

When his eyes landed on hers, her heart seemed to float, and she smiled. His deep, open stare made her want to part the sea of people between them to find his arms.

Until his look slid to the man on her right. He frowned. No, scowled. At her.

Jamie's heart sank. She hadn't seen him in two weeks, and he was upset before they even said hello.

He moved to the buffet, purposely avoiding her. Filling a plate, he took it over to the round table where Creighton and Ellie sat with a few teenagers, never once looking her way.

Glancing to Dale Carter, who'd sat next to her, Jamie sighed. Why did he have to sit there? And tonight of all nights, Andy came early. The evening seemed doomed to an argument.

Tables began to empty as the group left for their break. Jamie scavenged her brain. What to do? She could just go to the lodge and let him swim in his assumptions, but that was risky. If she walked out, there was a small possibility that he would take off, which would be awful.

Feeling terrible and angry at the same time, she glanced at Andy's profile and then over to the buffet. The freezer sat at the end of the counter, and a jolt of inspiration hit.

She emptied her tray before grabbing two ice creams, and then she joined the trio at the round table. Smiles welcomed her, even from him, although she knew it was pasted. They exchanged a cool greeting as she sat by his side.

"This should take you back a few years." She slid a small frozen cup his way. "Orange sherbet, complete with the tongue-depressor spoon."

A tiny grin lifted his mouth, and she released the breath she'd been holding.

"It does." He picked up the wooden paddle. "I haven't seen one of these since our grade-school days. You used to ask me to save the wooden stick."

Ellie and Creighton both laughed, their looks begging for the rest of the story.

Her face warmed, but she laughed. "I did. I would use them to make little people. If you press them into play dough they stand upright, and you can draw faces and add hair and clothes. It was perfect for a little girl's play world."

Andy actually chuckled. "That was about the only 'little girl' thing she ever played."

Creighton grinned. "I would imagine she was far too busy riding a bike or climbing trees to be much of a princess."

"Usually." Jamie nodded. So true. Dress up and baby dolls and playing house had never been her first choice activities. Even as a kid, she'd always wanted to be outside, to smell the subtle musk of the dirt, to feel the wind rearrange her hair and the sun warm on her skin. "Although I managed to rope this guy into playing stick people with me on a few occasions."

She looked at his eyes and was relieved to see that some of the displeasure had softened. "Poor guy." She nudged him with her shoulder. "Our older brothers would go off to baseball practice or Boy Scouts, and Andy had to stick it out with the only girl in the bunch."

Again the group laughed, but Ellie commented that he didn't look like it did him any harm, and then the Nelsons excused themselves.

Their audience gone, thick silence hung between them. Andy averted his face, concentrating on the ice cream he punctured with angry stabs.

So much for smoothing things over.

The silence became an unbearable ringing. Someone had to call a truce.

"You must have taken off early today," she said.

"Yeah." His glare actually made her flinch. "I guess I should have called first."

The jab penetrated deep. Why would he think that about her? "No, it was a good surprise."

Andy eyed her and looked toward the table where she'd been sitting. "How long have you kept in contact with Dale Carter?"

She knew it. She knew exactly what he'd been thinking when his eyes raked over Dale. Hurt took a back seat, and anger stepped up. She hadn't done anything wrong. Andy was just being Andy—overbearing and condescending.

"I haven't," she snapped. "He took a new position at the Academy and had to come up for training. I haven't seen or heard from him since I left Applewood."

Andy's scowl didn't soften, and Jamie stood to leave. He followed, dropping his tray off at the kitchen portal first. But it didn't take much effort for him to catch up before she reached the lodge, and he jerked the door open for her. She stomped inside the empty room, not looking at him as she passed.

She'd made it halfway to the stage when his low, angry tone stopped her. "Jamie, wait."

She crossed her arms and turned, examining him in cold silence. The muscles in his jaw tightened, his irritated expression reminding her of their worst fight. Something clenched in her stomach. Not really fear. Not really anger either. More like regret.

One hand pushed through his hair, and his eyebrows pulled together. "What were you doing?"

She should bridge the gap. He was upset, and maybe he had a reason. Except… except, well, he didn't. He was just operating on assumptions. And unfounded jealousy.

"I always eat at the staff table." She couldn't keep the defensive edge out of her voice. "I didn't single him out. He sat down after I did."

"You never see it, do you? Men don't just sit next to a pretty woman to gain a new friend." His arms crossed over his chest. "They don't hang around after class to meet a new fishing buddy. They don't ask an attractive woman to go mountain biking because they can't read a map."

Why did he have to lecture her as if she were an ignorant child? "I haven't done anything wrong, Andy." She stepped closer, crossing her arms. "This is my job, and I do the best I can. If you think I'm a flirt, just say it outright. I've still got work to do."

Something flashed in his eyes at the word *flirt*.

Was that what he thought of her?

Voices floated just outside the window. Heat burned her face, and she dropped her gaze to the floor.

Andy's voice fell. "I'm going to get my bag."

Biting her lip, Jamie nodded. Maybe she should stop him—sort this out now and not let it simmer for the next hour. She should probably take a softer approach. Dale had been a sore spot between them, and that was her fault.

The door burst open, and in piled a gaggle of giggling girls followed by a trio of young men.

Andy walked out.

***

Andrew slung his bag over his shoulder, not really feeling the impact of his hiking shoes smacking his back. The day just kept getting longer.

As of yet, he still had an office with Matthison and Locke, but he could feel the matter thickening daily. The tension was nerve-wracking, which was why he'd taken an early leave that afternoon. He needed a breath, a place where he didn't feel contempt gathering just beyond his door.

Once in the dorm, he let his pack fall onto the thin mattress. Not ready to go back to the lodge, Andrew dropped to his bunk alongside the bag. Staring at his hands, he let Jamie's last sentence roll through his mind.

It frustrated him, though he wasn't really sure why. Jamie was the last person he would call a flirt. She just wasn't. She was sincerely nice to everyone, and she had the kind of spirit that simply drew people to her.

Male people.

Well, not entirely. She had plenty of girlfriends, and she kept good boundaries with the other variety. She couldn't help it if men found her attractive.

Except that she gave the impression of availability.

That was the problem. Men wouldn't flock around a woman who was emotionally attached elsewhere. It wouldn't be worth the time or the risk. Jamie still sent the available signal to them. That confused him—and made him angry.

He balled his fists. It was unfair, really. Jamie didn't know one way or the other, and trying to explain it to her would be like asking her to understand instructions given in an unknown language. The language of men.

It shouldn't matter. She wasn't trying to make him jealous. But… but she still hadn't told him where he stood.

More than a friend…

That conversation happened two weeks ago, and that was all he had. He'd resolved not to press her, but hanging out in ambiguity was so much more difficult than he'd expected.

Still frustrated and now doubtful, Andrew headed to the men's bathroom, intending to wash his face. He made it just inside the door when a conversation stalled his feet.

"You could ask her." Dale Carter's irritating, arrogant voice was unmistakable. "She might even agree. All I'm saying is that for the two years I worked with her, even when she wasn't seeing anyone, she really wasn't available."

"Are you saying that because she turned you down?" another man asked.

"Nope. I never asked."

Because arrogant men don't take real risks.

"There were a couple guys who did. It was always the same. She's single, but not available. But you do whatever you want."

Andrew stepped back into the hall and walked back to his room.

He'd been an idiot.

***

Jamie began to worry as her class neared the end of the hour. Andy hadn't come back. Though still mad at him, she didn't want him to leave.

Teaching. That's what she was supposed to be doing. She buried her irritation and tried to focus on questions coming from the group. She'd stumbled over information that she should have presented clearly and the session went on longer than usual.

She was ready to be done.

Why did Andy have to be so overbearing?

Yet, she knew why he'd been so mad—known from the moment he first scowled in the dining hall. The hard grip of anger softened and a heaviness took its place in her stomach. She never did apologize. Andy had been working to make things right between them, and she hadn't owned up to her own failures.

Plus, she still held him at arm's length. Who wouldn't feel at least a little threatened when they were kept in constant uncertainty? Not to mention she had yet to offer any support for his current case. She should have. For all of Andy's missteps, all of the rebellion and bad decisions he'd made, he was a gifted lawyer. He was appointed for this—and she was discouraging him.

If only the dreams would stop. If only she could let go.

Jamie finally dismissed the group. Creighton announced that he'd built a bonfire and that Ellie had broken out the marshmallows. Almost in unison, the group moved toward the gazebo.

Jamie caught Creighton. "Have you seen Andy?"

"He helped me with the fire, then went to the draw to get more wood."

The draw was a small alcove in the hill opposite the pond where they kept a mountain of firewood. Jamie thanked him and headed down the Jeep path.

Andy sat on the large stump they used to split logs, and she hesitated when his eyes met hers. He'd changed out of his dress clothes. Jeans and a tee shirt covered by his puffer vest completed the look she preferred.

He stood, a single hand held out.

Jamie didn't need any more invitation. She stepped into his waiting embrace.

"I was being a jerk." He snuggled her close. "I'm sorry."

Jamie wrapped her arms around his waist and nodded against his shoulder. For many breaths they let the silence wash away their conflict.

But she owed him more than silence. "Andy?"

"Yeah?"

She took a small step back, searching his face. "I'm sorry about what happened before, with Dale."

His eyes slid shut, and he shook his head. "James, don't."

"No, I never told you—and I should have. Even before everything else happened, I knew I should have apologized, and maybe if I had..." The words caught in her throat. Her eyes burned. Things had gone so bad back then—and some of it they could have avoided if she'd just said sorry when she should have. "I am sorry, Andy. You wouldn't ever stand for someone else treating me the way Dale treated you, and I didn't do anything."

In the heavy silence, Andy's gaze moved from her face, traveling up the hill to where the crowd hummed from the gazebo. To Dale.

After several breaths, he turned his attention back to her and pulled her head back to his chest.

Did that mean that she was forgiven?

Chapter Thirty-Eight

The crowd had dwindled by the time the flames grew dim, and Creighton asked Andrew if he and Jamie would be sure the fire was out.

When the footsteps died away and the cabin doors ceased their creaking, Andrew lowered himself to her side. She snuggled against him as the burning twigs snapped. It'd been such a long week— long night. Two hours earlier they'd both brought up an armload of wood, joining the larger group. While it was easy to visit as darkness fell, Andrew longed for the time he'd have her to himself again. Leaning his head on hers, he shut his eyes.

She'd apologized. He'd been dumbfounded. He'd never expected an apology from her. That fight so many months before was the last thing he wanted to think about, but when he did, it was always with guilt. He'd been horrible.

But she'd apologized, whether he thought she ought to or not.

He kissed the top of her head. "You know I never minded playing stick people with you, right?"

She pulled away from his chest to look up at him. Even in the dim shadows, he could make out her affectionate smile. With one hand, he cradled her face, and she covered it with her own before she settled against him again.

Rustling pines and quaking aspen whispered secrets on the cool breeze while they listened in comfortable silence. Clouds made the night sky matte black, but an occasional star winked through the gaps. This was how life was supposed to have been all along. Peaceful. Happy. Something he hadn't shared with anyone since… since they were kids.

Had she? Maybe. She'd seemed pretty happy with Ryan.

"Jamie," Andrew whispered against her hair, "can I ask you something?"

She tipped her head, her eyes searching his. "Okay."

"I overheard a conversation earlier—one about you. Dale said you were single, but not really available." Andrew swallowed, fidgeting. Why was he doing this? "Why did you break up with Ryan?"

Jamie moved away, sliding her elbows to her knees.

The silence actually hurt. Did he really want to know the truth? "Sorry, James. I don't know why I asked. You don't—"

"He broke up with me."

Andrew thought back to the day Jamie had told him they'd broken up. Hadn't she said she'd done it? Maybe he'd assumed. At the time, he couldn't imagine that Ryan would end things.

The truth crashed onto his shoulders. She'd been happy with Ryan—maybe she had loved him. Practically speaking, it didn't matter now. But emotionally—well, it mattered. He could hardly measure up to the other man as it was.

"I'm sorry. I must have misunderstood." He swallowed, looking at the fire. It wasn't hard to recall the times Ryan had confronted him. Had he come between them?

Suddenly it all made sense. "It was because of me, wasn't it?"

Jamie sighed. She stood and walked over to the pit.

Andrew's stomach knotted. He loved her, almost desperately. Wanted her to love him. But he didn't want to be her second choice. Locking his hands behind his head, he slumped over and stared at his feet.

"You were the only thing we ever fought over, Andy."

He sat up, made himself look at her.

"But that wasn't why we broke up. Ryan figured out before I did that I didn't love him. It wasn't your fault."

She didn't love him. Andrew's lungs emptied.

She was in love with you long before she understood it. Andrew worked through the subtle implication. Ryan had figured out that she didn't love him... because her priorities never changed. Andrew always took precedence. Always.

His heart knocked against his ribs.

Jamie held still near the fire, looking exposed. Vulnerable. He pushed to his feet and approached her with measured steps, his hands wrapping around her upper arms. If he could make it okay for her to love him, make her see that she was safe, maybe everything bad in their past wouldn't matter anymore. He held her eyes, his pulse racing. Framing her face, he brushed his lips against her forehead.

Her fingers curled into his vest and her eyes slid shut. But when his head dipped toward her mouth, she stiffened.

"No," she cried softly, then pushed away.

Disappointed and bewildered, Andrew released her. He waited a few heart-wrenching seconds, wondering what to do. Even from an arm's length away, he could feel her tremble. What had passed through her mind? When it came to bad memories, he'd provided her with some options. Which scene had she just replayed?

He closed the space she'd put between them. "What just happened, Jamie?"

Sudden tears spilled over her lids. "I'm sorry."

"Tell me what happened."

"I—I thought you were going to kiss me."

Tipping her chin up, he looked at her with silent intensity. "I was."

She nodded, shutting her eyes. Her lips quivered.

"You don't want me to kiss you?"

"No. Yes." Jamie sniffed. "I do but I—"

Breathing hurt. Every natural instinct screamed to walk away. Leaving would be easier than seeing what he'd done. But this was never going to go away on its own.

Break down the walls.

Some things could only be done through pain. He held himself steady. It was time to reckon with it.

Gently cradling her cheek, he brought her gaze back. "Talk to me." His voice barely worked around his closed throat. "Don't shut me away."

Abruptly her body went rigid. She gripped his wrists as her glare burned through him. "Do you have any idea what you put me through?"

Andrew pulled in a breath. Finally. She was done pretending. "Tell me."

"I can't even begin, Andrew!" Her fists came up against his chest, her low voice hot. "You tied me in knots. One minute you were my favorite hero, and the next you were the worst person I'd ever known. I never knew what I was walking into when you called. I still have nightmares. You're either dead or—or…"

Even enraged, she couldn't spit the ugly words out. Choking on her sobs, she clutched at his vest. "You begged me not to give up on you, and then you pushed me until I had no other choice. And yet I loved you! I loved you, Andy, and you broke my heart."

Andrew covered the hands that clawed at him, silently taking the blows. Nothing had ever hurt so much, and seeing the damage of her wounded heart caused his own to rend in two. He rubbed her shoulders, and his own eyes stung. When she buried her face against him, he held her as if they were falling into blackness.

Maybe they were. The barrier between them seemed insurmountable. She'd loved him. He'd torn her apart. He had broken her trust, destroyed her hope. Broken her heart. He couldn't amend for it. Trying to was ripping her apart.

His voice wavered with emotion. "Would it be better if I left you alone?"

She didn't answer.

Andrew felt his heart shatter. He'd do it. If leaving would give her peace, he would go.

"No." She tightened her grip. "I missed you—I want to be with you. I want everything to be okay. But I can't seem to let go…"

His arms tightened, and the pit in his stomach turned. Why had he been so foolish, so destructive? What had he hoped to gain? It was all worthless. His hard-fought autonomy and everything that came with it was completely hollow. No, much worse than that. It had cost him more than he'd understood.

Jamie shook as she cried.

What could he do? He had nothing but apologies to give her, nothing to make it right.

As her hot tears slowed, her fists unfurled. "I'm sorry, Andy."

Why did she continue to apologize for the mess he'd made? If only he could go back. All the way back—and change his life to what it should have been. He would have been there for her when her mom died. He'd have held her hand, and she wouldn't have been alone. The drinking would've never started. They would have been happy. He wouldn't have broken her heart.

"I don't want you to be sorry." None of it had been her fault. "I want you to be honest. I know when you're not right, James, and I don't want it to be because of me anymore. Keep talking to me."

She wrapped her arms around him and clutched the back of his vest.

He'd known that when they finally reached this conversation it would be hard. He thought he was ready for it, that he could take it. But the helplessness swallowed him—it swallowed them both. He couldn't see past the darkness. How would they ever make it out of this abyss?

"Don't leave us here." Andrew clutched her while emotion wavered in his voice. "Please, God, don't leave us like this. I don't know what else to do."

***

Jamie stretched in the warmth of her bed. Rested. Oh, how glorious!

Turning toward the single window in her room, she basked in the morning sunlight. Light followed darkness. Tears flooded her eyes.

The night had been such a roller coaster. She was so ashamed of her rage. Christian love forgave, didn't it? Then why hadn't she been able to heal?

She hadn't wanted Andy to see the mess in her heart, but it all came pouring out.

But hearing him pray… there were no words.

It was a first between them. Even as children they'd never prayed together. It felt more intimate than a kiss, more bonding than the sharing of breath.

It felt like a miracle.

Brushing aside the tears, she readied for the day, renewed. In the kitchen, she found her favorite brew ready and waiting. She smiled as she fixed a cup, knowing where he'd be.

Andy looked up and smiled as Jamie passed through the back door.

"You're turning us into coffee snobs," she said.

She dropped to his side, and he drew her close. Though his eyes were tired, his expression was warm. "Did you sleep well?"

"I did." For the first night in way too long she'd gone to bed without fear. She'd drifted to sleep without the claws of turmoil snatching her peace.

He relaxed against the backrest. "I was praying you would."

Jamie snuggled against him. "I think hearing that will always thrill me."

"Hearing what?"

"That you pray."

Andy combed her hair with his fingers and kissed her forehead. "I wanted to share what I was reading today. Would you mind?"

Jamie straightened, wonder taking her captive. He was a total transformation.

He reopened his Bible, the pages falling to Matthew seven, and he moved the Word so they could share it. "I was looking at verses seven through eleven, where it begins with the ask, seek, knock promises. But I wanted to read verses nine, ten and eleven.

"Which of you, if your son asks for bread, will give him a stone? Or if he asks for a fish, will give him a snake? If you, then, though you are evil, know how to give good gifts to your children, how much more will your Father in heaven give good gifts to those who ask Him!"

An uneasy feeling swirled in her stomach as Jamie sat back. She didn't believe life was easy-peasy for the redeemed. Losing her mother to cancer, her family to grief, Andy to alcohol... her own life had proved otherwise. Jesus had warned his followers that there would be a cross involved in the Christian walk.

"Pastor Bartley reminds me often to cross reference to make sure I'm getting a good understanding." Andy thumbed through the pages. "Luke records the same thing, only he is more specific about the gift. It's the Holy Spirit."

Jamie leaned over his Bible, flipping to Luke eleven-thirteen to read his account.

Andy waited until she finished. "It made me think of a verse that became my lifeline last fall. Second Timothy one seven says that God has not given us a Spirit of fear, but one of power, of love, and of self-control.

"James, you know better than anyone that I had no power over addiction, no self-control, and a love only to serve myself. But God gives us His Spirit to accomplish the impossible in our lives. Not just in the long run, but in the now, the everyday."

Andy turned, setting aside his Bible and taking her hand. "I know you're afraid. It kills me to see fear bind you. But I know the Spirit that is in you is greater than the fear that is holding you captive."

Jamie stared at him her mouth open. *Andrew Harris* had just delivered a word from God! Scanning his face, she took in every feature. So familiar, but... but not. She slid her hand from his and with two fingers traced the scar running down his nose.

He looked at his hands. "It's pretty awful, isn't it?"

He hates his scar.

She hadn't realized he thought about it. Clearly he did. A lot. But it had become her favorite part of his handsome face.

"That's not what I was thinking at all." She grazed it again, this time with her thumb. "It's like the branding of a miracle. By all accounts, you should've died. God was so good—to both of us."

He searched her again, looking relieved. Grateful. Pressing a kiss to her hair, he pulled her close. "It's a new day."

Jamie melted a little more. "It's a new day."

Chapter Thirty-Nine

Andrew submitted his client's claim on Monday. Gary Matthison requested a private audience the following morning. The man didn't pull any punches.

Jamie called him that evening and within thirty seconds asked what was wrong.

He sighed, slumping onto his worn-out recliner. "I'm out."

"You're out?" she repeated. "You mean they fired you?"

"Not exactly, but yes." He stared at the ceiling. "I was asked to take an indefinite leave of absence. Matthison wants to see how this unravels without getting his name muddied. I can tell you right now that I won't be asked back."

"I'm sorry, Andy." She sighed. "What can I do?"

He shoved a hand through his hair, fighting defeat. "It'll be okay, James." He couldn't fake a convincing tone. "Just pray for me, okay?"

"Okay." She hesitated. "About the case? Or a new job? Or something else?"

"All of it." He swallowed. Getting up, he walked to the bathroom and looked in the mirror. He fingered the scar on his face—an ugly gash announcing to the world, *Hey, I'm a total mess. An alcoholic. A failure.*

Jamie saw redemption. What did she call it?

The branding of a miracle.

His eyes slid shut. "James, insecurity is a weak spot with me."

God, give me strength. Opening his eyes, the same man stared back at him. The one with the conspicuous gash.

He relived Jamie's touch as her fingers traced the blemish.

Maybe it wasn't so bad.

She cut into his thoughts."We could pray now."

Andrew agreed through the emotional vise in his throat. Praying with Jamie had been the single most intimate experience he'd ever shared with a woman. It seemed impossible—to his inexpressible regret he was no stranger to women—but nothing had ever bonded him to any of them. Praying, though, was an exposure of his soul, and there had been a oneness with Jamie that had no equivalent.

Love swept over him as she prayed, chasing anxiety and lending fresh strength.

***

Jamie worried herself to sleep and woke up anxious. Andy sounded okay by the time they'd said goodnight, but she couldn't stand the separation anymore. Hurrying through the day's work, she left camp, heading for town.

It was close to three by the time she pulled in front of his house. Noting the vehicle she'd parked behind, Jamie went to the door, wondering if he had company. She asked that very question when he answered. She thought he'd be surprised, and he was, but she couldn't quite read his look.

Maybe guilt?

Her heart tumbled, and she couldn't mask the hint of accusation. "Andy, what's going on?"

Shaking his head, he looked crestfallen. "Don't think what you're thinking."

She stood unmoving, hating those thoughts, despising her mistrust. "Is someone here?"

"My client—and her husband." He still looked wounded. "I don't have an office anymore, and I needed to meet with her."

Jamie's eyes slid shut. She kept stabbing him with her doubt. How would they ever make it if she didn't build some faith in the man he'd become? "I'll come back later."

She turned to go when a voice caught her midstride.

"Miss Carson?"

Looking back, she saw a familiar young woman stepping past Andy. Recognizing her former student, her mouth fell open. "Lacey Taylor?"

"It's Stewart now," Lacey answered, a pleased smile growing. She moved to Jamie with a ready embrace.

Shock rippled through her. *Lacey Taylor* was Andy's client? She'd been an outstanding student. Not the kind of kid to cause problems.

"I was so sad when my dad told me you'd moved. How great is it that I run into you now?"

"Pretty amazing." Jamie looked at Andy. The guilt on his face said it all. He'd known Lacey had been her student, and he hadn't told her.

"This is my husband, Aaron." Lacey introduced the man standing behind her, who stepped forward with an open hand. Jamie took it, hoping her smile didn't look forced.

"I'm so excited to see you." Lacey grinned again. "I wanted to be able to tell you what an impact you had on my life."

"You're in quite a pickle." Dragging her eyes from Andy, Jamie tried to narrow her focus on Lacey. "I'm not sure that's a good legacy."

Lacey scrunched her nose. "I just did what you always did. I encouraged questions, and pointed out some of the problems Darwinism encounters."

Jamie nodded, hoping she hadn't given Lacey the impression that she disapproved. "I know. It's not fair. I just meant that I wish that it'd been me instead. I'm sorry this happened."

"Lacey's not." Aaron stepped forward, dropping an arm around his wife's shoulders. "Don't get us wrong. A job would be really good right now. But nothing will ever change unless someone challenges the status quo. Lacey didn't set out to cause a disruption, but the whole deal just played out that way. If she's the stepping-stone to change, we're okay with it."

Lacey gave her husband an approving look before her attention swung back to Andy. "I think this tactic might work," she said. "I hope you'll be able to work in some of the science crediting intelligent design, but the philosophy angle is probably the best way to go."

"I've got a lot of work yet to do." Andy pushed his hands into his pockets. "But I'm fairly certain this is the right direction. I'll need more of your help with the science, though, so we'll be meeting frequently."

Lacey agreed. "I'm certain Ms. Carson can explain much better than I can."

The couple said goodbye and headed for their car. Andy dipped his head with a half-smile. Jamie was sure Lacey and Aaron didn't catch Andy's hesitancy, but she certainly hadn't missed it.

Andy held the door for her as Aaron and Lacey drove off. Jamie passed through the entry, waiting for him to say something.

He didn't.

"You knew she was my student, didn't you?"

"Yes." He shut the front door. "I figured it out when I was going through her background. She graduated from Applewood Academy with honors." He raised his eyes and met hers. "I couldn't tell you."

A fine cop-out. "You couldn't tell me one of my students was in trouble?"

"You know I couldn't." He rubbed his forehead, looking exhausted.

What was she doing picking a fight? He couldn't tell her. That was the nature of his job. Client confidentiality.

But now she knew.

"She's right." Her head dipped toward the door as if Lacey was still there.

Andy knew exactly what Jamie was talking about, and his head moved with precision. "No."

"You haven't even asked for my help."

"Which was intentional."

"I can help." Her chin rose. "I could even give testimony."

His hands settled on his hips. "Absolutely not."

He'd said he needed her on his side, then rejected the first offer she gave?

Andy's hands fell to his side and his shoulders slumped. He moved toward her, took her hand, and led her to the couch. "James, Lacey was denied her degree." He leaned closer, tracing her face. "I've lost my job. I'm not going to ask you to sacrifice your career as well."

"You didn't." She snagged his hand and held it. "I volunteered."

"No."

That was it? Just no? Weren't they supposed to talk through things like this? "Why is it okay for Lacey to make her stand and for you to sacrifice your job, but not for me? My voice may not count for much, but it would be better than staying silent."

He pulled away, that stern, don't-argue-with-me look creeping over his expression. "You'll lose your job."

"I know." She did understand how this worked, thank you very much.

"You'll put the Nelsons in a position to have to fire you or lose their jobs."

Okay, she hadn't thought of that. But surely the Nelsons would agree with her. This had to be the right thing to do. "Please, Andy." She reached for his hand again. "She was my student. This is my world you're trying to shake up. Don't make me watch in silence."

His mouth twisted, and as he stared at the wall, his Adam's apple bobbed several times.

Jamie shifted, waiting until she could no longer stand the silence. "What are you thinking?"

He stood and walked a few paces, his fingers again rubbing at his head. "I can't. Jamie, you hate confrontation." He paused for a moment and then turned to her. "I'm not saying what you have to offer wouldn't be useful, but I can't do that to you."

She felt his concern like a shield of safety, which was sweet, but she wasn't flimsy. "You're always protecting me."

Agony crossed his expression. "Not always."

Oh. That shadow from their past—that's what this was about. Jamie let it go.

***

The Sixteenth Street Mall was lively, lit up with twinkling lights and saturated with the noise of corner bands, horse-drawn carriages, and crowds—the night life of LoDo.

"Explain the scientific method to me." Andrew tugged on Jamie's hand as they wandered through the crowds.

Jamie grinned and the teacher in her took over as she explained the process of asking questions, diving into research, forming hypotheses, and pursuing answers.

Andrew nodded as she explained. The hearing date had been set for the end of September. As the appointment drew nearer, Andrew worked harder. Researching, rechecking his facts, trying to understand the complexities that twined around philosophy and science. It was not his expertise, but he poured himself into it. Almost as an obsession, which was exhausting.

"Why did you need all that?" Jamie walked by his side, her hand warm in his.

He shrugged, trying not to look discouraged. "I've got a roadblock to work around."

"Can you tell me?"

His chest tightened. Everything they'd done or talked about recently wound their way around this, monopolizing their lives. He was driven in his work. Always had been, but this was more than a contest that challenged his competitive nature. This was personal. And it demanded more of him than he'd ever given.

Ironically, the more he poured into it, the more he doubted the outcome. Case study after case study pounded his confidence.

"There was this case in Pennsylvania in 2005." A dull ache throbbed in his head, and he rubbed his temples with his free hand. "This board of education wrote up a statement that was to be read in every high school science class. Basically it said that evolution is a theory and that there were other theories that were worth looking into. If students wanted, the school would have material available. The material was specific to intelligent design. The board was sued and lost. The judge said that the whole thing was unconstitutional because ID is religious. He said that ID begins with a theistic pretext, it fails to employ scientific method, and any ideas produced by its research are not subject to peer review."

Jamie chewed on her bottom lip, quiet in her thoughts. Her stare focused on the sidewalk. Why hadn't he taken her to the movies or something? Being with him shouldn't be a downer.

"Do you wish you hadn't taken this on?" she asked.

"No." He squeezed her hand, attempting a smile. "I just wish I had more to go on. I can find cases that support our position, but for every one I find, I come across two that are contrary."

"How is that possible? Why is it so ambiguous?"

"Because it's an indistinguishable line." He sighed, rubbing his head again. It hurt. Thinking too much and sleeping too little gave him an ever-present dull ache. "The Joint Statement of Current Law from 1995 states that 'any genuinely scientific evidence for or against any explanation of life may be taught,' but the courts are aware that teachers can and do use that as license to promote their personal beliefs."

Jamie's thumb ran over his knuckles, and she glanced up at him, her eyes soft with concern.

Just drop it. This is a date, not a consultation. Andrew shook his head. Man, it really hurt.

"There's more to it than that, isn't there?" she asked. "I mean, surely the courts would draw a clear boundary, right?"

"Not yet." They could have gone bowling. Dancing. Stargazing. Anything else. Jamie deserved a man who wasn't so self-involved. But she kept asking, and her support meant more than he could put into words. "Most of the rulings in this matter were not appealed — they never went to the Supreme Court. So there are contradictions galore. For example, there was a case in 1987 that affirms the right of a teacher to employ academic freedom. But then there's this more recent case in Pennsylvania. Though it doesn't carry the force of federal law, it still sets a precedent."

Jamie looked lost in the inconsistency. "Will Lacey's case help set a new precedent?"

Andrew jammed a hand through his hair. He felt as if iron were pressing down on him.

"That depends on how far it goes." He stopped near a bakery and sighed. "Honestly, James, that prospect scares me to death. If she needs to appeal, if this continues to a higher court, she needs a better lawyer. I'm not equipped for this."

People scurried all around them. Life in LoDo moved fast, and it would have been easy to simply keep pace. But they stood still in the middle of the clamor. Jamie studied him, warmth softening her eyes. "You're a good lawyer, Andy." Two fingers traced his scar. "Such a good man."

Her featherlight touch soothed the pounding in his brain. Pulling her close, his eyes slid shut. Nothing from her lips, save three small words, could have affected him more profoundly.

***

Jamie sat on Andy's couch, her legs tucked beneath her, while Andy worked at his small dining table. She'd come down to see him, and Andy had takeout waiting.

He needed to work, though. The hearing began on Monday, just two days away. Jamie tried not to think about it. Every time she did, her stomach twisted.

She'd brought her MacBook and worked on her own project while Andy poured over his. She was reformatting a frame, highlighting the shadows to best contrast the peaks and valleys, when Andy dropped onto the couch beside her.

"Whatcha got?" He leaned close, pulling the screen so he could see

Jamie shifted, snuggling next to him. "Independence Pass."

"Where is that?"

"It connects Aspen to Twin Lakes, by Buena Vista. It's really gorgeous."

"I can see that." He studied the frame. Layers of enormous peaks stood purple in the late-day sun. "Are you putting this in your book?"

"Yeah, I think so."

Andy settled back further, wrapping an arm around her. "How's that coming?"

She pushed her hair from her face. "Andy, I know you have work to do. I'm really okay with it. I don't want my coming here to distract you."

"I need a distraction."

He moved the cursor, opening her *Colorado in the Raw* file. He began to read the rough background and histories she'd been working on.

Jamie stared at him, drawing his attention back. "What are you looking for?" he asked.

"Signs of guilt."

He pulled his eyebrows in. "Why?"

"Because I don't want you to feel guilty." She sat up, turning so she could face him. "What you're doing is important, and I don't feel neglected."

He wove her fingers with his. "I don't feel guilty, James. This case is a big deal, and I'm not blowing it off. But there will be life beyond it. What you do is important to me. I don't want to miss it."

Her heart soared. He was so much the boy she'd loved. It hardly seemed possible that he'd been anything less.

He smiled as if he could hear her heart. "So let's see it."

Together, they shuffled through the photos she'd selected. His approving smile and compliments made her believe that what she was attempting might be truly possible.

"I need your help," she said.

"No, you don't."

"I really do, Andy. These histories—the written part—it's not going well at all. I just don't have a way with words like you. You make language captivating, persuading your audience as though you were charmed."

Andy's grin spread wide. "That was poetic."

"It's all I've got."

He laughed, weaving his fingers through her hair. "Keep at it. I'll help you, but you need to keep at it. I know you can do this."

Chapter Forty

"How did Lacey do today?"

Jamie had waited on edge the entire day to ask that question. Andy had been in court for five days, and each one had felt like a week as she waited to hear from him in the evenings.

"She took a pounding. Reese poked at every emotional angle he could imagine." Andy chuckled. "But she held her own."

"Was she able to go into the science that supports intelligent design?"

"Some. I really wanted to focus on the questions that call evolutionary dogma into question, though. She went into the problems of complexity and how Darwin's theory requires small, random mutations over time, rather than a giant leap. Reese accused her of bringing religion into the classroom, and she got a little feisty."

"How'd she clear that one?"

"She said that she never brought any religious belief into it at all. She had her outline for that particular lesson, which I'd submitted on direct, so she referred to that. Reese asked her if she was, in fact, a Christian. Without flinching she said, 'Yes. Does that disqualify me?'"

Jamie couldn't help but smirk. "What did he do?"

"He turned pretty ugly, but she sat stoic. He railed about the subtle manipulation she'd attempted in a public classroom and outlined a fictional scheme for evangelism if people like Ms. Stewart were allowed to take a foothold."

Jamie's heart pounded. Lacey had been a sponge when it came to technical information, and she had an insatiable curiosity about the mechanisms of life. It hadn't been surprising to learn that she should have graduated college with honors.

"Andy, this is tying me in knots." Jamie stared out her window, watching the golden hues of the aspen leaves ripple in the breeze. "I wish I could be there."

"I know, James." His deep voice sent warmth through her. "But I'll do battle in court, if you'll fight for me on your knees. Okay?"

Tears pushed against her eyelids. It still thrilled her. Andrew Harris, passionate Christian, seeking the God of all creation. How awesome was that?

***

Unbelievable. Andrew called Jamie before he even made it to the car. He would deliver his final argument tomorrow, but right now his head buzzed with the way the day had played out.

"Andy." She sounded breathless, like she was taking on a mountain. "I was just praying for you."

"Really? You sound like you're on a trail."

"I am."

So Jamie. She usually felt closest to her Savior when she was out in His vast cathedral. Andrew smiled.

"So," she continued. "I'm dying to know how things went today."

"Amazing." He slid into his car and dropped back against the seat, letting the whole of it wash over him again. "Reese reserved his biggest guns for the final round. He brought in Dr. Patrick Daniels. Do you know him?"

"Yeah, I know who he is." Her breathing sounding even, and Andrew could picture her sitting on the dirt, propped up against a tree. "You said it was a good day? He's pretty hard-core. He hates ID and creationism with a violent passion."

Hard-core was putting it mildly. Daniels didn't have any problem voicing—shouting—his opinion with multi-degree-backed eloquence. But things had taken an interesting twist. "It was crazy, James. Daniels basically equated teaching anything other than evolution with child abuse and then totally opened the door to the philosophical angle I needed."

"Really?" Her voice went up. "How'd you pull that off?"

"That's just it. I didn't." Wonder made Andrew's skin prickle. "God was so there, James. I can't explain how it happened. But everything Daniels gave me worked for my argument. He even agreed that teaching any of the theories shaped a worldview. It set me up perfectly for my closing tomorrow."

The air between them held still, and then he heard her exhale a breathless laugh. "Are you serious? Daniels is probably the country's biggest opponent of ID in public education."

"I know. I can't even begin to tell you how much anxiety I had about him. But it just happened—everything just worked." *Because God can do what I can't.* Andrew trembled.

"Andy, I could come down tomorrow. Can I come for your closing?"

He swallowed, his throat almost too thick to talk. "That would mean the world to me."

***

"Evolution has reigned as a tyrant across these states." Andy leaned against the podium. "Qualified, well-educated, and gifted teachers are being excluded because of their beliefs. According to the freedom guaranteed in this country, this discrimination is unconstitutional."

Jamie sat forward, listening as though his words could change lives. Because maybe they could. He'd begun his closing argument more than ten minutes before, meticulously recounting Lacey Stewart's qualifications, the legal base she had operated within, and the consequences she'd faced because of her courage.

"The directive to maintain a separation of church and state was set forth to guard against a government-mandated system of beliefs. And yet, when our public schools are only given sanction to educate our students in the area of historical science under one *unproven* and very *philosophical* point of view, it is effectually stepping backward into a state-appointed belief system. This is the breach in separation. Not that a religious worldview is given voice, but in that the government demands selectively that one must be silent. The writers of our constitution would be appalled."

His hands fell at his side. "Lacey Stewart's career has been grounded because she held to her beliefs, which do *not* inherently contradict science, and she did so within the parameters of the constitution. How many others have lived in the shadow of fear, knowing that if they were so bold, they would be expelled? Our country was not formed to propagate that kind of bondage. Freedom in study is equally as important as freedom in worship. When one is stifled, it is not presumptuous to fear for the other."

Fervor lifted his voice, and he spoke with an authority, a passion Jamie hadn't heard from him before. Everything else faded. The panel of judges, the other players in the court, and the people in the gallery melted away as a surreal moment washed over her. His voice, his words, reverberated against their past, and wonder overtook her emotions.

Who is this man? Her eyes flooded. *God, is this Andrew Harris?* She choked back a cry. *You have called him from the grave. Plucked him out of the grip of alcoholism. Redeemed every moment of pain.* Her hand came to her mouth as powerful emotion shook her body.

How wonderful are your works, oh Lord. My soul knows it very well.
The new legacy of his life. Of hers... of theirs. Praise God.

They wouldn't have a decision until Monday. But the outcome wasn't nearly as important as what she'd witnessed that day. Life had changed. It became what it should have been.

Several hours later, after a shared dinner with the Stewarts, Andy drove to a lake surrounded by open space and pulled his car into the parking lot. Sliding her hand in his, she matched his stride as they made their way around the walking path.

The October evening had grown dark, and an autumn chill marked their breaths in white puffs. Andy's pace was a challenge since she was not used to heels, but she didn't complain.

They were about halfway around the mile-and-a-half loop before he slowed his pace and began to relax. He led her to an abandoned dock, the city lights flickering over the black water.

Jamie pulled her hand free and rubbed his back. "You did well, Andy. Lacey couldn't have asked for more."

His arm slipped around her, and she leaned into his side.

Andy sighed deeply. "She's done, you know."

Jamie turned to him, and her heart squeezed. If she could only smooth away his discouragement.

"No matter how this turns out, for all practical purposes, she's done." His shoulders slumped as he stared across the lake. "The university could award her a degree, but it won't make a difference. Her career will be restricted to parochial schools and the few charter academies like Applewood. It was professional suicide."

How could he feel like a failure when he had shown her the miracle she'd begged God for? "I think she knew that going into this." She slid her hand along his arm. "Coming to you wasn't an attempt to rescue her career. She did it to expose the truth. You did that."

Andy's smile was halfhearted.

Jamie understood. It didn't matter that his career, salary, and prestige were cut off at the knees. He felt responsible for Lacey.

"Andy." Her fingers skimmed his cheek. "I'm so proud of you."

He pushed away from the rail to pull her close.

Jamie ran her fingers over his neck and shoulders, willing the tension to drain away, wanting him to know her heart. Leaning back, she framed his face with both hands. "I love you, Andrew Harris."

A tender silence enveloped them as her confession draped around her heart. She did love him. Believed in him. Trusted him.

More miracles.

His hands moved to her shoulders, his eyes deep and warm. Jamie held his gaze as his head came to rest against hers.

The warmth of his breath brushed her mouth. "How is that possible?"

Her fingers curled through his hair. "When I was a girl, my best friend brought me a bunch of blue columbine. He was the kindest, most wonderful boy I ever knew."

Regret marked his face. "That was a long time ago, James. So many things went wrong since then."

"I know. But I can't believe what God has done. I am amazed at the man you've become." She paused, waiting for his gaze. "I wouldn't change any of it. Not one moment. You're a living, breathing miracle, Andy, and I'm so glad I got to see it."

The sheen in his eyes spilled over onto his cheeks, and she brushed them away with her fingertips. He closed the small space between them, and she raised her lips to his. She felt only the love of a good man, and her heart rejoiced as he whispered those wonderful words against her mouth.

Love warmed her down to the marrow as he claimed her lips again.

Epilogue

Andrew rescued his wailing daughter. He couldn't help but smile as the two-month-old crammed her fist into her mouth, studying him through light brown eyes. His eyes. And thus far, she seemed to have his will.

He lifted her tiny head to his lips. "Grow in beauty and grace, sweet girl, and you will avoid much heartache."

She studied him before scrunching her face in offense. He laughed, and his son came through the door, hopping onto the bed as Andrew bounced the baby.

"Gracie's mad." Michael spoke with authority. "She wants Mommy."

"Mommy's sleeping," Andrew whispered.

Sweet green eyes took him in before he scooted closer. "Grace is a Bible name."

Andrew smiled. "It is."

"My name is a Bible name."

"You're right again, buddy. Do you know what your name means?"

Michael puffed out his four-year-old chest. "Mighty is our God."

Andrew chuckled, and Grace seemed to take interest in their conversation. They cooed at the small girl, and Michael announced that he would teach her all about God.

"I have my Bible words in my head, Dad." He tapped his blond crew cut. "I can tell her all about how mighty He is."

Andrew felt a sting of tears. Looking toward the head of the bed, his gaze settled on Jamie, and love rushed over him. He still found it perfectly amazing that she'd married him.

His gaze moved to the wall by the window where she'd hung a collage of photos. In the middle, an outdated frame sheltered faded blue flowers and a lifetime of memories.

His mind went back to the day he'd returned it. He'd planned to save it for Christmas, but Thanksgiving came around and he couldn't wait. She'd met him at his duplex where they were to leave to meet his parents at the airport. But instead of climbing in the car, he took her hand and led her back to the house. "I have to tell you something."

He guided her to the secondhand couch. She sat, her expression growing more solemn with each breath. He slid next to her as though he were preparing for a confession. "I did something while you were gone last summer." He rubbed the top of his head. "I want to make it right."

Jamie's green eyes were huge. "What did you do?"

"I stole a picture from the trash pile after you moved." He pulled the thieved item, complete with new glass, out from under the couch.

She exhaled and smiled. "Andy..." She traced the papery flowers as tears glazed her eyes.

His voice cracked. "I didn't want you to throw it away."

Jamie hugged the chintzy frame. Her hand stopped on something anchored to the back, and Andrew's grin began to spread. She eyed him, unable to keep those emeralds from dancing, as she flipped the picture over.

Scotch tape held the simple ring. It wasn't flowery or extravagant. He simply said, "I love you, James. Please marry me."

It was one of his best days.

Looking at those old, dried flowers, he could visualize the backside. Andy, 1986. Right below her little girl penmanship, she'd traced an outline of his ring. Andy, 2007.

Somehow five years had flown by. He'd been right about Lacey's case—she was awarded her degree, but her opportunities were limited. The Stewarts were okay with that, though. They'd walked the path God had given and left the rest in His hands. A good example for Andrew, because his path had narrowed too. After Lacey's case, his ties with Matthison severed. But he'd found a fresh calling and a new passion. He'd joined a legal group that specialized in cases like Lacey's. The money wasn't great, and he lost more than he won in court. It was worth it, though.

Jamie delivered their firstborn, Michael, eighteen months into their marriage. She quit her job, though doing so was bittersweet, not to mention financially risky. But through it all, they melded together, he and Jamie Carson—no, Harris.

They still had their standoff moments. He could still make her mad with his overbearing tendencies, and she could still drive him crazy with her perfectionism. But they were one, and happier that way than he'd dreamed could be possible. A truth confirmed by the genuine smiles captured and hung on the wall. Their wedding, hikes, long weekends spent at the farm in Iowa and summer trips to California. Good times, good memories.

His eyes slid to the side table by their window. One book sat solitary on the top. She wouldn't let him display it on the coffee table, so this was their compromise. Colorado in the Raw. His lips tipped up. He knew it would happen.

Andrew's attention went back to his children. He needed no further testimony to God's life-changing power than to look at the family he'd been given. His eyes slid shut as gratitude swelled in his chest.

Grace. Unmerited favor. Praise God.

Jamie stirred. He moved to greet her with a soft kiss before he transferred Grace into her arms.

"Good morning." She yawned.

Andrew smiled. "Good morning."

"Another new day."

Her eyes captured his, and he leaned forward for another kiss. "Another new day."

"...celebrate and rejoice,
for this brother of yours was dead and has come to life again;
he was lost and has been found."
Luke 15:32

Dear reader,

Thank you for journeying with me through Andrew and Jamie's lives. It wasn't always pretty—life is that way sometimes. But God's redemption is something to behold, isn't it? It is my prayer that this story will encourage you to lift your hands in praise for the amazing things that you have seen God do.

While I know that life, and the messy stories that are in it, doesn't always work out happily ever after, I have seen God do miracles. Miracles that have made me weep for joy and shout praise to the God of redemption. There isn't a soul in the darkest places of existence that the hand of grace cannot reach. If you know and love those with captive hearts, as do I, may this work of fiction encourage you to pray for their redemption. He is able—don't ever doubt it.

This has been a long path, but I would absolutely do it over again—and I plan to. My second novel, *Reclaimed*, is slated for release in 2016. I would love for you to join me in Paul and Suzanna's story—a different flavor as far as books go, but one I enjoyed every bit as much as I did *Blue*.

I'd love to hear from you! Please visit me at my website, or on my Facebook page at Author Jen Rodewald. If you'd like to be notified when my next book will be released, please join my mailing list here. Also, reviews are always helpful and greatly appreciated!

Thank you again! I hope this work has blessed you as you have blessed me.

For His Glory,

Jen

Acknowledgments

I would be remiss if I didn't relay my gratitude to the many people who made this book possible.

My crit partners; you encourage me, push me to be better, put up with my rants, and called me out when I needed it. Thank you.

Kristin, you didn't laugh when I told you I wanted to be a writer. First hurdle cleared! Thank you for reading, even when it was awful! You are amazing, and I am blessed to call you friend.

E,K,SJ, and B, you often lost your mommy to her imaginary world, and you did it with grace and love. Thank you for letting me chase my dreams. I can't imagine a better cheering section, and I'm so proud that you are mine.

Finally, most especially, Superman. You never stopped believing. That is the world. You have my heart. Forever.

Coming Soon...

A place of her own and the love of a good man...
shouldn't that be enough?

Suzanna Wilton has had a hefty share of heartache in her twenty-seven years. Left heartbroken by a marriage cut short, she leaves city life to take up residency in a tiny Nebraska town. Her introduction to her neighbor Paul Rustin is a disaster. Assuming he's as undermining as the other local cowboys she's already met, Suzanna greets him with a heavy dose of hostility.

Though Paul is offended by Suzanna's unfriendliness, she often invades his thoughts. Intrigued by the woman who lives down the road, and propelled by a sense that she carries a painful burden, he frequently drops by to offer help as she adjusts to rural living.

Just as Paul's kindness begins to melt Suzanna's frozen heart, a conflict regarding her land escalates in town. Even in the warmth of Paul's love, resentment continues to strangle her fragile soul. Will Suzanna ever find peace?

Winning title for the 2014 Clash of the Title's Olympia
Second place winner for the 2014 FCRW Beacon Contest
Third place winner for the 2015 NTRW Great Expectations Contest

Look for award-winning novel *Reclaimed* in September, 2015.

About the Author

Jennifer Rodewald is passionate about the Word of God and the powerful vehicle of story. The draw to fiction has tugged hard on her heart since childhood, and when she began pursuing writing she set on stories that reveal the grace of God.

Aiming to live with boundless enthusiasm, her creed is vision, pursuit and excellence. Blessed with a robust curiosity, she loves to research. Whether she's investigating the history of a given area, the biography of a Christian icon, or how nature declares the glory of God, her daily goal is to learn something new.

Jen lives and writes in a lovely speck of a town where she watches with amazement while her children grow up way too fast, gardens, plays with her horses, and marvels at God's mighty hand in everyday life. Four kids and her own personal superman make her home in southwestern Nebraska delightfully chaotic.

She would love to hear from you! Please visit her at authorjenrodewald.com.

Made in the USA
Columbia, SC
17 December 2019